THE NOVELS OF
MRS APHRA BEHN

THE NOVELS OF
MRS APHRA BEHN

WITH AN INTRODUCTION BY

ERNEST A. BAKER, M.A.

GREENWOOD PRESS, PUBLISHERS
WESTPORT, CONNECTICUT

823.4
B419w

Originally published in 1913
by George Routledge & Sons, Ltd.

First Greenwood Reprinting 1969

SBN 8371-2824-2

PRINTED IN UNITED STATES OF AMERICA

CONTENTS

INTRODUCTION

To most people nowadays the name of Aphra Behn conveys nothing more intelligible than certain vague associations of license and impropriety. She is dimly remembered as the author of plays and novels, now unread, that embodied the immorality of Restoration times, and were all the more scandalous in that they were written by a woman. Her works are to be found in few libraries, and are rarely met with at the booksellers'. Although they were republished in an expensive form and in a limited edition in 1871, they have now been many years out of print. Nor is this much to be regretted. Her novels are worth reprinting now and again, not because they are more clever, but because they are less offensive to modern taste than her comedies; and in addition to their intrinsic merits, they have an interest for the student of literature. But a general reprint of the plays would hardly be justified, at least, in anything like a cheap and popular form. This is a case where, for many reasons, it is best to have one's reading done by proxy.

The obstacles which she herself has set to our appreciation have done her an injustice. In dismissing her merely as a purveyor of scandalous amusement in a profligate age, we are apt to give her none of the credit due to a long career of arduous work and of persevering struggle against adverse circumstances. Mrs. Behn was not only the first Englishwoman who became a novelist and a playwright, but the first of all those numerous women who have earned their livelihood by their pens.

We can form a better idea of the once popular Astrea from her works than from the scanty memorials that have come down to us; more is known of her personal character than about the events of her life. The so-called *History of the Life and Memoirs of Mrs. Aphra Behn, written by one of the Fair Sex*, and prefixed to the collection of her histories and novels published in 1735, is rather of the nature of a eulogium and of a vindication from certain aspersions on her conduct and originality than of any biographical value. The admiring writer, although she describes herself as an intimate friend, seems to have known less about her subject than the average journalist who is called upon to produce an obituary notice in a hurry, and to have pressed into her service a great deal of gossip, with letters, presumably written by Mrs. Behn, but undated, recounting tender episodes from Astrea's own history and that of her acquaintances, which read more like studies for her novels than authentic epistles. Astrea, probably, whilst she affected to pour out the secrets of her heart into the bosom of her friend, preferred to wrap the actual incidents of her life in romantic obscurity. Thus we are told that "She was a gentlewoman by birth, of a good family in the city of Canterbury in Kent; her father's name was Johnson, whose relation to the Lord Willoughby drew him for the advantageous post of Lieutenant-General of many isles, besides the continent of Surinam, from his quiet retreat at Canterbury, to run the hazardous voyage of the West-Indies. With him he took his chief riches, his wife and children, and in that number, Afra, his promising darling, our future heroine, and admired Astrea, who even in the first bud of infancy discovered such early hopes of her riper years, that she was equally her parents' joy and fears." But the recent discovery of Aphra's baptismal register has shown that she was born at Wye, and that her father was a barber; and, furthermore, whoever the friend or relative was with whom she went to Surinam, there is little reason to believe that he was her father. However that may be, this protector died on the voyage out; whilst the family did not return forthwith, but settled at St. John's Hill, the best house in Surinam—a house described very seductively in the pages of *Oroonoko*. Here befell the chapter of tragic events afterwards related, with a certain amount of idealisation, in the story of that famous negro prince. "One of the fair sex" makes it her business to defend Astrea from the scandalous gossip that arose about her friendship for Oroonoko—quite an unnecessary task. When the colony was ceded to the Dutch, Aphra, an attractive girl of eighteen, returned to England. As a matter of fact, this was before the Restoration, but her fair biographer states that she gave Charles II. "so pleasant and rational an account of his affairs there, and particularly of the misfortunes of Oroonoko, that he desired her to deliver them publicly to the world, and was satisfied of her abilities in the management of business, and the fidelity of our heroine to his interest." It was most likely through her marriage, later on, to Mr. Behn, a Dutchman who had become a wealthy merchant of the city of London, that she gained admittance to the Court. By the year 1666 he was dead, and Astrea was sent by the Government as a secret agent to the Low Countries, which were then at war with England.

Her memoirist gives a flowery account of her love adventures in Antwerp, with the letters of one of her suitors, Van Bruin—who was about twice the age and bulk of a more favoured lover, Van der Albert—and Astrea's replies. The episode and the letters, as they are given us, are like the burlesque of some tale of high-flown sentiment. "Most Transcendent Charmer," writes that elephantine euphuist, Van Bruin, "I have strove often to tell you the tempests of my heart, and with my own mouth scale the walls of your affections; but terrified with the strength of your fortifications, I concluded to make more regular approaches, and first attack you at a farther distance, and try first what a bombardment of letters would do; whether these carcasses of love, thrown into the sconces of your eyes, would break into the midst of your breast, beat down the court of guard of your aversion, and blow up the magazine of your cruelty, that you might be brought to a capitulation, and yield upon reasonable terms." This warlike language, perhaps, derives some appropriateness from the fact that the bulky Dutchman was addressing one of his country's foes. But Van Bruin was at no loss for metaphors, and he goes on to compare his inamorata, somewhat indelicately, with a ship, in a style that reminds one of a facetious dialogue in *Sam Slick*, clinching the simile with a rhetorical appeal: "Is it not a pity that so spruce a ship should be unmanned, should lie in the harbour for want of her crew?" Though she had the cruelty to encourage this "Most Magnificent Hero," as she addresses him in her reply, by answering him in the same rhapsodical vein, Mrs. Behn eventually dismissed him, and turned her attention to Albert. What follows is too like an incident repeatedly utilised in her comedies, and taxes credulity to the utmost. Albert, as wicked a young man as any of her favourite heroes, Willmore, Wilding, or the Rover, is already married, but has deserted his bride on the wedding day. To punish him Mrs. Behn contrives, like Isabella in *Measure for Measure*, to put the forsaken wife in her place, but, unfortunately, without succeeding in re-tying the marriage knot. Albert's subsequent stratagem for retaliating the affront in kind upon Astrea, is discomfited in a farcical manner by the substitution of a young gallant for the heroine.

The end of it was that Mrs. Behn promised to marry Albert, but before the union could be consummated he died; and soon after she returned to England, all but losing her life by shipwreck on the way. Her services as a spy had met with a severe snub from the Government. Through Van der Albert she had obtained early information of De Witt's intended raid upon the Thames. Though she sent instant intelligence of this to London, her warning was treated with ridicule; the Dutch fleet sailed, and she had the painful satisfaction of seeing her accuracy verified by the misfortunes of her country. She seems to have received no reward from the Government, and having been left by her husband without means, she now found herself obliged to write for a living. Henceforward tragedies, comedies, novels, and poems came in rapid succession from her pen. No literary task came amiss to her: she translated Van Dale's Latin *History of Oracles*, La Rochefoucauld's *Maxims*, and Fontenelle's *Plurality of Worlds*, prefixing to the last an able essay on translated prose. She collaborated in an English translation of Ovid's *Heroical Epistles* in 1683; and few occasions of public rejoicing passed uncelebrated by an ode from Astrea. The brief memoir already quoted contains a series of perfervid letters, signed Astrea, to one Lycidas, who appears to have treated her advances with indifference. Doubtless, her life was as free and unconventional for the seventeenth century as that of certain emancipated women of letters was for the nineteenth; but we must not suppose her own conduct was as irregular as the life depicted in her comedies. Let the warm affection of her friend speak once more as to her personal character:—

She was of a generous and open temper, something passionate, very serviceable to her friends in all that was in her power; and could sooner forgive an injury than do one. She was mistress of all the pleasing arts of conversation, but used 'em not to any but those who love plain-dealing. She was a woman of sense, and by consequence a lover of pleasure, as indeed all, both men and women, are; but only some would be thought to be above the conditions of humanity, and place their chief pleasure in a proud vain hypocrisy. For my part, I knew her intimately, and never saw aught unbecoming the just modesty of our sex, tho' more gay and free than the folly of the precise will allow. She was, I'm satisfied, a greater honour to our sex than all the canting tribe of dissemblers that die with the false reputation of saints.

She died on the 16th of April, 1689, and was buried in Westminster Abbey, the marble slab that covered her being inscribed with "two wretched verses," made, so her friend relates, "by a very ingenious gentleman, tho' no poet— the very person whom the envious of our sex, and the malicious of the other, would needs have the author of most of hers." The person referred to is the playwright, Edward Ravenscroft, with whom she was on very intimate terms. There is no reason to believe that he was the author or part-author of any of her works, although he wrote a number of her epilogues.

It is usual to add a piquancy to reminiscences of ladies who write by giving particulars as to their earnings. All that we may be sure of in the case of Mrs. Aphra Behn is that she must have obtained a good deal more by her plays than by her novels. In her collected works, the latter are scarcely able to fill out two volumes of large print; whereas the former occupy four thick and closely printed volumes, even with the omission of one or two inferior productions. Then, as now, there was a huge disproportion between the profits of fiction and of writing for the stage. Astrea's first attempt was a tragedy, written partly in rhyme and partly in prose, and entitled *The Young King; or, the Mistake.* It was adapted from a romance by La Calprenède. The scene is Dacia; the Dacians and the Scythians are at war; and the *dramatis personæ* consist of the hostile princes and their soldiers, with a crowd of shepherds and shepherdesses. No further description is necessary. The play failed to obtain either a manager or a publisher. Her next effort was more fortunate. This was *The Forc'd Marriage; or, the Jealous Bridegroom*, a tragi-comedy in blank verse, which was produced at the Duke's Theatre in 1671. Betterton and his wife took the part of the two lovers, and young Otway, a boy from college, appeared on the boards for the first and only time as the king. I need say no more about this work than that the scene is laid "within the Court of France," and the characters bear such names as Alcippus, Orgulius, Cleontius, Galatea. A very gross and immoral comedy, *The Amorous Prince*, was brought out the same year at the Duke's Theatre, and afterwards published.

An equally objectionable play, *The Dutch Lover*, was published in 1673. Here, though she drew upon her Dutch experiences in depicting the boorish Haunce van Ezel, a sort of gasconading Van Bruin, there is not much advance in realism. The plot is a series of errors of identity, blunders in the dark, mistaken relationships, with the ensuing complications. We have a man in love with his supposed sister, and engaged in mortal combat with his alleged brother; a gallant colonel impersonating the Dutch fop, in order to secure a bride with whom he falls in love by accident; stage tears, and conventional passion to excess. But if the incidents are far-fetched, they are brought about with exemplary skill. In spite of its intricacy, the plot is clearly developed; the dialogue is smooth and tripping, always lively, and sometimes witty. The play has, at all events, one excellence— that of workmanship. The blank verse, however, and the serious passages generally, are the most arrant bombast.

The next play was all in blank verse. *Abdelazar; or, the Moor's Revenge*, which was played at the Duke's Theatre in 1676, is an adaptation of the old tragedy, *Lust's Dominion*, erroneously ascribed to Marlowe; it reads like a travesty of *Macbeth*, ambition, however, playing in the long run a secondary part to sexual passion, as might be expected in a drama by Mrs. Behn. The usurper who murders his trusting sovereign, and puts to death all who oppose his way to the throne, is the Moorish chieftain, Abdelazar; and the woman who assists at his career of crime, and hopes to reign by his side, is the wife of the betrayed king. She helps on the death of her husband to pave the way for her paramour, and then by coquetting with another lover paralyses the opposition to Abdelazar. He meanwhile makes a handle of the new king's passion for his own wife, whom he loves, but sacrifices without a scruple to ambition. His rivals are overthrown, the crown of Spain is in his grasp, the infamous queen is no longer of use as an instrument of his villainy. He murders her. But, according to the ideas of Mrs. Behn and her public, what swayed most potently the greatest saint and the greatest sinner was sexual passion. The ferocious Abdelazar, who has slaughtered friend and foe without a qualm, now gives way to a fatal madness for the daughter of the royal house, throws the crown into her lap, and becomes the prey of his enemies.

This is a theme worthy of the early unchastened Elizabethans, Marlowe, Nash, and Kyd, who preceded Shakespeare, or of the school of Dryden, who succeeded him; it is what the age considered a pre-eminently tragic theme. As Mrs. Behn treated it, *Abdelazar* is merely rant and melodrama, masquerading as tragedy. Yet there are echoes of Elizabethan poetry in the distichs at the end of the scenes; and some of the lyrics are pure in feeling. Let me quote two, the second of them a favourite of Mr. Swinburne's, who justly styles it "that melodious and magnificent song."

I

Make haste, Amyntas, come away,
The sun is up and will not stay;
And oh! how very short's a lover's day!
Make haste, Amyntas, to this grove,
Beneath whose shade so oft I've sat,
And heard my dear lov'd swain repeat
How much he Galatea lov'd;
Whilst all the list'ning birds around,
Sung to the music of the blessed sound.
Make haste, Amyntas, come away,
The sun is up and will not stay;
And oh! how very short's a lover's day!

II

Love in fantastic triumph sat,
    Whilst bleeding hearts around him flow'd,
For whom fresh pains he did create,
    And strange tyrannic power he showed ;
From thy bright eyes he took his fires,
    Which round about in sport he hurl'd ;
But 'twas from mine he took desires,
    Enough t' undo the amorous world.

From me he took his sighs and tears,
    From thee his pride and cruelty ;
From me his languishments and fears,
    And every killing dart from thee ;
Thus thou and I the god have arm'd,
    And set him up a deity ;
But my poor heart alone is harm'd,
    Whilst thine the victor is, and free.

Often in reading *Abdelazar* one seems to recognise a suggestion from Shakespeare used or misused, travestied, yet not deprived entirely of dramatic force. Edmund, in *King Lear*, is brought to mind when we read :

Abd. So I thank thee, Nature, that in making me
Thou did'st design me villain,
Hitting each faculty for active mischief :
Thou skilful artist, thank thee for my face,
It will discover nought that's hid within.
Thus arm'd for ills,
Darkness and Horror, I invoke your aid ;
And thou dread Night, shade all your busy stars
In blackest clouds,
And let my dagger's brightness only serve
To guide me to the mark, and guide it so,
It may undo a kingdom at one blow.

Abdelazar's speech before the king's murder, on the other hand, is a crude parody of the famous prelude to Duncan's murder.

'Tis now dead time of night, when rapes, and murders
Are hid beneath the horrid veil of darkness—
I'll ring through all the court, with doleful sound,
The sad alarms of murder—Murder—Zarrack—
Take up thy standing yonder—Osmin, thou
At the queen's apartment—cry out Murder—
Whilst I, like his ill genius, do awake the king ;
Perhaps in this disorder I may kill him.

But we get bombast surpassing this as we approach the climax.

> Prince Philip and the Cardinal now ride
> Like Jove in thunder ; we in storms must meet them.
> To arms ! to arms ! and then to victory,
> Resolv'd to conquer, or resolv'd to die.

This grandiloquence subsides into the most astounding bathos.

> *Sebast.* Advance, advance, my lord, with all your force,
> Or else the prince and victory is lost,
> Which now depends upon his single valour ;
> Who, like some ancient hero, or some god,
> Thunders amongst the thickest of his enemies,
> Destroying all before him in such numbers,
> That piles of dead obstruct his passage to the living—
> Relieve him straight, my lord, with our last cavalry and hopes.

Perhaps in this case, the faulty scansion and doubtful grammar are evidence of a corrupt text. Here is a sentimental passage, a description of night, intended to be poetical.

> *Queen.* Let all the chambers too be filled with lights :
> There's a solemnity, methinks, in night,
> That does insinuate love into the soul,
> And makes the bashful lover more assured.

> *Elvira.* Madam,
> You speak as if this were your first enjoyment.

> *Queen.* My first ! Oh, Elvira, his powers, like his charms,
> His wit, or bravery, every hour renews ;
> Love gathers sweets like flowers, which grow more fragrant
> The nearer they approach maturity.   [*Knock.*
> —Hark ! 'tis my Moor,—give him admittance straight.
> The thought comes o'er me like a gentle gale,
> Raising my blood into a thousand curls.

There are ranting passages, too long to quote, that merit the ridicule cast upon the Drydenian drama in *Chrononhotonthologos*, with its inimitable—

> *Bom.* A blow !—Shall Bombardinian take a blow ?
> Blush—blush, thou sun !—start back, thou rapid ocean !
> Hills ! vales ! seas ! mountains !—all commixing, crumble,
> And into chaos pulverise the world !
> For Bombardinian has received a blow,
> And Chrononhotonthologos shall die !

In her next play, *The Rover*, Mrs. Behn left these crude heroics for what was to be her most prolific comedy vein. It appeared anonymously, and was so successful that she followed it up immediately with another anonymous play, *The Debauchee*, which has been described as the worst and least original of all her dramatic works. *The Rover* was produced in 1677, and held the stage the longest of any of her plays. In 1681 she brought out a second part, changing the scene from Naples to Madrid; otherwise the sequel is almost a replica of the first.

What helped to make *The Rover* so popular was the subject. As she said in the Epilogue—

> The banished Cavaliers ! a roving blade !
> A Popish carnival ! a masquerade !
> The devil's in't if this will please the nation,
> In these our blessed times of reformation,
> When conventicling is so much in fashion,
> And yet——

Her argument is in the aposiopesis. This was the year before Titus Oates denounced the alleged Popish Plot; Shaftesbury was in opposition, the champion of Nonconformity, the idol of the populace, and the bugbear of the Court party, who believed him to be fomenting heresy and sedition. A year or two later, Mrs. Behn was to caricature him at full length in *The City Heiress; or, Sir Timothy Treat-all.* In *The Rover*, she was making the same political appeal to the party prejudices of the Tories. *Almighty rabble*, says the Prologue to the second part, "'tis to you this day our humble author dedicates the play."

A band of exiled Royalists are engaged in the chase of pleasure in a foreign capital. The most reckless and dissipated of the merry crew is Willmore, the Rover, one of those swaggering inconstants whom, according to Mrs. Behn, no woman can resist. A certain lady, nevertheless, observes, "I should as soon be enamoured on the north wind, a tempest, or a clap of thunder. Bless me from such a blast." The most prominent female character in each of the two plays bearing the name of "The Rover" is set down in the bill as "a famous curtezan' ; so the indescribable nature of the incidents may be imagined. Willmore was born to dash the matrimonial schemes of soberer men;

he cuts the knot of all the intrigues, licit or illicit; he is the impersonation of Astrea's code of sexual morality, of which the two most salient definitions are summed up as follows :—

"Conscience : a cheap pretence to cozen fools withal—"
"Constancy, that current coin for fools."

The dialogue is always full of life and vigour, often sparkling with wit, never quotable; and it is the same with the highly diverting scenes of both these plays. One marvels at the state of society when such impudent things could be put on the stage, and an audience applaud them.

In *Sir Patient Fancy*, Mrs. Behn borrowed her plot from Molière's *Malade Imaginaire*. It is one of the most vivacious of her plays, and the most completely devoid of moral feeling. The valetudinarian is a rich old alderman, married to a beautiful young wife, who has a gallant. His suspicions being awakened, the jealous old man is persuaded, on what must be confessed very inadequate evidence, that Wittmore, the gallant, is really a suitor for his daughter. But the daughter has a lover already whom he dislikes, and so we have two intrigues going on—with divers others, be it understood—the lover and the gallant both in seeming rivalry courting the daughter of the house, whilst Wittmore and Lady Fancy are scheming to outwit the doubly deluded husband. The usual complications are provided in the usual way. There is a double assignation in the dark; the gallant is mistaken for the lover, and the lover for the gallant; and at the critical moment Sir Patient appears on the scene. Lady Fancy is one of the shameless and absolutely unscrupulous women Astrea loved to portray. She carries off the situation with unabashed address, continues to hoodwink her spouse, until, by a combination of accidents, her perfidy is revealed. But all the characters are so entirely absorbed in self that there is no bias in the reader's mind in favour either of the hypochondriacal knight the clever unfaithful wife, or the honest lovers; and the con fusion of the intriguers gives real satisfaction to nobody.

Betterton took the part of Wittmore, and Mrs. Gwyn that of the affected learned woman Lady Knowell, who must have been a very comic figure on the stage, well acted. She is one of those who think there is no learning but what

is comprised in the tongues of antiquity: she is a Mrs.
Malaprop in Latin.

O faugh! Mr. Fancy, what have you said, mother tongue!
Can anything that's great or moving be expressed in filthy
English?—I'll give you an energetic proof, Mr. Fancy; observe
but divine Homer in the Grecian language—*Ton apanibomenos
prosiphe podas ochus Achilles!* ah, how it sounds! which
English'd dwindles into the most grating stuff—Then the
swift-foot Achilles made reply; oh faugh!

Her niece has very different views, and expresses the com-
moner opinion of her sex in the remark, " Sure he's too
much a gentleman to be a scholar."

Lady Knowell's excessive conversation bores Sir Patient
dreadfully, though he is no less a bore with his anxious
absorption in the progress of his imaginary ailments. Says
one of the characters, " He has been on the point of going
off this twenty years." He is continually setting his affairs
in order. His favourite reading is furnished by prescriptions and apothecaries' bills, which provide him with a sort
of diary. " By this rule, good Mr. Doctor," says he, " I am
sicker this month than I was the last."

Broader farce comes in with the daughter's clownish
suitor, Sir Credulous Easy, " a foolish Devonshire squire."

Sir Cred. Come, undo my portmantle, and equip me, that
I may look like some body before I see the ladies—Curry, thou
shalt e'en remove now from groom to footman; for I'll ne'er
keep horse more, no, nor mare neither, since my poor Gillian's
departed this life.

Cur. Nay, to say truth, sir, 'twas a good-natur'd civil beast,
and so she remained to her last gasp, for she cou'd never have
left this world in a better time, as the saying is, so near her
journey's end.

Sir Cred. A civil beast! Why was it civilly done of her,
thinkest thou, to die at Brentford, when had she liv'd till
to-morrow, she had been converted into money and have been
in my pocket? for now I am to marry and live in town, I'll sell
off all my pads; poor fool, I think she e'en died of grief I
wou'd have sold her.

Cur. Well, well, sir, her time was come you must think, and
we are all mortal as the saying is.

Sir Cred. Well, 'twas the loving'st tit—but grass and hay,
she's gone—where be her shoes, Curry?

Cur. Here, sir, her skin went for good ale at Brentford.
　　　　　　　　　　　　　　　　　[Gives him the shoes.

Sir Cred. Ah, how often has she carried me upon these shoes to Mother Jumbles. What pure ale she brewed!

At a later stage Sir Credulous enacts the part of Falstaff, taking refuge in a basket, in which he has to submit to various indignities without daring to move a muscle lest he betray himself. Mrs. Behn must have had indulgent audiences, who were satisfied with a very cheap kind of humour. In one scene, which has no more affectation of probability than a harlequinade, Sir Credulous is persuaded to feign dumbness, and to court his mistress by signs, whilst his pretended interpreter relieves him of his diamond ring, his cambric handkerchief, and his purse, as presents to the lady.

The *enfant terrible* is already a figure in low comedy. Sir Patient's seven-year-old daughter admonishes her father, when he tries to escape the loquacious Lady Knowell, in these terms :—

Fan. Shou'd I tell a lie, Sir Father, and to a lady of her quality?

Sir Pat. Her quality and she are a couple of impertinent things, which are very troublesome, and not to be endur'd I take it.

Fan. Sir, we shou'd bear with things we do not love sometimes, 'tis a sort of trial, sir, a kind of mortification fit for a good Christian.

Sir Pat. Why, what a notable talking baggage is this? How came you by this doctrine?

Fan. I remember, sir, you preached it once to my sister, when the old alderman was the text, whom you exhorted her to marry, but the wicked creature made ill use on't.

Unfortunately, Mrs. Behn's sense of propriety is so defective that she makes this precocious child the confidante of her elder sister's highly improper love affairs. 'For I have heard you say,' this budding coquette remarks, 'women were born to no other end than to love; and 'tis fit I should learn to live and die in my calling.' Such is the cynicism of one who has no faith in the virtue of her own sex, and less in that of men. Yet she could say, in her epilogue, to the coxcomb who cried 'Ah rot it—'tis a woman's comedy,'

> 'What has poor woman done, that she must be
> Debar'd from sense, and sacred poetry?'

Sacred poetry indeed!

In 1682, her most successful year, she brought out, besides *The False Count*, two political comedies, or at least, comedies that owed much of their popularity to their direct appeal to party feeling. *The Roundheads; or, the Good Old Cause* is a scurrilous lampoon on the Commonwealth. It represents the Parliamentarian generals, Fleetwood, Lambert, and Desborough, as sanctimonious hypocrites, each scheming to betray his comrades and raise himself to supreme office in the state, largely by the efforts of his wife. A traitor in the camp, Corporal Right, is described in the playbill as, 'An Oliverian commander, but honest and a cavalier in his heart.' This is an index to the character of the piece, which, if a man had written it, we should speak of as a cowardly attack on the fallen—a shameless appeal to the basest instincts of the mob. For the most part the abuse is too offensive to quote, but the following scene representing a meeting of the council of ladies will illustrate the spirit of Mrs. Behn's satire :—

Enter page with women, and Loveless dressed as a woman.

Lady Lambert. Gentlewomen, what's your business with us?

Lov. Gentlewomen! some of us are ladies.

L. Lam. Ladies, in good time; by what authority, and from whom do you derive your title of ladies?

Lov. From our husbands.

Gill. Husbands, who are they, and of what standing?

2 Lady. Of no long standing, I confess.

Gill. That's a common grievance indeed.

L. Desborough. And ought to be redressed.

L. Lam. And that shall be taken into consideration; write it down, Gilliflower, who made your husband a knight, woman?

Lov. Oliver the first, an't please ye.

L. Lam. Of horrid memory; write that down—who yours?

2 Lady. Richard the fourth, an't like your honour.

Gill. Of sottish memory; shall I write that down too?

L. Des. Most remarkably.

L. Cromwell. Heav'ns! can I hear this profanation of our Royal Family.

*   *   *   *   *   *

Lov. I petition for a pension ; my husband, deceas'd, was a constant active man, in all the late rebellion, against the Man ; he plundered my Lord Capel, he betray'd his dearest friend, Brown Bushel, who trusted his life in his hands, and several others ; plundering their wives and children even to their smocks.

L. Lam. Most considerable service, and ought to be considered.

2 Lady. And most remarkably, at the trial of the late Man, I spit in's face, and betrayed the Earl of Holland to the Parliament.

L. Crom. In the king's face, you mean—it showed your zeal for the good cause.

2 Lady. And 'twas my husband that headed the rabble, to pull down Gog and Magog, the bishops, broke the idols in the windows, and turned the churches into stables and dens of thieves ; robb'd the altar of the cathedral of the twelve pieces of plate called the twelve Apostles, turn'd eleven of 'em into money, and kept Judas for his own use at home.

L. Fleetwood. On my word, most wisely perform'd, note it down—

3 Lady. And my husband made libels on the Man from the first troubles to this day, defam'd and profaned the Woman and her children, printed all the Man's letters to the Woman with burlesque marginal notes, pull'd down the sumptuous shrines in churches, and with the golden and popish spoils adorn'd his house and chimney-pieces.

L. Lam. We shall consider these great services.

We must stop here ; the rest of the scene is a more ribald kind of invective even than the foregoing.

In *The City Heiress* (1682), based on Middleton's *A Mad World, My Masters*, the satire is not so heavy, and has far more wit. There is no need to describe the plot, which has a family resemblance to most of the others. The hero is a certain Tom Wilding, the very counterpart of Wittmore and Willmore the Rover. He is the scapegrace nephew of Sir Timothy Treat-all, who is undisguisedly intended for Shaftesbury, Dryden's 'false Achitophel.' Sir Timothy is, of course, the general butt of the satire, being cozened of his property, tricked by his nephew into receiving him as an emissary from the Polish electors, and, to cap the whole, married to a supposed heiress, who turns out to be an impostor. In the scene where Wilding carries out his trickery the political meaning is very obvious.

Enter Wilding in disguise, Dresswell, footmen and pages.

Wild. Sir, by your reverend aspect, you shou'd be the renown'd Maitre de Hotel.

Sir Tim. Mater de Otell! I have not the honour to know any of that name, I am called Sir Timothy Treat-all. [*Bowing.*

Wild. The same, sir; I have been bred abroad, and thought all persons of quality had spoke French.

Sir Tim. Not City persons of quality, my lord.

Wild. I'm glad on't, sir; for 'tis a nation I hate, as indeed I do all monarchies.

Sir Tim. Hum! Hate monarchy! Your lordship is most welcome.   [*Bows.*

Wild. Unless elective monarchies, which so resemble a commonwealth.

Sir Tim. Right, my lord; where every man may hope to take his turn—Your lordship is most singularly welcome.
                                                      [*Bows low.*

Wild. And though I am a stranger to your person, I am not to your fame, amongst the sober party of the Amsterdamians, all the French Hugonots throughout Geneva; even to Hungary and Poland, fame's trumpet sounds your praise, making the Pope to fear, the rest to admire you.

Sir Tim. I'm much obliged to the renowned mobile.

Wild. So you will say, when you shall hear my embassy. The Polanders by me salute you, sir, and have in the next new election pricked ye down for their succeeding king.

Sir Tim. How, my lord, pricked me down for their king! Why this is wonderful! pricked me, unworthy me down for a king! How cou'd I merit this amazing glory!

Wild. They know, he that can be so great a patriot to his native country, when but a private person, what must he be when power is on his side?

Sir Tim. Ay, my lord, my country, my bleeding country! there's the stop to all my rising greatness. Shall I be so ungrateful to disappoint this big expecting nation? defeat the sober party, and my neighbours, for any Polish crown? But yet, my lord, I will consider on't: meantime my house is yours.

Wild. I've brought you, sir, the measure of the crown: ha, it fits you to a hair. [*Pulls out a riband, measures his head.*] You were by heaven and nature fram'd that monarch.

When Sir Timothy finds out the trick that has been played upon him, he cries, 'Undone, undone! I shall never make Guildhall speech more: but he shall hang for't, if there be e'er a witness between this and Salamanca for money.' There are many more hits against false witnesses and credulous juries. When hard pressed, Sir Timothy is quite ready to protest himself a good friend even to the Pope.

Sir Tim. Nay, gentlemen, not but I love and honour his Holiness with all my soul ; and if his Grace did but know what I've done for him, d'ye see——

Fop. You done for the Pope, sirrah ! Why what have you done for the Pope?

Sir Tim. Why, sir, an't like ye, I have done you very great service, very great service ; for I have been, d'ye see, in a small trial I had, the cause and occasion of invalidating the evidence to that degree, that I suppose no jury in Christendom will ever have the impudence to believe 'em hereafter, shou'd they swear against his Holiness and all the conclave of cardinals.

And when his house is found to be full of 'knavery, sedition, libels, rights and privileges, with a new fashion'd oath of abjuration, call'd the Association,' he shouts,

'Why I'll deny it, sir ; for what jury will believe so wise a magistrate as I cou'd communicate such secrets to such as you? I'll say you forged 'em, and put 'em in—or print every one of 'em, and own 'em, as long as they were writ and published in London, sir. Come, come, the world is not so bad yet, but a man may speak treason within the walls of London, thanks be to God, and honest conscientious jurymen.'

Two later plays, *The Lucky Chance*, a comedy, and *The Emperor of the Moon*, a farce, were both failures. In *The Widow Ranter* Astrea tells the story of Bacon's rebellion in Virginia, and makes use of her own experiences of life in the American colonies.

It was the truth and power with which she recounted what she had herself witnessed in Surinam that has singled out for permanence the best of her novels, the story of the royal slave, Oroonoko. We need not give ear to the whispers of a liaison with the heroic black. A very different emotion inspires the tale, the same feeling of outraged humanity that in after days inflamed Mrs. Stowe. *Oroonoko* is the first emancipation novel. It is also the first glorification of the Natural Man. Mrs. Behn was, in a manner, the precursor of Bernardin de Saint-Pierre ; and in her attempts to depict the splendour of tropical scenery she foreshadows, though feebly, the prose-epics of Chateaubriand. There is fierce satire in *Oroonoko*. Who would think that Astrea, who entertained the depraved pit at the

Duke's Theatre, could have drawn those idyllic pictures of Oroonoko in his native Coromantien, of the truth and purity of the savage uncontaminated with the vices of Christian Europe, or have written such vehement invectives against the baseness and utter falsehood of the whites?

'These people represented to me,' she said, 'an absolute idea of the first state of innocence, before man knew how to sin: and 'tis most evident and plain that simple nature is the most harmless, inoffensive and virtuous mistress. 'Tis she alone, if she were permitted, that better instructs the world than all the inventions of man : religion would here but destroy that tranquillity they possess by ignorance ; and laws would teach 'em to know offences of which now they have no notion. They once made mourning and fasting for the death of the English governor, who had given his hand to come on such a day to 'em, and neither came nor sent ; believing when a man's word was past, nothing but death could or should prevent his keeping it : and when they saw he was not dead, they ask'd him what name they had for a man who promis'd a thing he did not do? The governor told them such a man was a lyar, which was a word of infamy to a gentleman. Then one of 'em replied, 'Governor, you are a lyar, and guilty of that infamy.'

It is said further on, 'Such ill morals are only practis'd in Christian countries, where they prefer the bare name of religion ; and, without virtue and morality, think that sufficient.'

Oroonoko is no savage, but the ideal man, as conceived by Mrs. Behn, the man out of Eden ; and in him she has an absolute criterion by which to judge and condemn the object of her satire—European civilisation. His bravery, wisdom, chastity, his high sense of honour, are the idealisations of a sentimental young lady, carried away by her admiration for a truly heroic figure, and disgusted by the vicious manners of the colonists, whom she describes as 'rogues and runagades, that have abandoned their own countries for rapine, murder, theft and villainies.' 'Do you not hear,' says Oroonoko, 'how they upbraid each other with infamy of life, below the wildest savages? And shall we render obedience to such a degenerate race, who have no one human virtue left, to distinguish them from the vilest creatures ?'

The story has the natural elements of drama. Southern wrote a very bad tragedy on the theme of Mrs. Behn's narrative, altering it slightly, and adding a great deal of foulness that is, happily, not in the original. Oroonoko loves the beautiful Imoinda, a maiden of his own race, not the child of a European who has adopted a savage life, as in Southern's play. But when they are on the brink of happiness, the old king, Oroonoko's grandfather, demands her for his harem. Imoinda acts the part of Abishag the Shunamite, and her lover that of Adonijah. The vengeful monarch discovers their attachment, and sells her into slavery. Oroonoko, soon afterwards, is kidnapped, and finds himself in Surinam, where Imoinda is already famous as the beautiful slave, as chaste as she is beautiful. They recognise each other in a touching scene, and are suffered to be re-united. Oroonoko distinguishes himself by his virtue and prowess. But he quickly finds that his tyrants promise freedom to himself and Imoinda merely to delude them into good behaviour. He flies into the wilderness at the head of a body of slaves. The planters follow, the blacks fling down their arms, and Oroonoko surrenders on the assurance that they shall not be chastised. The white governor is a scoundrel. The magnanimous negro is put in irons and tortured. Imoinda is set apart for a worse fate. But she prefers to die at his beloved hands, rather than bear dishonour. Oroonoko, with Roman fortitude, slays his wife, and with the stoicism of the Indian smokes a pipe of tobacco while his captors execute him piecemeal.

The Fair Jilt; or, the Amours of Prince Tarquin and Miranda, also purports to be a recital of incidents Astrea herself had witnessed. 'As Love,' it begins, 'is the most noble and divine passion of the soul, so it is that to which we may justly attribute all the real satisfactions of life; and without it man is unfinish'd and unhappy." She hardly succeeds in proving the divinity of the passion she portrays. Miranda is only a false name for a Beguine at Antwerp, who had many lovers; Tarquin is the real name of a German prince, the most illustrious of her votaries. It is the story of a fair hypocrite, whose beauty drives men mad. Miranda, whose raging fever of desire reminds one of Phaedra, being repulsed by a handsome young friar, falls back on the device of Potiphar's wife, to secure revenge. This episode is full of force and vigour; but 'Tarquin's subjugation to the enchantress, his complaisant obedience to her criminal schemes, which is offered for our admiration as an example of the illimitable power of love, does not strike us so. Passion, Mrs. Behn maintains, condones everything. There is nothing too heinous, too flagitious, to attain a sort of dignity if done in the cause of love. Tarquin attempts to assassinate the Fair Jilt's sister, and is deservedly condemned to death. The novelist depicts him as a martyr, and has a tear to spare even for the more culpable Miranda.

> At last the bell toll'd, and he was to take leave of the princess, as his last work of life, and the most hard he had to accomplish. He threw himself at her feet, and gazing on her as she sat more dead than alive, overwhelm'd with silent grief, they both remained some moments speechless ; and then, as if one rising tide of tears had supplied both their eyes, it burst out in tears at the same instant: and when his sighs gave way, he utter'd a thousand farewells, so soft, so passionate, and moving, that all who were by were extremely touch'd with it, and said, 'That nothing could be seen more deplorable and melancholy.'

All that can be said in comment is, that there have been novelists since Mrs. Behn who have written stuff that is quite as false, lurid, and depraved, and readers who have gushed over it. Only the sinners begotten of later romancers do not sin with such abandon. Astrea has never lacked successors, though the cut of her mantle has been altered to suit the changes of the mode.

The omnipotence of love is again the theme in another 'true novel,' *The Nun ; or, the Perjured Beauty*, in which a similar heroine is also the villain of the plot. Astrea frankly accepted Charles the Second's well-known opinion as to the frailty of woman. 'Virtue,' she makes one of her characters say, 'is but a name kept from scandal, which the most base of women best preserve.' But Ardelia does not even trouble about appearances. She is one of those passionate, insatiable, capricious women who play a leading rôle in every one of Astrea's comedies, and are always drawn with energy and truth because their author's heart was in them. The plot is worked out with great ingenuity in this story, and also in a later one, *The Lucky Mistake*, in which the reader is kept in the titillations of suspense to the final page. In the last-named, also, there is some attempt at character-drawing.

Oroonoko was not the only novel in which Mrs. Behn

tried to portray ideal feelings and elevated morality. *Agnes de Castro* is a sweet, sentimental tragedy, which at least has the merit of being free from errors of taste. Agnes is maid-of-honour to Donna Constantia, wife of the Prince of Portugal, and has the misfortune to be loved by her mistress's husband. But there is no foul intrigue in the story. Don Pedro struggles honourably against his passion: 'his fault was not voluntary': . . . 'a commanding power, a fatal star, had forc'd him to love in spite of himself.' The Princess is so high-minded—after the seventeenth-century pattern of high-mindedness—that she admits his innocence. ' I have no reproaches to make against you, knowing that 'tis inclination that disposes hearts, and not reason." Her complaisance goes so far that she even conjures Agnes not to deprive him of her society, since it is necessary to his happiness. But the truce is brought to a fatal ending by the malice of an envious woman, who persuades Constantia that the lovers are guilty, and so breaks her heart. The novel is painfully stilted, and reads like the discarded sketch for a tragedy, which had been worked up to suit another style.

It must be confessed that, apart from *Oroonoko*, Mrs. Behn's fiction is of very little importance in the history of our literature. Her best work was put into her comedies, which contain, not only much diversion, but also strong, and perhaps too highly coloured, pictures of the manners and morals of the pleasure-seekers of her time, in all classes. Unfortunately, it would be difficult indeed to compile even a book of elegant extracts that would give the modern reader any adequate idea of their merits, without either emasculating them altogether or nauseating him with their coarseness.

ERNEST A. BAKER

February, 1905.

THE HISTORY OF
THE ROYAL SLAVE

I DO not pretend, in giving you the history of this *ROYAL SLAVE*, to entertain my Reader with the adventures of a feigned hero, whose life and fortunes fancy may manage at the poet's pleasure; nor, in relating the truth, design to adorn it with any accidents, but such as arrived in earnest to him: and it shall come simply into the world, recommended by its own proper merits, and natural intrigues; there being enough of reality to support it, and to render it diverting, without the addition of invention.

I was myself an eye-witness to a great part of what you will find here set down; and what I could not be witness of, I received from the mouth of the chief actor in this history, the hero himself, who gave us the whole transactions of his youth: and I shall omit, for brevity's sake, a thousand little accidents of his life, which, however pleasant to us, where history was scarce, and adventures very rare, yet might prove tedious and heavy to my reader, in a world where he finds diversions for every minute, new and strange. But we who were perfectly charmed with the character of this great man, were curious to gather every circumstance of his life.

The scene of the last part of his adventures lies in a colony in America, called Surinam, in the West Indies.

But before I give you the story of this gallant slave,

it is fit I tell you the manner of bringing them to
these new colonies; those they make use of there,
not being natives of the place: for those we live with
in perfect amity, without daring to command them;
but, on the contrary, caress them with all the brotherly
and friendly affection in the world; trading with
them for their fish, venison, buffaloes' skins, and little
rarities; as marmosets, a sort of monkey, as big as
a rat or weasel, but of a marvellous and delicate
shape, having face and hands like a human creature;
and cousheries, a little beast in the form and fashion
of a lion, as big as a kitten, but so exactly made in
all parts like that noble beast, that it is it in
miniature: then for little parrakeets, great parrots,
mackaws and a thousand other birds and beasts of
wonderful and surprising forms, shapes, and colours:
for skins of prodigious snakes, of which there are
some three-score yards in length; as is the skin of
one that may be seen at his Majesty's Antiquary's;
where are also some rare flies, of amazing forms and
colours, presented to them by myself: some as big
as my fist, some less; and all of various excellences,
such as art cannot imitate. Then we trade for
feathers, which they order into all shapes, make
themselves little short habits of them, and glorious
wreaths for their heads, necks, arms and legs, whose
tinctures are inconceivable. I had a set of these
presented to me, and I gave them to the King's
Theatre; it was the dress of the Indian Queen,
infinitely admired by persons of quality; and was
inimitable. Besides these, a thousand little knacks,
and rarities in nature; and some of art, as their
baskets, weapons, aprons, etc. We dealt with them
with beads of all colours, knives, axes, pins, and
needles, which they used only as tools to drill holes
with in their ears, noses, and lips, where they hang
a great many little things; as long beads, bits of tin,
brass or silver beat thin, and any shining trinket.
The beads they weave into aprons about a quarter

of an ell long, and of the same breadth; working
them very prettily in flowers of several colours;
which apron they wear just before them, as Adam
and Eve did the fig-leaves; the men wearing a long
strip of linen, which they deal with us for. They
thread these beads also on long cotton-threads, and
make girdles to tie their aprons to, which come
twenty times, or more, about the waist, and then
cross, like a shoulder-belt, both ways, and round
their necks, arms and legs. This adornment, with
their long black hair, and the face painted in little
specks or flowers here and there, makes them a
wonderful figure to behold. Some of the beauties,
which indeed are finely shaped, as almost all are, and
who have pretty features, are charming and novel;
for they have all that is called beauty, except the
colour, which is a reddish yellow; or after a new
oiling, which they often use to themselves, they are
of the colour of a new brick, but smooth, soft and
sleek. They are extreme modest and bashful, very
shy, and nice of being touched. And though they
are all thus naked, if one lives for ever among them,
there is not to be seen an indecent action, or glance:
and being continually used to see one another so
unadorned, so like our first parents before the fall, it
seems as if they had no wishes, there being nothing
to heighten curiosity: but all you can see, you see at
once, and every moment see; and where there is no
novelty, there can be no curiosity. Not but I have
seen a handsome young Indian, dying for love of a
very beautiful young Indian maid; but all his courtship was, to fold his arms, pursue her with his eyes, and
sighs were all his language: whilst she, as if no such
lover were present, or rather as if she desired none
such, carefully guarded her eyes from beholding him;
and never approached him, but she looked down with
all the blushing modesty I have seen in the most
severe and cautious of our world. And these people
represented to me an absolute idea of the first state

of innocence, before man knew how to sin: And 'tis most evident and plain, that simple Nature is the most harmless, inoffensive and virtuous mistress. It is she alone, if she were permitted, that better instructs the world, than all the inventions of man: religion would here but destroy that tranquillity they possess by ignorance; and laws would but teach them to know offences, of which now they have no notion. They once made mourning and fasting for the death of the English Governor, who had given his hand to come on such a day to them, and neither came nor sent; believing when, a man's word was past, nothing but death could or should prevent his keeping it: and when they saw he was not dead, they asked him what name they had for a man who promised a thing he did not do? The Governor told them such a man was a liar, which was a word of infamy to a gentleman. Then one of them replied, 'Governor, you are a liar, and guilty of that infamy.' They have a native justice, which knows no fraud; and they understand no vice, or cunning, but when they are taught by the white men. They have plurality of wives; which when they grow old, serve those that succeed them, who are young, but with a servitude easy and respected; and unless they take slaves in war, they have no other attendants.

Those on that continent where I was, had no King; but the oldest War-Captain was obeyed with great resignation.

A War-Captain is a man who has led them on to battle with conduct and success; of whom I shall have occasion to speak more hereafter, and of some other of their customs and manners, as they fall in my way.

With these people, as I said, we live in perfect tranquillity, and good understanding, as it behoves us to do; they knowing all the places where to seek the best food of the country, and the means of getting it; and for very small and invaluable trifles, supplying

us with what it is almost impossible for us to get: for
they do not only in the woods, and over the Sevana's,
in hunting, supply the parts of hounds, by swiftly
scouring through those almost impassable places, and
by the mere activity of their feet, run down the
nimblest deer, and other eatable beasts; but in the
water, one would think they were gods of the rivers,
or fellow-citizens of the deep; so rare an art they
have in swimming, diving, and almost living in water;
by which they command the less swift inhabitants of
the floods. And then for shooting, what they cannot
take, or reach with their hands, they do with arrows;
and have so admirable an aim, that they will split
almost a hair, and at any distance that an arrow can
reach: they will shoot down oranges, and other
fruit, and only touch the stalk with the dart's point,
that they may not hurt the fruit. So that they being
on all occasions very useful to us, we find it absolutely
necessary to caress them as friends, and not to treat
them as slaves; nor dare we do otherwise, their
numbers so far surpassing ours in that continent.

Those then whom we make use of to work in our
plantations of sugar, are Negroes, black-slaves altogether, who are transported thither in this manner.

Those who want slaves, make a bargain with a
master, or a captain of a ship, and contract to pay
him so much apiece, a matter of twenty pound a head,
for as many as he agrees for, and to pay for them
when they shall be delivered on such a plantation: so
that when there arrives a ship laden with slaves, they
who have so contracted, go aboard, and receive their
number by lot; and perhaps in one lot that may be
for ten, there may happen to be three or four men,
the rest women and children. Or be there more or
less of either sex, you are obliged to be contented
with your lot.

Coramantien, a country of blacks so called, was one
of those places in which they found the most advantageous trading for these slaves, and thither most of

our great traders in that merchandise traffic; for that nation is very warlike and brave: and having a continual campaign, being always in hostility with one neighbouring Prince or other, they had the fortune to take a great many captives: for all they took in battle were sold as slaves; at least those common men who could not ransom themselves. Of these slaves so taken, the General only has all the profit; and of these Generals our captains and masters of ships buy all their freights.

The King of Coramantien was of himself a man of an hundred and odd years old, and had no son, though he had many beautiful black wives: for most certainly there are beauties that can charm of that colour. In his younger years he had had many gallant men to his sons, thirteen of whom died in battle, conquering when they fell; and he had only left him for his successor, one grandchild, son to one of these dead victors, who, as soon as he could bear a bow in his hand, and a quiver at his back, was sent into the field, to be trained up by one of the oldest Generals to war; where, from his natural inclination to arms, and the occasions given him, with the good conduct of the old General, he became, at the age of seventeen, one of the most expert Captains, and bravest soldiers that ever saw the field of Mars: so that he was adored as the wonder of all that world, and the darling of the soldiers. Besides, he was adorned with a native beauty, so transcending all those of his gloomy race, that he struck an awe and reverence, even into those that knew not his quality; as he did into me, who beheld him with surprise and wonder, when afterwards he arrived in our world.

He had scarce arrived at his seventeenth year, when, fighting by his side, the General was killed with an arrow in his eye, which the Prince Oroonoko (for so was this gallant Moor called) very narrowly avoided; nor had he, if the General who saw the arrow shot, and perceiving it aimed at the Prince,

had not bowed his head between, on purpose to
receive it in his own body, rather than it should touch
that of the Prince, and so saved him.

It was then, afflicted as Oroonoko was, that he was
proclaimed General in the old man's place: and then
it was, at the finishing of that war, which had continued for two years, that the Prince came to Court,
where he had hardly been a month together, from
the time of his fifth year to that of seventeen: and it
was amazing to imagine where it was he learned
so much humanity; or to give his accomplishments a
juster name, where it was he got that real greatness
of soul, those refined notions of true honour, that
absolute generosity, and that softness that was capable
of the highest passions of love and gallantry, whose
objects were almost continually fighting men, or those
mangled or dead, who heard no sounds but those of
war and groans. Some part of it we may attribute to
the care of a Frenchman of wit and learning, who
finding it turn to a very good account to be a sort of
royal tutor to this young black, and perceiving him
very ready, apt, and quick of apprehension, took a
great pleasure to teach him morals, language and
science; and was for it extremely beloved and valued
by him. Another reason was, he loved when he came
from war, to see all the English gentlemen that
traded thither; and did not only learn their language,
but that of the Spaniard also, with whom he traded
afterwards for slaves.

I have often seen and conversed with this great
man, and been a witness to many of his mighty
actions, and do assure my reader, the most illustrious
Courts could not have produced a braver both for
greatness of courage and mind, a judgment more solid,
a wit more quick, and a conversation more sweet and
diverting. He knew almost as much as if he had read
much: he had heard of and admired the Romans:
he had heard of the late Civil Wars in England,
and the deplorable death of our great Monarch; and

would discourse of it with all the sense and abhorrence of the injustice imaginable. He had an extreme good and graceful mien, and all the civility of a well-bred great man. He had nothing of barbarity in his nature, but in all points addressed himself as if his education had been in some European Court.

This great and just character of Oroonoko gave me an extreme curiosity to see him, especially when I knew he spoke French and English, and that I could talk with him. But though I had heard so much of him, I was as greatly surprised when I saw him, as if I had heard nothing of him; so beyond all report I found him. He came into the room, and addressed himself to me, and some other women, with the best grace in the world. He was pretty tall, but of a shape the most exact that can be fancied: the most famous statuary could not form the figure of a man more admirably turned from head to foot. His face was not of that brown rusty black which most of that nation are, but a perfect ebony, or polished jet. His eyes were the most awful that could be seen, and very piercing; the white of them being like snow, as were his teeth. His nose was rising and Roman, instead of African and flat: his mouth the finest shaped that could be seen; far from those great turned lips, which are so natural to the rest of the Negroes. The whole proportion and air of his face was so nobly and exactly formed, that, bating his colour, there could be nothing in nature more beautiful, agreeable and handsome. There was no one grace wanting, that bears the standard of true beauty. His hair came down to his shoulders, by the aids of art, which was by pulling it out with a quill, and keeping it combed; of which he took particular care. Nor did the perfections of his mind come short of those of his person; for his discourse was admirable upon almost any subject: and whoever had heard him speak, would have been convinced of their errors, that all fine wit is confined to the white men,

especially to those of Christendom ; and would have
confessed that Oroonoko was as capable even of
reigning well, and of governing as wisely, had as great
a soul, as politic maxims, and was as sensible of
power, as any Prince civilised in the most refined
schools of humanity and learning, or the most illustrious courts.

This Prince, such as I have described him, whose
soul and body were so admirably adorned, was (while
yet he was in the Court of his grandfather, as I said)
as capable of love, as it was possible for a brave and
gallant man to be ; and in saying that, I have named
the highest degree of love : for sure great souls are
most capable of that passion.

I have already said, the old General was killed by
the shot of an arrow, by the side of this Prince, in
battle; and that Oroonoko was made General.   This
old dead hero had one only daughter left of his
race, a beauty, that to describe her truly, one need
say only, she was female to the noble male ; the beautiful black Venus to our young Mars ; as charming in
her person as he, and of delicate virtues.   I have seen
a hundred white men sighing after her, and making a
thousand vows at her feet, all in vain and unsuccessful.   And she was indeed too great for any but a
prince of her own nation to adore.

Oroonoko coming from the wars (which were now
ended) after he had made his Court to his grandfather, he thought in honour he ought to make a visit
to Imoinda, the daughter of his foster-father, the dead
General; and to make some excuses to her, because
his preservation was the occasion of her father's
death ; and to present her with those slaves that had
been taken in this last battle, as the trophies of her
father's victories.   When he came, attended by all the
young soldiers of any merit, he was infinitely surprised at the beauty of this fair Queen of Night,
whose face and person were so exceeding all he had
ever beheld, that lovely modesty with which she

received him, that softness in her look and sighs, upon the melancholy occasion of this honour that was done by so great a man as Oroonoko, and a Prince of whom she had heard such admirable things; the awfulness wherewith she received him, and the sweetness of her words and behaviour while he stayed, gained a perfect conquest over his fierce heart, and made him feel, the victor could be subdued. So that having made his first compliments, and presented her an hundred and fifty slaves in fetters, he told her with his eyes, that he was not insensible of her charms; while Imoinda, who wished for nothing more than so glorious a conquest, was pleased to believe, she understood that silent language of new-born love; and, from that moment, put on all her additions to beauty.

The Prince returned to Court with quite another humour than before; and though he did not speak much of the fair Imoinda, he had the pleasure to hear all his followers speak of nothing but the charms of that maid, insomuch, that, even in the presence of the old King, they were extolling her, and heightening, if possible, the beauties they had found in her: so that nothing else was talked of, no other sound was heard in every corner where there were whisperers, but Imoinda! Imoinda!

It will be imagined Oroonoko stayed not long before he made his second visit; nor, considering his quality, not much longer before he told her, he adored her. I have often heard him say, that he admired by what strange inspiration he came to talk things so soft, and so passionate, who never knew love, nor was used to the conversation of women; but (to use his own words) he said, 'Most happily, some new, and, till then, unknown power instructed his heart and tongue in the language of love; and at the same time, in favour of him, inspired Imoinda with a sense of his passion.' She was touched with what he said, and returned it all in such answers as went to his very heart, with a pleasure unknown before. Nor did he use those obligations ill, that love had done him, but turned all his happy moments to the best advantage; and as he knew no vice, his flame aimed at nothing but honour, if such a distinction may be made in love; and especially in that country, where men take to themselves as many as they can maintain; and where the only crime and sin against a woman, is, to turn her off, to abandon her to want, shame and misery; such ill morals are only practised in Christian countries, where they prefer the bare name of religion; and, without religion or morality, think that sufficient. But Oroonoko was none of these professors; but as he had right notions of honour, so he made her such propositions as were not only and barely such; but, contrary to the custom of his country, he made her, vows she should be the only woman he would possess while he lived; that no age or wrinkles should incline him to change: for her soul would be always fine, and always young; and he should have an eternal idea in his mind of the charms she now bore; and should look into his heart for that idea, when he could find it no longer in her face.

After a thousand assurances of his lasting flame, and her eternal empire over him, she condescended to receive him for her husband; or rather, receive him, as the greatest honour the gods could do her.

There is a certain ceremony in these cases to be observed, which I forgot to ask how it was performed; but it was concluded on both sides, that in obedience to him, the grandfather was to be first made acquainted with the design: for they pay a most absolute resignation to the monarch, especially when he is a parent also.

On the other side, the old King, who had many wives, and many concubines, wanted not court-flatterers to insinuate into his heart a thousand tender thoughts for this young beauty; and who represented her to his fancy, as the most charming he had ever possessed in all the long race of his numerous years. At this character, his old heart, like an extinguished brand, most apt to take fire, felt new sparks of love, and began to kindle; and now grown to his second childhood, longed with impatience to behold this gay thing, with whom, alas! he could but innocently play. But how he should be confirmed she was this wonder, before he used his power to call her to Court, (where maidens never came, unless for the King's private use) he was next to consider; and while he was so doing, he had intelligence brought him, that Imoinda was most certainly mistress to the Prince Oroonoko. This gave him some chagrin: however, it gave him also an opportunity, one day, when the Prince was a hunting, to wait on a man of quality, as his slave and attendant, who should go and make a present to Imoinda, as from the Prince; he should then, unknown, see this fair maid, and have an opportunity to hear what message she would return the Prince for his present, and from thence gather the state of her heart, and degree of her inclination. This was put in execution, and the old monarch saw, and burned: he found her all he had heard, and would not delay his happiness, but found he should have some obstacle to overcome her heart; for she expressed her sense of the present the Prince had sent her, in terms so sweet, so soft and pretty, with an air of love and joy that could not be dissembled, insomuch that it was past doubt whether she loved Oroonoko entirely. This gave the old King some affliction; but he salved it with this, that the obedience the people pay their King, was not at all inferior to what they paid their gods; and what love would not oblige Imoinda to do, duty would compel her to.

He was therefore no sooner got into his apartment, but he sent the Royal Veil to Imoinda; that is the ceremony of invitation: he sends the lady he has a mind to honour with his bed, a veil, with which she is covered, and secured for the King's use; and it is

death to disobey ; besides, held a most impious disobedience.

It is not to be imagined the surprise and grief that
seized the lovely maid at this news and sight. However, as delays in these cases are dangerous, and
pleading worse than treason ; trembling, and almost
fainting, she was obliged to suffer herself to be
covered, and led away.

They brought her thus to Court; and the King,
who had caused a very rich bath to be prepared, was
led into it, where he sat under a canopy, in state, to
receive this longed-for virgin ; whom he having commanded to be brought to him, they (after disrobing
her) led her to the bath, and making fast the doors,
left her to descend. The King, without more courtship, bade her throw off her mantle, and come to his
arms. But Imoinda, all in tears, threw herself on the
marble, on the brink of the bath, and besought him to
hear her. She told him, as she was a maid, how
proud of the divine glory she should have been of
having it in her power to oblige her King : but as by
the laws he could not, and from his Royal goodness
would not take from any man his wedded wife ; so she
believed she should be the occasion of making him
commit a great sin, if she did not reveal her state and
condition ; and tell him she was another's, and could
not be so happy to be his.

The King, enraged at this delay, hastily demanded
the name of the bold man, that had married a woman
of her degree, without his consent. Imoinda seeing
his eyes fierce, and his hands tremble (whether with
age or anger, I know not, but she fancied the last)
almost repented she had said so much, for now she
feared the storm would fall on the Prince ; she therefore said a thousand things to appease the raging of
his flame, and to prepare him to hear who it was with
calmness : but before she spoke, he imagined who she
meant, but would not seem to do so, but commanded
her to lay aside her mantle, and suffer herself to receive

his caresses, or, by his gods he swore, that happy man whom she was going to name should die, though it were even Oroonoko himself. 'Therefore,' said he, 'deny this marriage, and swear thyself a maid.' 'That,' replied Imoinda, 'by all our powers I do; for I am not yet known to my husband.' 'It is enough,' said the King, 'it is enough both to satisfy my conscience and my heart.' And rising from his seat, he went and led her into the bath; it being in vain for her to resist.

In this time, the Prince, who was returned from hunting, went to visit his Imoinda, but found her gone; and not only so, but heard she had received the Royal Veil. This raised him to a storm; and in his madness, they had much ado to save him from laying violent hands on himself. Force first prevailed, and then reason: they urged all to him, that might oppose his rage; but nothing weighed so greatly with him as the King's old age, incapable of injuring him with Imoinda. He would give way to that hope, because it pleased him most, and flattered best his heart. Yet this served not altogether to make him cease his different passions, which sometimes raged within him, and softened into showers. It was not enough to appease him, to tell him, his grandfather was old, and could not that way injure him, while he retained that awful duty which the young men are used there to pay to their grave relations. He could not be convinced he had no cause to sigh and mourn for the loss of a mistress, he could not with all his strength and courage retrieve, and he would often cry, 'Oh, my friends! were she in walled cities, or confined from me in fortifications of the greatest strength; did enchantments or monsters detain her from me; I would venture any hazard to free her: but here, in the arms of a feeble old man, my youth, my violent love, my trade in arms, and all my vast desire of glory, avail me nothing. Imoinda is as irrecoverably lost to me, as if she were snatched

by the cold arms of death.   Oh ' she is never to be
retrieved.   If I would wait tedious years ; till fate
should bow the old King to his grave, even that
would not leave me Imoinda free ; but still that
custom that makes it so vile a crime for a son to
marry his father's wives or mistresses, would hinder
my happiness ; unless I would either ignobly set an
ill precedent to my successors, or abandon my country,
and fly with her to some unknown world who never
heard our story.'

But it was objected to him, that his case was not
the same : for Imoinda being his lawful wife by
solemn contract, it was he was the injured man, and
might, if he so pleased, take Imoinda back, the breach
of the law being on his grandfather's side ; and that
if he could circumvent him, and redeem her from the
Otan, which is the Palace of the King's Women, a
fort of Seraglio, it was both just and lawful for him so
to do.

This reasoning had some force upon him, and he
should have been entirely comforted, but for the
thought that she was possessed by his grandfather.
However, he loved her so well, that he was resolved to
believe what most favoured his hope, and to endeavour
to learn from Imoinda's own mouth, what only she
could satisfy him in, whether she was robbed of that
blessing which was only due to his faith and love.
But as it was very hard to get a sight of the women
(for no men ever entered into the Otan, but when the
King went to entertain himself with some one of his
wives or mistresses ; and it was death, at any other
time, for any other to go in) so he knew not how to
contrive to get a sight of her.

While Oroonoko felt all the agonies of love, and
suffered under a torment the most painful in the
world, the old King was not exempted from his share
of affliction. He was troubled, for having been forced,
by an irresistible passion, to rob his son of a treasure,
he knew, could not but be extremely dear to him ;

since she was the most beautiful that ever had been seen, and had besides, all the sweetness and innocence of youth and modesty, with a charm of wit surpassing all. He found, that however she was forced to expose her lovely person to his withered arms, she could only sigh and weep there, and think of Oroonoko; and oftentimes could not forbear speaking of him, though her life were, by custom, forfeited by owning her passion. But she spoke not of a lover only, but of a Prince dear to him to whom she spoke; and of the praises of a man, who, till now, filled the old man's soul with joy at every recital of his bravery, or even his name. And it was this dotage on our young hero, that gave Imoinda a thousand privileges to speak of him without offending, and this condescension in the old King, that made her take the satisfaction of speaking of him so very often.

Besides, he many times inquired how the Prince bore himself: and those of whom he asked, being entirely slaves to the merits and virtues of the Prince, still answered what they thought conduced best to his service; which was, to make the old King fancy that the Prince had no more interest in Imoinda, and had resigned her willingly to the pleasure of the King; that he diverted himself with his mathematicians, his fortifications, his officers, and his hunting.

This pleased the old lover, who failed not to report these things again to Imoinda, that she might, by the example of her young lover, withdraw her heart, and rest better contented in his arms. But, however she was forced to receive this unwelcome news, in all appearance, with unconcern and content; her heart was bursting within, and she was only happy when she could get alone, to vent her griefs and moans with sighs and tears.

What reports of the Prince's conduct were made to the King, he thought good to justify, as far as possibly he could by his actions; and when he ap-

peared in the presence of the King, he showed a face
not at all betraying his heart: so that in a little time,
the old man, being entirely convinced that he was no
longer a lover of Imoinda, he carried him with him,
in his train, to the Otan, often to banquet with his
mistresses.   But as soon as he entered, one day, into
the apartment of Imoinda, with the King, at the first
glance from her eyes, notwithstanding all his determined resolution, he was ready to sink in the place
where he stood; and had certainly done so, but for
the support of Aboan, a young man who was next
to him; which, with his change of countenance, had
betrayed him, had the King chanced to look that
way.   And I have observed, it is a very great error
in those who laugh when one says, 'A Negro can
change colour': for I have seen them as frequently
blush, and look pale, and that as visibly as ever I saw
in the most beautiful white.   And it is certain, that
both these changes were evident, this day, in both
these lovers.   And Imoinda, who saw with some joy
the change in the Prince's face, and found it in her
own, strove to divert the King from beholding either,
by a forced caress, with which she met him; which
was a new wound in the heart of the poor dying
Prince.   But as soon as the King was busied in looking on some fine thing of Imoinda's making, she had
time to tell the Prince, with her angry, but love-
darting eyes, that she resented his coldness, and bemoaned her own miserable captivity.   Nor were his
eyes silent, but answered hers again, as much as eyes
could do, instructed by the most tender and most
passionate heart that ever loved: and they spoke so
well, and so effectually, as Imoinda no longer doubted
but she was the only delight and darling of that soul
she found pleading in them its right of love, which
none was more willing to resign than she.   And it
was this powerful language alone that in an instant
conveyed all the thoughts of their souls to each
other; that they both found there wanted but oppor-

tunity to make them both entirely happy. But when he saw another door opened by Onahal (a former old wife of the King's, who now had charge of Imoinda) and saw the prospect of a bed of state made ready, with sweets and flowers for the dalliance of the King, who immediately led the trembling victim from his sight, into that prepared repose; what rage! what wild frenzies seized his heart! which forcing to keep within bounds, and to suffer without noise, it became the more insupportable, and rent his soul with ten thousand pains. He was forced to retire to vent his groans, where he fell down on a carpet, and lay struggling a long time, and only breathing now and then—Oh Imoinda! When Onahal had finished her necessary affair within, shutting the door, she came forth, to wait till the King called; and hearing some one sighing in the other room, she passed on, and found the Prince in that deplorable condition, which she thought needed her aid. She gave him cordials, but all in vain; till finding the nature of his disease, by his sighs, and naming Imoinda, she told him he had not so much cause as he imagined to afflict himself: for if he knew the King so well as she did, he would not lose a moment in jealousy; and that she was confident that Imoinda bore, at this minute, part in his affliction. Aboan was of the same opinion, and both together persuaded him to re-assume his courage; and all sitting down on the carpet, the Prince said so many obliging things to Onahal, that he half persuaded her to be of his party: and she promised him, she would thus far comply with his just desires, that she would let Imoinda know how faithful he was, what he suffered, and what he said.

This discourse lasted till the King called, which gave Oroonoko a certain satisfaction; and with the hope Onahal had made him conceive, he assumed a look as gay as it was possible a man in his circumstances could do: and presently after, he was called in with the rest who waited without. The King com-

manded music to be brought, and several of his
young wives and mistresses came all together by his
command, to dance before him ; where Imoinda performed her part with an air and grace so surpassing
all the rest, as her beauty was above them, and received the present ordained as a prize. The Prince
was every moment more charmed with the new
beauties and graces he beheld in this fair one ; and
while he gazed, and she danced, Onahal was retired
to a window with Aboan.

This Onahal, as I said, was one of the Cast-
Mistresses of the old King ; and it was these (now
past their beauty) that were made guardians or
governantes to the new and the young ones, and
whose business it was to teach them all those wanton
arts of love, with which they prevailed and charmed
heretofore in their turn ; and who now treated the
triumphing happy-ones with all the severity, as to
liberty and freedom, that was possible, in revenge of
the honours they rob them of; envying them those
satisfactions, those gallantries and presents, that were
once made to themselves, while youth and beauty
lasted, and which they now saw pass, as it were regardless by, and paid only to the bloomings. And certainly,
nothing is more afflicting to a decayed beauty, than
to behold in itself declining charms, that were once
adored ; and to find those caresses paid to new
beauties, to which once she laid claim ; to hear them
whisper, as she passes by, that once was a delicate
woman. Those abandoned ladies therefore endeavour
to revenge all the despites and decays of time, on
these flourishing happy-ones. And it was this
severity that gave Oroonoko a thousand fears he
should never prevail with Onahal to see Imoinda.
But, as I said, she was now retired to a window with
Aboan.

This young man was not only one of the best
quality, but a man extremely well made, and beautiful ; and coming often to attend the King to the Otan,

he had subdued the heart of the antiquated Onahal, which had not forgot how pleasant it was to be in love. And though she had some decays in her face, she had none in her sense and wit; she was there agreeable still, even to Aboan's youth: so that he took pleasure in entertaining her with discourses of love. He knew also, that to make his court to these she-favourites, was the way to be great; these being the persons that do all affairs and business at Court. He had also observed that she had given him glances more tender and inviting than she had done to others of his quality. And now, when he saw that her favour could so absolutely oblige the Prince, he failed not to sigh in her ear, and look with eyes all soft upon her, and gave her hope that she had made some impressions on his heart. He found her pleased at this, and making a thousand advances to him: but the ceremony ending, and the King departing, broke up the company for that day, and his conversation.

Aboan failed not that night to tell the Prince of his success, and how advantageous the service of Onahal might be to his amour with Imoinda. The Prince was overjoyed with this good news, and besought him, if it were possible, to caress her so, as to engage her entirely, which he could not fail to do, if he complied with her desires: 'For then,' said the Prince, 'her life lying at your mercy, she must grant you the request you make in my behalf.' Aboan understood him, and assured him he would make love so effectually, that he would defy the most expert mistress of the art to find out whether he dissembled it, or had it really. And it was with impatience they waited the next opportunity of going to the Otan.

The wars came on, the time of taking the field approached; and it was impossible for the Prince to delay his going at the head of his Army to encounter the enemy; so that every day seemed a tedious year, till he saw his Imoinda: for he believed he could not live, if he were forced away without being so happy.

It was with impatience therefore that he expected the next visit the King would make ; and, according to his wish, it was not long.

The parley of the eyes of these two lovers had not passed so secretly, but an old jealous lover could spy it ; or rather, he wanted not flatterers who told him they observed it : so that the Prince was hastened to the camp, and this was the last visit he found he should make to the Otan ; he therefore urged Aboan to make the best of this last effort, and to explain himself so to Onahal, that she deferring her enjoyment of her young lover no longer, might make way for the Prince to speak to Imoinda.

The whole affair being agreed on between the Prince and Aboan, they attended the King, as the custom was, to the Otan ; where, while the whole company was taken up in beholding the dancing and antic postures the Women-Royal made to divert the King, Onahal singled out Aboan, whom she found most pliable to her wish. When she had him where she believed she could not be heard, she sighed to him, and softly cried, 'Ah, Aboan ! when will you be sensible of my passion ? I confess it with my mouth, because I would not give my eyes the lie ; and you have but too much already perceived they have confessed my flame : nor would I have you believe that because I am the abandoned mistress of a King, I esteem myself altogether divested of charms : No, Aboan ; I have still a rest of beauty enough engaging, and have learned to please too well, not to be desirable. I can have lovers still, but will have none but Aboan.' 'Madam,' replied the half-feigning youth, 'you have already, by my eyes, found you can still conquer ; and I believe it is in pity of me you condescend to this kind confession. But, Madam, words are used to be so small a part of our country-courtship, that it is rare one can get so happy an opportunity as to tell one's heart ; and those few minutes we have, are forced to be snatched for more

certain proofs of love than speaking and sighing,
and such I languish for.'

He spoke this with such a tone, that she hoped it
true, and could not forbear believing it; and being
wholly transported with joy for having subdued the
finest of all the King's subjects to her desires, she
took from her ears two large pearls, and commanded
him to wear them in his. He would have refused
them crying, 'Madam, these are not the proofs of
your love that I expect; it is opportunity, it is a lone
hour only that can make me happy." But forcing
the pearls into his hand, she whispered softly to him,
'Oh! do not fear a woman's invention, when love
sets her a thinking.' And pressing his hand, she
cried, 'This night you shall be happy. Come to the
gate of the orange-grove, behind the Otan, and I will
be ready about midnight to receive you.' It was thus
agreed, and she left him that no notice might be taken
of their speaking together.

The ladies were still dancing, and the King, laid on
a carpet, with a great deal of pleasure was beholding
them, especially Imoinda, who that day appeared
more lovely than ever, being enlivened with the good
tidings Onahal had brought her, of the constant
passion the Prince had for her. The Prince was
laid on another carpet at the other end of the room,
with his eyes fixed on the object of his soul; and as
she turned or moved, so did they; and she alone
gave his eyes and soul their motions. Nor did
Imoinda employ her eyes to any other use, than in
beholding with infinite pleasure the joy she produced
in those of the Prince. But while she was more
regarding him than the steps she took, she chanced
to fall, and so near him, as that leaping with extreme
force from the carpet, he caught her in his arms as
she fell; and it was visible to the whole presence, the
joy wherewith he received her. He clasped her close
to his bosom, and quite forgot that reverence that was
due to the mistress of a King, and that punishment

that is the reward of a boldness of this nature. And had not the presence of mind of Imoinda (fonder of his safety than her own) befriended him, in making her spring from his arms, and fall into her dance again, he had at that instant met his death; for the old King, jealous to the last degree, rose up in rage, broke all the diversion, and led Imoinda to her apartment, and sent out word to the Prince, to go immediately to the camp; and that if he were found another night in Court, he should suffer the death ordained for disobedience to offenders.

You may imagine how welcome this news was to Oroonoko, whose unseasonable transport and caress of Imoinda was blamed by all men that loved him: and now he perceived his fault, yet cried, 'That for such another moment he would be content to die.'

All the Otan was in disorder about this accident; and Onahal was particularly concerned because on the Prince's stay depended her happiness; for she could no longer expect that of Aboan: so that ere they departed, they contrived it so that the Prince and he should both come that night to the grove of the Otan, which was all of oranges and citrons, and that there they would wait her orders.

They parted thus with grief enough till night, leaving the King in possession of the lovely maid. But nothing could appease the jealousy of the old lover; he would not be imposed on, but would have it that Imoinda made a false step on purpose to fall into Oroonoko's bosom, and that all things looked like a design on both sides; and it was in vain she protested her innocence; he was old and obstinate, and left her, more than half assured that his fear was true.

The King going to his apartment, sent to know where the Prince was, and if he intended to obey his command. The messenger returned, and told him, he found the Prince pensive, and altogether unprepared for the campaign; that he lay negligently on

the ground, and answered very little. This confirmed
the jealousy of the King, and he commanded that
they should very narrowly and privately watch his
motions; and that he should not stir from his apartment, but one spy or other should be employed to
watch him: so that the hour approaching, wherein
he was to go to the citron-grove; and taking only
Aboan along with him, he leaves his apartment, and
was watched to the very gate of the Otan; where he
was seen to enter, and where they left him, to carry
back the tidings to the King.

Oroonoko and Aboan were no sooner entered, but
Onahal led the Prince to the apartment of Imoinda;
who, not knowing any thing of her happiness, was
laid in bed. But Onahal only left him in her
chamber, to make the best of his opportunity, and
took her dear Aboan to her own; where he showed
the height of complaisance for his Prince, when, to
give him an opportunity, he suffered himself to be
caressed in bed by Onahal.

The Prince softly wakened Imoinda, who was not
a little surprised with joy to find him there; and yet
she trembled with a thousand fears. I believe he
omitted saying nothing to this young maid, that
might persuade her to suffer him to seize his own,
and take the rights of love. And I believe she was
not long resisting those arms where she so longed to
be; and having opportunity, night, and silence, youth,
love, and desire, he soon prevailed, and ravished in a
moment what his old grandfather had been endeavouring for so many months.

It is not to be imagined the satisfaction of these
two young lovers; nor the vows she made him, that
she remained a spotless maid till that night, and that
what she did with his grandfather had robbed him
of no part of her virgin honour; the gods, in mercy
and justice, having reserved that for her plighted
lord, to whom of right it belonged. And it is impossible to express the transports he suffered, while

he listened to a discourse so charming from her loved lips; and clasped that body in his arms, for whom he had so long languished; and nothing now afflicted him, but his sudden departure from her; for he told her the necessity, and his commands, but should depart satisfied in this, that since the old King had hitherto not been able to deprive him of those enjoyments which only belonged to him, he believed for the future he would be less able to injure him; so that, abating the scandal of the veil, which was no otherwise so, than that she was wife to another, he believed her safe, even in the arms of the King, and innocent; yet would he have ventured at the conquest of the world, and have given it all to have had her avoided that honour of receiving the Royal Veil. It was thus, between a thousand caresses, that both bemoaned the hard fate of youth and beauty, so liable to that cruel promotion : it was a glory that could well have been spared here, though desired and aimed at by all the young females of that kingdom.

But while they were thus fondly employed, forgetting how time ran on, and that the dawn must conduct him far away from his only happiness, they heard a great noise in the Otan, and unusual voices of men; at which the Prince, starting from the arms of the frighted Imoinda, ran to a little battle-axe he used to wear by his side; and having not so much leisure as to put on his habit, he opposed himself against some who were already opening the door : which they did with so much violence, that Oroonoko was not able to defend it; but was forced to cry out with a commanding voice, 'Whoever ye are that have the boldness to attempt to approach this apartment thus rudely; know, that I, the Prince Oroonoko, will revenge it with the certain death of him that first enters; therefore stand back, and know, this place is sacred to love and me this night; to-morrow 'tis the King's.'

This he spoke with a voice so resolved and assured,

that they soon retired from the door; but cried, "'Tis by the King's command we are come; and being satisfied by thy voice, O Prince, as much as if we had entered, we can report to the King the truth of all his fears, and leave thee to provide for thy own safety, as thou art advised by thy friends.'

At these words they departed, and left the Prince to take a short and sad leave of his Imoinda; who, trusting in the strength of her charms, believed she should appease the fury of a jealous King, by saying, she was surprised, and that it was by force of arms he got into her apartment. All her concern now was for his life, and therefore she hastened him to the camp, and with much ado prevailed on him to go. Nor was it she alone that prevailed; Aboan and Onahal both pleaded, and both assured him of a lie that should be well enough contrived to secure Imoinda. So that at last, with a heart sad as death, dying eyes, and sighing soul, Oroonoko departed, and took his way to the camp.

It was not long after, the King in person came to the Otan; where beholding Imoinda, with rage in his eyes, he upbraided her wickedness, and perfidy; and threatening her royal lover, she fell on her face at his feet, bedewing the floor with her tears, and imploring his pardon for a fault which she had not with her will committed; as Onahal, who was also prostrate with her, could testify: that, unknown to her, he had broken into her apartment, and ravished her. She spoke this much against her conscience; but to save her own life, it was absolutely necessary she should feign this falsity. She knew it could not injure the Prince, he being fled to an army that would stand by him, against any injuries that should assault him. However, this last thought of Imoinda's being ravished, changed the measures of his revenge; and whereas before he designed to be himself her executioner, he now resolved she should not die. But as it is the greatest crime in nature amongst them, to touch a woman after having been possessed by a son, a father, or a brother, so now he looked on Imoinda as a polluted thing wholly unfit for his embrace; nor would he resign her to his grandson, because she had received the Royal Veil: he therefore removes her from the Otan, with Onahal; whom he put into safe hands, with the order they should be both sold off as slaves to another country, either Christian or heathen, it was no matter where.

This cruel sentence, worse than death, they implored might be reversed; but their prayers were vain, and it was put in execution accordingly, and that with so much secrecy, that none, either without or within the Otan, knew anything of their absence, or their destiny.

The old King nevertheless executed this with a great deal of reluctancy; but he believed he had made a very great conquest over himself, when he had once resolved, and had performed what he resolved. He believed now, that his love had been unjust; and that he could not expect the gods, or Captain of the Clouds (as they call the unknown power) would suffer a better consequence from so ill a cause. He now begins to hold Oroonoko excused; and to say, he had reason for what he did. And now every body could assure the King how passionately Imoinda was beloved by the Prince; even those confessed it now, who said the contrary before his flame was not abated. So that the King being old, and not able to defend himself in war, and having no sons of all his race remaining alive, but only this to maintain him on his throne; and looking on this as a man disobliged, first by the rape of his mistress, or rather wife, and now by depriving him wholly of her, he feared, might make him desperate, and do some cruel thing, either to himself or his old grandfather the offender, he began to repent him extremely of the contempt he had, in his rage, put on Imoinda. Besides, he considered he ought in honour to have

killed her for this offence, if it had been one. He
ought to have had so much value and consideration
for a maid of her quality, as to have nobly put her to
death, and not to have sold her like a common slave;
the greatest revenge, and the most disgraceful of any,
and to which they a thousand times prefer death, and
implore it; as Imoinda did, but could not obtain that
honour. Seeing therefore it was certain that Oroonoko would highly resent this affront, he thought
good to make some excuse for his rashness to him;
and to that end, he sent a messenger to the camp,
with orders to treat with him about the matter, to
gain his pardon, and endeavour to mitigate his grief:
but that by no means he should tell him she was sold,
but secretly put to death; for he knew he should
never obtain his pardon for the other.

When the messenger came, he found the Prince
upon the point of engaging with the enemy; but as soon
as he heard of the arrival of the messenger, he commanded him to his tent, where he embraced him, and
received him with joy; which was soon abated by the
downcast looks of the messenger, who was instantly
demanded the cause by Oroonoko; who, impatient of
delay, asked a thousand questions in a breath, and all
concerning Imoinda. But there needed little return;
for he could almost answer himself of all he demanded, from his sight and eyes. At last the messenger casting himself at the Prince's feet, and kissing
them with all the submission of a man that had something to implore which he dreaded to utter, besought
him to hear with calmness what he had to deliver to
him, and to call up all his noble and heroic courage,
to encounter with his words, and defend himself
against the ungrateful things he had to relate. Oroonoko replied, with a deep sigh, and a languishing
voice, 'I am armed against their worst efforts, for I
know they will tell me, Imoinda is no more—— And
after that, you may spare the rest.' Then, commanding him to rise, he laid himself on a carpet, under a

rich pavilion, and remained a good while silent, and was hardly heard to sigh. When he was come a little to himself, the messenger asked him leave to deliver that part of his embassy which the Prince had not yet divined: and the Prince cried, 'I permit thee.' Then he told him the affliction the old King was in, for the rashness he had committed in his cruelty to Imoinda; and how he deigned to ask pardon for his offence, and to implore the Prince would not suffer that loss to touch his heart too sensibly, which now all the gods could not restore him, but might recompense him in glory, which he begged he would pursue; and that death, that common revenger of all injuries, would soon even the account between him and a feeble old man.

Oroonoko bad him return his duty to his lord and master; and to assure him, there was no account of revenge to be adjudged between them: if there was, he was the aggressor, and that death would be just, and, maugre his age, would see him righted; and he was contented to leave his share of glory to youths more fortunate and worthy of that favour from the gods: that henceforth he would never lift a weapon, or draw a bow, but abandon the small remains of his life to sighs and tears, and the continual thoughts of what his lord and grandfather had thought good to send out of the world, with all that youth, that innocence and beauty.

After having spoken this, whatever his greatest officers and men of the best rank could do, they could not raise him from the carpet, or persuade him to action, and resolutions of life; but commanding all to retire, he shut himself into his pavilion all that day, while the enemy was ready to engage: and wondering at the delay, the whole body of the chief of the army then addressed themselves to him, and to whom they had much ado to get admittance. They fell on their faces at the foot of his carpet, where they lay, and besought him with earnest prayers and tears to lead them forth to battle, and not let the enemy take advantages of them; and implored him to have regard to his glory, and to the world, that depended on his courage and conduct. But he made no other reply to all their supplications than this, that he had now no more business for glory; and for the world, it was a trifle not worth his care: 'Go,' continued he, sighing, 'and divide it amongst you, and reap with joy what you so vainly prize, and leave me to my more welcome destiny.'

They then demanded what they should do, and whom he would constitute in his room, that the confusion of ambitious youth and power might not ruin their order, and make them a prey to the enemy. He replied, he would not give himself that trouble, but wished them to choose the bravest man amongst them, let his quality or birth be what it would: 'For, oh my friends!' says he, 'it is not titles make men brave or good; or birth that bestows courage and generosity, or makes the owner happy. Believe this, when you behold Oroonoko the most wretched, and abandoned by fortune, of all the creation of the gods.' So turning himself about, he would make no more reply to all they could urge or implore.

The army beholding their officers return unsuccessful, with sad faces and ominous looks, that presaged no good luck, suffered a thousand fears to take possession of their hearts, and the enemy to come even upon them before they could provide for their safety by any defence: and though they were assured by some who had a mind to animate them, that they should be immediately headed by the Prince: and that in the mean time Aboan had orders to command as General; yet they were so dismayed for want of that great example of bravery, that they could make but a very feeble resistance; and, at last, downright fled before the enemy, who pursued them to the very tents, killing them: nor could all Aboan's courage, which that day gained him immortal glory, shame them into a manly defence of themselves. The guards that were left behind about the Prince's tent, seeing the soldiers flee before the enemy, and scatter themselves over the plain, in great disorder, made such outcries, as roused the Prince from his amorous slumber, in which he had remained buried for two days, without permitting any sustenance to approach him. But, in spite of all his resolutions, he had not the constancy of grief to that degree, as to make him insensible of the danger of his army; and in that instant he leaped from his couch, and cried— 'Come, if we must die, let us meet death the noblest way; and it will be more like Oroonoko to encounter him at an army's head, opposing the torrent of a conquering foe, than lazily on a couch, to wait his lingering pleasure, and die every moment by a thousand racking thoughts; or be tamely taken by an enemy, and led a whining, love-sick slave to adorn the triumphs of Jamoan, that young victor, who already is entered beyond the limits I have prescribed him.'

While he was speaking, he suffered his people to dress him for the field; and sallying out of his pavilion, with more life and vigour in his countenance than ever he showed, he appeared like some Divine Power descended to save his country from destruction: and his people had purposely put him on all things that might make him shine with most splendour, to strike a reverend awe into the beholders. He flew into the thickest of those that were pursuing his men; and being animated with despair, he fought as if he came on purpose to die, and did such good things as will not be believed that human strength could perform; and such, as soon inspired all the rest with new courage, and new ardour. And now it was that they began to fight indeed; and so, as if they would not be outdone even by their adored hero; who turning the tide of the victory, changing absolutely the fate of the day, gained an entire conquest: and

Oroonoko having the good fortune to single out Jamoan, he took him prisoner with his own hand, having wounded him almost to death.

This Jamoan afterwards became very dear to him, being a man very gallant, and of excellent graces, and fine parts; so that he never put him amongst the rank of captives as they used to do, without distinction, for the common sale, or market, but kept him in his own court, where he retained nothing of the prisoner but the name, and returned no more into his own country; so great an affection he took for Oroonoko, and by a thousand tales and adventures of love and gallantry, flattered his disease of melancholy and languishment; which I have often heard him say had certainly killed him, but for the conversation of this prince and Aboan, and the French Governor he had from his childhood, of whom I have spoken before, and who was a man of admirable wit, great ingenuity and learning; all which he had infused into his young pupil. This Frenchman was banished out of his own country for some heretical notions he held; and though he was a man of very little religion, yet he had admirable morals, and a brave soul.

After the total defeat of Jamoan's army, which all fled, or were left dead upon the place, they spent some time in the camp; Oroonoko choosing rather to remain awhile there in his tents, than to enter into a Palace, or live in a Court where he had so lately suffered so great a loss; the officers therefore, who saw and knew his cause of discontent, invented all sorts of diversions and sports to entertain their Prince: so that what with those amusements abroad, and others at home, that is, within their tents, with the persuasions, arguments, and care of his friends and servants that he more peculiarly prized, he wore off in time a great part of that chagrin, and torture of despair, which the first efforts of Imoinda's death had given him; insomuch, as having received a thousand kind embassies from the King, and invitation to return to Court, he obeyed, though with no little reluctancy; and when he did so, there was a visible change in him, and for a long time he was much more melancholy than before. But time lessens all extremes, and reduces them to mediums, and unconcern; but no motives of beauties, though all endeavoured it, could engage him in any sort of amour, though he had all the invitations to it, both from his own youth, and other ambitions and designs.

Oroonoko was no sooner returned from this last conquest, and received at Court with all the joy and magnificence that could be expressed to a young victor, who was not only returned triumphant, but beloved like a deity, than there arrived in the port an English ship.

The master of it had often before been in these countries, and was very well known to Oroonoko, with whom he had trafficked for slaves, and had used to do the same with his predecessors.

This commander was a man of a finer sort of address and conversation, better bred, and more engaging, than most of that sort of men are; so that he seemed rather never to have been bred out of a Court, than almost all his life at sea. This captain therefore was always better received at Court, than most of the traders to those countries were; and especially by Oroonoko, who was more civilised, according to the European mode, than any other had been, and took more delight in the white nations; and, above all, men of parts and wit. To this captain he sold abundance of his slaves; and for the favour and esteem he had for him, made him many presents, and obliged him to stay at Court as long as possibly he could. Which the captain seemed to take as a very great honour done him, entertaining the Prince every day with globes and maps, and mathematical discourses and instruments;

eating, drinking, hunting, and living with him with so much familiarity, that it was not to be doubted but he had gained very greatly upon the heart of this gallant young man. And the captain, in return of all these mighty favours, besought the Prince to honour his vessel with his presence some day or other at dinner, before he should set sail; which he condescended to accept, and appointed his day. The captain, on his part, failed not to have all things in a readiness, in the most magnificent order he could possibly; and the day being come, the captain, in his boat, richly adorned with carpets and velvet cushions, rowed to the shore to receive the Prince; with another long-boat, where was placed all his music and trumpets, with which Oroonoko was extremely delighted; who met him on the shore, attended by his French Governor, Jamoan, Aboan, and about a hundred of the noblest of the youths of the Court; and after they had first carried the Prince on board, the boats fetched the rest off; where they found a very splendid treat, with all sorts of fine wines; and were as well entertained, as it was possible in such a place to be.

The Prince having drunk hard of punch, and several sorts of wine, as did all the rest, (for great care was taken they should want nothing of that part of the entertainment) was very merry, and in great admiration of the ship, for he had never been in one before; so that he was curious of beholding every place where he decently might descend. The rest, no less curious, who were not quite overcome with drinking, rambled at their pleasure fore and aft, as their fancies guided them; so that the captain, who had well laid his design before, gave the word, and seized on all his guests; then, clapping great irons suddenly on the Prince, when he was leaped down into the hold, to view that part of the vessel, and locking him fast down, secured him. The same treachery was used to all the rest; and all in one

instant, in several places of the ship, were lashed
fast in irons, and betrayed to slavery. That great
design over, they set all hands at work to hoist sail;
and with as treacherous as fair a wind they made
from the shore with this innocent and glorious
prize, who thought of nothing less than such an
entertainment.

Some have commended this act, as brave in the
captain; but I will spare my sense of it, and leave
it to my reader to judge as he pleases. It may
be easily guessed, in what manner the Prince resented
this indignity, who may be best resembled to a lion
taken in a toil; so he raged, so he struggled for
liberty, but all in vain; and they had so wisely
managed his fetters, that he could not use a hand
in his defence, to quit himself of a life that would by
no means endure slavery; nor could he move from
the place where he was tied, to any solid part of the
ship, against which he might have beat his head, and
have finished his disgrace that way. So that being
deprived of all other means, he resolved to perish for
want of food; and pleased at last with that thought,
and toiled and tired by rage and indignation, he laid
himself down, and sullenly resolved upon dying, and
refused all things that were brought him.

This did not a little vex the captain, and the more
so, because he found almost all of them of the same
humour; so that the loss of so many brave slaves,
so tall and goodly to behold, would have been very
considerable; he therefore ordered one to go from
him (for he would not be seen himself) to Oroonoko,
and to assure him, he was afflicted for having rashly
done so inhospitable a deed, and which could not be
now remedied, since they were far from shore; but
since he resented it in so high a nature, he assured
him he would revoke his resolution, and set both him
and his friends ashore on the next land they should
touch at; and of this the messenger gave him his
oath, provided he would resolve to live. And

Oroonoko, whose honour was such, as he never had violated a word in his life himself, much less a solemn asseveration, believed in an instant what this man said; but replied, he expected, for a confirmation of this, to have his shameful fetters dismissed. This demand was carried to the captain; who returned him answer, that the offence had been so great which he had put upon the Prince, that he durst not trust him with liberty while he remained in the ship, for fear, lest by a valour natural to him, and a revenge that would animate that valour, he might commit some outrage fatal to himself, and the King his master, to whom the vessel did belong. To this Oroonoko replied, He would engage his honour to behave himself in all friendly order and manner, and obey the command of the captain, as he was lord of the King's vessel, and General of those men under his command.

This was delivered to the still doubting captain, who could not resolve to trust a heathen, he said, upon his parole, a man that had no sense or notion of the god that he worshipped. Oroonoko then replied, He was very sorry to hear that the captain pretended to the knowledge and worship of any gods, who had taught him no better principles, than not to credit as he would be credited. But they told him, the difference of their faith occasioned that distrust; for the captain had protested to him upon the word of a Christian, and sworn in the name of a great God; which if he should violate, he must expect eternal torments in the world to come. 'Is that all the obligations he has to be just to his oath?' replied Oroonoko. 'Let him know, I swear by my honour; which to violate, would not only render me contemptible and despised by all brave and honest men, and so give myself perpetual pain, but it would be eternally offending and displeasing to all mankind; harming, betraying, circumventing, and outraging a'l men. But punishments hereafter are suffered by one's self; and the world takes no cognizance whether this God has revenged them or not, it is done so secretly, and deferred so long; while the man of no honour suffers every moment the scorn and contempt of the honester world, and dies every day ignominiously in his fame, which is more valuable than life. I speak not this to move belief, but to show you how you mistake, when you imagine, that he who will violate his honour, will keep his word with his gods.' So, turning from him with a disdainful smile, he refused to answer him, when he urged him to know what answer he should carry back to his captain; so that he departed without saying any more.

The captain pondering and consulting what to do, it was concluded, that nothing but Oroonoko's liberty would encourage any of the rest to eat, except the Frenchman, whom the captain could not pretend to keep prisoner, but only told him, he was secured, because he might act something in favour of the Prince; but that he should be freed as soon as they came to land. So that they concluded it wholly necessary to free the Prince from his irons, that he might show himself to the rest; that they might have an eye upon him, and that they could not fear a single man.

This being resolved, to make the obligation the greater, the captain himself went to Oroonoko; where, after many compliments, and assurances of what he had already promised, he receiving from the Prince his parole, and his hand, for his good behaviour, dismissed his irons, and brought him to his own cabin; where, after having treated and reposed him a while, (for he had neither eaten nor slept in four days before) he besought him to visit those obstinate people in chains, who refused all manner of sustenance; and entreated him to oblige them to eat, and assure them of their liberty the first opportunity.

Oroonoko, who was too generous not to give credit to his words, showed himself to his people, who were transported with excess of joy at the sight of their darling Prince; falling at his feet, and kissing and embracing them; believing, as some divine oracle, all he assured them. But he besought them to bear their chains with that bravery that became those whom he had seen act so nobly in arms; and that they could not give him greater proofs of their love and friendship, since it was all the security the captain (his friend) could have against the revenge, he said, they might possibly justly take for the injuries sustained by him. And they all, with one accord, assured him, that they could not suffer enough, when it was for his repose and safety.

After this, they no longer refused to eat, but took what was brought them, and were pleased with their captivity, since by it they hoped to redeem the Prince, who, all the rest of the voyage, was treated with all the respect due to his birth, though nothing could divert his melancholy; and he would often sigh for Imoinda, and think this a punishment due to his misfortune, in having left that noble maid behind him, that fatal night, in the Otan, when he fled to the camp.

Possessed with a thousand thoughts of past joys with this fair young person, and a thousand griefs for her eternal loss, he endured a tedious voyage, and at last arrived at the mouth of the River of Surinam, a colony belonging to the King of England, and where they were to deliver some part of their slaves. There the merchants and gentlemen of the country going on board, to demand those lots of slaves they had already agreed on; and amongst those, the overseers of those plantations where I then chanced to be. The captain, who had given the word, ordered his men to bring up those noble slaves in fetters, whom I have spoken of; and having put them, some in one, and some in other lots, with women and children (which they call pick-

aninnies) they sold them off, as slaves to several
merchants and gentlemen ; not putting any two in
one lot, because they would separate them far from
each other ; nor daring to trust them together, lest
rage and courage should put them upon contriving
some great action, to the ruin of the colony.

Oroonoko was first seized on, and sold to our overseer, who had the first lot, with seventeen more of all
sorts and sizes, but not one of quality with him.
When he saw this, he found what they meant ; for,
as I said, he understood English pretty well; and
being wholly unarmed and defenceless, so as it was
in vain to make any resistance, he only beheld the
captain with a look all fierce and disdainful, upbraid-
ing him with eyes that forced blushes on his guilty
cheeks, he only cried in passing over the side of the
ship : ' Farewell, sir, 'tis worth my sufferings to gain
so true a knowledge, both of you, and of your gods,
by whom you swear.'   And desiring those that held
him to forbear their pains, and telling them he would
make no resistance, he cried, ' Come, my fellow-slaves,
let us descend, and see if we can meet with more
honour and honesty in the next world we shall touch
upon.'   So he nimbly leapt into the boat, and showing no more concern, suffered himself to be rowed up
the river, with his seventeen companions.

The gentleman that bought him was a young
Cornish gentleman, whose name was Trefry ; a man
of great wit, and fine learning, and was carried into
those parts by the Lord ——, Governor, to manage
all his affairs.   He reflecting on the last words of
Oroonoko to the captain, and beholding the richness
of his vest, no sooner came into the boat, but he fixed
his eyes on him ; and finding something so extraordinary in his face, his shape and mien, a greatness
of look, and haughtiness in his air, and finding he
spoke English, had a great mind to be inquiring into
his quality and fortune ; which, though Oroonoko
endeavoured to hide, by only confessing he was above

the rank of common slaves, Trefry soon found he was yet something greater than he confessed; and from that moment began to conceive so vast an esteem for him, that he ever after loved him as his dearest brother, and showed him all the civilities due to so great a man.

Trefry was a very good mathematician, and a linguist; could speak French and Spanish; and in the three days they remained in the boat, (for so long were they going from the ship to the plantation) he entertained Oroonoko so agreeably with his art and discourse, that he was no less pleased with Trefry, than he was with the Prince; and he thought himself, at least, fortunate in this, that since he was a slave, as long as he would suffer himself to remain so, he had a man of so excellent wit and parts for a master. So that before they had finished their voyage up the river, he made no scruple of declaring to Trefry all his fortunes, and most part of what I have here related, and put himself wholly into the hands of his new friend, who he found resented all the injuries were done him, and was charmed with all the greatnesses of his actions; which were recited with that modesty, and delicate sense, as wholly vanquished him, and subdued him to his interest. And he promised him, on his word and honour, he would find the means to reconduct him to his own country again; assuring him, he had a perfect abhorrence of so dishonourable an action; and that he would sooner have died, than have been the author of such a perfidy. He found the Prince was very much concerned to know what became of his friends, and how they took their slavery; and Trefry promised to take care about the inquiring after their condition, and that he should have an account of them.

Though, as Oroonoko afterwards said, he had little reason to credit the words of a *Backearary;* yet he knew not why, but he saw a kind of sincerity, and awful truth in the face of Trefry; he saw honesty in

his eyes, and he found him wise and witty enough to
understand honour : for it was one of his maxims, *A
man of wit could not be a knave or villain.*

In their passage up the river, they put in at several
houses for refreshment ; and ever when they landed,
numbers of people would flock to behold this man :
not but their eyes were daily entertained with the
sight of slaves ; but the fame of Oroonoko was gone
before him, and all people were in admiration of his
beauty.   Besides, he had a rich habit on, in which he
was taken, so different from the rest, and which the
captain could not strip him of, because he was forced
to surprise his person in the minute he sold him.
When he found his habit made him liable, as he
thought, to be gazed at the more, he begged Trefry
to give him something more befitting a slave, which
he did, and took off his robes : nevertheless, he shone
through all, and his osenbrigs (a sort of brown
Holland suit he had on) could not conceal the graces
of his looks and mien ; and he had no less admirers
than when he had his dazzling habit on.   The Royal
Youth appeared in spite of the slave, and people
could not help treating him after a different manner,
without designing it.   As soon as they approached
him, they venerated and esteemed him ; his eyes insensibly commanded respect, and his behaviour insinu-
ated it into every soul.   So that there was nothing
talked of but this young and gallant slave, even by
those who yet knew not that he was a prince.

I ought to tell you that the Christians never buy
any slaves but they give them some name of their
own, their native ones being likely very barbarous,
and hard to pronounce ; so that Mr. Trefry gave
Oroonoko that of Cæsar ; which name will live in
that country as long as that (scarce more) glorious
one of the great Roman : for it is most evident he
wanted no part of the personal courage of that
Cæsar, and acted things as memorable, had they been
done in some part of the world replenished with

people and historians, that might have given him his
due. But his misfortune was, to fall in an obscure
world, that afforded only a female pen to celebrate
his fame; though I doubt not but it had lived from
others' endeavours, if the Dutch, who immediately
after his time took that country, had not killed,
banished and dispersed all those that were capable
of giving the world this great man's life, much better
than I have done. And Mr. Trefry, who designed it,
died before he began it, and bemoaned himself for
not having undertaken it in time.

For the future therefore I must call Oroonoko
Cæsar; since by that name only he was known in
our western world, and by that name he was received
on shore at Parham House, where he was destined a
slave. But if the king himself (God bless him) had
come ashore there could not have been greater expectation by all the whole plantation, and those
neighbouring ones, than was on ours at that time:
and he was received more like a governor than a
slave: notwithstanding, as the custom was, they
assigned him his portion of land, his house and his
business up in the plantation. But as it was more
for form, than any design to put him to his task, he
endured no more of the slave but the name, and
remained some days in the house, receiving all visits
that were made him, without stirring towards that
part of the plantation where the negroes were.

At last, he would needs go view his land, his house,
and the business assigned him. But he no sooner
came to the houses of the slaves, which are like a
little town by itself, the negroes all having left work,
but they all came forth to behold him, and found he
was that Prince who had, at several times, sold most
of them to these parts; and from a veneration they
pay to great men, especially if they know them, and
from the surprise and awe they had at the sight of
him, they all cast themselves at his feet, crying out,
in their language, 'Live, O King! Long live, O

King!' and kissing his feet, paid him even divine homage.

Several English gentlemen were with him, and what Mr. Trefry had told them was here confirmed; of which he himself before had no other witness than Cæsar himself. But he was infinitely glad to find his grandeur confirmed by the adoration of all the slaves.

Cæsar, troubled with their over-joy, and over-ceremony, besought them to rise, and to receive him as their fellow-slave; assuring them he was no better. At which they set up with one accord a most terrible and hideous mourning and condoling, which he and the English had much ado to appease: but at last they prevailed with them, and they prepared all their barbarous music, and every one killed and dressed something of his own stock (for every family has their land apart, on which, at their leisure times, they breed all eatable things) and clubbing it together, made a most magnificent supper, inviting their *Grandee Captain*, their *Prince*, to honour it with his presence; which he did, and several English with him, where they all waited on him, some playing, others dancing before him all the time, according to the manners of their several nations, and with un-wearied industry endeavouring to please and delight him.

While they sat at meat, Mr. Trefry told Cæsar, that most of these young slaves were undone in love with a fine she-slave, whom they had had about six months on their land; the Prince, who never heard the name of love without a sigh, nor any mention of it without the curiosity of examining further into that tale, which of all discourses was most agreeable to him, asked, how they came to be so unhappy, as to be all undone for one fair slave? Trefry, who was naturally amorous, and delighted to talk of love as well as anybody, proceeded to tell him, they had the most charming black that ever was beheld on their plantation, about fifteen or sixteen years old, as he guessed; that for his part he had done nothing but sigh for her ever since she came; and that all the white beauties he had seen, never charmed him so absolutely as this fine creature had done; and that no man, of any nation, ever beheld her, that did not fall in love with her; and that she had all the slaves perpetually at her feet; and the whole country resounded with the fame of Clemene, for so (said he) we have christened her: but she denies us all with such a noble disdain, that 'tis a miracle to see, that she who can give such eternal desires, should herself be all ice and unconcern. She is adorned with the most graceful modesty that ever beautified youth; the softest sigher——that, if she were capable of love, one would swear she languished for some absent happy man; and so retired, as if she feared a rape even from the God of Day, or that the breezes would steal kisses from her delicate mouth. Her task of work, some sighing lover every day makes it his petition to perform for her; which she accepts blushing, and with reluctancy, for fear he will ask her a look for a recompense, which he dares not presume to hope: so great an awe she strikes into the hearts of her admirers. 'I do not wonder,' replied the Prince, 'that Clemene should refuse slaves, being, as you say, so beautiful; but wonder how she escapes those that can entertain her as you can do; or why, being your slave, you do not oblige her to yield?' 'I confess,' said Trefry, 'when I have, against her will, entertained her with love so long, as to be transported with my passion even above decency, I have been ready to make use of those advantages of strength and force nature has given me. But, oh! she disarms me with that modesty and weeping, so tender and so moving, that I retire, and thank my stars she overcame me.' The company laughed at his civility to a slave, and Cæsar only applauded the nobleness of his passion and nature, since that slave might be noble, or, what was better, have true notions of honour and virtue in her. Thus passed they this night, after having received from the slaves all imaginable respect and obedience.

The next day, Trefry asked Cæsar to walk when the heat was allayed, and designedly carried him by the cottage of the fair slave; and told him she whom he spoke of last night lived there retired: 'But,' says he, 'I would not wish you to approach; for I am sure you will be in love as soon as you behold her.' Cæsar assured him, he was proof against all the charms of that sex; and that if he imagined his heart could be so perfidious to love again after Imoinda, he believed he should tear it from his bosom. They had no sooner spoken, but a little shock-dog, that Clemene had presented her, which she took great delight in, ran out; and she, not knowing anybody was there, ran to get it in again, and bolted out on those who were just speaking of her: when seeing them, she would have run in again, but Trefry caught her by the hand, and cried, 'Clemene, however you fly a lover, you ought to pay some respect to this stranger,' pointing to Cæsar. But she, as if she had resolved never to raise her eyes to the face of a man again, bent them the more to the earth, when he spoke, and gave the Prince the leisure to look the more at her. There needed no long gazing, or consideration, to examine who this fair creature was; he soon saw Imoinda all over her; in a minute he saw her face, her shape, her air, her modesty, and all that called forth his soul with joy at his eyes, and left his body destitute of almost life: it stood without motion, and for a minute knew not that it had a being; and, I believe, he had never come to himself, so oppressed he was with over-joy, if he had not met with this allay, that he perceived Imoinda fall dead in the hands of Trefry. This awakened him, and he ran to her aid, and caught her in his arms, where by degrees she came to herself; and it is needless to tell with what transports, what ecstasies of joy, they both a while beheld each other, without speaking; then snatched each other to their arms; then gazed again, as if they still doubted whether they possessed the blessing they grasped: but when they recovered their speech, it is not to be imagined what tender things they expressed to each other; wondering what strange fate had brought them again together. They soon informed each other of their fortunes, and equally bewailed their fate; but at the same time they mutually protested, that even fetters and slavery were soft and easy, and would be supported with joy and pleasure, while they could be so happy to possess each other, and to be able to make good their vows. Cæsar swore he disdained the empire of the world, while he could behold his Imoinda; and she despised grandeur and pomp, those vanities of her sex, when she could gaze on Oroonoko. He adored the very cottage where she resided, and said, That little inch of the world would give him more happiness than all the universe could do; and she vowed it was a palace, while adorned with the presence of Oroonoko.

Trefry was infinitely pleased with this novel, and found this Clemene was the fair mistress of whom Cæsar had before spoke; and was not a little satisfied, that heaven was so kind to the Prince as to sweeten his misfortunes by so lucky an accident; and leaving the lovers to themselves, was impatient to come down to Parham House (which was on the same plantation) to give me an account of what had happened. I was as impatient to make these lovers a visit, having already made a friendship with Cæsar, and from his own mouth learned what I have related; which was confirmed by his Frenchman, who was set on shore to seek his fortune, and of whom they could not make a slave, because a Christian; and he came daily to Parham Hill to see and pay his respects to his pupil Prince. So that concerning and interesting myself in all that related to Cæsar, whom I had assured of liberty as soon as the Governor arrived, I hasted presently to the place where these lovers were, and was infinitely glad to find this beautiful young slave (who had already gained all our esteems, for her modesty and extraordinary prettiness) to be the same I had heard Cæsar speak so much of. One may imagine then we paid her a treble respect; and though from her being carved in fine flowers and birds all over her body, we took her to be of quality before, yet when we knew Clemene was Imoinda, we could not enough admire her.

I had forgot to tell you, that those who are nobly born of that country, are so delicately cut and raised all over the fore-part of the trunk of their bodies, that it looks as if it were japanned, the works being raised like high point round the edges of the flowers. Some are only carved with a little flower, or bird, at the sides of the temples, as was Cæsar; and those who are so carved over the body, resemble our ancient Picts that are figured in the chronicles, but these carvings are more delicate.

From that happy day Cæsar took Clemene for his wife, to the general joy of all people; and there was as much magnificence as the country could afford at the celebration of this wedding: and in a very short time after she conceived with child, which made Cæsar even adore her, knowing he was the last of his great race. This new accident made him more impatient of liberty, and he was every day treating with Trefry for his and Clemene's liberty, and offered either gold, or a vast quantity of slaves, which should be paid before they let him go, provided he could have any security that he should go when his ransom was paid. They fed him from day to day with promises, and delayed him till the Lord-Governor should come; so that he began to suspect them of falsehood, and that they would delay him till the time of his wife's delivery, and make a slave of the child too; for all the breed is theirs to whom the

parents belong. This thought made him very uneasy, and his sullenness gave them some jealousies
of him ; so that I was obliged, by some persons who
feared a mutiny (which is very fatal sometimes in
those colonies that abound so with slaves, that they
exceed the whites in vast numbers), to discourse with
Cæsar, and to give him all the satisfaction I possibly
could. They knew he and Clemene were scarce an
hour in a day from my lodgings ; that they ate with
me, and that I obliged them in all things I was
capable. I entertained them with the lives of the
Romans, and great men, which charmed him to my
company ; and her, with teaching her all the pretty
works that I was mistress of, and telling her stories
of nuns, and endeavouring to bring her to the knowledge of the true God. But of all discourses, Cæsar
liked that the worst, and would never be reconciled
to our notions of the trinity, of which he ever made
a jest ; it was a riddle he said would turn his brain
to conceive, and one could not make him understand
what faith was. However, these conversations failed
not altogether so well to divert him, that he liked the
company of us women much above the men, for he
could not drink, and he is but an ill companion in
that country that cannot. So that obliging him to
love us very well, we had all the liberty of speech
with him, especially myself, whom he called his *Great
Mistress ;* and indeed my word would go a great way
with him. For these reasons I had opportunity to
take notice of him, that he was not well pleased of
late, as he used to be; was more retired and thought-
ful ; and told him, I took it ill he should suspect we
would break our words with him, and not permit both
him and Clemene to return to his own kingdom,
which was not so long a way, but when he was once
on his voyage he would quickly arrive there. He
made me some answers that showed a doubt in him,
which made me ask, what advantage it would be to
doubt? It would but give us a fear of him, and

possibly compel us to treat him so as I should be very loth to behold; that is, it might occasion his confinement. Perhaps this was not so luckily spoke of me, for I perceived he resented that word, which I strove to soften again in vain : however, he assured me, that whatsoever resolutions he should take, he would act nothing upon the white people; and as for myself, and those upon that plantation where he was, he would sooner forfeit his eternal liberty, and life itself, than lift his hand against his greatest enemy on that place. He besought me to suffer no fears upon his account, for he could do nothing that honour should not dictate; but he accused himself for having suffered slavery so long; yet he charged that weakness on love alone, who was capable of making him neglect even glory itself; and, for which, now he reproaches himself every moment of the day. Much more to this effect he spoke, with an air impatient enough to make me know he would not be long in bondage; and though he suffered only the name of a slave, and had nothing of the toil and labour of one, yet that was sufficient to render him uneasy; and he had been too long idle, who used to be always in action, and in arms. He had a spirit all rough and fierce, and that could not be tamed to lazy rest: and though all endeavours were used to exercise himself in such actions and sports as this world afforded, as running, wrestling, pitching the bar, hunting and fishing, chasing and killing tigers of a monstrous size, which this continent affords in abundance; and wonderful snakes, such as Alexander is reported to have encountered at the river of Amazons, and which Cæsar took great delight to overcome; yet these were not actions great enough for his large soul, which was still panting after more renowned actions.

Before I parted that day with him, I got, with much ado, a promise from him to rest yet a little longer with patience, and wait the coming of the

Lord-Governor, who was every day expected on our shore. He assured me he would, and this promise he desired me to know was given perfectly in complaisance to me, in whom he had an entire confidence.

After this, I neither thought it convenient to trust him much out of our view, nor did the country, who feared him; but with one accord it was advised to treat him fairly, and oblige him to remain within such a compass, and that he should be permitted, as seldom as could be, to go up to the plantations of the negroes; or, if he did, to be accompanied by some that should be rather, in appearance, attendants than spies. This care was for some time taken, and Cæsar looked upon it as a mark of extraordinary respect, and was glad his discontent had obliged them to be more observant to him; he received new assurance from the overseer, which was confirmed to him by the opinion of all the gentlemen of the country, who made their court to him. During this time that we had his company more frequently than hitherto we had had, it may not be unpleasant to relate to you the diversions we entertained him with, or rather he us.

My stay was to be short in that country; because my father died at sea, and never arrived to possess the honour designed him, (which was Lieutenant-General of six-and-thirty islands, besides the continent of Surinam) nor the advantages he hoped to reap by them: so that, though we were obliged to continue on our voyage, we did not intend to stay upon the place. Though, in a word, I must say thus much of it; that certainly had his late Majesty, of sacred memory, but seen and known what a vast and charming world he had been master of in that continent, he would never have parted so easily with it to the Dutch. It is a continent, whose vast extent was never yet known, and may contain more noble earth than all the universe beside; for, they say, it reaches from east to west one way as far as China,

and another to Peru. It affords all things both for
beauty and use; it is there eternal spring, always the
very months of April, May, and June; the shades are
perpetual, the trees bearing at once all degrees of
leaves, and fruit, from blooming buds to ripe autumn:
groves of oranges, lemons, citrons, figs, nutmegs, and
noble aromatics, continually bearing their fragrances:
the trees appearing all like nosegays, adorned with
flowers of different kinds; some are all white, some
purple, some scarlet, some blue, some yellow; bearing
at the same time ripe fruit, and blooming young, or
producing every day new. The very wood of all
these trees has an intrinsic value, above common
timber; for they are, when cut, of different colours,
glorious to behold, and bear a price considerable, to
inlay withal. Besides this, they yield rich balm, and
gums; so that we make our candles of such an
aromatic substance, as does not only give a sufficient
light, but as they burn, they cast their perfumes all
about. Cedar is the common firing, and all the houses
are built with it. The very meat we eat, when set on
the table, if it be native, I mean of the country, perfumes the whole room; especially a little beast called
an Armadillo, a thing which I can liken to nothing
so well as a rhinoceros; it is all in white armour,
so jointed, that it moves as well in it, as if it had
nothing on. This beast is about the bigness of a pig
of six weeks old. But it were endless to give an
account of all the divers wonderful and strange things
that country affords, and which he took a great
delight to go in search of; though those adventures
are oftentimes fatal, and at least dangerous. But
while we had Cæsar in our company on these designs,
we feared no harm, nor suffered any.

As soon as I came into the country, the best house
in it was presented me, called St. John's Hill. It
stood on a vast rock of white marble, at the foot of
which the river ran a vast depth down, and not to be
descended on that side; the little waves still dashing

and washing the foot of this rock, made the softest
murmurs and purlings in the world; and the opposite
bank was adorned with such vast quantities of different flowers eternally blowing, and every day and
hour new, fenced behind them with lofty trees of a
thousand rare forms and colours, that the prospect was
the most ravishing that fancy can create. On the
edge of this white rock, towards the river, was a walk,
or grove, of orange and lemon trees, about half the
length of the Mall here, whose flowery and fruit-
bearing branches met at the top, and hindered the
sun, whose rays are very fierce there, from entering
a beam into the grove; and the cool air that came
from the river made it not only fit to entertain people
in, at all the hottest hours of the day, but refresh the
sweet blossoms, and made it always sweet and charming; and sure, the whole globe of the world cannot
show so delightful a place as this grove was: not all
the gardens of boasted Italy can produce a shade to
outvie this, which nature has joined with art to
render so exceeding fine; and it is a marvel to see
how such vast trees, as big as English oaks, could
take footing on so solid a rock, and in so little earth
as covered that rock. But all things by nature there
are rare, delightful, and wonderful. But to our sports.
    Sometimes we would go surprising, and in search
of young tigers in their dens, watching when the old
ones went forth to forage for prey: and oftentimes we
have been in great danger, and have fled apace for
our lives, when surprised by the dams. But once,
above all other times, we went on this design, and
Cæsar was with us; who had no sooner stolen a young
tiger from her nest, but going off, we encountered the
dam, bearing a buttock of a cow, which she had torn
off with her mighty paw, and going with it towards
her den. We had only four women, Cæsar, and an
English gentleman, brother to Harry Martin the
great Oliverian; we found there was no escaping this
enraged and ravenous beast. However, we women

fled as fast as we could from it; but our heels had
not saved our lives, if Cæsar had not laid down her
cub, when he found the tiger quit her prey to make
the more speed towards him; and taking Mr. Martin's
sword, desired him to stand aside, or follow the ladies.
He obeyed him; and Cæsar met this monstrous beast
of mighty size, and vast limbs, who came with open
jaws upon him; and fixing his awful stern eyes full
upon those of the beast, and putting himself into
a very steady and good aiming posture of defence,
ran his sword quite through his breast, down to his
very heart, home to the hilt of the sword. The dying
beast stretched forth her paw, and going to grasp his
thigh, surprised with death in that very moment, did
him no other harm than fixing her long nails in his
flesh very deep, feebly wounded him, but could not
grasp the flesh to tear off any. When he had done
this, he halloaed us to return; which, after some
assurance of his victory, we did, and found him
lugging out the sword from the bosom of the tiger,
who was laid in her blood on the ground. He took
up the cub, and with an unconcern that had nothing
of the joy or gladness of victory, he came and laid
the whelp at my feet. We all extremely wondered
at his daring, and at the bigness of the beast, which
was about the height of a heifer, but of mighty
great and strong limbs.

Another time, being in the woods, he killed a tiger,
that had long infested that part, and borne away
abundance of sheep and oxen, and other things, that
were for the support of those to whom they belonged.
Abundance of people assailed this beast, some affirm-
ing they had shot her with several bullets quite
through the body at several times; and some swearing they shot her through the very heart; and they
believed she was a devil, rather than a mortal thing.
Cæsar had often said, he had a mind to encounter
this monster, and spoke with several gentlemen who
had attempted her; one crying, I shot her with so

many poisoned arrows, another with his gun in this part of her, and another in that; so that he remarking all the places where she was shot, fancied still he should overcome her, by giving her another sort of a wound than any had yet done; and one day said (at the table) 'What trophies and garlands, ladies, will you make me, if I bring you home the heart of this ravenous beast that eats up all your lambs and pigs?' We all promised he should be rewarded at our hands. So taking a bow, which he chose out of a great many, he went up into the wood, with two gentlemen, where he imagined this devourer to be. They had not passed very far into it when they heard her voice, growling and grumbling, as if she were pleased with something she was doing. When they came in view, they found her nuzzling in the belly of a new ravished sheep, which she had torn open; and seeing herself approached, she took fast hold of her prey with her fore-paws, and set a very fierce raging look on Cæsar, without offering to approach him, for fear at the same time of losing what she had in possession. So that Cæsar remained a good while, only taking aim, and getting an opportunity to shoot her where he designed. It was some time before he could accomplish it; and to wound her, and not kill her, would but have enraged her the more, and endangered him. He had a quiver of arrows at his side, so that if one failed, he could be supplied. At last, retiring a little, he gave her opportunity to eat, for he found she was ravenous, and fell to as soon as she saw him retire, being more eager of her prey, than of doing new mischiefs; when he going softly to one side of her, and hiding his person behind certain herbage, that grew high and thick, he took so good aim that, as he intended he shot her just into the eye, and the arrow was sent with so good a will, and so sure a hand, that it stuck in her brain, and made her caper, and become mad for a moment or two; but being seconded by another arrow, she fell dead upon the prey. Cæsar cut her open with a knife, to see where those wounds were that had been reported to him, and why she did not die of them. But I shall now relate a thing that, possibly, will find no credit among men; because it is a notion commonly received with us, that nothing can receive a wound in the heart, and live. But when the heart of this courageous animal was taken out, there were seven bullets of lead in it, the wound seamed up with great scars, and she lived with the bullets a great while, for it was long since they were shot. This heart the conqueror brought up to us, and it was a very great curiosity, which all the country came to see; and which gave Cæsar occasion of many fine discourses of accidents in war, and strange escapes.

At other times he would go a-fishing; and discoursing on that diversion, he found we had in that country a very strange fish, called a Numb-Eel, (an eel of which I have eaten) that while it is alive, it has a quality so cold, that those who are angling, though with a line of ever so great a length, with a rod at the end of it, it shall in the same minute the bait is touched by this eel, seize him or her that holds the rod with a numbness, that shall deprive them of sense for a while; and some have fallen into the water, and others dropped, as dead, on the banks of the rivers where they stood, as soon as this fish touches the bait. Cæsar used to laugh at this, and believed it impossible a man could lose his force at the touch of a fish; and could not understand that philosophy, that a cold quality should be of that nature; however, he had a great curiosity to try whether it would have the same effect on him it had on others, and often tried, but in vain. At last, the sought-for fish came to the bait, as he stood angling on the bank; and instead of throwing away the rod, or giving it

a sudden twitch out of the water, whereby he might
have caught both the eel, and have dismissed the rod,
before it could have too much power over him; for
experiment-sake, he grasped it but the harder, and
fainting, fell into the river; and being still possessed
of the rod, the tide carried him, senseless as he was, a
great way, till an Indian boat took him up; and perceived when they touched him, a numbness seize them,
and by that knew the rod was in his hand; which
with a paddle, (that is a short oar) they struck away,
and snatched it into the boat, eel and all. If Cæsar
was almost dead, with the effect of this fish, he was
more so with that of the water, where he had remained the space of going a league, and they found
they had much ado to bring him back to life; but
at last they did, and brought him home, where he
was in a few hours well recovered and refreshed, and
not a little ashamed to find he should be overcome
by an eel, and that all the people, who heard his
defiance, would laugh at him. But we cheered him
up; and he being convinced, we had the eel at
supper, which was a quarter of an ell about, and
most delicate meat; and was of the more value,
since it cost so dear as almost the life of so gallant
a man.

About this time we were in many mortal fears,
about some disputes the English had with the
Indians; so that we could scarce trust ourselves,
without great numbers, to go to any Indian towns,
or place where they abode, for fear they should fall
upon us, as they did immediately after my coming
away; and the place being in the possession of the
Dutch, they used them not so civilly as the English;
so that they cut in pieces all they could take, getting
into houses, and hanging up the mother, and all her
children about her; and cut a footman I left behind
me, all in joints, and nailed him to trees.

This feud began while I was there: so that I lost
half the satisfaction I proposed, in not seeing and

visiting the Indian towns. But one day, bemoaning of our misfortunes on this account, Cæsar told us, we need not fear, for if we had a mind to go, he would undertake to be our guard. Some would, but most would not venture. About eighteen of us resolved, and took barge, and after eight days, arrived near an Indian town. But approaching it, the hearts of some of our company failed; and they would not venture on shore; so we polled, who would, and who would not. For my part, I said, if Cæsar would, I would go. He resolved; so did my brother, and my woman, a maid of good courage. Now none of us speaking the language of the people, and imagining we should have a half diversion in gazing only; and not knowing what they said, we took a fisherman that lived at the mouth of the river, who had been a long inhabitant there, and obliged him to go with us. But because he was known to the Indians as trading among them, and being, by long living there, become a perfect Indian in colour, we, who had a mind to surprise them, by making them see something they never had seen (that is, white people), resolved only myself, my brother and woman should go. So Cæsar, the fisherman, and the rest, hiding behind some thick reeds and flowers that grew in the banks, let us pass on towards the town, which was on the bank of the river all along. A little distant from the houses, or huts, we saw some dancing, others busied in fetching and carrying of water from the river. They had no sooner spied us, but they set up a loud cry, that frighted us at first; we thought it had been for those that should kill us, but it seems it was of wonder and amazement. They were all naked; and we were dressed, so as is most commode for the hot countries, very glittering and rich; so that we appeared extremely fine; my own hair was cut short, and I had a taffety cap, with black feathers on my head; my brother was in a stuff-suit, with silver loops and buttons, and abundance of green ribbon. This was all infinitely surprising to them : and because we saw them stand still till we approached them, we took heart and advanced, came up to them, and offered them our hands ; which they took, and looked on us round about, calling still for more company; who came swarming out, all wondering, and crying out *Tepeeme;* taking their hair up in their hands, and spreading it wide to those they called out to ; as if they would say (as indeed it signified) *Numberless Wonders*, or not to be recounted, no more than to number the hair of their heads. By degrees they grew more bold, and from gazing upon us round, they touched us, laying their hands upon all the features of our faces, feeling our breasts and arms, taking up one petticoat, then wondering to see another; admiring our shoes and stockings, but more our garters, which we gave them, and they tied about their legs, being laced with silver lace at the ends; for they much esteem any shining things. In fine, we suffered them to survey us as they pleased, and we thought they never would have done admiring us. When Cæsar, and the rest, saw we were received with such wonder, they came up to us; and finding the Indian trader whom they knew, (for it is by these fishermen, called Indian traders, we hold a commerce with them ; for they love not to go far from home, and we never go to them) when they saw him therefore, they set up a new joy, and cried in their language, 'Oh, here's our Tiguamy, and we shall know whether these things can speak.' So advancing to him, some of them gave him their hands, and cried, 'Amora Tiguamy'; which is as much as, *How do you do ?* or, *Welcome, friend ;* and all, with one din, began to gabble to him, and asked, if we had sense and wit ? If we could talk of affairs of life and war, as they could do ? If we could hunt, swim, and do a thousand things they use? He answered them, We could. Then they invited us into their houses, and dressed venison and buffalo for us ; and going out, gathered

a leaf of a tree, called a *Sarumbo* leaf, of six yards
long, and spread it on the ground for a table-cloth ;
and cutting another in pieces instead of plates, set us
on little low Indian stools, which they cut out of one
entire piece of wood, and paint in a sort of Japan-
work. They serve every one their mess on these pieces
of leaves ; and it was very good, but too high-seasoned
with pepper. When we had eaten, my brother and I
took out our flutes, and played to them, which gave
them new wonder ; and I soon perceived, by an
admiration that is natural to these people, and by the
extreme ignorance and simplicity of them, it were not
difficult to establish any unknown or extravagant
religion among them, and to impose any notions
or fictions upon them. For seeing a kinsman of mine
set some paper on fire with a burning-glass, a trick
they had never before seen, they were like to have
adored him for a god, and begged he would give
them the characters or figures of his name, that they
might oppose it against winds and storms : which he
did, and they held it up in those seasons, and fancied
it had a charm to conquer them, and kept it like a
holy relic. They are very superstitious, and called
him the Great Peeie, that is, *Prophet*. They showed
us their Indian Peeie, a youth of about sixteen years
old, as handsome as nature could make a man.
They consecrate a beautiful youth from his infancy,
and all arts are used to complete him in the finest
manner, both in beauty and shape. He is bred to all
the little arts and cunning they are capable of ; to all
the legerdemain tricks and sleight of hand whereby
he imposes on the rabble, and is both a doctor in
physic and divinity : and by these tricks makes the
sick believe he sometimes eases their pains, by drawing from the afflicted part little serpents, or odd flies,
or worms, or any strange thing : and though they
have besides undoubted good remedies for almost all
their diseases, they cure the patient more by fancy
than by medicines, and make themselves feared,

loved, and reverenced. This young Peeie had a very young wife, who seeing my brother kiss her, came running and kissed me. After this they kissed one another, and made it a great jest, it being so novel; and new admiration and laughing went round the multitude, that they never will forget that ceremony, never before used or known. Cæsar had a mind to see and talk with their war-captains, and we were conducted to one of their houses, where we beheld several of the great captains, who had been at council. But so frightful a vision it was to see them, no fancy can create; no sad dreams can represent so dreadful a spectacle. For my part, I took them for hobgoblins, or fiends, rather than men. But however their shapes appeared, their souls were very humane and noble; but some wanted their noses, some their lips, some both noses and lips, some their ears, and others cut through each cheek, with long slashes, through which their teeth appeared. They had several other formidable wounds and scars, or rather dismemberings. They had *Comitias*, or little aprons before them, and girdles of cotton, with their knives naked stuck in it; a bow at their back, and a quiver of arrows on their thighs; and most had feathers on their heads of divers colours. They cried 'Amora Tiguamy' to us at our entrance, and were pleased we said as much to them. They seated us, and gave us drink of the best sort, and wondered as much as the others had done before to see us. Cæsar was marvelling as much at their faces, wondering how they should be all so wounded in war; he was impatient to know how they all came by those frightful marks of rage or malice, rather than wounds got in noble battle. They told us by our interpreter, that when any war was waging, two men, chosen out by some old captain whose fighting was past, and who could only teach the theory of war, were to stand in competition for the generalship, or great war-captain; and being brought before the old judges, now past

labour, they are asked, what they dare do to show
they are worthy to lead an army? When he who is
first asked, making no reply, cuts off his nose, and
throws it contemptibly on the ground ; and the other
does something to himself that he thinks surpasses
him, and perhaps deprives himself of lips and an eye.
So they slash on till one gives out, and many have
died in this debate. And it is by a passive valour
they show and prove their activity; a sort of courage
too brutal to be applauded by our black hero ; nevertheless, he expressed his esteem of them.

In this voyage Cæsar begat so good an understanding between the Indians and the English, that there
were no more fears or heart-burnings during our stay,
but we had a perfect, open, and free trade with them.
Many things remarkable, and worthy reciting, we
met with in this short voyage ; because Cæsar made
it his business to search out and provide for our entertainment, especially to please his dearly adored
Imoinda, who was a sharer in all our adventures ; we
being resolved to make her chains as easy as we
could, and to compliment the Prince in that manner
that most obliged him.

As we were coming up again, we met with some
Indians of strange aspects ; that is, of a larger size, and
other sort of features than those of our country.
Our Indian slaves, that rowed us, asked them some
questions ; but they could not understand us, but
showed us a long cotton string, with several knots on
it, and told us, they had been coming from the
mountains so many moons as there were knots : they
were habited in skins of a strange beast, and brought
along with them bags of gold-dust ; which, as well
as they could give us to understand, came streaming
in little small channels down the high mountains,
when the rains fell ; and offered to be the convoy to
anybody, or persons, that would go to the mountains.
We carried these men up to Parham, where they were
kept till the Lord-Governor came. And because all

the country was mad to be going on this golden adventure, the Governor, by his letters, commanded (for they sent some of the gold to him) that a guard should be set at the mouth of the river of Amazons (a river so called, almost as broad as the river of Thames) and prohibited all people from going up that river, it conducting to those mountains of gold. But we going off for England before the project was further prosecuted, and the Governor being drowned in a hurricane, either the design died, or the Dutch have the advantage of it. And it is to be bemoaned what his Majesty lost, by losing that part of America.

Though this digression is a little from my story, however, since it contains some proofs of the curiosity and daring of this great man, I was content to omit nothing of his character.

It was thus for some time we diverted him; but now Imoinda began to show she was with child, and did nothing but sigh and weep for the captivity of her lord, herself, and the infant yet unborn; and believed, if it were so hard to gain the liberty of two, it would be more difficult to get that for three. Her griefs were so many darts in the great heart of Cæsar, and taking his opportunity, one Sunday, when all the whites were overtaken in drink, as there were abundance of several trades, and slaves for four years, that inhabited among the negro houses; and Sunday being their day of debauch, (otherwise they were a sort of spies upon Cæsar) he went, pretending out of goodness to them, to feast among them, and sent all his music, and ordered a great treat for the whole gang, about three hundred negroes, and about a hundred and fifty were able to bear arms, such as they had, which were sufficient to do execution, with spirits accordingly. For the English had none but rusty swords, that no strength could draw from a scabbard; except the people of particular quality, who took care to oil them, and keep them in good order. The guns also, unless here and there one, or those newly carried from England, would do no good or harm; for it is the nature of that country to rust and eat up iron, or any metals but gold and silver. And they are very expert at the bow, which the negroes and Indians are perfect masters of.

Cæsar, having singled out these men from the women and children, made a harangue to them of the miseries and ignominies of slavery; counting up all their toils and sufferings, under such loads, burdens and drudgeries, as were fitter for beasts than men; senseless brutes, than human souls. He told them, it was not for days, months or years, but for eternity; there was no end to be of their misfortunes. They suffered not like men, who might find a glory and fortitude in oppression; but like dogs, that loved the whip and bell, and fawned the more they were beaten; that they had lost the divine quality of men, and were become insensible asses, fit only to bear: nay, worse; an ass, or dog, or horse, having done his duty, could lie down in retreat, and rise to work again, and while he did his duty, endured no stripes; but men, villainous, senseless men, such as they, toiled on all the tedious week till Black Friday; and then, whether they worked or not, whether they were faulty or meriting, they, promiscuously, the innocent with the guilty, suffered the infamous whip, the sordid stripes, from their fellow-slaves, till their blood trickled from all parts of their body; blood, whose every drop ought to be revenged with a life of some of those tyrants that impose it. 'And why,' said he, 'my dear friends and fellow-sufferers, should we be slaves to an unknown people? Have they vanquished us nobly in fight? Have they won us in honourable battle? And are we by the chance of war become their slaves? This would not anger a noble heart; this would not animate a soldier's soul. No, but we are bought and sold like apes or monkeys, to be the sport of women, fools and cowards; and the support of rogues and runagates, that have abandoned their own countries for rapine, murders, theft and villainies. Do you not hear every day how they upbraid each other with infamy of life, below the wildest savages? And shall we render obedience to such a degenerate race, who have no one human virtue left, to distingush them from the vilest creatures? Will you, I say, suffer the lash from such hands?' They all replied with one accord, 'No, no, no; Cæsar has spoke like a great captain, like a great king.'

After this he would have proceeded, but was interrupted by a tall negro, of some more quality than the rest, his name was Tuscan; who bowing at the feet of Cæsar, cried, 'My lord, we have listened with joy and attention to what you have said; and, were we only men, would follow so great a leader through the world. But O! consider we are husbands and parents too, and have things more dear to us than life; our wives and children, unfit for travel in those unpassable woods, mountains and bogs. We have not only difficult lands to overcome, but rivers to wade, and mountains to encounter; ravenous beasts of prey.'

To this Cæsar replied, that honour was the first principle in nature, that was to be obeyed; but as no man would pretend to that, without all the acts of virtue, compassion, charity, love, justice and reason, he found it not inconsistent with that, to take equal care of their wives and children as they would of themselves; and that he did not design, when he led them to freedom, and glorious liberty, that they should leave that better part of themselves to perish by the hand of the tyrant's whip. But if there were a woman among them so degenerate from love and virtue, to choose slavery before the pursuit of her husband, and with the hazard of her life, to share with him in his fortunes; that such a one ought to be abandoned, and left as a prey to the common enemy.

THE ROYAL SLAVE 65

To which they all agreed—and bowed. After
this, he spoke of the impassable woods and rivers ;
and convinced them, the more danger the more glory.
He told them, that he had heard of one Hannibal,
a great captain, had cut his way through mountains
of solid rocks ; and should a few shrubs oppose them,
which they could fire before them ? No, it was a
trifling excuse to men resolved to die, or overcome.
As for bogs, they are with a little labour filled and
hardened ; and the rivers could be no obstacle, since
they swam by nature, at least by custom, from the
first hour of their birth. That when the children
were weary, they must carry them by turns, and the
woods and their own industry would afford them
food. To this they all assented with joy.

Tuscan then demanded, what he would do. He
said he would travel towards the sea, plant a new
colony, and defend it by their valour ; and when they
could find a ship, either driven by stress of weather,
or guided by providence that way, they would seize
it, and make it a prize, till it had transported them to
their own countries : at least they should be made
free in his kingdom, and be esteemed as his fellow-
sufferers, and men that had the courage and the
bravery to attempt, at least, for liberty ; and if they
died in the attempt, it would be more brave, than to
live in perpetual slavery.

They bowed and kissed his feet at this resolution,
and with one accord vowed to follow him to death ;
and that night was appointed to begin their march.
They made it known to their wives, and directed
them to tie their hammocks about their shoulders, and
under their arms, like a scarf, and to lead their
children that could go, and carry those that could
not. The wives, who pay an entire obedience to
their husbands, obeyed, and stayed for them where
they were appointed. The men stayed but to furnish themselves with what defensive arms they could
get ; and all met at the rendezvous, where Cæsar

made a new encouraging speech to them and led them out.

But as they could not march far that night, on Monday early, when the overseers went to call them all together, to go to work, they were extremely surprised, to find not one upon the place, but all fled with what baggage they had. You may imagine this news was not only suddenly spread all over the plantation, but soon reached the neighbouring ones; and we had by noon about six hundred men, they call the Militia of the country, that came to assist us in the pursuit of the fugitives. But never did one see so comical an army march forth to war. The men of any fashion would not concern themselves, though it were almost the common cause; for such revoltings are very ill examples, and have very fatal consequences oftentimes, in many colonies. But they had a respect for Cæsar, and all hands were against the Parhamites (as they called those of Parham Plantation) because they did not in the first place love the Lord-Governor; and secondly, they would have it, that Cæsar was ill-used, and baffled with: and it is not impossible but some of the best in the country was of his council in this flight, and depriving us of all the slaves; so that they of the better sort would not meddle in the matter. The Deputy-Governor, of whom I have had no great occasion to speak, and who was the most fawning fair-tongued fellow in the world, and one that pretended the most friendship to Cæsar, was now the only violent man against him; and though he had nothing, and so need fear nothing, yet talked and looked bigger than any man. He was a fellow, whose character is not fit to be mentioned with the worst of the slaves. This fellow would lead his army forth to meet Cæsar, or rather to pursue him. Most of their arms were of those sort of cruel whips they call *Cat with nine tails;* some had rusty useless guns for show; others old basket-hilts, whose blades

had never seen the light in this age; and others had
long staffs and clubs. Mr. Trefry went along, rather
to be a mediator than a conqueror in such a battle;
for he foresaw and knew, if by fighting they put the
negroes into despair, they were a sort of sullen fel-
lows, that would drown or kill themselves before they
would yield; and he advised that fair means was
best. But Byam was one that abounded in his own
wit, and would take his own measures.

It was not hard to find these fugitives; for as they
fled, they were forced to fire and cut the woods before
them; so that night or day they pursued them by the
light they made, and by the path they had cleared.
But as soon as Cæsar found he was pursued, he put
himself in a posture of defence, placing all the women
and children in the rear; and himself, with Tuscan
by his side, or next to him, all promising to die or
conquer. Encouraged thus, they never stood to parley, but fell on pell-mell upon the English, and killed
some, and wounded a great many; they having recourse to their whips, as the best of their weapons.
And as they observed no order, they perplexed the
enemy so sorely, with lashing them in the eyes; and
the women and children seeing their husbands so
treated, being of fearful and cowardly dispositions, and
hearing the English cry out, 'Yield, and live! Yield,
and be pardoned!' they all ran in amongst their
husbands and fathers, and hung about them, crying
out, 'Yield! Yield! and leave Cæsar to their revenge,'
that by degrees the slaves abandoned Cæsar, and
left him only Tuscan and his heroic Imoinda, who
grown as big as she was, did nevertheless press near
her lord, having a bow and a quiver full of poisoned
arrows, which she managed with such dexterity, that
she wounded several, and shot the Governor into the
shoulder; of which wound he had liked to have died,
but that an Indian woman, his mistress, sucked the
wound, and cleansed it from the venom. But however, he stirred not from the place till he had parleyed

with Cæsar, who he found was resolved to die fighting, and would not be taken; no more would Tuscan or Imoinda. But he, more thirsting after revenge of another sort, than that of depriving him of life, now made use of all his art of talking and dissembling, and besought Cæsar to yield himself upon terms which he himself should propose, and should be sacredly assented to, and kept by him. He told him, it was not that he any longer feared him, or could believe the force of two men, and a young heroine, could overthrow all them, and with all the slaves now on their side also; but it was the vast esteem he had for his person, the desire he had to serve so gallant a man, and to hinder himself from the reproach hereafter, of having been the occasion of the death of a Prince, whose valour and magnanimity deserved the empire of the world. He protested to him, he looked upon his action as gallant and brave, however tending to the prejudice of his lord and master, who would by it have lost so considerable a number of slaves; that this flight of his should be looked on as a heat of youth, and a rashness of a too forward courage, and an unconsidered impatience of liberty, and no more; and that he laboured in vain to accomplish that which they would effectually perform as soon as any ship arrived that would touch on his coast: 'So that if you will be pleased,' continued he, 'to surrender yourself, all imaginable respect shall be paid you; and yourself, your wife and child, if it be born here, shall depart free out of our land.' But Cæsar would hear of no composition; though Byam urged, if he pursued and went on in his design, he would inevitably perish, either by great snakes, wild beasts or hunger; and he ought to have regard to his wife, whose condition required ease, and not the fatigues of tedious travel, where she could not be secured from being devoured. But Cæsar told him there was no faith in the white men, or the gods they adored; who instructed them in principles so false, that honest men

could not live amongst them; though no people professed so much, none performed so little: that he knew
what he had to do when he dealt with men of honour;
but with them a man ought to be eternally on his
guard, and never to eat and drink with Christians,
without his weapon of defence in his hand; and, for
his own security, never to credit one word they spoke.
As for the rashness and inconsiderateness of his
action, he would confess the Governor is in the right;
and that he was ashamed of what he had done, in
endeavouring to make those free, who were by
nature slaves, poor wretched rogues, fit to be used as
Christians' tools; dogs, treacherous and cowardly, fit
for such masters; and they wanted only but to be
whipped into the knowledge of the Christian gods, to
be the vilest of all creeping things; to learn to worship such deities as had not power to make them just,
brave, or honest. In fine, after a thousand things of
this nature, not fit here to be recited, he told Byam
he had rather die than live upon the same earth with
such dogs. But Trefry and Byam pleaded and protested together so much, that Trefry believing the
Governor to mean what he said, and speaking very
cordially himself, generously put himself into Cæsar's
hands, and took him aside, and persuaded him, even
with tears, to live, by surrendering himself, and to
name his conditions. Cæsar was overcome by his wit
and reasons, and in consideration of Imoinda; and
demanding what he desired, and that it should be
ratified by their hands in writing, because he had
perceived that was the common way of contract
between man and man amongst the whites; all this
was performed, and Tuscan's pardon was put in, and
they surrendered to the Governor, who walked peace-
ably down into the plantation with them, after giving
order to bury their dead. Cæsar was very much
toiled with the bustle of the day, for he had fought
like a fury; and what mischief was done, he and
Tuscan performed alone; and gave their enemies a

fatal proof, that they durst do anything, and feared
no mortal force.

But they were no sooner arrived at the place where
all the slaves receive their punishments of whipping,
but they laid hands on Cæsar and Tuscan, faint with
heat and toil; and surprising them, bound them to two
several stakes, and whipped them in a most deplorable and inhuman manner, rending the very flesh
from their bones, especially Cæsar, who was not perceived to make any moan or to alter his face, only
to roll his eyes on the faithless Governor, and those
he believed guilty, with fierceness and indignation;
and to complete his rage, he saw every one of those
slaves who but a few days before adored him as something more than mortal, now had a whip to give him
some lashes, while he strove not to break his fetters;
though if he had, it were impossible: but he pronounced
a woe and revenge from his eyes, that darted fire, which
was at once both awful and terrible to behold.

When they thought they were sufficiently revenged
on him, they untied him, almost fainting with loss of
blood from a thousand wounds all over his body,
from which they had rent his clothes, and led him
bleeding and naked as he was, and loaded him all
over with irons; and then rubbed his wounds, to complete their cruelty, with Indian pepper, which had
like to have made him raving mad; and, in this condition made him so fast to the ground, that he could not
stir, if his pains and wounds would have given him
leave. They spared Imoinda, and did not let her see
this barbarity committed towards her lord, but carried
her down to Parham, and shut her up; which was not
in kindness to her, but for fear she should die with
the sight, or miscarry, and then they should lose a
young slave, and perhaps the mother.

You must know, that when the news was brought
on Monday morning, that Cæsar had betaken himself
to the woods, and carried with him all the negroes,
we were possessed with extreme fear, which no per-

suasions could dissipate, that he would secure himself till night, and then would come down and cut all our throats. This apprehension made all the females of us fly down the river, to be secured; and while we were away, they acted this cruelty; for I suppose I had authority and interest enough there, had I suspected any such thing, to have prevented it: but we had not gone many leagues, but the news overtook us, that Cæsar was taken and whipped like a common slave. We met on the river with Colonel Martin, a man of great gallantry, wit, and goodness, and whom I have celebrated in a character of my new comedy, by his own name, in memory of so brave a man. He was wise and eloquent, and, from the fineness of his parts, bore a great sway over the hearts of all the colony. He was a friend to Cæsar, and resented this false dealing with him very much. We carried him back to Parham, thinking to have made an accommodation; when he came, the first news we heard, was, that the Governor was dead of a wound Imoinda had given him; but it was not so well. But it seems, he would have the pleasure of beholding the revenge he took on Cæsar; and before the cruel ceremony was finished, he dropped down; and then they perceived the wound he had on his shoulder was by a venomed arrow, which, as I said, his Indian mistress healed, by sucking the wound.

We were no sooner arrived, but we went up to the plantation to see Cæsar; whom we found in a very miserable and inexpressible condition; and I have a thousand times admired how he lived in so much tormenting pain. We said all things to him, that trouble, pity and good-nature could suggest, protesting our innocency of the fact, and our abhorrence of such cruelties; making a thousand professions and services to him, and begging as many pardons for the offenders, till we said so much, that he believed we had no hand in his ill-treatment; but told us, he could never pardon Byam; as for Trefry, he confessed he saw his 'grief and sorrow for his suffering, which he could not hinder, but was like to have been beaten down by the very slaves, for speaking in his defence. But for Byam, who was their leader, their head—and should, by his justice and honour, have been an example to them—for him, he wished to live to take a dire revenge of him; and said, 'It had been well for him, if he had sacrificed me, instead of giving me the contemptible whip.' He refused to talk much; but begging us to give him our hands, he took them, and protested never to lift up his to do us any harm. He had a great respect for Colonel Martin, and always took his counsel like that of a parent; and assured him, he would obey him in anything, but his revenge on Byam: 'Therefore,' said he, 'for his own safety, let him speedily despatch me; for if I could despatch myself, I would not, till that justice were done to my injured person, and the contempt of a soldier. No, I would not kill myself, even after a whipping, but will be content to live with that infamy, and be pointed at by every grinning slave, till I have completed my revenge; and then you shall see, that Oroonoko scorns to live with the indignity that was put on Cæsar.' All we could do, could get no more words from him; and we took care to have him put immediately into a healing bath, to rid him of his pepper, and ordered a chirurgeon to anoint him with healing balm, which he suffered, and in some time he began to be able to walk and eat. We failed not to visit him every day, and to that end had him brought to an apartment at Parham.

The Governor had no sooner recovered, and had heard of the menaces of Cæsar, but he called his Council, who (not to disgrace them, or burlesque the Government there) consisted of such notorious villains as Newgate never transported; and, possibly, originally were such who understood neither the laws of God or man, and had no sort of principles to make them worthy the name of men; but at the very council-table would contradict and fight with one another, and swear so bloodily, that it was terrible to hear and see them. (Some of them were afterwards hanged, when the Dutch took possession of the place, others sent off in chains.) But calling these special rulers of the nation together, and requiring their counsel in this weighty affair, they all concluded, that (damn them) it might be their own cases; and that Cæsar ought to be made an example to all the negroes, to fright them from daring to threaten their betters, their lords and masters; and at this rate no man was safe from his own slaves; and concluded, *nemine contradicente*, that Cæsar should be hanged.

Trefry then thought it time to use his authority, and told Byam, his command did not extend to his lord's plantation; and that Parham was as much exempt from the law as White Hall; and that they ought no more to touch the servants of the Lord —— (who there represented the King's person) than they could those about the King himself; and that Parham was a sanctuary; and though his lord were absent in person, his power was still in being there, which he had entrusted with him, as far as the dominions of his particular plantations reached, and all that belonged to it; the rest of the country, as Byam was lieutenant to his lord, he might exercise his tyranny upon. Trefry had others as powerful, or more, that interested themselves in Cæsar's life, and absolutely said, he should be defended. So turning the Governor, and his wise Council, out of doors, (for they sat at Parham House) we set a guard upon our lodging-place, and would admit none but those we called friends to us and Cæsar.

The Governor having remained wounded at Parham, till his recovery was completed, Cæsar did not know but he was still there, and indeed for the most part, his time was spent there: for he was one that loved to live at other people's expense, and if he were a day absent, he was ten present there; and used to

play, and walk, and hunt, and fish with Cæsar. So
that Cæsar did not at all doubt, if he once recovered
strength, but he should find an opportunity of being
revenged on him; though, after such a revenge, he
could not hope to live: for if he escaped the fury of
the English mobile, who perhaps would have been
glad of the occasion to have killed him, he was resolved not to survive his whipping; yet he had some
tender hours, a repenting softness, which he called his
fits of cowardice, wherein he struggled with love for
the victory of his heart, which took part with his
charming Imoinda there; but for the most part, his
time was passed in melancholy thoughts, and black
designs. He considered, if he should do this deed,
and die either in the attempt, or after it, he left his
lovely Imoinda a prey, or at best a slave to the enraged multitude; his great heart could not endure
that thought: 'Perhaps,' said he, 'she may be first
ravished by every brute; exposed first to their nasty
lusts, and then a shameful death.' No, he could not
live a moment under that apprehension, too insupportable to be borne. These were his thoughts, and
his silent arguments with his heart, as he told us
afterwards. So that now resolving not only to kill
Byam, but all those he thought had enraged him;
pleasing his great heart with the fancied slaughter he
should make over the whole face of the plantation;
he first resolved on a deed (that however horrid it
first appeared to us all) when we had heard his
reasons, we thought it brave and just. Being able to
walk, and, as he believed, fit for the execution of his
great design, he begged Trefry to trust him into the
air, believing a walk would do him good; which was
granted him; and taking Imoinda with him, as he
used to do in his more happy and calmer days, he led
her up into a wood, where (after with a thousand
sighs, and long gazing silently on her face, while tears
gushed, in spite of him, from his eyes) he told her his
design, first of killing her, and then his enemies, and

next himself, and the impossibility of escaping, and therefore he told her the necessity of dying. He found the heroic wife faster pleading for death, than he was to propose it, when she found his fixed resolution; and, on her knees, besought him not to leave her a prey to his enemies. He (grieved to death) yet pleased at her noble resolution, took her up, and embracing of her with all the passion and languishment of a dying lover, drew his knife to kill this treasure of his soul, this pleasure of his eyes; while tears trickled down his cheeks, hers were smiling with joy she should die by so noble a hand, and be sent into her own country (for that is their notion of the next world) by him she so tenderly loved, and so truly adored in this. For wives have a respect for their husbands equal to what any other people pay a deity; and when a man finds any occasion to quit his wife, if he love her, she dies by his hand; if not, he sells her, or suffers some other to kill her. It being thus, you may believe the deed was soon resolved on; and it is not to be doubted, but the parting, the eternal leave-taking of two such lovers, so greatly born, so sensible, so beautiful, so young, and so fond, must be very moving, as the relation of it was to me afterwards.

All that love could say in such cases, being ended, and all the intermitting irresolutions being adjusted, the lovely, young and adored victim lays herself down before the sacrificer; while he, with a hand resolved, and a heart-breaking within, gave the fatal stroke, first cutting her throat, and then severing her yet smiling face from that delicate body, pregnant as it was with the fruits of tenderest love. As soon as he had done, he laid the body decently on leaves and flowers, of which he made a bed, and concealed it under the same cover-lid of nature; only her face he left yet bare to look on. But when he found she was dead, and past all retrieve, never more to bless him with her eyes, and soft language, his grief swelled up to rage; he tore, he raved, he roared like some monster of the wood, calling on the loved name of Imoinda. A thousand times he turned the fatal knife that did the deed toward his own heart, with a resolution to go immediately after her; but dire revenge, which was now a thousand times more fierce in his soul than before, prevents him; and he would cry out, 'No, since I have sacrificed Imoinda to my revenge, shall I lose that glory which I have purchased so dear, as at the price of the fairest, dearest, softest creature that ever nature made? No, no!' Then at her name grief would get the ascendant of rage, and he would lie down by her side, and water her face with showers of tears, which never were wont to fall from those eyes; and however bent he was on his intended slaughter, he had not power to stir from the sight of this dear object, now more beloved, and more adored than ever.

He remained in this deplorable condition for two days, and never rose from the ground where he had made her sad sacrifice; at last rousing from her side, and accusing himself with living too long, now Imoinda was dead, and that the deaths of those barbarous enemies were deferred too long, he resolved now to finish the great work: but offering to rise, he found his strength so decayed, that he reeled to and fro, like boughs assailed by contrary winds; so that he was forced to lie down again, and try to summon all his courage to his aid. He found his brains turned round, and his eyes were dizzy, and objects appeared not the same to him they were wont to do; his breath was short, and all his limbs surprised with a faintness he had never felt before. He had not eaten in two days, which was one occasion of his feebleness, but excess of grief was the greatest; yet still he hoped he should recover vigour to act his design, and lay expecting it yet six days longer; still mourning over the dead idol of his heart, and striving every day to rise, but could not.

In all this time you may believe we were in no little affliction for Cæsar and his wife; some were of opinion he was escaped, never to return; others thought some accident had happened to him. But however, we failed not to send out a hundred people several ways, to search for him. A party of about forty went that way he took, among whom was Tuscan, who was perfectly reconciled to Byam. They had not gone very far into the wood, but they smelt an unusual smell, as of a dead body; for stinks must be very noisome, that can be distinguished among such a quantity of natural sweets, as every inch of that land produces: so that they concluded they should find him dead, or somebody that was so; they passed on towards it, as loathsome as it was, and made such rustling among the leaves that lie thick on the ground, by continual falling, that Cæsar heard he was approached; and though he had, during the space of these eight days, endeavoured to rise, but found he wanted strength, yet, looking up, and seeing his pursuers, he rose, and reeled to a neighbouring tree, against which he fixed his back; and being within a dozen yards of those that advanced and saw him, he called out to them, and bid them approach no nearer, if they would be safe. So that they stood still, and hardly believing their eyes, that would persuade them that it was Cæsar that spoke to them, so much he was altered; they asked him what he had done with his wife, for they smelt a stink that almost struck them dead? He, pointing to the dead body, sighing, cried, 'Behold her there.' They put off the flowers that covered her, with their sticks, and found she was killed, and cried out, 'Oh, monster! thou hast murdered thy wife.' Then asking him, why he did so cruel a deed? He replied, he had no leisure to answer impertinent questions: 'You may go back,' continued he, 'and tell the faithless Governor, he may thank fortune that I am breathing my last; and that my arm is too feeble to obey my heart, in what it

had designed him.' But his tongue faltering, and
trembling, he could scarce end what he was saying.
The English taking advantage by his weakness, cried,
'Let us take him alive by all means.' He heard
them; and, as if he had revived from a fainting, or
a dream, he cried out, 'No, gentlemen, you are
deceived; you will find no more Cæsars to be
whipped; no more find a faith in me. Feeble as you
think me, I have strength yet left to secure me from
a second indignity.' They swore all anew; and he
only shook his head, and beheld them with scorn.
Then they cried out, 'Who will venture on this single
man? Will nobody?' They stood all silent, while
Cæsar replied, 'Fatal will be the attempt of the first
adventurer, let him assure himself,' and, at that word,
held up his knife in a menacing posture. 'Look ye,
ye faithless crew,' said he, ''tis not life I seek, nor am
I afraid of dying,' and at that word, cut a piece of
flesh from his own throat, and threw it at them, 'yet
still I would live if I could, till I had perfected my
revenge. But, oh! it cannot be; I feel life gliding
from my eyes and heart; and if I make not haste,
I shall fall a victim to the shameful whip.' At that,
he ripped up his own belly, and took his bowels and
pulled them out, with what strength he could; while
some, on their knees imploring, besought him to hold
his hand. But when they saw him tottering, they
cried out, 'Will none venture on him?' A bold
Englishman cried, 'Yes, if he were the Devil,' (taking
courage when he saw him almost dead) and swearing
a horrid oath for his farewell to the world, he rushed
on him. Cæsar with his armed hand, met him so
fairly, as stuck him to the heart, and he fell dead
at his feet. Tuscan seeing that, cried out, 'I love
thee, O Cæsar! and therefore will not let thee die, if
possible'; and running to him, took him in his arms;
but, at the same time, warding a blow that Cæsar
made at his bosom, he received it quite through his
arm; and Cæsar having not strength to pluck the knife

forth, though he attempted it, Tuscan neither pulled
it out himself nor suffered it to be pulled out, but
came down with it sticking in his arm; and the
reason he gave for it, was, because the air should not
get into the wound. They put their hands across,
and carried Cæsar between six of them, fainting as he
was, and they thought dead, or just dying; and they
brought him to Parham, and laid him on a couch,
and had the chirurgeon immediately to him, who
dressed his wounds, and sewed up his belly, and used
means to bring him to life, which they effected. We
ran all to see him! and, if before we thought him
so beautiful a sight, he was now so altered, that
his face was like a death's-head blacked over, nothing
but teeth and eye-holes. For some days we suffered
nobody to speak to him, but caused cordials to be
poured down his throat; which sustained his life, and
in six or seven days he recovered his senses. For,
you must know, that wounds are almost to a miracle
cured in the Indies; unless wounds in the legs, which
they rarely ever cure.

When he was well enough to speak, we talked
to him, and asked him some questions about his wife,
and the reasons why he killed her; and he then told
us what I have related of that resolution, and of his
parting, and he besought us we would let him die,
and was extremely afflicted to think it was possible
he might live. He assured us, if we did not despatch
him, he would prove very fatal to a great many. We
said all we could to make him live, and gave him new
assurances; but he begged we would not think so
poorly of him, or of his love to Imoinda, to imagine
we could flatter him to life again. But the chirurgeon
assured him he could not live, and therefore he need
not fear. We were all (but Cæsar) afflicted at this
news, and the sight was ghastly. His discourse was
sad; and the earthy smell about him so strong, that
I was persuaded to leave the place for some time,
(being myself but sickly, and very apt to fall into fits

of dangerous illness upon any extraordinary melancholy). The servants, and Trefry, and the chirurgeons, promised all to take what possible care they could of the life of Cæsar; and I, taking boat, went with other company to Colonel Martin's, about three days' journey down the river. But I was no sooner gone, than the Governor taking Trefry, about some pretended earnest business, a day's journey up the river, having communicated his design to one Banister, a wild Irishman, one of the Council, a fellow of absolute barbarity, and fit to execute any villainy, but rich; he came up to Parham, and forcibly took Cæsar, and had him carried to the same post where he was whipped; and causing him to be tied to it, and a great fire made before him, he told him he should die like a dog, as he was. Cæsar replied, This was the first piece of bravery that ever Banister did, and he never spoke sense till he pronounced that word; and if he would keep it, he would declare, in the other world, that he was the only man, of all the whites, that ever he heard speak truth. And turning to the men that had bound him, he said, ' My friends, am I to die, or to be whipt?' And they cried, ' Whipt! no, you shall not escape so well.' And then he replied, smiling, ' A blessing on thee '; and assured them they need not tie him, for he would stand fixed like a rock, and endure death so as should encourage them to die: ' But if you whip me,' said he, ' be sure you tie me fast.'

He had learned to take tobacco; and when he was assured he should die, he desired they would give him a pipe in his mouth, ready lighted; which they did. And the executioner came, and first cut off his members, and threw them into the fire; after that, with an ill-favoured knife, they cut off his ears and his nose, and burned them; he still smoked on, as if nothing had touched him; then they hacked off one of his arms, and still he bore up and held his pipe; but at the cutting off the other arm, his head sunk, and his pipe dropped, and he gave up the ghost, without a groan, or a reproach. My mother and sister were by him all the while, but not suffered to save him ; so rude and wild were the rabble, and so inhuman were the justices who stood by to see the execution, who after paid dear enough for their insolence. They cut Cæsar into quarters, and sent them to several of the chief plantations : one quarter was sent to Colonel Martin ; who refused it, and swore, he had rather see the quarters of Banister, and the Governor himself, than those of Cæsar, on his plantations ; and that he could govern his negroes, without terrifying and grieving them with frightful spectacles of a mangled king.

Thus died this great man, worthy of a better fate, and a more sublime wit than mine to write his praise. Yet, I hope, the reputation of my pen is considerable enough to make his glorious name to survive to all ages, with that of the brave, the beautiful and the constant Imoinda.

THE FAIR JILT

OR THE AMOURS OF PRINCE TARQUIN
AND MIRANDA

As love is the most noble and divine passion of the soul, so it is that to which we may justly attribute all the real satisfactions of life; and without it man is unfinished and unhappy.

There are a thousand things to be said of the advantages this generous passion brings to those, whose hearts are capable of receiving its soft impressions; for it is not every one that can be sensible of its tender touches. How many examples, from history and observation, could I give of its wondrous power; nay, even to a degree of transmigration! How many idiots has it made wise! How many fools eloquent! How many home-bred squires accomplished! How many cowards brave! And there is no sort of species of mankind on whom it cannot work some change and miracle, if it be a noble well-grounded passion, except on the fop in fashion, the hardened incorrigible fop; so often wounded, but never reclaimed. For still, by a dire mistake, conducted by vast opiniatrety, and a greater portion of self-love, than the rest of the race of man, he believes that affectation in his mien and dress, that mathematical movement, that formality in every action, that a face managed with care, and softened into ridicule, the languishing turn, the toss, and the back-shake of the periwig, is the direct way to the

heart of the fine person he adores; and instead of
curing love in his soul, serves only to advance his
folly; and the more he is enamoured, the more
industriously he assumes (every hour) the coxcomb.
These are love's playthings, a sort of animals with
whom he sports; and whom he never wounds, but
when he is in good humour, and always shoots
laughing. It is the diversion of the little god, to see
what a fluttering and bustle one of these sparks, new-
wounded, makes; to what fantastic fooleries he has
recourse. The glass is every moment called to
counsel, the valet consulted and plagued for new
invention of dress, the footman and scrutore perpetually employed; billet-doux and madrigals take
up all his mornings, till playtime in dressing, till
night in gazing; still, like a sun-flower, turned towards the beams of the fair eyes of his Cælia, ad-
justing himself in the most amorous posture he can
assume, his hat under his arm, while the other hand
is put carelessly into his bosom, as if laid upon his
panting heart; his head a little bent to one side, supported with a world of cravat-string, which he takes
mighty care not to put into disorder; as one may
guess by a never-failing and horrid stiffness in his
neck; and if he had any occasion to look aside, his
whole body turns at the same time, for fear the
motion of the head alone should incommode the
cravat or periwig. And sometimes the glove is well
managed, and the white hand displayed. Thus, with
a thousand other little motions and formalities, all in
the common place or road of foppery, he takes
infinite pains to show himself to the pit and boxes,
a most accomplished ass. This is he, of all human
kind, on whom love can do no miracles, and who can
nowhere, and upon no occasion, quit one grain of his
refined foppery, unless in a duel, or a battle, if ever
his stars should be so severe and ill-mannered, to
reduce him to the necessity of either. Fear then
would ruffle that fine form he had so long preserved

in nicest order, with grief considering, that an unlucky chance-wound in his face, if such a dire misfortune should befall him, would spoil the sale of it
for ever.

Perhaps it will be urged, that since no metamor-
phosis can be made in a fop by love, you must consider him one of those that only talks of love, and
thinks himself that happy thing, a lover; and wanting fine sense enough for the real passion, believes
what he feels to be it. There are in the quiver of the
god a great many different darts; some that wound
for a day, and others for a year; they are all fine,
painted, glittering darts, and show as well as those
made of the noblest metal; but the wounds they
make reach the desire only, and are cured by possess-
ing, while the short-lived passion betrays the cheat.
But it is that refined and illustrious passion of the
soul whose aim is virtue, and whose end is honour,
that has the power of changing nature, and is capable
of performing all those heroic things, of which history is full.

How far distant passions may be from one another,
I shall be able to make appear in these following
rules. I'll prove to you the strong effects of love in
some unguarded and ungoverned hearts; where it
rages beyond the inspirations of 'a God all soft and
gentle,' and reigns more like 'a Fury from Hell.'

I do not pretend here to entertain you with a
feigned story, or anything pieced together with romantic accidents; but every circumstance, to a tittle,
is truth. To a great part of the main I myself was
an eye-witness; and what I did not see, I was confirmed of by actors in the intrigue, holy men, of the
order of St. Francis. But for the sake of some of her
relations, I shall give my Fair Jilt a feigned name,
that of Miranda; but my hero must retain his own, it
being too illustrious to be concealed.

You are to understand, that in all the Catholic
countries, where Holy Orders are established, there

are abundance of differing kinds of religious, both of men and women. Amongst the women, there are those we call Nuns, that make solemn vows of perpetual chastity; there are others who make but a simple vow, as for five or ten years, or more or less; and that time expired, they may contract anew for longer time, or marry, or dispose of themselves as they shall see good; and these are ordinarily called Galloping Nuns. Of these there are several Orders; as Canonesses, Begines, Quests, Swart-Sisters, and Jesuitesses, with several others I have forgot. Of those of the Begines was our fair votress.

These Orders are taken up by the best persons of the town, young maids of fortune, who live together, not inclosed, but in palaces that will hold about fifteen hundred or two thousand of these *filles devotes;* where they have a regulated government, under a sort of Abbess, or Prioress, or rather a *Governante.* They are obliged to a method of devotion, and are under a sort of obedience. They wear a habit much like our widows of quality in England, only without a bando; and their veil is of a thicker crape than what we have here, through which one cannot see the face; for when they go abroad, they cover themselves all over with it; but they put them up in the churches, and lay them by in the houses. Every one of these has a confessor, who is to them a sort of steward. For, you must know, they that go into these places, have the management of their own fortunes, and what their parents design them. Without the advice of this confessor, they act nothing, nor admit of a lover that he shall not approve; at least, this method ought to be taken, and is by almost all of them; though Miranda thought her wit above it, as her spirit was.

But as these women are, as I said, of the best quality, and live with the reputation of being retired from the world a little more than ordinary, and because there is a sort of difficulty to approach them, they are the people the most courted, and liable to

the greatest temptations; for as difficult as it seems
to be, they receive visits from all the men of the best
quality, especially strangers. All the men of wit and
conversation meet at the apartments of these fair
filles devotes, where all manner of gallantries are
performed, while all the study of these maids is
to accomplish themselves for these noble conversations. They receive presents, balls, serenades, and
billets. All the news, wit, verses, songs, novels, music,
gaming, and all fine diversion, is in their apartments,
they themselves being of the best quality and fortune.
So that to manage these gallantries, there is no sort
of female arts they are not practised in, no intrigue
they are ignorant of, and no management of which
they are not capable.

Of this happy number was the fair Miranda, whose
parents being dead, and a vast estate divided between
herself and a young sister, (who lived with an unmarried old uncle, whose estate afterwards was all
divided between them) she put herself into this unin-
closed religious house; but her beauty, which had all
the charms that ever nature gave, became the envy of
the whole sisterhood. She was tall, and admirably
shaped; she had a bright hair, and hazel eyes, all full
of love and sweetness. No art could make a face so
fair as hers by nature, which every feature adorned
with a grace that imagination cannot reach. Every
look, every motion charmed, and her black dress
showed the lustre of her face and neck. She had an
air, though gay as so much youth could inspire, yet
so modest, so nobly reserved, without formality, or
stiffness, that one who looked on her would have
imagined her soul the twin-angel of her body; and
both together made her appear something divine. To
this she had a great deal of wit, read much, and
retained all that served her purpose. She sang
delicately, and danced well, and played on the lute to
a miracle. She spoke several languages naturally; for,
being co-heiress to so great a fortune, she was bred

with the nicest care, in all the finest manners of education; and was now arrived to her eighteenth year.

It were needless to tell you how great a noise the fame of this young beauty, with so considerable a fortune, made in the world. I may say, the world, rather than confine her fame to the scanty limits of a town; it reached to many others. And there was not a man of any quality that came to Antwerp, or passed through the city, but made it his business to see the lovely Miranda, who was universally adored. Her youth and beauty, her shape, and majesty of mien, and air of greatness, charmed all her beholders; and thousands of people were dying by her eyes, while she was vain enough to glory in her conquests, and make it her business to wound. She loved nothing so much as to behold sighing slaves at her feet, of the greatest quality; and treated them all with an affability that gave them hope. Continual music, as soon as it was dark, and songs of dying lovers, were sung under her windows; and she might well have made herself a great fortune (if she had not been so already) by the rich presents that were hourly made her; and everybody daily expected when she would make some one happy, by suffering herself to be conquered by love and honour, by the assiduities and vows of some one of her adorers. But Miranda accepted their presents, heard their vows with pleasure, and willingly admitted all their soft addresses; but would not yield her heart, or give away that lovely person to the possession of one, who could please itself with so many. She was naturally amorous, but extremely inconstant. She loved one for his wit, another for his face, and a third for his mien; but above all, she admired quality. Quality alone had the power to attach her entirely; yet not to one man, but that virtue was still admired by her in all. Wherever she found that, she loved, or at least acted the lover with such art, that (deceiving well) she failed not to complete her conquest; and yet she never

durst trust her fickle humour with marriage. She
knew the strength of her own heart, and that it could
not suffer itself to be confined to one man, and wisely
avoided those inquietudes, and that uneasiness of life
she was sure to find in that married state, which
would, against her nature, oblige her to the embraces
of one, whose humour was, to love all the young and
the gay. But Love, who had hitherto only played with
her heart, and given it nought but pleasing wanton
wounds, such as afforded only soft joys, and not pains,
resolved, either out of revenge to those numbers she
had abandoned, and who had sighed so long in vain, or
to try what power he had upon so fickle a heart, to send
an arrow dipped in the most tormenting flames that
rage in hearts most sensible. He struck it home and
deep, with all the malice of an angry god.

There was a church belonging to the Cordeliers,
whither Miranda often repaired to her devotion ; and
being there one day, accompanied with a young sister
of the Order, after the Mass was ended, as it is the
custom, some one of the Fathers goes about the
church with a box for contribution, or charity-money.
It happened that day, that a young Father, newly
initiated, carried the box about, which, in his turn, he
brought to Miranda. She had no sooner cast her
eyes on this young friar but her face was overspread
with blushes of surprise. She beheld him steadfastly,
and saw in his face all the charms of youth, wit, and
beauty ; he wanted no one grace that could form him
for love, he appeared all that is adorable to the fair
sex, nor could the misshapen habit hide from her the
lovely shape it endeavoured to cover, nor those
delicate hands that approached her too near with the
box. Besides the beauty of his face and shape, he
had an air altogether great, in spite of his professed
poverty, it betrayed the man of quality ; and that
thought weighed greatly with Miranda. But love,
who did not design she should now feel any sort of
those easy flames, with which she had heretofore

burnt, made her soon lay all those considerations
aside, which used to invite her to love, and now loved
she knew not why.

She gazed upon him, while he bowed before her, and
waited for her charity, till she perceived the lovely
friar to blush, and cast his eyes to the ground. This
awakened her shame, and she put her hand into her
pocket, and was a good while in searching for her
purse, as if she thought of nothing less than what she
was about; at last she drew it out, and gave him a
pistole; but with so much deliberation and leisure, as
easily betrayed the satisfaction she took in looking on
him; while the good man, having received her bounty,
after a very low obeisance, proceeded to the rest; and
Miranda casting after him a look all languishing, as
long as he remained in the church, departed with a
sigh as soon as she saw him go out, and returned to
her apartment without speaking one word all the way
to the young *fille devote* who attended her; so absolutely was her soul employed with this young holy
man. Cornelia (so was this maid called who was with
her) perceiving she was so silent, who used to be all
wit and good humour, and observing her little disorder at the sight of the young father, though she
was far from imagining it to be love, took an occasion,
when she was come home, to speak of him. 'Madam,'
said she, 'did you not observe that fine young
Cordelier, who brought the box?' At a question
that named that object of her thoughts, Miranda
blushed; and she finding she did so, redoubled her
confusion, and she had scarce courage enough to say,
'Yes, I did observe him.' And then, forcing herself
to smile a little, continued, 'And I wondered to see
so jolly a young friar of an Order so severe and
mortified.' 'Madam', replied Cornelia, 'when you
know his story, you will not wonder.' Miranda, who
was impatient to know all that concerned her new
conqueror, obliged her to tell his story; and Cornelia
obeyed, and proceeded.

THE STORY OF PRINCE HENRICK

'You must know, Madam, that this young holy man is a Prince of Germany, of the House of ——, whose fate it was to fall most passionately in love with a fair young lady, who loved him with an ardour equal to what he vowed her. Sure of her heart, and wanting only the approbation of her parents, and his own, which her quality did not suffer him to despair of, he boasted of his happiness to a young Prince, his elder brother, a youth amorous and fierce, impatient of joys, and sensible of beauty, taking fire with all fair eyes. He was his father's darling, and delight of his fond mother; and, by an ascendant over both their hearts, ruled their wills.

'This young Prince no sooner saw, but loved the fair mistress of his brother; and with an authority of a sovereign, rather than the advice of a friend, warned his brother Henrick (this now young friar) to approach no more this lady, whom he had seen; and, seeing, loved.

'In vain the poor surprised Prince pleads his right of love, his exchange of vows, and assurance of a heart that could never be but for himself. In vain he urges his nearness of blood, his friendship, his passion, or his life, which so entirely depended on the possession of the charming maid. All his pleading served but to blow his brother's flame; and the more he implores, the more the other burns; and while Henrick follows him, on his knees, with humble submissions, the other flies from him in rages of transported love; nor could his tears, that pursued his brother's steps, move him to pity. Hot-headed, vain-conceited of his beauty, and greater quality, as elder brother, he doubts not of success, and resolved to sacrifice all to the violence of his new-born passion.

'In short, he speaks of his design to his mother, who promised him her assistance; and accordingly proposing it first to the Prince her husband, urging the languishment of her son, she soon wrought so on him, that a match being concluded between the parents of this young beauty and Henrick's brother, the hour was appointed before she knew of the sacrifice she was to be made. And while this was in agitation, Henrick was sent on some great affairs, up into Germany, far out of the way; not but his boding heart, with perpetual sighs and throbs, eternally foretold him his fate.

'All the letters he wrote were intercepted, as well as those she wrote to him. She finds herself every day perplexed with the addresses of the Prince she hated; he was ever sighing at her feet. In vain were all her reproaches, and all her coldness, he was on the surer side; for what he found love would not do, force of parents would.

'She complains, in her heart, of young Henrick, from whom she could never receive one letter; and at last could not forbear bursting into tears, in spite of all her force, and feigned courage, when, on a day, the Prince told her, that Henrick was withdrawn to give him time to court her; to whom he said, he confessed he had made some vows, but did repent of them, knowing himself too young to make them good : that it was for that reason he brought him first to see her; and for that reason, that after that he never saw her more, nor so much as took leave of her; when, indeed, his death lay upon the next visit, his brother having sworn to murder him; and to that end, put a guard upon him, till he was sent into Germany.

'All this he uttered with so many passionate asseverations, vows, and seeming pity for her being so inhumanly abandoned, that she almost gave credit to all he had said, and had much ado to keep herself within the bounds of moderation and silent grief. Her heart was breaking, her eyes languished, and her cheeks grew pale, and she had like to have fallen dead into the treacherous arms of him that had reduced her to this discovery ; but she did what she could to assume her courage, and to show as little resentment as possible for a heart, like hers, oppressed with love, and now abandoned by the dear subject of its joys and pains.

'But, Madam, not to tire you with this adventure, the day arrived wherein our still weeping fair unfortunate was to be sacrificed to the capriciousness of love ; and she was carried to Court by her parents, without knowing to what end, where she was even compelled to marry the Prince.

'Henrick, who all this while knew no more of his unhappiness, than what his fears suggested, returns, and passes even to the presence of his father, before he knew anything of his fortune ; where he beheld his mistress and his brother, with his father, in such a familiarity, as he no longer doubted his destiny. It is hard to judge, whether the lady, or himself, was most surprised ; she was all pale and unmovable in her chair, and Henrick fixed like a statue ; at last grief and rage took place of amazement, and he could not forbear crying out, 'Ah, traitor ! Is it thus you have treated a friend and brother ? And you, O perjured charmer ! Is it thus you have rewarded all my vows ?' He could say no more ; but reeling against the door, had fallen in a swoon upon the floor, had not his page caught him in his arms, who was entering with him. The good old Prince, the father, who knew not what all this meant, was soon informed by the young weeping Princess ; who, in relating the story of her amour with Henrick, told her tale in so moving a manner, as brought tears to the old man's eyes, and rage to those of her husband ; he immediately grew jealous to the last degree. He finds himself in possession ('tis true) of the beauty he adored, but the beauty adoring another ; a Prince young and charming as the light, soft, witty, and raging with an equal passion. He finds this dreaded rival in the same house with him, with an authority equal to his own; and fancies, where two hearts are so entirely agreed, and have so good an understanding, it would not be impossible to find opportunities to satisfy and ease that mutual flame, that burned so equally in both; he therefore resolved to send him out of the world, and to establish his own repose by a deed, wicked, cruel, and unnatural, to have him assassinated the first opportunity he could find. This resolution set him a little at ease, and he strove to dissemble kindness to Henrick, with all the art he was capable of, suffering him to come often to the apartment of the Princess, and to entertain her oftentimes with discourse, when he was not near enough to hear what he spoke; but still watching their eyes, he found those of Henrick full of tears, ready to flow, but restrained, looking all dying, and yet reproaching, while those of the Princess were ever bent to the earth, and she as much as possible, shunning his conversation. Yet this did not satisfy the jealous husband; it was not her complaisance that could appease him; he found her heart was panting within, whenever Henrick approached her, and every visit more and more confirmed his death.

'The father often found the disorders of the sons; the softness and address of the one gave him as much fear, as the angry blushings, the fierce looks, and broken replies of the other, whenever he beheld Henrick approach his wife; so that the father, fearing some ill consequence of this, besought Henrick to withdraw to some other country, or travel into Italy, he being now of an age that required a view of the world. He told his father that he would obey his commands, though he was certain, that moment he was to be separated from the sight of the fair Princess, his sister, would be the last of his life; and, in fine, made so pitiful a story of his suffering love, as almost moved the old Prince to compassionate him so far, as to permit him to stay; but he saw inevitable danger in that, and therefore bid him prepare for his journey.

'That which passed between the father and Henrick, being a secret, none talked of his departing from Court; so that the design the brother had went on; and making a hunting-match one day, where most young people of quality were, he ordered some whom he had hired to follow his brother, so as if he chanced to go out of the way, to despatch him; and accordingly, fortune gave them an opportunity; for he lagged behind the company, and turned aside into a pleasant thicket of hazels, where alighting, he walked on foot in the most pleasant part of it, full of thought, how to divide his soul between love and obedience. He was sensible that he ought not to stay; that he was but an affliction to the young Princess, whose honour could never permit her to ease any part of his flame; nor was he so vicious to entertain a thought that should stain her virtue. He beheld her now as his brother's wife, and that secured his flame from all loose desires, if her native modesty had not been sufficient of itself to have done it, as well as that profound respect he paid her; and he considered, in obeying his father, he left her at ease, and his brother freed of a thousand fears; he went to seek a cure, which if he could not find, at last he could but die; and so he must, even at her feet. However, that it was more noble to seek a remedy for his disease, than expect a certain death by staying. After a thousand reflections on his hard fate, and bemoaning himself, and blaming his cruel stars, that had doomed him to die so young, after an infinity of sighs and tears, resolvings and unresolvings, he, on the sudden, was interrupted by the trampling of some horses he heard, and their rushing through the boughs, and saw four men make towards him. He had not time to mount, being walked some paces from his horse. One of the men advanced, and cried, 'Prince, you must die.' 'I do believe thee,' replied

Henrick, 'but not by a hand so base as thine,' and at the same time drawing his sword, ran him into the groin. When the fellow found himself so wounded, he wheeled off and cried, 'Thou art a prophet, and hast rewarded my treachery with death.' The rest came up, and one shot at the Prince, and shot him in the shoulder; the other two hastily laying hold (but too late) on the hand of the murderer, cried, 'Hold, traitor; we relent, and he shall not die.' He replied, ''Tis too late, he is shot; and see, he lies dead. Let us provide for ourselves, and tell the Prince, we have done the work; for you are as guilty as I am.' At that they all fled, and left the Prince lying under a tree, weltering in his blood.

'About the evening, the forester going his walks, saw the horse richly caparisoned, without a rider, at the entrance of the wood; and going farther, to see if he could find its owner, found there the Prince almost dead; he immediately mounts him on the horse, and himself behind, bore him up, and carried him to the lodge; where he had only one old man, his father, well skilled in surgery, and a boy. They put him to bed; and the old forester, with what art he had, dressed his wound, and in the morning sent for an abler surgeon, to whom the Prince enjoined secrecy, because he knew him. The man was faithful, and the Prince in time was recovered of his wound; and as soon as he was well, he came for Flanders, in the habit of a pilgrim, and after some time took the Order of St. Francis, none knowing what became of him, till he was professed; and then he wrote his own story to the Prince his father, to his mistress, and his ungrateful brother. The young Princess did not long survive his loss, she languished from the moment of his departure; and he had this to confirm his devout life, to know she died for him.

'My brother, Madam, was an officer under the Prince his father, and knew his story perfect y well; from whose mouth I had it.

'What!' replied Miranda then, 'is Father Henrick a man of quality?' 'Yes, Madam,' said Cornelia, 'and has changed his name to Francisco.' But Miranda, fearing to betray the sentiments of her heart, by asking any more questions about him, turned the discourse; and some persons of quality came in to visit her (for her apartment was about six o'clock, like the presence-chamber of a queen, always filled with the greatest people). There meet all the *beaux esprits*, and all the beauties. But it was visible Miranda was not so gay as she used to be; but pensive, and answering *mal à propos* to all that was said to her. She was a thousand times going to speak, against her will, something of the charming friar, who was never from her thoughts; and she imagined, if he could inspire love in a coarse, grey, ill-made habit, a shorn crown, a hair-cord about his waist, bare-legged, in sandals instead of shoes; what must he do, when looking back on time, she beholds him in a prospect of glory, with all that youth, and illustrious beauty, set off by the advantage of dress and equipage? She frames an idea of him all gay and splendid, and looks on his present habit as some disguise proper for the stealths of love; some feigned put-on shape, with the more security to approach a mistress, and make himself happy; and that the robe laid by, she has the lover in his proper beauty, the same he would have been, if any other habit (though ever so rich) were put off. In the bed, the silent gloomy night, and the soft embraces of her arms, he loses all the friar, and assumes all the prince; and that awful reverence, due alone to his holy habit, he exchanges for a thousand dalliances, for which his youth was made: for love, for tender embraces, and all the happiness of life. Some moments she fancies him a lover, and that the fair object that takes up all his heart, has left no room for her there; but that was a thought that did not long perplex her, and which, almost as soon as born, she turned to her advantage. She beholds him a lover, and therefore finds he has a heart sensible and tender; he had youth to be fired, as well as to inspire; he was far from the loved object, and totally without hope; and she reasonably considered, that flame would of itself soon die, that had only despair to feed on. She beheld her own charms; and experience, as well as her glass, told her, they never failed of conquest, especially where they designed it. And she believed Henrick would be glad, at least, to quench that flame in himself, by an amour with her, which was kindled by the young Princess of —— his sister.

These, and a thousand other self-flatteries, all vain and indiscreet, took up her waking nights, and now more retired days; while love, to make her truly wretched, suffered her to soothe herself with fond imaginations; not so much as permitting her reason to plead one moment to save her from undoing. She would not suffer it to tell her, he had taken Holy Orders, made sacred and solemn vows of everlasting chastity, that it was impossible he could marry her, or lay before her any argument that might prevent her ruin; but love, mad malicious love, was always called to counsel, and like easy monarchs, she had no ears, but for flatterers.

Well then, she is resolved to love, without considering to what end, and what must be the consequence of such an amour. She now missed no day of being at that little church, where she had the happiness, or rather the misfortune (so love ordained) to see this ravisher of her heart and soul; and every day she took new fire from his lovely eyes. Unawares, unknown, and unwillingly, he gave her wounds, and the difficulty of her cure made her rage the more. She burned, she languished, and died for the young innocent, who knew not he was the author of so much mischief.

Now she resolves a thousand ways in her tortured mind, to let him know her anguish, and at last pitched upon that of writing to him soft billets, which she had

learned the art of doing ; or if she had not, she had
now fire enough to inspire her with all that could
charm and move. These she delivered to a young
wench, who waited on her, and whom she had entirely
subdued to her interest, to give to a certain lay-
brother of the Order, who was a very simple harmless
wretch, and who served in the kitchen, in the nature
of a cook, in the monastery of Cordeliers. She gave
him gold to secure his faith and service ; and not
knowing from whence they came (with so good
credentials) he undertook to deliver the letters to
Father Francisco ; which letters were all afterwards,
as you shall hear, produced in open court. These
letters failed not to come every day ; and the sense of
the first was, to tell him, that a very beautiful young
lady, of a great fortune, was in love with him, without
naming her ; but it came as from a third person, to
let him know the secret, that she desired he would
let her know whether she might hope any return from
him ; assuring him, he needed but only see the fair
languisher, to confess himself her slave.

This letter being delivered him, he read by himself,
and was surprised to receive words of this nature,
being so great a stranger in that place ; and could
not imagine, or would not give himself the trouble of
guessing who this should be, because he never designed to make returns.

The next day, Miranda, finding no advantage from
her messenger of love, in the evening sends another
(impatient of delay) confessing that she who suffered
the shame of writing and imploring, was the person
herself who adored him. It was there her raging
love made her say all things that discovered the
nature of its flame, and propose to flee with him to
any part of the world, if he would quit the convent ;
that she had a fortune considerable enough to make
him happy ; and that his youth and quality were not
given him to so unprofitable an end as to lose themselves in a convent, where poverty and ease was all

the business. In fine, she leaves nothing unurged
that might debauch and invite him; not forgetting to
send him her own character of beauty, and left him
to judge of her wit and spirit by her writing, and her
love by the extremity of passion she professed. To
all which the lovely friar made no return, as believing
a gentle capitulation or exhortation to her would
but inflame her the more, and give new occasions for
her continuing to write. All her reasonings, false
and vicious, he despised, pitied the error of her love,
and was proof against all she could plead. Yet notwithstanding his silence, which left her in doubt, and
more tormented her, she ceased not to pursue him
with her letters, varying her style; sometimes all
wanton, loose and raving; sometimes feigning a
virgin-modesty all over, accusing herself, blaming
her conduct, and sighing her destiny, as one compelled
to the shameful discovery by the austerity of his vow
and habit, asking his pity and forgiveness; urging
him in charity to use his fatherly care to persuade
and reason with her wild desires, and by his counsel
drive the god from her heart, whose tyranny was worse
than that of a fiend; and he did not know what his
pious advice might do. But still she writes in vain,
in vain she varies her style, by a cunning, peculiar to
a maid possessed with such a sort of passion.

This cold neglect was still oil to the burning lamp,
and she tries yet more arts, which for want of right
thinking were as fruitless. She has recourse to
presents; her letters came loaded with rings of great
price, and jewels, which fops of quality had given her.
Many of this sort he received, before he knew where
to return them, or how; and on this occasion alone
he sent her a letter, and restored her trifles, as he
called them. But his habit having not made him
forget his quality and education, he wrote to her with
all the profound respect imaginable; believing by her
presents, and the liberality with which she parted
with them, that she was of quality. But the whole

letter, as he told me afterwards, was to persuade her
from the honour she did him, by loving him; urging
a thousand reasons, solid and pious, and assuring her,
he had wholly devoted the rest of his days to heaven,
and had no need of those gay trifles she had sent
him, which were only fit to adorn ladies so fair as
herself, and who had business with this glittering
world, which he disdained, and had for ever abandoned. He sent her a thousand blessings, and told
her, she should be ever in his prayers, though not in
his heart, as she desired. And abundance of goodness more he expressed, and counsel he gave her,
which had the same effect with his silence; it made
her love but the more, and the more impatient she
grew. She now had a new occasion to write, she now
is charmed with his wit; this was the new subject.
She rallies his resolution, and endeavours to recall
him to the world, by all the arguments that human
invention is capable of.

But when she had above four months languished
thus in vain, not missing one day, wherein she went
not to see him, without discovering herself to him;
she resolved, as her last effort, to show her person,
and see what that, assisted by her tears, and soft
words from her mouth, could do, to prevail upon him.

It happened to be on the eve of that day when she
was to receive the Sacrament, that she, covering herself with her veil, came to vespers, purposing to make
choice of the conquering friar for her confessor.

She approached him; and as she did so, she
trembled with love. At last she cried, 'Father, my
confessor is gone for some time from the town, and
I am obliged to-morrow to receive, and beg you will
be pleased to take my confession.'

He could not refuse her; and led her into the
sacristy, where there is a confession-chair, in which
he seated himself; and on one side of him she
kneeled down, over against a little altar, where the
priests' robes lie, on which were placed some lighted

wax-candles, that made the little place very light and splendid, which shone full upon Miranda.

After the little preparation usual in confession, she turned up her veil, and discovered to his view the most wondrous object of beauty he had ever seen, dressed in all the glory of a young bride; her hair and stomacher full of diamonds, that gave a lustre all dazzling to her brighter face and eyes. He was surprised at her amazing beauty, and questioned whether he saw a woman, or an angel at his feet. Her hands, which were elevated, as if in prayer, seemed to be formed of polished alabaster; and he confessed, he had never seen anything in nature so perfect, and so admirable.

He had some pain to compose himself to hear her confession, and was obliged to turn away his eyes, that his mind might not be perplexed with an object so diverting; when Miranda, opening the finest mouth in the world, and discovering new charms, began her confession.

'Holy father,' said she, 'amongst the number of my vile offences, that which afflicts me to the greatest degree, is, that I am in love. Not,' continued she, 'that I believe simple and virtuous love a sin, when it is placed on an object proper and suitable; but, my dear father,' said she, and wept, 'I love with a violence which cannot be contained within the bounds of reason, moderation, or virtue. I love a man whom I cannot possess without a crime, and a man who cannot make me happy without being perjured.' 'Is he married?' replied the father. 'No,' answered Miranda. 'Are you so?' continued he. 'Neither,' said she. 'Is he too near allied to you?' said Francisco, 'a brother, or relation?' 'Neither of these,' said she. 'He is unenjoyed, unpromised; and so am I. Nothing opposes our happiness, or makes my love a vice, but you——'Tis you deny me life: 'tis you that forbid my flame: 'tis you will have me die, and seek my remedy in my grave, when I complain of tortures, wounds, and flames. O cruel charmer! 'tis for you I languish; and here, at your feet, implore that pity, which all my addresses have failed of procuring me.'

With that, perceiving he was about to rise from his seat, she held him by his habit, and vowed she would in that posture follow him, wherever he flew from her. She elevated her voice so loud, he was afraid she might be heard, and therefore suffered her to force him into his chair again; where being seated, he began, in the most passionate terms imaginable, to dissuade her; but finding she the more persisted in eagerness of passion, he used all the tender assurances that he could force from himself, that he would have for her all the respect, esteem, and friendship that he was capable of paying; that he had a real compassion for her: and at last she prevailed so far with him, by her sighs and tears, as to own he had a tenderness for her, and that he could not behold so many charms, without being sensibly touched by them, and finding all those effects, that a maid so fair and young causes in the souls of men of youth and sense. But that, as he was assured, he could never be so happy to marry her, and as certain he could not grant anything but honourable passion, he humbly besought her not to expect more from him than such. And then began to tell her how short life was, and transitory its joys; how soon she would grow weary of vice, and how often change to find real repose in it, but never arrive to it. He made an end, by new assurance of his eternal friendship, but utterly forbad her to hope.

Behold her now denied, refused and defeated, with all her pleading youth, beauty, tears, and knees, imploring, as she lay, holding fast his scapular, and embracing his feet. What shall she do? She swells with pride, love, indignation and desire; her burning heart is bursting with despair, her eyes grow fierce, and from grief she rises to a storm; and in her agony of passion, with looks all disdainful, haughty, and full of rage, she began to revile him, as the poorest of animals; tells him his soul was dwindled to the meanness of his habit, and his vows of poverty, were suited to his degenerate mind. 'And,' said she, 'since all my nobler ways have failed me; and that, for a little hypocritical devotion, you resolve to lose the greatest blessings of life, and to sacrifice me to your religious pride and vanity, I will either force you to abandon that dull dissimulation, or you shall die, to prove your sanctity real. Therefore answer me immediately, answer my flame, my raging fire, which your eyes have kindled; or here, in this very moment, I will ruin thee; and make no scruple of revenging the pains I suffer, by that which shall take away your life and honour.'

The trembling young man, who, all this while, with extreme anguish of mind, and fear of the dire result, had listened to her ravings, full of dread, demanded what she would have him do? When she replied, 'Do what thy youth and beauty were ordained to do: this place is private, a sacred silence reigns here, and no one dares to pry into the secrets of this holy place. We are as secure from fears of interruption, as in deserts uninhabited, or caves forsaken by wild beasts. The tapers too shall veil their lights, and only that glimmering lamp shall be witness of our dear stealths of love. Come to my arms, my trembling, longing arms: and curse the folly of thy bigotry, that has made thee so long lose a blessing, for which so many princes sigh in vain.'

At these words she rose from his feet, and snatching him in her arms, he could not defend himself from receiving a thousand kisses from the lovely mouth of the charming wanton; after which, she ran herself, and in an instant put out the candles. But he cried to her, 'In vain, O too indiscreet fair one, in vain you put out the light! for Heaven still has eyes, and will look down upon my broken vows. I own your power, I own I have all the sense in the world of your charming touches; I am frail flesh and blood, but——yet——yet I can resist; and I prefer my vows to all your powerful temptations. I will be deaf and blind, and guard my heart with walls of ice, and make you know, that when the flames of true devotion are kindled in a heart, it puts out all other fires; which are as ineffectual, as candles lighted in the face of the sun. Go, vain wanton, and repent, and mortify that blood which has so shamefully betrayed thee, and which will one day ruin both thy soul and body.'

At these words, Miranda, more enraged, the nearer she imagined herself to happiness, made no reply; but throwing herself, in that instant, into the confessing-chair, and violently pulling the young friar into her lap, she elevated her voice to such a degree, in crying out, 'Help, help! A rape! Help, help!' that she was heard all over the church, which was full of people at the evening's devotion; who flocked about the door of the sacristy, which was shut with a spring-lock on the inside, but they durst not open the door.

It is easily to be imagined in what condition our young friar was, at this last devilish stratagem of his wicked mistress. He strove to break from those arms that held him so fast; and his bustling to get away, and hers to retain him, disordered her hair and habit to such a degree, as gave the more credit to her false accusation.

The fathers had a door on the other side, by which they usually entered, to dress in this little room; and at the report that was in an instant made them, they hasted thither, and found Miranda and the good Father very indecently struggling; which they misinterpreted, as Miranda desired; who, all in tears, immediately threw herself at the feet of the Provincial, who was one of those that entered; and cried, 'O holy father! revenge an innocent maid, undone and lost to fame and honour, by that vile monster, born of goats, nursed by tigers, and bred up on savage mountains, where humanity and religion

are strangers. For, O holy father, could it have
entered into the heart of man, to have done so barbarous and horrid a deed, as to attempt the virgin-
honour of an unspotted maid, and one of my degree,
even in the moment of my confession, in that holy
time, when I was prostrate before him and heaven,
confessing those sins that pressed my tender conscience, even then to load my soul with the blackest
of infamies, to add to my number a weight that must
sink me to hell? Alas! under the security of his
innocent looks, his holy habit, and his awful function,
I was led into this room to make my confession;
where, he locking the door, I had no sooner began,
but he gazing on me, took fire at my fatal beauty;
and starting up, put out the candles and caught me
in his arms; and raising me from the pavement, set
me in the confession-chair; and then—— Oh, spare
me the rest.'

With that a shower of tears burst from her fair
dissembling eyes, and sobs so naturally acted, and so
well managed, as left no doubt upon the good men,
but all she had spoken was truth.

'At first,' proceeded she, 'I was unwilling to bring
so great a scandal on his Order, as to cry out; but
struggled as long as I had breath; pleaded the
heinousness of the crime, urging my quality, and the
danger of the attempt. But he, deaf as the winds,
and ruffling as a storm, pursued his wild design with
so much force and insolence, as I at last, unable to
resist, was wholly vanquished, robbed of my native
purity. With what life and breath I had, I called for
assistance, both from men and heaven; but oh, alas!
your succours came too late. You find me here a
wretched, undone, and ravished maid. Revenge me,
fathers; revenge me on the perfidious hypocrite, or
else give me a death that may secure your cruelty
and injustice from ever being proclaimed over the
world; or my tongue will be eternally reproaching
you, and cursing the wicked author of my infamy.'

She ended as she began, with a thousand sighs and tears ; and received from the Provincial all assurances of revenge.

The innocent betrayed victim, all the while she was speaking, heard her with an astonishment that may easily be imagined ; yet showed no extravagant signs of it, as those would do, who feign it, to be thought innocent ; but being really so, he bore with a humble, modest, and blushing countenance, all her accusations ; which silent shame they mistook for evident signs of his guilt.

When the Provincial demanded, with an unwonted severity in his eyes and voice, what he could answer for himself ? calling him profaner of his sacred vows, and infamy to the Holy Order ; the injured, but innocently accused, only replied : ' May Heaven forgive that bad woman, and bring her to repentance !' For his part, he was not so much in love with life, as to use many arguments to justify his innocence ; unless it were to free that Order from a scandal, of which he had the honour to be professed. But as for himself, life or death were things indifferent to him, who heartily despised the world.

He said no more, and suffered himself to be led before the magistrate ; who committed him to prison, upon the accusation of this implacable beauty ; who, with so much feigned sorrow, prosecuted the matter, even to his trial and condemnation ; where he refused to make any great defence for himself. But being daily visited by all the religious, both of his own and other Orders, they obliged him (some of them knowing the austerity of his life, others his cause of griefs that first brought him into Orders, and others pretending a nearer knowledge, even of his soul itself) to stand upon his justification, and discover what he knew of that wicked woman ; whose life had not been so exemplary for virtue, not to have given the world a thousand suspicions of her lewdness and prostitutions.

The daily importunities of these fathers made him produce her letters. But as he had all the gown-men on his side, she had all the hats and feathers on hers; all the men of quality taking her part, and all the church-men his. They heard his daily protesta-tions and vows, but not a word of what passed at confession was yet discovered. He held that as a secret sacred on his part; and what was said in nature of a confession, was not to be revealed, though his life depended on the discovery. But as to the letters, they were forced from him, and exposed; however, matters were carried with so high a hand against him, that they served for no proof at all of his innocence, and he was at last condemned to be burned at the market-place.

After his sentence was passed, the whole body of priests made their addresses to the Marquis Castel Roderigo, the then Governor of Flanders, for a re-prieve; which, after much ado, was granted him for some weeks, but with an absolute denial of pardon. So prevailing were the young cavaliers of his Court, who were all adorers of this fair jilt.

About this time, while the poor innocent young Henrick was thus languishing in prison, in a dark and dismal dungeon, and Miranda, cured of her love, was triumphing in her revenge, expecting and daily giving new conquests: and who, by this time, had re-assumed all her wonted gaiety; there was a great noise about the town, that a Prince of mighty name, and famed for all the excellences of his sex, was arrived; a Prince young, and gloriously attended, called Prince Tarquin.

We had often heard of this great man, and that he was making his travels in France and Germany. And we had also heard, that some years before, he being about eighteen years of age, in the time when our King Charles, of blessed memory, was in Brussels, in the last year of his banishment, that all on a-sudden, this young man rose up upon them like the sun all glorious and dazzling, demanding place of all the princes in that Court. And when his pretence was demanded, he owned himself Prince Tarquin, of the race of the last Kings of Rome, made good his title, and took his place accordingly. After that he travelled for about six years up and down the world, and then arrived at Antwerp, about the time of my being sent thither by King Charles.

Perhaps there could be nothing seen so magnificent as this Prince. He was, as I said, extremely handsome, from head to foot exactly formed, and he wanted nothing that might adorn that native beauty to the best advantage. His parts were suitable to the rest. He had an accomplishment fit for a Prince, an air haughty, but a carriage affable, easy in conversation, and very entertaining, liberal and good-natured, brave and inoffensive. I have seen him pass the streets with twelve footmen, and four pages ; the pages all in green velvet coats laced with gold, and white velvet tunics ; the men in cloth, richly laced with gold ; his coaches, and all other officers suitable to a great man.

He was all the discourse of the town ; some laughing at his title, others reverencing it. Some cried that he was an impostor ; others, that he had made his title as plain, as if Tarquin had reigned but a year ago. Some made friendships with him, others would have nothing to say to him. But all wondered where his revenue was, that supported this grandeur ; and believed, though he could make his descent from the Roman kings very well out, that he could not lay so good a claim to the Roman land. Thus everybody meddled with what they had nothing to do ; and, as in other places, thought themselves on the surer side, if, in these doubtful cases, they imagined the worst.

But the men might be of what opinion they pleased concerning him ; the ladies were all agreed that he was a prince, and a young handsome prince, and a

prince not to be resisted. He had all their wishes, all
their eyes, and all their hearts. They now dressed
only for him; and what church he graced, was sure,
that day, to have the beauties, and all that thought
themselves so.

You may believe, our amorous Miranda was not
the least conquest he made. She no sooner heard of
him, which was as soon as he arrived, but she fell
in love with his very name. 'Jesu! A young King
of Rome!' Oh, it was so novel, that she doted on
the title; and had not cared whether the rest had
been man or monkey almost. She was resolved
to be the Lucretia that this young Tarquin should
ravish.

To this end, she was no sooner up the next day,
but she sent him a *billet doux*, assuring him how
much she admired his fame; and that being a
stranger in the town, she begged the honour of intro-
ducing him to all the *belle* conversations, etc., which
he took for the invitation of some coquette, who had
interest in fair ladies; and civilly returned her an
answer, that he would wait on her. She had him
that day watched to church; and impatient to see
what she heard so many people flock to see, she went
also to the same church; those sanctified abodes
being too often profaned by such devotees, whose business is to ogle and ensnare.

But what a noise and humming was heard all over
the church, when Tarquin entered! His grace, his
mien, his fashion, his beauty, his dress, and his equipage, surprised all that were present. And by the
good management and care of Miranda, she got to
kneel at the side of the altar, just over against the
Prince, so that, if he would, he could not avoid looking full upon her. She had turned up her veil, and all
her face and shape appeared such, and so enchanting,
as I have described; and her beauty heightened with
blushes, and her eyes full of spirit and fire, with joy,
to find the young Roman monarch so charming, she

appeared like something more than mortal, and compelled his eyes to a fixed gazing on her face ; she
never glanced his way, but she met them ; and then
would feign so modest a shame, and cast her eyes
downwards with such inviting art, that he was wholly
ravished and charmed, and she overjoyed to find he
was so.

The ceremony being ended, he sent a page to
follow that lady home, himself pursuing her to the
door of the church, where he took some holy water,
and threw upon her, and made her a profound reverence. She forced an innocent look, and a modest
gratitude in her face, and bowed, and passed forward,
half assured of her conquest; leaving her, to go
home to his lodging, and impatiently wait the return
of his page. And all the ladies who saw this first
beginning between the Prince and Miranda, began to
curse and envy her charms, who had deprived them
of half their hopes.

After this, I need not tell you, he made Miranda a
visit; and from that day never left her apartment, but
when he went home at nights, or unless he had
business; so entirely was he conquered by this fair
one. But the Bishop, and several men of quality, in
Orders, that professed friendship to him, advised him
from her company ; and spoke several things to him,
that might (if love had not made him blind) have
reclaimed him from the pursuit of his ruin. But
whatever they trusted him with, she had the art to
wind herself about his heart, and make him unravel
all his secrets; and then knew as well, by feigned
sighs and tears, to make him disbelieve all ; so that
he had no faith but for her ; and was wholly en-
chanted and bewitched by her. At last, in spite of
all that would have opposed it, he married this
famous woman, possessed by so many great men and
strangers before, while all the world was pitying his
shame and misfortunes.

Being married, they took a great house; and as

she was indeed a great fortune, and now a great princess, there was nothing wanting that was agreeable to their quality; all was splendid and magnificent. But all this would not acquire them the world's esteem; they had an abhorrence for her former life, and despised her; and for his espousing a woman so infamous, they despised him. So that though they admired, and gazed upon their equipage, and glorious dress, they foresaw the ruin that attended it, and paid her quality little respect.

She was no sooner married, but her uncle died; and dividing his fortune between Miranda and her sister, leaves the young heiress, and all her fortune, entirely in the hands of the Princess.

We will call this sister Alcidiana; she was about fourteen years of age, and now had chosen her brother, the Prince, for her guardian. If Alcidiana were not altogether so great a beauty as her sister, she had charms sufficient to procure her a great many lovers, though her fortune had not been so considerable as it was; but with that addition, you may believe, she wanted no courtships from those of the best quality; though everybody deplored her being under the tutorage of a lady so expert in all the vices of her sex, and so cunning a manager of sin, as was the Princess; who, on her part, failed not, by all the caresses, and obliging endearments, to engage the mind of this young maid, and to subdue her wholly to her government. All her senses were eternally regaled with the most bewitching pleasures they were capable of. She saw nothing but glory and magnificence, heard nothing but music of the sweetest sounds; the richest perfumes employed her smelling; and all she ate and touched was delicate and inviting; and being too young to consider how this state and grandeur was to be continued, little imagined her vast fortune was every day diminishing, towards its needless support.

When the Princess went to church, she had her

gentleman bare before her, carrying a great velvet
cushion, with great golden tassels, for her to kneel
on, and her train borne up a most prodigious length,
led by a gentleman usher, bare; followed by innumerable footmen, pages, and women. And in this
state she would walk in the streets, as in those
countries it is the fashion for the great ladies to do,
who are well; and in her train two or three coaches,
and perhaps a rich velvet chair embroidered, would
follow in state.

It was thus for some time they lived, and the
Princess was daily pressed by young sighing lovers,
for her consent to marry Alcidiana; but she had still
one art or other to put them off, and so continually
broke all the great matches that were proposed to
her, notwithstanding their kindred and other friends
had industriously endeavoured to make several great
matches for her; but the Princess was still positive
in her denial, and one way or other broke all. At
last it happened, there was one proposed, yet more
advantageous, a young count, with whom the young
maid grew passionately in love, and besought her
sister to consent that she might have him, and got
the Prince to speak in her behalf; but he had no
sooner heard the secret reasons Miranda gave him,
but (entirely her slave) he changed his mind, and
suited it to hers, and she, as before, broke off that
amour: which so extremely incensed Alcidiana, that
she, taking an opportunity, got from her guard, and
ran away, putting herself into the hands of a wealthy
merchant, her kinsman, and one who bore the greatest
authority in the city; him she chose for her guardian,
resolving to be no longer a slave to the tyranny of
her sister. And so well she ordered matters, that she
writ to this young cavalier, her last lover, and retrieved him; who came back to Antwerp again, to
renew his courtship.

Both parties being agreed, it was no hard matter
to persuade all but the Princess. But though she

opposed it, it was resolved on, and the day appointed for marriage, and the portion demanded; demanded only, but never to be paid, the best part of it being spent. However, she put them off from day to day, by a thousand frivolous delays; and when she saw they would have recourse to force, and that all her magnificence would be at an end, if the law should prevail against her; and that without this sister's fortune, she could not long support her grandeur; she bethought herself of a means to make it all her own, by getting her sister made away; but she being out of her tuition, she was not able to accomplish so great a deed of darkness. But since it was resolved it must be done, she contrives a thousand stratagems; and at last pitches upon an effectual one.

She had a page called Van Brune, a youth of great address and wit, and one she had long managed for her purpose. This youth was about seventeen years of age, and extremely beautiful; and in the time when Alcidiana lived with the Princess, she was a little in love with this handsome boy; but it was checked in its infancy, and never grew up to a flame. Nevertheless, Alcidiana retained still a sort of tenderness for him, while he burned in good earnest with love for the Princess.

The Princess one day ordering this page to wait on her in her closet, she shut the door; and after a thousand questions of what he would undertake to serve her, the amorous boy finding himself alone, and caressed by the fair person he adored, with joyful blushes that beautified his face, told her 'There was nothing upon earth he would not do, to obey her least commands.' She grew more familiar with him, to oblige him; and seeing love dance in his eyes, of which she was so good a judge, she treated him more like a lover, than a servant; till at last the ravished youth, wholly transported out of himself, fell at her feet, and impatiently implored to receive her commands quickly, that he might fly to execute them; for he was not able to bear her charming words, looks, and touches, and retain his duty. At this she smiled, and told him, the work was of such a nature, as would mortify all flames about him; and he would have more need of rage, envy, and malice, than the aids of a passion so soft as what she now found him capable of. He assured her, he would stick at nothing, though even against his nature, to recompense for the boldness he now, through his indiscretion, had discovered. She smiling, told him, he had committed no fault; and that possibly, the pay he should receive for the service she required at his hands, should be—what he most wished for in the world. At this he bowed to the earth; and kissing her feet, bade her command. And then she boldly told him, it was to kill her sister Alcidiana. The youth, without so much as starting or pausing upon the matter, told her, it should be done; and bowing low, immediately went out of the closet. She called him back, and would have given him some instruction; but he refused it, and said, 'The action and the contrivance should be all his own.' And offering to go again, she again recalled him; putting into his hand a purse of a hundred pistoles, which he took, and with a low bow departed.

He no sooner left her presence, but he goes directly, and buys a dose of poison, and went immediately to the house where Alcidiana lived; where desiring to be brought to her presence, he fell a-weeping; and told her, his lady had fallen out with him, and dismissed him her service; and since from a child he had been brought up in the family, he humbly besought Alcidiana to receive him into hers, she being in a few days to be married. There needed not much entreaty to a thing that pleased her so well, and she immediately received him to pension. And he waited some days on her, before he could get an opportunity to administer his devilish potion. But one night, when she drank wine with roasted apples, which was usual with her; instead of sugar, or with the sugar, the baneful drug was mixed, and she drank it down.

About this time, there was a great talk of this page's coming from one sister, to go to the other. And Prince Tarquin, who was ignorant of the design from the beginning to the end, hearing some men of quality at his table speaking of Van Brune's change of place (the Princess then keeping her chamber upon some trifling indisposition), he answered, 'That surely they were mistaken, that he was not dismissed from the Princess's service': and calling some of his servants, he asked for Van Brune; and whether anything had happened between her Highness and him, that had occasioned his being turned off. They all seemed ignorant of this matter; and those who had spoken of it, began to fancy there was some juggle in the case, which time would bring to light.

The ensuing day it was all about the town, that Alcidiana was poisoned; and though not dead, yet very near it; and that the doctors said, she had taken mercury. So that there was never so formidable a sight as this fair young creature; her head and body swollen, her eyes starting out, her face black, and all deformed. So that diligent search was made, who it should be that did this; who gave her drink and meat. The cook and butler were examined, the footmen called to account; but all concluded, she received nothing but from the hand of her new page, since he came into her service. He was examined, and showed a thousand guilty looks. And the apothecary, then attending among the doctors, proved he had bought mercury of him three or four days before; which he could not deny; and making many excuses for his buying it, betrayed him the more; so ill he chanced to dissemble. He was immediately sent to be examined by the Margrave or Justice, who made his *Mittimus*, and sent him to prison.

It is easy to imagine, in what fears and confusion the Princess was at this news. She took her chamber upon it, more to hide her guilty face, than for any indisposition. And the doctors applied such remedies to Alcidiana, such antidotes against the poison, that in a short time she recovered; but lost the finest hair in the world, and the complexion of her face ever after.

It was not long before the trials for criminals came on; and the day being arrived, Van Brune was tried the first of all; everybody having already read his destiny, according as they wished it; and none would believe, but just indeed as it was. So that for the revenge they hoped to see fall upon the Princess, every one wished he might find no mercy, that she might share of his shame and misery.

The sessions-house was filled that day with all the ladies, and chief of the town, to hear the result of his trial; and the sad youth was brought, loaded with chains, and pale as death; where every circumstance being sufficiently proved against him, and he making but a weak defence for himself, he was convicted, and sent back to prison, to receive his sentence of death on the morrow; where he owned all, and who set him on to do it. He owned it was not reward of gain he did it for, but hope he should command at his pleasure the possession of his mistress, the Princess, who should deny him nothing, after having entrusted him with so great a secret; and that besides, she had elevated him with the promise of that glorious reward, and had dazzled his young heart with so charming a prospect, that blind and mad with joy, he rushed forward to gain the desired prize, and thought on nothing but his coming happiness. That he saw too late the follies of his presumptuous flame, and cursed the deluding flatteries of the fair hypocrite, who had soothed him to his undoing. That he was a miserable victim to her wickedness; and hoped he should warn all young

men, by his fall, to avoid the dissimulation of the
deceiving fair.   That he hoped they would have pity
on his youth, and attribute his crime to the subtle
persuasions alone of his mistress the Princess : and
that since Alcidiana was not dead, they would grant
him mercy, and permit him to live to repent of his
grievous crime, in some part of the world, whither
they might banish him.

He ended with tears, that fell in abundance from
his eyes ; and immediately the Princess was apprehended, and brought to prison, to the same prison
where yet the poor young Father Francisco was
languishing, he having been from week to week re-
prieved, by the intercession of the fathers ; and
possibly she there had time to make some reflections.

You may imagine Tarquin left no means un-
essayed, to prevent the imprisonment of the Princess,
and the public shame and infamy she was likely to
undergo in this affair.   But the whole city being
overjoyed that she should be punished, as an author
of all this mischief, were generally bent against her,
both priests, magistrates and people ; the whole force
of the stream running that way, she found no more
favour than the meanest criminal.   The Prince therefore, when he saw it was impossible to rescue her
from the hands of justice, suffered with grief unspeakable, what he could not prevent, and led her
himself to the prison, followed by all his people,
in as much state as if he had been going to his
marriage ; where, when she came, she was as well-
attended and served as before, he never stirring one
moment from her.

The next day she was tried in open and common
court ; where she appeared in glory, led by Tarquin,
and attended according to her quality.   And she
could not deny all the page had alleged against her,
who was brought thither also in chains ; and after a
great many circumstances, she was found guilty, and
both received sentence ; the page to be hanged till he

was dead, on a gibbet in the market-place; and the Princess to stand under the gibbet, with a rope about her neck, the other end of which was to be fastened to the gibbet where the page was hanging; and to have an inscription, in large characters, upon her back and breast, of the cause why; where she was to stand from ten in the morning to twelve.

This sentence, the people with one accord, believed too favourable for so ill a woman, whose crimes deserved death, equal to that of Van Brune. Nevertheless, there were some who said, it was infinitely more severe than death itself.

The following Friday was the day of execution, and one need not tell of the abundance of people, who were flocked together in the market-place. And all the windows were taken down, and filled with spectators, and the tops of houses; when at the hour appointed, the fatal beauty appeared. She was dressed in a black velvet gown, with a rich row of diamonds all down the fore-part of her breast, and a great knot of diamonds at the peak behind; and a petticoat of flowered gold, very rich, and laced; with all things else suitable. A gentleman carried her great velvet cushion before her, on which her prayer-book, embroidered, was laid; her train was borne up by a page, and the Prince led her, bare; followed by his footmen, pages, and other officers of his house.

When they arrived at the place of execution, the cushion was laid on the ground, upon a Portugal mat, spread there for that purpose; and the Princess stood on the cushion, with her prayer-book in her hand, and a priest by her side; and was accordingly tied up to the gibbet.

She had not stood there ten minutes, but she had the mortification (at least one would think it so to her) to see her sad page, Van Brune, approach, fair as an angel, but languishing and pale. That sight moved all the beholders with as much pity, as that of the Princess did with disdain and pleasure.

He was dressed all in mourning, and very fine linen, bare-headed, with his own hair, the fairest that could be seen, hanging all in curls on his back and shoulders, very long. He had a prayer-book of black velvet in his hand, and behaved himself with much penitence and devotion.

When he came under the gibbet, he seeing his mistress in that condition, showed an infinite concern, and his fair face was covered over with blushes; and falling at her feet, he humbly asked her pardon for having been the occasion of so great an infamy to her, by a weak confession, which the fears of youth, and hopes of life, had obliged him to make, so greatly to her dishonour; for indeed he wanted that manly strength, to bear the efforts of dying, as he ought, in silence, rather than of committing so great a crime against his duty, and honour itself; and that he could not die in peace, unless she would forgive him. The Princess only nodded her head, and cried, ' I do.'

And after having spoken a little to his father-confessor, who was with him, he cheerfully mounted the ladder, and in sight of the Princess he was turned off, while a loud cry was heard through all the market-place, especially from the fair sex; he hanged there till the time the Princess was to depart; and then she was put into a rich embroidered chair, and carried away, Tarquin going into his, for he had all that time stood supporting the Princess under the gallows, and was very weary. She was sent back, till her releasement came, which was that night about seven o'clock; and then she was conducted to her own house in great state, with a dozen white wax flambeaux about her chair.

If the guardian of Alcidiana, and her friends, before were impatient of having the portion out of the hands of these extravagants, it is not to be imagined but they were now much more so; and the next day they sent an officer, according to law, to demand it, or to summon the Prince to give reasons why he would not pay it. The officer received for answer, that the money should be called in, and paid in such a time, setting a certain time, which I have not been so curious as to retain, or put in my journal-observations; but I am sure it was not long, as may be easily imagined, for they every moment suspected the Prince would pack up, and be gone, some time or other, on the sudden ; and for that reason they would not trust him without bail, or two officers to remain in his house, to watch that nothing should be removed or touched. As for bail, or security, he could give none; every one slunk their heads out of the collar, when it came to that. So that he was obliged, at his own expense, to maintain officers in his house.

The Princess finding herself reduced to the last extremity, and that she must either produce the value of a hundred thousand crowns, or see the Prince her husband lodged for ever in a prison, and all their glory vanish ; and that it was impossible to fly, since guarded; she had recourse to an extremity, worse than the affair of Van Brune. And in order to this, she first puts on a world of sorrow and concern, for what she feared might arrive to the Prince. And indeed, if ever she shed tears which she did not dissemble, it was upon this occasion. But here she almost over-acted. She stirred not from her bed, and refused to eat, or sleep, or see the light; so that the day being shut out of her chamber, she lived by wax-lights, and refused all comfort and consolation.

The Prince, all raving with love, tender compassion and grief, never stirred from her bedside, nor ceased to implore, that she would suffer herself to live. But she, who was not now so passionately in love with Tarquin, as she was with the Prince ; nor so fond of the man as his titles, and of glory, foresaw the total ruin of the last, if not prevented by avoiding the payment of this great sum ; which could not otherwise be, than by the death of Alcidiana. And therefore, without ceasing, she wept, and cried out, 'She could

not live, unless Alcidiana died. This Alcidiana,'
continued she, 'who has been the author of my
shame; who has exposed me under a gibbet, in the
public market-place! Oh! I am deaf to all reason,
blind to natural affection. I renounce her, I hate her
as my mortal foe, my stop to glory, and the finisher
of my days, ere half my race of life be run.'

Then throwing her false, but snowy charming arms
about the neck of her heart-breaking lord and lover,
who lay sighing, and listening by her side, he was
charmed and bewitched into saying all things that
appeased her; and lastly, told her, 'Alcidiana should
be no longer any obstacle to her repose; but that, if
she would look up, and cast her eyes of sweetness
and love upon him, as heretofore; forget her sorrow,
and redeem her lost health; he would take what
measures she should propose to despatch this fatal
stop to her happiness, out of the way.'

These words failed not to make her caress him in
the most endearing manner that love and flattery
could invent; and she kissed him to an oath, a solemn
oath, to perform what he had promised; and he
vowed liberally. And she assumed in an instant her
good-humour, and suffered a supper to be prepared,
and did eat; which in many days before she had not
done. So obstinate and powerful was she in dissembling well.

The next thing to be considered was, which way
this deed was to be done; for they doubted not, but
when it was done all the world would lay it upon the
Princess, as done by her command. But she urged,
suspicion was no proof; and that they never put to
death any one, but when they had great and certain
evidence who were the offenders. She was sure of
her own constancy, that racks and tortures should
never get the secret from her breast; and if he were
as confident on his part, there was no danger. Yet
this preparation she made towards laying the fact on
others, that she caused several letters to be wrote

from Germany, as from the relations of Van Brune, who threatened Alcidiana with death, for depriving their kinsman (who was a gentleman) of his life, though he had not taken away hers. And it was the report of the town, how this young maid was threatened. And indeed, the death of the page had so afflicted a great many, that Alcidiana had procured herself abundance of enemies upon that account, because she might have saved him if she had pleased; but, on the contrary, she was a spectator, and in full health and vigour, at his execution. And people were not so much concerned for her at this report, as they would have been.

The Prince, who now had, by reasoning the matter soberly with Miranda, found it absolutely necessary to despatch Alcidiana, resolved himself, and with his own hand, to execute it; not daring to trust any of his most favourite servants, though he had many, who possibly would have obeyed him; for they loved him as he deserved, and so would all the world, had he not been so purely deluded by this fair enchantress. He therefore, as I said, resolved to keep this great secret to himself; and taking a pistol, charged well with two bullets, he watched an opportunity to shoot her as she should go out or into her house, or coach, some evening.

To this end he waited several nights near her lodgings, but still, either she went not out, or when she returned, she was so guarded with friends, her lover, and flambeaux, that he could not aim at her without endangering the life of some other. But one night above the rest, upon a Sunday, when he knew she would be at the theatre, for she never missed that day seeing the play, he waited at the corner of the Stadt House, near the theatre, with his cloak cast over his face, and a black periwig, all alone, with his pistol ready cocked; and remained not very long but he saw her kinsman's coach come along; it was almost dark, day was just shutting up her beauties, and left

such a light to govern the world, as served only just
to distinguish one object from another, and a convenient help to mischief. He saw alight out of the
coach only one young lady, the lover, and then the
destined victim ; which he (drawing near) knew rather
by her tongue than shape. The lady ran into the
play-house, and left Alcidiana to be conducted by
her lover into it, who led her to the door, and went to
give some order to the coachman ; so that the lover
was about twenty yards from Alcidiana ; when she
stood the fairest mark in the world, on the threshold
of the entrance of the theatre, there being many
coaches about the door, so that hers could not come
so near. Tarquin was resolved not to lose so fair an
opportunity, and advanced, but went behind the
coaches ; and when he came over against the door,
through a great booted velvet coach, that stood
between him and her, he shot ; and she having the
train of her gown and petticoat on her arm, in great
quantity, he missed her body, and shot through her
clothes, between her arm and her body. She, frightened to find something hit her, and to see the smoke,
and hear the report of the pistol ; running in, cried, 'I
am shot, I am dead.'

This noise quickly alarmed her lover ; and all the
coachmen and footmen immediately ran, some one
way, and some another. One of them seeing a man
haste away in a cloak ; he being a lusty bold German,
stopped him ; and drawing upon him, bid him stand,
and deliver his pistol, or he would run him through.

Tarquin being surprised at the boldness of this
fellow to demand his pistol, as if he positively knew
him to be the murderer (for so he thought himself,
since he believed Alcidiana dead), had so much
presence of mind as to consider, if he suffered himself
to be taken, he should poorly die a public death ; and
therefore resolved upon one mischief more, to secure
himself from the first. And in the moment that the
German bade him deliver his pistol, he cried, 'Though

I have no pistol to deliver, I have a sword to chastise thy insolence.' And throwing off his cloak, and flinging his pistol from him, he drew, and wounded, and disarmed the fellow.

This noise of swords brought everybody to the place; and immediately the bruit ran, 'The murderer was taken, the murderer was taken.' Yet none knew which was he, nor as yet so much as the cause of the quarrel between the two fighting men; for it was now darker than before. But at the noise of the murderer being taken, the lover of Alcidiana, who by this time found his lady unhurt, all but the trains of her gown and petticoat, came running to the place, just as Tarquin had disarmed the German, and was ready to kill him; when laying hold of his arm, they arrested the stroke, and redeemed the footman.

They then demanded who this stranger was, at whose mercy the fellow lay; but the Prince, who now found himself venturing for his last stake, made no reply; but with two swords in his hands went to fight his way through the rabble. And though there were above a hundred persons, some with swords, others with long whips (as coachmen), so invincible was the courage of this poor unfortunate gentleman at that time, that all these were not able to seize him; but he made his way through the ring that encompassed him, and ran away; but was, however, so closely pursued, the company still gathering as they ran, that toiled with fighting, oppressed with guilt, and fear of being taken, he grew fainter and fainter, and suffered himself, at last, to yield to his pursuers, who soon found him to be Prince Tarquin in disguise. And they carried him directly to prison, being Sunday, to wait the coming day, to go before a magistrate.

In an hour's time the whole fatal adventure was carried all over the city, and every one knew that Tarquin was the intended murderer of Alcidiana; and not one but had a real sorrow and compassion for him. They heard how bravely he had defended himself, how many he had wounded before he could be taken, and what numbers he had fought through. And even those that saw his valour and bravery, and who had assisted at his being seized, now repented from the bottom of their hearts their having any hand in the ruin of so gallant a man ; especially since they knew the lady was not hurt. A thousand addresses were made to her not to prosecute him ; but her lover, a hot-headed fellow, more fierce than brave, would by no means be pacified, but vowed to pursue him to the scaffold.

The Monday came, and the Prince being examined, confessed the matter of fact, since there was no harm done ; believing a generous confession the best of his game. But he was sent back to closer imprisonment, loaded with irons, to expect the next sessions. All his household goods were seized, and all they could find, for the use of Alcidiana. And the Princess, all in rage, tearing her hair, was carried to the same prison, to behold the cruel effects of her hellish designs.

One need not tell here how sad and horrid this meeting appeared between her lord and her. Let it suffice, it was the most melancholy and mortifying object that ever eyes beheld. On Miranda's part, it was sometimes all rage and fire, and sometimes all tears and groans ; but still it was sad love, and mournful tenderness on his. Nor could all his sufferings, and the prospect of death itself, drive from his soul one spark of that fire the obstinate god had fatally kindled there. And in the midst of all his sighs, he would recall himself, and cry, ‘I have Miranda still.’

He was eternally visited by his friends and acquaintance ; and this last action of bravery had got him more than all his former conduct had lost. The fathers were perpetually with him ; and all joined with one common voice in this, that he ought to abandon a woman so wicked as the Princess ; and that however fate dealt with him, he could not show himself a true penitent, while he laid the author of so much evil in his bosom : that heaven would never bless him, till he had renounced her: and on such conditions he would find those that would employ their utmost interest to save his life, who else would not stir in this affair. But he was so deaf to all, that he could not so much as dissemble a repentance of having married her.

He lay a long time in prison, and all that time the poor Father Francisco remained there also. And the good fathers who daily visited these two amorous prisoners, the Prince and Princess; and who found, by the management of matters, it would go very hard with Tarquin, entertained them often with holy matters relating to the life to come; from which, before his trial, he gathered what his stars had appointed, and that he was destined to die.

This gave an unspeakable torment to the now repenting beauty, who had reduced him to it; and she began to appear with a more solid grief: which being perceived by the good fathers, they resolved to attack her on the yielding side; and after some discourse upon the judgment for sin, they came to reflect on the business of Father Francisco; and told her, she had never thriven since her accusing of that father, and laid it very home to her conscience; assuring her that they would do their utmost in her service, if she would confess that secret sin to all the world, so that she might atone for the crime, by the saving that good man. At first she seemed inclined to yield; but shame of being her own detector, in so vile a matter, recalled her goodness, and she faintly persisted in it.

At the end of six months, Prince Tarquin was called to his trial; where I will pass over the circumstances, which are only what is usual in such criminal cases, and tell you, that he being found guilty of the intent of killing Alcidiana, was condemned to lose his head in the market-place, and the Princess to be banished her country.

After sentence pronounced, to the real grief of all the spectators, he was carried back to prison. And now the fathers attack her anew; and she, whose griefs daily increased, with a languishment that brought her very near her grave, at last confessed all her life, all the lewdness of her practices with several princes and great men, besides her lusts with people that served her, and others in mean capacity: and lastly, the whole truth of the young friar; and how she had drawn the page, and the Prince her husband, to this designed murder of her sister. This she signed with her hand, in the presence of the Prince, her husband, and several holy men who were present. Which being signified to the magistrates, the friar was immediately delivered from his irons (where he had languished more than two whole years) in great triumph, with much honour, and lives a most exemplary pious life, as he did before; for he is now living in Antwerp.

After the condemnation of these two unfortunate persons, who begot such different sentiments in the minds of the people (the Prince, all the compassion and pity imaginable; and the Princess, all the contempt and despite); they languished almost six months longer in prison: so great an interest there was made, in order to the saving his life, by all the men of the robe. On the other side, the Princes, and great men of all nations, who were at the Court of Brussels, who bore a secret revenge in their hearts against a man who had, as they pretended, set up a false title, only to take place of them; who indeed was but a merchant's son of Holland, as they said; so incensed them against him, that they were too hard at Court for the church-men. However, this dispute gave the Prince his life some months longer than was expected; which gave him also some hope, that a reprieve for ninety years would have been granted, as was desired. Nay, Father Francisco so interested himself in this concern, that he writ to his father, and several princes of Germany, with whom the Marquis Castel Roderigo was well acquainted, to intercede with him for the saving of Tarquin; since it was more by his persuasions, than those of all who attacked her, that made Miranda confess the truth of her affair with him. But at the end of six months, when all applications were found fruitless and vain, the Prince received news, that in two days he was to die, as his sentence had been before pronounced, and for which he prepared himself with all cheerfulness.

On the following Friday, as soon as it was light, all people of any condition came to take their leaves of him; and none departed with dry eyes, or hearts unconcerned to the last degree. For Tarquin, when he found his fate inevitable bore it with a fortitude that showed no signs of regret; but addressed himself to all about him with the same cheerful, modest, and great air, he was wont to do in his most flourishing fortune. His valet was dressing him all the morning, so many interruptions they had by visitors; and he was all in mourning, and so were all his followers; for even to the last he kept up his grandeur, to the amazement of all people. And indeed, he was so passionately beloved by them, that those he had dismissed, served him voluntarily, and would not be persuaded to abandon him while he lived.

The Princess was also dressed in mourning, and her two women; and notwithstanding the unheard-of lewdness and villainies she had confessed of herself, the Prince still adored her; for she had still those charms that made him first do so; nor, to his last moment, could he be brought to wish, that he had never seen her; but on the contrary, as a man yet vainly proud of his fetters, he said, 'All the satisfaction this short moment of life could afford him, was, that he died in endeavouring to serve Miranda, his adorable Princess.'

After he had taken leave of all, who thought it necessary to leave him to himself for some time, he retired with his confessor ; where they were about an hour in prayer, all the ceremonies of devotion that were fit to be done, being already passed. At last the bell tolled, and he was to take leave of the Princess, as his last work of life, and the most hard he had to accomplish. He threw himself at her feet, and gazing on her as she sat more dead than alive, overwhelmed with silent grief, they both remained some moments speechless ; and then, as if one rising tide of tears had supplied both their eyes, it burst out in streams at the same instant : and when his sighs gave way, he uttered a thousand farewells, so soft, so passionate, and moving, that all who were by were extremely touched with it, and said, that nothing could be seen more deplorable and melancholy. A thousand times they bade farewell, and still some tender look, or word, would prevent his going ; then embrace, and bid farewell again. A thousand times she asked his pardon for being the occasion of that fatal separation ; a thousand times assuring him, she would follow him, for she could not live without him. And Heaven knows when their soft and sad caresses would have ended, had not the officers assured him it was time to mount the scaffold. At which words the Princess fell fainting in the arms of her women, and they led Tarquin out of prison.

When he came to the market-place, whither he walked on foot, followed by his own domestics, and some bearing a black velvet coffin with silver hinges ; the headsman before him with his fatal scimitar drawn, his confessor by his side, and many gentlemen and church-men, with Father Francisco attending him, the people showering millions of blessings on him, and beholding him with weeping eyes, he mounted the scaffold ; which was strown with some sawdust, about the place where he was to kneel, to receive the blood. For they behead people kneeling,

and with the back-stroke of a scimitar; and not lying
on a block, and with an axe, as we in England. The
scaffold had a low rail about it, that everybody might
more conveniently see. This was hung with black,
and all that state that such a death could have, was
here in most decent order.

He did not say much upon the scaffold. The sum
of what he said to his friends was, to be kind, and
take care of the poor penitent his wife, To others,
recommending his honest and generous servants,
whose fidelity was so well known and commended,
that they were soon promised preferment. He was
some time in prayer, and a very short time in speaking to his confessor; then he turned to the headsman, and desired him to do his office well, and gave
him twenty louis d'ors; and undressing himself with
the help of his valet and page, he pulled off his coat,
and had underneath a white satin waistcoat. He
took off his periwig, and put on a white satin cap,
with a holland one done with point under it, which he
pulled over his eyes; then took a cheerful leave of
all, and kneeled down, and said, 'When he lifted up
his hands the third time, the headsman should do
his office.' Which accordingly was done, and the
headsman gave him his last stroke, and the Prince
fell on the scaffold. The people with one common
voice, as if it had been but one entire one, prayed for
his soul; and murmurs of sighs were heard from the
whole multitude, who scrambled for some of the
bloody sawdust, to keep for his memory.

The headsman going to take up the head, as the
manner is, to show it to the people, he found he had
not struck it off, and that the body stirred; with that
he stepped to an engine, which they always carry with
them, to force those who may be refractory; thinking, as he said, to have twisted the head from the
shoulders, conceiving it to hang but by a small matter
of flesh. Though it was an odd shift of the fellow's,
yet it was done, and the best shift he could suddenly

propose. The Margrave, and another officer, old
men, were on the scaffold, with some of the Prince's
friends and servants; who seeing the headsman put
the engine about the neck of the Prince, began to
call out, and the people made a great noise. The
Prince, who found himself yet alive; or rather, who
was past thinking but had some sense of feeling left,
when the headsman took him up, and set his back
against the rail, and clapped the engine about his
neck, got his two thumbs between the rope and his
neck, feeling himself pressed there; and struggling
between life and death, and bending himself over the
rail backward, while the headsman pulled forward,
he threw himself quite over the rail, by chance, and
not design, and fell upon the heads and shoulders of
the people, who were crying out with amazing shouts
of joy. The headsman leaped after him, but the
rabble had liked to have pulled him to pieces. All
the city was in an uproar, but none knew what the
matter was, but those who bore the body of the
Prince, whom they found yet living; but how, or by
what strange miracle preserved, they knew not, nor
did examine; but with one accord, as if the whole
crowd had been one body, and had but one motion,
they bore the Prince on their heads about a hundred
yards from the scaffold, where there is a monastery of
Jesuits; and there they secured him. All this was
done, his beheading, his falling, and his being secured,
almost in a moment's time; the people rejoicing, as
at some extraordinary victory won. One of the
officers being, as I said, an old timorous man, was so
frightened at the accident, the bustle, the noise, and
the confusion, of which he was wholly ignorant, that
he died with amazement and fear; and the other was
fain to be let blood.

The officers of justice went to demand the prisoner,
but they demanded in vain; the Jesuits had now
a right to protect him, and would do so. All his
overjoyed friends went to see in what condition he

was, and all of quality found admittance. They saw him in bed, going to be dressed by the most skilful surgeons, who yet could not assure him of life. They desired nobody should speak to him, or ask him any questions. They found that the headsman had struck him too low, and had cut him into the shoulder-bone. A very great wound, you may be sure; for the sword, in such executions, carries an extreme force. However, so great care was taken on all sides, and so greatly the fathers were concerned for him, that they found an amendment, and hopes of a good effect of their incomparable charity and goodness.

At last, when he was permitted to speak, the first news he asked was after the Princess. And his friends were very much afflicted to find, that all his loss of blood had not quenched that flame, nor let out that which made him still love that bad woman. He was solicited daily to think no more of her. And all her crimes are laid so open to him, and so shame-fully represented; and on the other side, his virtues so admired; and which, they said, would have been eternally celebrated, but for his folly with this infamous creature; that at last, by assuring him of all their assistance if he abandoned her; and to re-nounce him, and deliver him up, if he did not; they wrought so far upon him, as to promise he would suffer her to go alone into banishment, and would not follow her, or live with her any more. But alas! this was but his gratitude that compelled this com-plaisance, for in his heart he resolved never to aban-don her; nor was he able to live, and think of doing it. However, his reason assured him, he could not do a deed more justifiable, and one that would regain his fame sooner.

His friends asked him some questions concerning his escape; and since he was not beheaded, but only wounded, why he did not immediately rise up. But he replied, he was so absolutely prepossessed, that at the third lifting up his hands he should receive the stroke of death, that at the same instant the sword touched him, he had no sense; nay, not even of pain, so absolutely dead he was with imagination; and knew not that he stirred, as the headsman found he did; nor did he remember anything, from the lifting up of his hands, to his fall; and then awakened, as out of a dream, or rather a moment's sleep without dream, he found he lived, and wondered what was arrived to him, or how he came to live; having not, as yet, any sense of his wound, though so terrible an one.

After this, Alcidiana, who was extremely afflicted for having been the prosecutor of this great man; who, bating this last design against her, which she knew was at the instigation of her sister, had obliged her with all the civility imaginable; now sought all means possible of getting his pardon, and that of her sister; though of a hundred thousand crowns, which she should have paid her, she could get but ten thousand; which was from the sale of her rich beds, and some other furniture. So that the young Count, who before should have married her, now went off for want of fortune; and a young merchant (perhaps the best of the two) was the man to whom she was destined.

At last, by great intercession, both their pardons were obtained; and the Prince, who would be no more seen in a place that had proved every way so fatal to him, left Flanders, promising never to live with the fair hypocrite more; but ere he departed, he wrote her a letter, wherein he ordered her, in a little time, to follow him into Holland; and left a bill of exchange with one of his trusty servants, whom he had left to wait upon her, for money for her accommodation; so that she was now reduced to one woman, one page, and this gentleman. The Prince, in this time of his imprisonment, had several bills of great sums from his father, who was exceeding rich, and this all the children he had in the world, and whom he tenderly loved.

As soon as Miranda was come into Holland, she was welcomed with all imaginable respect and endearment by the old father; who was imposed upon so, as that he knew not she was the fatal occasion of all these disasters to his son; but rather looked on her as a woman, who had brought him a hundred and fifty thousand crowns, which his misfortunes had consumed. But, above all, she was received by Tarquin with a joy unspeakable; who, after some time, to redeem his credit, and gain himself a new fame, put himself into the French army, where he did wonders; and after three campaigns, his father dying, he returned home, and retired to a country-house: where, with his Princess, he lived as a private gentleman, in all the tranquillity of a man of good fortune. They say Miranda has been very penitent for her life past, and gives Heaven the glory for having given her these afflictions that have reclaimed her, and brought her to as perfect a state of happiness, as this troublesome world can afford.

Since I began this relation, I heard that Prince Tarquin died about three-quarters of a year ago.

THE NUN

OR THE PERJURED BEAUTY

A TRUE NOVEL

DON HENRIQUE was a person of great birth, of a great estate, of a bravery equal to either, of a most generous education, but of more passion than reason. He was besides of an opener and freer temper than generally his countrymen are (I mean, the Spaniards) and always engaged in some love-intrigue or other.

One night as he was retreating from one of those engagements, Don Sebastian, whose sister he had abused with a promise of marriage, set upon him at the corner of a street, in Madrid, and by the help of three of his friends, designed to have despatched him on a doubtful embassy to the Almighty Monarch. But he received their first instructions with better address than they expected, and dismissed his envoy first, killing one of Don Sebastian's friends. Which so enraged the injured brother, that his strength and resolution seemed to be redoubled, and so animated his two surviving companions, that (doubtless) they had gained a dishonourable victory, had not Don Antonio accidentally come in to the rescue; who after a short dispute, killed one of the two who attacked him only; whilst Don Henrique, with the greatest difficulty, defended his life, for some moments, against Sebastian, whose rage deprived him of strength, and gave his adversary the unwished advantage of his seeming death, though not without bequeathing some bloody legacies to Don Henrique. Antonio had received but one slight wound in the left arm, and his surviving antagonist none; who however thought it not advisable to begin a fresh dispute against two, of whose courage he had but too fatal a proof, though one of them was sufficiently disabled. The conquerors on the other side, politically retreated, and quitting the field to the conquered, left the living to bury the dead, if he could, or thought convenient.

As they were marching off, Don Antonio, who all this while knew not whose life he had so happily preserved, told his companion in arms, that he thought it indispensably necessary that he should quarter with him that night for his further preservation. To which he prudently consented, and went, with no little uneasiness, to his lodgings; where he surprised Antonio with the sight of his dearest friend. For they had certainly the nearest sympathy in all their thoughts, that ever made two brave men unhappy. And, undoubtedly, nothing but death, or more fatal love, could have divided them. However, at present, they were united and secure.

In the meantime, Don Sebastian's friend was just going to call help to carry off the bodies, as the ——— came by; who seeing three men lie dead, seized the fourth: who as he was about to justify himself, by discovering one of the authors of so much bloodshed, was interrupted by a groan from his supposed dead friend Don Sebastian; whom, after a brief account of some part of the matter, and a knowledge of his quality, they took up, and carried to his house; where, within a few days he was recovered past the fear of death. All this while Henrique and Antonio durst not appear, so much as by night; nor could be found, though diligent and daily search was made after the first; but upon Don Sebastian's recovery, the search ceasing, they took the advantage of the night, and, in disguise, retreated to Seville. It was there they thought themselves most secure, where indeed they were in the greatest danger; for though (haply) they might there have escaped the murderous attempt of Don Sebastian and his friends, yet they could not there avoid the malicious influence of their stars.

This city gave birth to Antonio, and to the cause of his greatest misfortunes, as well as of his death. Dona Ardelia was born there, a miracle of beauty and falsehood. It was more than a year since Don Antonio had first seen and loved her. For it was impossible any man should do one without the other. He had had the unkind opportunity of speaking and conveying a billet to her at church; and to his greater misfortune, the next time he found her there, he met with too kind a return both from her eyes and from her hand, which privately slipped a paper into his; in which he found abundantly more than he expected, directing him in that, how he should proceed, in order to carry her off from her father with the least danger he could look for in such an attempt; since it would have been vain and fruitless to have asked her of her father, because their families had been at enmity for several years; though Antonio was as well descended as she, and had as ample a fortune; nor was his person, according to his sex, any way inferior to hers; and certainly, the beauties of his mind were more excellent, especially if it be an excellence to be constant.

He had made several attempts to take possession of her, but all proved ineffectual; however, he had the good fortune not to be known, though once or twice he narrowly escaped with life, bearing off his wounds with difficulty. (Alas, that the wounds of love should cause those of hate!) Upon which she was strictly confined to one room, whose only window was towards the garden, and that too was grated with iron; and, once a month, when she went to church, she was constantly and carefully attended by her father, and a mother-in-law, worse than a *Duegna*. Under this miserable confinement Antonio under-

stood she still continued, at his return to Seville, with
Don Henrique, whom he acquainted with his invincible passion for her; lamenting the severity of
her present circumstances, that admitted of no
prospect of relief; which caused a generous concern
in Don Henrique, both for the sufferings of his friend,
and of the lady. He proposed several ways to Don
Antonio, for the release of the fair prisoner; but
none of them was thought practicable, or at least
likely to succeed. But Antonio, who (you may
believe) was then more nearly engaged, bethought
himself of an expedient that would undoubtedly
reward their endeavours. It was, that Don Henrique,
who was very well acquainted with Ardelia's father,
should make him a visit, with pretence of begging
his consent and admission to make his addresses to
his daughter; which, in all probability, he could not
refuse to Don Henrique's quality and estate; and
then this freedom of access to her would give him the
opportunity of delivering the lady to his friend. This
was thought so reasonable, that the very next day it
was put in practice; and with so good success, that
Don Henrique was received by the father of Ardelia
with the greatest and most respectful ceremony
imaginable. And when he made the proposal to him
of marrying his daughter, it was embraced with a
visible satisfaction and joy in the air of his face.
This their first conversation ended with all imaginable content on both sides; Don Henrique being
invited by the father to dinner the next day, when
Dona Ardelia was to be present; who, at that time,
was said to be indisposed, (as it is very probable she
was, with so close an imprisonment). Henrique returned to Antonio, and made him happy with the
account of his reception; which could not but have
terminated in the perfect felicity of Antonio, had his
fate been just to the merits of his love. The day
and hour came which brought Henrique, with a
private commission from his friend, to Ardelia. He

saw her; (ah! would he had only seen her veiled!) and, with the first opportunity, gave her the letter, which held so much love, and so much truth, as ought to have preserved him in the empire of her heart. It contained, besides, a discovery of his whole design upon her father, for the completing of their happiness; which nothing then could obstruct but herself. But Henrique had seen her; he had gazed, and swallowed all her beauties at his eyes. How greedily his soul drank the strong poison in! But yet his honour and his friendship were strong as ever, and bravely fought against the usurper love, and got a noble victory; at least he thought and wished so. With this, and a short answer to his letter, Henrique returned to the longing Antonio; who, receiving the paper with the greatest devotion, and kissing it with the greatest zeal, opened and read these words to himself:—

DON ANTONIO,

You have, at last, made use of the best and only expedient for my enlargement; for which I thank you, since I know it is purely the effect of your love. Your agent has a mighty influence on my father: and you may assure yourself, that as you have advised and desired me, he shall have no less on me, who am

Yours entirely,

And only yours,

ARDELIA.

Having respectfully and tenderly kissed the name, he could not choose but show the billet to his friend; who reading that part of it which concerned himself, started and blushed: which Antonio observing, was curious to know the cause of it. Henrique told him, that he was surprised to find her express so little love, after so long an absence. To which his friend replied for her, that, doubtless, she had not time enough to attempt so great a matter as a perfect account of her love; and added, that it was confirmation enough to

him of its continuance, since she subscribed herself
his entirely, and only his. How blind is love! Don
Henrique knew how to make it bear another meaning; which, however, he had the discretion to conceal.
Antonio, who was as real in his friendship, as constant
in his love, asked him what he thought of her beauty?
To which the other answered, that he thought it
irresistible to any, but to a soul prepossessed, and
nobly fortified with a perfect friendship: 'Such as is
thine, my Henrique,' added Antonio; 'yet as sincere
and perfect as that is, I know you must, nay, I know,
you do love her.' 'As I ought to do,' replied Henrique. 'Yes, yes,' returned his friend, 'it must be so;
otherwise the sympathy which unites our souls would
be wanting, and consequently our friendship were in
a state of imperfection.' 'How industriously you
would argue me into a crime, that would tear and
destroy the foundation of the strongest ties of truth
and honour!' said Henrique. 'But,' he continued, 'I
hope within a few days, to put it out of my power to
be guilty of so great a sacrilege.' 'I can't determine,'
said Antonio, 'if I knew that you loved one another,
whether I could easier part with my friend, or my
mistress.' 'Though what you say is highly generous,
replied Henrique, 'yet give me leave to urge, that it
looks like a trial of friendship, and argues you inclin-
able to jealousy. But, pardon me, I know it to be
sincerely meant by you; and must therefore own,
that it is the best, because it is the noblest way of
securing both your friend and mistress.' 'I need not
make use of any arts to secure me of either,' replied
Antonio, 'but expect to enjoy them both in a little
time.'

Henrique, who was a little uneasy with a discourse
of this nature, diverted it, by reflecting on what had
passed at Madrid, between them two and Don Sebastian and his friends; which caused Antonio to bethink
himself of the danger to which he exposed his friend,
by appearing daily, though in disguise. For, doubt-

less, Don Sebastian would pursue his revenge to the utmost extremity. These thoughts put him upon desiring his friend, for his own sake, to hasten the performance of his attempt; and accordingly, each day Don Henrique brought Antonio nearer the hopes of happiness, while he himself was hourly sinking into the lowest state of misery. The last night before the day in which Antonio expected to be blessed in her love, Don Henrique had a long and fatal conference with her about her liberty. Being then with her alone in an arbour of the garden, which privilege he had had for some days; after a long silence, and observing Don Henrique in much disorder, by the motion of his eyes, which were sometimes steadfastly fixed on the ground, then lifted up to her or heaven, (for he could see nothing more beautiful on earth) she made use of the privilege of her sex, and began the discourse first, to this effect: 'Has anything happened, sir, since our retreat hither, to occasion that disorder which is but too visible in your face, and too dreadful in your continued silence? Speak, I beseech you, sir, and let me know if I have any way unhappily contributed to it!' 'No, madam,' replied he, 'my friendship is now likely to be the only cause of my greatest misery; for to-morrow I must be guilty of an unpardonable crime, in betraying the generous confidence which your noble father has placed in me. To-morrow,' added he, with a piteous sigh, 'I must deliver you into the hands of one whom your father hates even to death, instead of doing myself the honour of becoming his son-in-law within a few days more.—But—I will consider and remind myself, that I give you into the hands of my friend; of my friend, that loves you better than his life, which he has often exposed for your sake; and what is more than all, to my friend, whom you love more than any consideration on earth.' 'And must this be done?' she asked. 'Is it inevitable as fate?' 'Fixed as the laws of nature, madam,' replied he. 'Don't you find the

necessity of it, Ardelia?' continued he, by way of
question. 'Does not your love require it? Think,
you are going to your dear Antonio, who alone can
merit you, and whom only you can love.' 'Were
your last words true,' returned she, 'I should yet be
unhappy in the displeasure of a dear and tender
father, and infinitely more, in being the cause of your
infidelity to him. No, Don Henrique,' continued she,
'I could with greater satisfaction return to my miserable confinement, than by any means disturb the
peace of your mind, or occasion one moment's interruption of your quiet.' 'Would to Heaven you did
not,' sighed he to himself. Then addressing his words
more distinctly to her, cried he, 'Ah, cruel! ah,
unjust Ardelia! these words belong to none but
Antonio; why then would you endeavour to persuade me, that I do, or ever can merit the tenderness
of such an expression? Have a care!' pursued he,
'have a care, Ardelia! your outward beauties are too
powerful to be resisted; even your frowns have such
a sweetness that they attract the very soul that is not
strongly prepossessed with the noblest friendship,
and the highest principles of honour. Why then,
alas! did you add such sweet and charming accents?
Why——' 'Ah, Don Henrique!' she interrupted,
'why did you appear to me so charming in your
person, so great in your friendship, and so illustrious
in your reputation? Why did my father, ever since
your first visit, continually fill my ears and thoughts
with noble characters and glorious ideas, which yet
but imperfectly and faintly represent the inimitable
original! But (what is most severe and cruel) why,
Don Henrique, why will you defeat my father in his
ambition of your alliance, and me of those glorious
hopes with which you had blessed my soul, by casting me away from you to Antonio!' 'Ha,' cried he,
starting, 'what said you, madam! What did Ardelia
say? That I had blessed your soul with hopes!
That I would cast you away to Antonio! Can they

who safely arrive in their wished-for port, be said to
be shipwrecked? Or, can an abject indigent wretch
make a king? These are more than riddles, madam;
and I must not think to expound them.' 'No,' said
she, 'let it alone, Don Henrique; I'll ease you of that
trouble, and tell you plainly that I love you.' 'Ah,'
cried he, 'now all my fears are come upon me!'
'How!' asked she, 'were you afraid I should love
you? Is my love so dreadful then?' 'Yes, when
misplaced,' replied he; 'but it was your falsehood that
I feared. Your love was what I would have sought
with the utmost hazard of my life, nay, even of my
future happiness, I fear, had you not been engaged;
strongly obliged to love elsewhere, both by your own
choice and vows, as well as by his dangerous services,
and matchless constancy.' 'For which,' said she, 'I
do not hate him, though his father killed my uncle.
Nay, perhaps,' continued she, 'I have a friendship for
him, but no more.' 'No more, said you, madam?'
cried he; 'but tell me, did you never love him?'
'Indeed I did,' replied she; 'but the sight of you has
better instructed me, both in my duty to my father,
and in causing my passion for you, without whom I
shall be eternally miserable. Ah, then pursue your
honourable proposal, and make my father happy in
my marriage!' 'It must not be,' returned Don Henrique, 'my honour, my friendship forbids it.' 'No,'
she returned, 'your honour requires it; and if your
friendship opposes your honour, it can have no sure
and solid foundation.' 'Female sophistry,' cried Henrique: 'but you need no art nor artifice, Ardelia, to
make me love you. Love you!' pursued he, 'by that
bright sun, the light and heat of all the world, you are
my only light and heat—— Oh, friendship! Sacred
friendship, now assist me!' [Here for a time he
paused, and then afresh proceeded thus,] 'You told
me, or my ears deceived me, that you loved me,
Ardelia.' 'I did,' she replied, 'and that I do love
you, is as true as that I told you so.' ''Tis well; but

would it were not so!' 'Did ever man receive a blessing thus?' 'Why, I could wish I did not love you, Ardelia! But that were impossible——' 'At least unjust,' interrupted she. 'Well then,' he went on, 'to show you that I do sincerely consult your particular happiness, without any regard to my own, to-morrow I will give you to Don Antonio; and as a proof of your love to me, I expect your ready consent to it.' 'To let you see, Don Henrique, how perfectly and tenderly I love you, I will be sacrificed to-morrow to Don Antonio, and to your quiet.' 'Oh, strongest, dearest obligation!' cried Henrique. 'To-morrow then, as I have told your father, I am to bring you to see the dearest friend I have on earth, who dares not appear within this city for some unhappy reasons, and therefore cannot be present at our nuptials; for which cause, I could not but think it my duty to one so nearly related to my soul, to make him happy in the sight of my beautiful choice, ere yet she be my bride.' 'I hope,' said she, 'my loving obedience may merit your compassion; and that at last, ere the fire is lighted that must consume the offering, I mean the marriage-tapers' (alluding to the old Roman ceremony) 'that you or some other pitying angel, will snatch me from the altar.' 'Ah, no more, Ardelia! say no more,' cried he, 'we must be cruel, to be just to ourselves.' [Here their discourse ended, and they walked into the house, where they found the good old gentleman and his lady, with whom he stayed till about an hour after supper, when he returned to his friend with joyful news, but a sorrowful heart.]

Antonio was all rapture with the thoughts of the approaching day; which though it brought Don Henrique and his dear Ardelia to him, about five o'clock in the evening, yet at the same time brought his last and greatest misfortune. He saw her then at a she relation's of his, above three miles from Seville, which was the place assigned for their fatal interview. He saw her, I say; but ah! how strange! how altered

from the dear, kind Ardelia she was when last he left
her! 'Tis true, he flew to her with arms expanded,
and with so swift and eager a motion, that she could
not avoid, nor get loose from his embrace, till he had
kissed, and sighed, and dropped some tears, which all
the strength of his mind could not restrain; whether
they were the effects of joy, or whether (which rather
may be feared) they were the heat-drops which preceded and threatened the thunder and tempest that
should fall on his head, I cannot positively say; yet
all this she was then forced to endure, ere she had
liberty to speak, or indeed to breathe. But as soon as
she had freed herself from the loving circle that
should have been the dear and loved confinement or
centre of a faithful heart, she began to dart whole
showers of tortures on him from her eyes; which that
mouth that he had just before so tenderly and sacredly
kissed, seconded with whole volleys of deaths crammed
in every sentence, pointed with the keenest affliction
that ever pierced a soul. 'Antonio,' she began, 'you
have treated me now as if you were never like to see
me more: and would to Heaven you were not!'
'Ha!' cried he, starting and staring wildly on her,
'What said you, madam? What said you, my Ardelia?'
'If you like the repetition, take it!' replied she, un-
moved. 'Would to Heaven you were never like to
see me more!' 'Good! very good!' cried he, with
a sigh that threw him trembling into a chair behind
him, and gave her the opportunity of proceeding thus.
'Yet, Antonio, I must not have my wish; I must
continue with you, not out of choice, but by command, by the strictest and severest obligation that
ever bound humanity. Don Henrique, your friend,
commands it; Don Henrique, the dearest object of
my soul, enjoins it; Don Henrique, whose only aversion I am, will have it so.' 'Oh, do not wrong me,
madam!' cried Don Henrique. 'Lead me, lead me
a little more by the light of your discourse, I beseech
you,' said Don Antonio, 'that I may see your mean-

ing! for hitherto 'tis darkness all to me.' 'Attend, therefore, with your best faculties,' pursued Ardelia, 'and know, that I do most sincerely and most passionately love Don Henrique; and as a proof of my love to him, I have this day consented to be delivered up to you by him; not for your sake in the least, Antonio, but purely to sacrifice all the quiet of my life to his satisfaction. And now, sir,' continued she, addressing herself to Don Henrique, 'now, sir, if you can be so cruel, execute your own most dreadful decree, and join our hands, though our hearts never can meet.' 'All this to try me! It's too much, Ardelia,' said Antonio. And then turning to Don Henrique, he went on, 'Speak, thou! if yet thou art not apostate to our friendship! Yet speak, however! Speak, though the Devil has been tampering with thee too! Thou art a man, a man of honour once.' 'And when I forfeit my just title to that,' interrupted Don Henrique, 'may I be made most miserable! May I lose the blessings of thy friendship! May I lose thee!' 'Say on then, Henrique,' cried Antonio, 'and I charge thee, by all the sacred ties of friendship, say, Is this a trial of me? Is't illusion, sport, or shameful murderous truth? Oh, my soul burns within me, and I can bear no longer. Tell! Speak! Say on!' [Here, with folded arms, and eyes fixed steadfastly on Henrique, he stood like a statue, without motion; unless sometimes, when his swelling heart raised his overcharged breast.] After a little pause, and a hearty sigh or two, Henrique began: 'Oh, Antonio! Oh my friend! prepare thyself to hear yet more dreadful accents! I am,' pursued he, 'unhappily the greatest and most innocent criminal that ere till now offended: I love her, Antonio, I love Ardelia with a passion strong and violent as thine! Oh! summon all that used to be more than man about thee, to suffer to the end of my discourse, which nothing but a resolution like thine can bear! I know it by myself.' 'Though there be wounds, horror, and death in each syllable,' interrupted Antonio, 'yet prithee now go on, but with all haste.' 'I will,' returned Henrique, 'though I feel my own words have the same cruel effects on me. I say again, my soul loves Ardelia. And how can it be otherwise? Have we not both the self-same appetites, the same disgusts? How then could I avoid my destiny, that has decreed that I should love and hate just as you do? Oh, hard necessity! that obliged you to use me in the recovery of this lady! Alas, can you think that any man of sense or passion could have seen, and not have loved her! Then how should I, whose thoughts are unisons to yours, evade those charms that had prevailed on you? And now, to let you know, 'tis no illusion, no sport, but serious and amazing woeful truth, Ardelia best can tell you whom she loves.' 'What I have already said, is true, by Heaven,' cried she, ''tis you, Don Henrique, whom I only love, and who alone can give me happiness. Ah, would you would! With you, Antonio, I must remain unhappy, wretched, cursed. Thou art my Hell; Don Henrique is my Heaven.' 'And thou art mine,' returned he, 'which here I part with to my dearest friend.' Then taking her hand, 'Pardon me, Antonio,' pursued he, 'that I thus take my last farewell of all the tastes of bliss from your Ardelia, at this moment.' [At which words he kissed her hand, and gave it to Don Antonio; who received it, and gently pressed it close to his heart, as if he would have her feel the disorders she had caused there.] 'Be happy, Antonio,' cried Henrique. 'Be very tender of her; to-morrow early I shall hope to see thee, Ardelia,' pursued he; 'All happiness and joy surround thee! May'st thou ne'er want those blessings thou canst give Antonio! Farewell to both!' added he, going out. 'Ah,' cried she, 'farewell to all joys, blessings, happiness, if you forsake me. Yet do not go! Ah, cruel!' continued she, seeing him quit the room, 'but you shall take my soul with you.' Here she swooned away in Don Antonio's arms; who, though he was happy that he had her fast there, yet was obliged to call in his cousin, and Ardelia's attendants, ere she could be perfectly recovered. In the meanwhile Don Henrique had not the power to go out of sight of the house, but wandered to and fro about it, distracted in his soul; and not being able longer to refrain her sight, her last words still resounding in his ears, he came again into the room where he left her with Don Antonio, just as she revived, and called him, exclaiming on his cruelty, in leaving her so soon. But when, turning her eyes towards the door, she saw him; oh! with what eager haste she flew to him! then clasped him round the waist, obliging him, with all the tender expressions that the soul of a lover, and a woman's too, is capable of uttering, not to leave her in the possession of Don Antonio. This so amazed her slighted lover, that he knew not, at first, how to proceed in this tormenting scene; but at last, summoning all his wonted resolution, and strength of mind, he told her, he would put her out of his power, if she would consent to retreat for some few hours to a nunnery that was not above half a mile distant from thence, till he had discoursed with his friend, Don Henrique, something more particularly than hitherto, about this matter. To which she readily agreed, upon the promise that Don Henrique made her, of seeing her with the first opportunity. They waited on her then to the convent, where she was kindly and respectfully received by the Lady Abbess; but it was not long before her grief renewing with greater violence, and more afflicting circumstances, had obliged them to stay with her till it was almost dark, when they once more begged the liberty of an hour's absence; and the better to palliate their design, Henrique told her, that he would make use of her father Don Richardo's coach, in which they came to Don Antonio's, for so small a time: which they did, leaving only Eleonora, her attendant, with her, without whom she had been at a loss, among so many fair strangers; strangers, I mean, to her unhappy circumstances. Whilst they were carried near a mile farther, where, just as it was dark, they lighted from the coach, Don Henrique ordering the servants not to stir thence till their return from their private walk, which was about a furlong, in a field that belonged to the convent. Here Don Antonio told Don Henrique, that he had not acted honourably; that he had betrayed him, and robbed him at once both of a friend and mistress. To which the other returned, that he understood his meaning, when he proposed a particular discourse about this affair, which he now perceived must end in blood. 'But you may remind yourself,' continued he, 'that I have kept my promise in delivering her to you.' 'Yes,' cried Antonio, 'after you had practised foully and basely on her.' 'Not at all!' returned Henrique. 'It was her fate that brought this mischief on her; for I urged the shame and scandal of inconstancy, but all in vain, to her.' 'But don't you love her, Henrique?' the other asked. 'Too well, and cannot live without her, though I fear I may feel the cursed effects of the same inconstancy. However, I had quitted her all to you, but you see how she resents it.' 'And you shall see, sir,' cried Antonio, drawing his sword in a rage, 'how I resent it.' Here, without more words, they fell to action; to bloody action. (Ah! how wretched are our sex, in being the unhappy occasion of so many fatal mischiefs, even between the dearest friends!) They fought on each side with the greatest animosity of rivals, forgetting all the sacred bonds of their former friendship; till Don Antonio fell, and said, dying, 'Forgive me, Henrique! I was to blame; I could not live without her: I fear she will betray thy life, which haste and preserve, for my sake——Let me not die all at once! Heaven pardon both of us! Farewell! Oh, haste!' 'Farewell!' returned Don Henrique, 'Farewell, thou bravest, truest friend! Farewell, thou noblest part of me! And farewell all the quiet of my soul.' Then stooping, he kissed his cheek; but, rising, he found he must retire in time, or else must perish through loss of blood, for he had received two or three dangerous wounds, besides others of less consequence. Wherefore, he made all the convenient haste he could to the coach, into which, by the help of the footmen, he got, and ordered them to drive him directly to Don Richardo's with all imaginable speed; where he arrived in little more than half an hour's time, and was received by Ardelia's father with the greatest confusion and amazement that is expressible, seeing him returned without his daughter, and so desperately wounded. Before he thought it convenient to ask him any question more than to inquire of his daughter's safety, to which he received a short but satisfactory answer, Don Richardo sent for an eminent and able surgeon, who probed and dressed Don Henrique's wounds, who was immediately put to bed; not without some despondency of his recovery: but (thanks to his kind stars, and kinder constitution!) he rested pretty well for some hours that night, and early in the morning, Ardelia's father, who had scarce taken any rest all that night, came to visit him, as soon as he understood from the servants who watched with him, that he was in a condition to suffer a short discourse; which, you may be sure, was to learn the circumstances of the past night's adventure; of which Don Henrique gave him a perfect and pleasant account, since he heard that Don Antonio, his mortal enemy, was killed; the assurance of whose death was the more delightful to him, since, by this relation, he found that Antonio was the man, whom his care of his daughter had so often frustrated. Don Henrique hardly made an end of his narration, ere a servant came hastily to give Richardo notice, that the officers were come to search for his son-in-law that should have been; whom the old gentleman's wise precaution had secured in a room so unsuspected, that they might as reasonably have imagined the entire walls of his house had a door made of stones, as that there should have been one to that close apartment. He went therefore boldly to the officers, and gave them all the keys of his house, with free liberty to examine every room and chamber; which they did, but to no purpose; and Don Henrique lay there undiscovered, till his cure was perfected.

In the meantime Ardelia, who that fatal night but too rightly guessed that the death of one or both her lovers was the cause that they did not return to their promise, the next day fell into a high fever, in which her father found her soon after he had cleared himself of those who come to search for a lover. The assurance which her father gave her of Henrique's life, seemed a little to revive her; but the severity of Antonio's fate was no way obliging to her, since she could not but retain the memory of his love and constancy; which added to her afflictions, and heightened her distemper, insomuch that Richardo was constrained to leave her under the care of the good Lady Abbess, and to the diligent attendance of Eleonora, not daring to hazard her life in a removal to his own house. All their care and diligence was however ineffectual; for she languished even to the least hope of recovery, till immediately after the first visit of Don Henrique, which was the first he made in a month's time, and that by night *incognito*, with her father, her distemper visibly retreated each day. Yet, when at last she enjoyed a perfect health of body, her mind grew sick, and she plunged into a deep melancholy; which made her entertain a positive resolution of taking the veil at the end of her novitiate; which accordingly she did, notwithstanding all the entreaties, prayers, and tears both of her father and lover. But she soon repented her vow, and often wished that she might by any means see and speak to Don Henrique, by whose help she promised to herself a deliverance out of her voluntary imprisonment: nor were his wishes wanting to the same effect, though he was forced to fly into Italy, to avoid the prosecution of Antonio's friends. Thither she pursued him; nor could he any way shun her, unless he could have left his heart at a distance from his body; which made him take a fatal resolution of returning to Seville in disguise, where he wandered about the convent every night like a ghost (for indeed his soul was within, while his inanimate trunk was without) till at last he found means to convey a letter to her, which both surprised and delighted her. The messenger that brought it her was one of her mother-in-law's maids whom he had known before, and met accidentally one night as he was going his rounds, and she coming out from Ardelia; with her he prevailed, and with gold obliged her to secrecy and assistance: which proved so successful, that he understood from Ardelia her strong desire of liberty, and the continuance of her passion for him, together with the means and time most convenient and likely to succeed for her enlargement. The time was the fourteenth night following, at twelve o'clock, which just completed a month since his return thither; at which time they both promised themselves the greatest happiness on earth. But you may observe the justice of Heaven, in their disappointment.

Don Sebastian, who still pursued him with a most implacable hatred, had traced him even to Italy, and there narrowly missing him, posted after him to Toledo; so sure and secret was his intelligence! As soon as he arrived, he went directly to the convent where his sister Elvira had been one of the professed, ever since Don Henrique had forsaken her, and where Ardelia had taken her repented vow. Elvira had all along concealed the occasion of her coming thither from Ardelia; and though she was her only confidant, and knew the whole story of her misfortunes, and heard the name of Don Henrique repeated a hundred times a day, whom still she loved most perfectly, yet never gave her beautiful rival any cause of suspicion that she loved him, either by words or looks. Nay more, when she understood that Don Henrique came to the convent with Ardelia and Antonio, and at other times with her father; yet she had so great a command of herself, as to refrain seeing him, or to be seen by him; nor ever intended to have spoken or writ to him, had not her brother Don Sebastian put her upon the cruel necessity of doing the last; who coming to visit his sister (as I have said before) found her with Dona Ardelia, whom he never remembered to have seen, nor who ever had seen him but twice, and that was about six years before, when she was but ten years of age, when she fell passionately in love with him, and continued her passion till about the fourteenth year of her empire, when unfortunate Antonio first began his court to her. Don Sebastian was really a very desirable person, being at that time very beautiful, his age not exceeding six-and-twenty, of a sweet conversation, very brave, but revengeful and irreconcilable (like most of his countrymen) and of an honourable family. At the sight of him Ardelia felt her former passion renew; which proceeded and continued with such violence, that it utterly defaced the ideas of Antonio and Henrique. (No wonder that she who could resolve to forsake her God for man, should quit one lover for another.) In short, she then only wished that he might love her equally, and then she doubted not of contriving the means of their happiness betwixt them. She had her wish, and more, if possible; for he loved her beyond the thought of any other present or future blessing, and failed not to let her know it, at the second interview; when he received the greatest pleasure he could have wished, next to the joys of a bridal bed. For she confessed her love to him, and presently put him upon thinking on the means of her escape; but not finding his designs so likely to succeed, as those measures she had sent to Don Henrique, she communicates the very same to Don Sebastian, and agreed with him to make use of them on that very night, wherein she had obliged Don Henrique to attempt her deliverance. The hour indeed was different, being determined to be at eleven. Elvira, who was present at the conference, took the hint; and not being willing to disoblige a brother who had so hazarded his life in vindication of her, either does not, or would not seem to oppose his inclinations at that time. However, when he retired with her to talk more particularly of his intended revenge on Don Henrique, who he told her lay somewhere absconded in Toledo, and whom he had resolved, as he assured her, to sacrifice to her injured honour, and his resentments; she opposed that his vindictive resolution with all the forcible arguments in a virtuous and pious lady's capacity, but in vain: so that immediately, upon his retreat from the convent, she took the opportunity of writing to Don Henrique as follows, the fatal hour not being then seven nights distant.

DON HENRIQUE,

My brother is now in town, in pursuit of your life; nay more, of your mistress, who has consented to make her escape from the convent, at the same place of it, and by the same means on which she had agreed to give herself entirely to you, but the hour is eleven. I know, Henrique, your Ardelia is dearer to you than your life: but your life, your dear life, is more desired than anything in this world, by

Your injured and forsaken
ELVIRA.

This she delivered to Richardo's servant, whom Henrique had gained that night, as soon as she came to visit Ardelia, at her usual hour, just as she went out of the cloister.

Don Henrique was not a little surprised with this

billet; however, he could hardly resolve to forbear his accustomed visits to Ardelia, at first. But upon more mature consideration, he only chose to converse with her by letters, which still pressed her to be mindful of her promise, and of the hour, not taking notice of any caution that he had received of her treachery. To which she still returned in words that might assure him of her constancy.

The dreadful hour wanted not a quarter of being perfect, when Don Henrique came; and having fixed his rope-ladder to that part of the garden-wall, where he was expected, Ardelia, who had not stirred from that very place for a quarter of an hour before, prepared to ascend by it; which she did, as soon as his servant had returned and fixed it on the inner side of the wall: on the top of which, at a little distance, she found another fastened, for her to descend on the outside, whilst Don Henrique eagerly waited to receive her. She came at last, and flew into his arms; which made Henrique cry out in a rapture, 'Am I at last once more happy in having my Ardelia in my possession!' She, who knew his voice, and now found she was betrayed, but knew not by whom, shrieked out, 'I am ruined! help! help! Loose me, I charge you, Henrique! Loose me!' At that very moment, and at those very words, came Sebastian, attended by only one servant; and hearing Henrique reply, 'Not all the powers of hell shall snatch you from me,' drawing his sword, without one word, made a furious pass at him. But his rage and haste misguided his arm, for his sword went quite through Ardelia's body, who only said, 'Ah, wretched maid!' and dropped from Henrique's arms, who then was obliged to quit her, to preserve his own life, if possible: however he had not had so much time as to draw, had not Sebastian been amazed at this dreadful mistake of his sword; but presently recollecting himself, he flew with redoubled rage to attack Henrique; and his servant had seconded him, had not Henrique's, who was now descended, otherwise diverted him. They fought with the greatest animosity on both sides, and with equal advantage ; for they both fell together : 'Ah, my Ardelia, I come to thee now !' Sebastian groaned out. 'Twas this unlucky arm, which now embraces thee, that killed thee.' 'Just Heaven !' she sighed out, 'Oh, yet have mercy !' [Here they both died.] 'Amen,' cried Henrique, dying, 'I want it most——Oh, Antonio ! Oh ! Elvira ! Ah, there's the weight that sinks me down. And yet I wish forgiveness. Once more, sweet Heaven, have mercy !' He could not outlive that last word ; which was echoed by Elvira, who all this while stood weeping, and calling out for help, as she stood close to the wall in the garden.

This alarmed the rest of the sisters, who rising, caused the bell to be rung out, as upon dangerous occasions it used to be ; which raised the neighbourhood, who came time enough to remove the dead bodies of the two rivals, and of the late fallen angel Ardelia. The injured and neglected Elvira, whose piety designed quite contrary effects, was immediately seized with a violent fever, which, as it was violent, did not last long : for she died within four-and-twenty hours, with all the happy symptoms of a departing saint.

THE HISTORY OF
AGNES DE CASTRO

THOUGH love, all soft and flattering, promises nothing but pleasures; yet its consequences are often sad and fatal. It is not enough to be in love, to be happy; since Fortune, who is capricious, and takes delight to trouble the repose of the most elevated and virtuous, has very little respect for passionate and tender hearts, when she designs to produce strange adventures.

Many examples of past ages render this maxim certain; but the reign of Don Alphonso IV., King of Portugal, furnishes us with one, the most extraordinary that history can produce.

He was the son of that Don Denis, who was so successful in all his undertakings, that it was said of him, that he was capable of performing whatever he designed, (and of Isabella, a Princess of eminent virtue) who when he came to inherit a flourishing and tranquil State, endeavoured to establish peace and plenty in abundance in his kingdom.

And to advance this his design, he agreed on a marriage between his son Don Pedro (then about eight years of age) and Bianca, daughter of Don Pedro, King of Castile; and whom the young Prince married when he arrived to his sixteenth year.

Bianca brought nothing to Coimbra but infirmities and very few charms. Don Pedro, who was full of sweetness and generosity, lived nevertheless very well

with her; but those distempers of the Princess de-
generating into the palsy, she made it her request
to retire, and at her intercession the Pope broke the
marriage, and the melancholy Princess concealed her
languishment in a solitary retreat: and Don Pedro,
for whom they had provided another match, married
Constantia Manuel, daughter of Don John Manuel,
a prince of the blood of Castile, and famous for the
enmity he had to his king.

Constantia was promised to the King of Castile;
but that King not keeping his word, they made no
difficulty of bestowing her on a young Prince, who
was one day to reign over a number of fine provinces.
He was but five-and-twenty years of age, and the man
of all Spain that had the best fashion and grace: and
with the most advantageous qualities of the body he
possessed those of the soul, and showed himself
worthy in all things of the crown that was destined
for him.

The Princess Constantia had beauty, wit, and
generosity, in as great a measure as it was possible
for a woman to be possessed with; her merit alone
ought to have attached Don Pedro eternally to her;
and certainly he had for her an esteem, mixed with so
great a respect, as might very well pass for love with
those that were not of a nice and curious observation:
but alas! his real care was reserved for another
beauty.

Constantia brought into the world, the first year
after her marriage, a son, who was called Don Louis:
but it scarce saw the light, and died almost as soon as
born. The loss of this little Prince sensibly touched
her, but the coldness she observed in the Prince her
husband, went yet nearer her heart; for she had
given herself absolutely up to her duty, and had made
her tenderness for him her only concern: but puissant
glory, which tied her so entirely to the interest of the
Prince of Portugal, opened her eyes upon his actions,
where she observed nothing in his caresses and civili-

ties that was natural, or could satisfy her delicate
heart.

At first she fancied herself deceived, but time
having confirmed her in what she feared, she sighed
in secret; yet had that consideration for the Prince,
as not to let him see her disorder : and which nevertheless she could not conceal from Agnes de Castro,
who lived with her, rather as a companion, than a
maid of honour, and whom her friendship made her
infinitely distinguish from the rest.

This maid, so dear to the Princess, very well
merited the preference her mistress gave her; she
was beautiful to excess, wise, discreet, witty, and had
more tenderness for Constantia than she had for
herself, having quitted her family, which was illustrious, to give herself wholly to the service of the
Princess, and to follow her into Portugal. It was
into the bosom of this maid, that the Princess un-
laded her first moans; and the charming Agnes
forgot nothing that might give ease to her afflicted
heart.

Nor was Constantia the only person who complained of Don Pedro before his divorce from
Bianca, he had expressed some care and tenderness
for Elvira Gonzales, sister to Don Alvaro Gonzales,
favourite to the King of Portugal; and this amusement in the young years of the Prince, had made
a deep impression on Elvira, who flattered her ambition with the infirmities of Bianca. She saw, with
a secret rage, Constantia take her place, who was
possessed with such charms, that quite divested her
of all hopes.

Her jealousy left her not idle, she examined all the
actions of the Prince, and easily discovered the little
regard he had for the Princess; but this brought him
not back to her. And it was upon very good grounds
that she suspected him to be in love with some other
person, and possessed with a new passion; and which
she promised herself, she would destroy as soon as

she could find it out. She had a spirit altogether
proper for bold and hazardous enterprises; and the
credit of her brother gave her so much vanity, as
all the indifference of the Prince was not capable
of humbling.

The Prince languished, and concealed the cause with
so much care, that it was impossible for any to find it
out. No public pleasures were agreeable to him, and
all conversations were tedious; and it was solitude
alone that was able to give him any ease.

This change surprised all the world. The King,
who loved his son very tenderly, earnestly pressed
him to know the reason of his melancholy; but the
Prince made no answer, but only this, that it was the
effect of his temper.

But time ran on, and the Princess was brought to
bed of a second son, who lived, and was called Fernando. Don Pedro forced himself a little to take
part in the public joy, so that they believed his
humour was changing; but this appearance of a calm
endured not long, and he fell back again into his
black melancholy.

The artful Elvira was incessantly agitating in
searching out the knowledge of this secret. Chance
wrought for her; and, as she was walking, full of
indignation and anger, in the garden of the palace of
Coimbra, she found the Prince of Portugal sleeping
in an obscure grotto.

Her fury could not contain itself at the sight of
this loved object, she rolled her eyes upon him, and
perceived, in spite of sleep, that some tears escaped
his eyes; the flame which burnt yet in her heart,
soon grew soft and tender there: but oh! she heard
him sigh, and after that utter these words, 'Yes,
divine Agnes, I will sooner die than let you know it.
Constantia shall have nothing to reproach me with.'
Elvira was enraged at this discourse, which represented to her immediately, the same moment, Agnes
de Castro with all her charms; and not at all doubt-

ing, but it was she who possessed the heart of Don Pedro, she found in her soul more hatred for this fair rival, than tenderness for him.

The grotto was not a fit place to make reflections in, or to form designs. Perhaps her first transports would have made her waken him, if she had not perceived a paper lying under his hand, which she softly seized on ; and that she might not be surprised in the reading it, she went out of the garden with as much haste as confusion.

When she was retired to her apartment, she opened the paper, trembling, and found in it these verses, writ by the hand of Don Pedro ; and which, in appearance, he had newly then composed.

> In vain, oh ! sacred honour, you debate
>   The mighty business in my heart :
> Love ! charming love ! rules all my fate ;
>   Interest and glory claim no part.
> The god, sure of his victory, triumphs there,
>   And will have nothing in his empire share.
>
> In vain, oh ! sacred duty, you oppose ;
>   In vain, your nuptial tie you plead :
> Those forced devoirs Love overthrows,
>   And breaks the vows he never made.
> Fixing his fatal arrows everywhere,
>   I burn and languish in a soft despair.
>
> Fair Princess, you to whom my faith is due ;
>   Pardon the destiny that drags me on :
> 'Tis not my fault my heart's untrue,
>   I am compelled to be undone.
> My life is yours, I gave it with my hand,
>   But my fidelity I can't command.

Elvira did not only know the writing of Don Pedro, but she knew also that he could write verses. And seeing the sad part which Constantia had in these which were now fallen into her hands, she made no scruple of resolving to let the Princess see them : but that she might not be suspected, she took care not to appear in this business herself ; and since it was not enough for Constantia to know that the

Prince did not love her, but that she must know also
that he was a slave to Agnes de Castro, Elvira caused
these few verses to be written in an unknown hand,
under those writ by the Prince.

Sleep betrayed th' unhappy lover,
While tears were streaming from his eyes;
His heedless tongue without disguise,
The secret did discover:
The language of his heart declare,
That *Agnes'* image triumphs there.

Elvira regarded neither exactness nor grace in
these lines: and if they had but the effect she designed,
she wished no more.

Her impatience could not wait till the next day to
expose them: she therefore went immediately to the
lodgings of the Princess, who was then walking in
the garden of the palace; and passing without resistance, even to her cabinet, she put the paper into
a book, in which the Princess used to read, and went
out again unseen, and satisfied with her good fortune.

As soon as Constantia was returned, she entered
into her cabinet, and saw the book open, and the
verses lying in it, which were to cost her so dear: she
soon knew the hand of the Prince which was so familiar
to her; and besides the information of what she had
always feared, she understood it was Agnes de Castro
(whose friendship alone was able to comfort her in her
misfortunes) who was the fatal cause of it: she read
over the paper a hundred times, desiring to give her
eyes and reason the lie; but finding but too plainly
she was not deceived, she found her soul possessed
with more grief than anger: when she considered, as
much in love as the Prince was, he had kept his torment secret. After having made her moan, without
condemning him, the tenderness she had for him, made
her shed a torrent of tears, and inspired her with a
resolution of concealing her resentment.

She would certainly have done it by a virtue extraordinary, if the Prince, who missing his verses when

he waked, and fearing they might fall into indiscreet hands, had not entered the palace, all troubled with his loss; and hastily going into Constantia's apartment, saw her fair eyes all wet with tears, and at the same instant cast his own on the unhappy verses that had escaped from his soul, and now lay before the Princess.

He immediately turned pale at this sight, and appeared so moved, that the generous Princess felt more pain than he did: 'Madam,' said he (infinitely alarmed), 'from whom had you that paper?' 'It cannot come but from the hand of some person,' answered Constantia, 'who is an enemy both to your repose and mine. It is the work, sir, of your own hand; and doubtless the sentiment of your heart. But be not surprised, and do not fear; for if my tenderness should make it pass for a crime in you, the same tenderness which nothing is able to alter, shall hinder me from complaining.'

The moderation and calmness of Constantia, served only to render the Prince more ashamed and confused. 'How generous are you, madam,' pursued he, 'and how unfortunate am I!' Some tears accompanied his words, and the Princess, who loved him with extreme ardour, was so sensibly touched, that it was a good while before she could utter a word. Constantia then broke silence, and showing him what Elvira had caused to be written, 'You are betrayed, sir,' added she, 'you have been heard speak, and your secret is known.' It was at this very moment that all the forces of the Prince abandoned him; and his condition was really worthy compassion: he could not pardon himself the involuntary crime he had committed, in exposing of the lovely and the innocent Agnes. And though he was convinced of the virtue and goodness of Constantia, the apprehensions that he had, that this modest and prudent maid might suffer by his conduct, carried him beyond all consideration.

The Princess, who heedfully surveyed him, saw so

many marks of despair in his face and eyes, that she was afraid of the consequences ; and holding out her hand, in a very obliging manner to him, she said, 'I promise you, sir, I will never more complain of you, and that Agnes shall always be very dear to me; you shall never hear me make you any reproaches : and since I cannot possess your heart, I will content myself with endeavouring to render myself worthy of it.' Don Pedro, more confused and dejected than before he had been, bent one of his knees at the feet of Constantia, and with respect kissed that fair kind hand she had given him, and perhaps forgot Agnes for a moment.

But love soon put a stop to all the little advances of Hymen ; the fatal star that presided over the destiny of Don Pedro had not yet vented its malignity; and one moment's sight of Agnes gave new force to his passion.

The wishes and desires of this charming maid had no part in this victory; her eyes were just, though penetrating, and they searched not in those of the Prince, what they had a desire to discover to her.

As she was never far from Constantia, Don Pedro was no sooner gone out of the closet, but Agnes entered; and finding the Princess all pale and languishing in her chair, she doubted not but there was some sufficient cause for her affliction : she put herself in the same posture the Prince had been in before, and expressing an inquietude, full of concern : 'Madam,' said she, 'by all your goodness, conceal not from me the cause of your trouble.' 'Alas, Agnes,' replied the Princess, 'what would you know ? And what should I tell you ? The Prince, the Prince, my dearest maid, is in love ; the hand that he gave me, was not a present of his heart ; and for the advantage of this alliance, I must become the victim of it.' 'What ! the Prince in love !' replied Agnes, with an astonishment mixed with indignation. 'What beauty can dispute the empire over a heart so much your due? Alas, madam, all the respect I owe him, cannot hinder me from murmuring against him.' 'Accuse him of nothing,' interrupted Constantia, 'he does what he can; and I am more obliged to him for desiring to be faithful, than if I possessed his real tenderness. It is not enough to fight, but to overcome; and the Prince does more in the condition wherein he is, than I ought reasonably to hope for. In fine, he is my husband, and an agreeable one; to whom nothing is wanting, but what I cannot inspire; that is, a passion which would have made me but too happy.' 'Ah! madam,' cried out Agnes, transported with her tenderness for the Princess, 'he is a blind and stupid Prince, who knows not the precious advantages he possesses.' 'He must surely know something,' replied the Princess modestly. 'But, madam,' replied Agnes, 'is there anything, not only in Portugal, but in all Spain, that can compare with you? And, without considering the charming qualities of your person, can we enough admire those of your soul?' 'My dear Agnes,' interrupted Constantia, sighing, 'she who robs me of my husband's heart, has but too many charms to plead his excuse; since it is thou, child, whom fortune makes use of, to give me the killing blow. Yes, Agnes, the Prince loves thee; and the merit I know thou art possessed of, puts bounds to my complaints, without suffering me to have the least resentment.'

The delicate Agnes little expected to hear what the Princess told her. Thunder would have less surprised, and less oppressed her. She remained a long time without speaking; but at last, fixing her looks all frightful on Constantia, 'What say you, madam?' cried she, 'and what thoughts have you of me? What, that I should betray you? And coming hither only full of ardour to be the repose of your life, do I bring a fatal poison to afflict it? What detestation must I have for the beauty they find in me, without aspiring to make it appear? And how ought I to

curse the unfortunate day, on which I first saw the
Prince? But, madam, it cannot be me whom Heaven
has chosen to torment you, and to destroy all your
tranquillity. No, it cannot be so much my enemy, to
put me to so great a trial. And if I were that odious
person, there is no punishment, to which I would not
condemn myself. It is Elvira, madam, the Prince
loves, and loved before his marriage with you, and
also before his divorce from Bianca; and somebody
has made an indiscreet report to you of this intrigue
of his youth. But, madam, what was in the time of
Bianca, is nothing to you.' 'It is certain that Don
Pedro loves you,' answered the Princess, 'and I have
vanity enough to believe, that none besides yourself
could have disputed his heart with me. But the secret
is discovered, and Don Pedro has not disowned it.'
'What,' interrupted Agnes, more surprised than ever,
'is it then from himself you have learned his weakness?' The Princess then showed her the verses, and
there was never any despair like to hers.

While they were both thus sadly employed, both
sighing, and both weeping, the impatient Elvira, who
was willing to learn the effect of her malice, returned
to the apartment of the Princess, where she freely
entered; even to the cabinet where these unhappy
persons were: who all afflicted and troubled as they
were, blushed at her approach, whose company they
did not desire. She had the pleasure to see Constantia
hide from her the paper which had been the cause of
all their trouble, and which the Princess had never
seen, but for her spite and revenge; and to observe
also in the eyes of the Princess, and those of Agnes,
an immoderate grief. She stayed in the cabinet as
long as it was necessary to be assured, that she had
succeeded in her design; but the Princess, who did
not desire such a witness of the disorder in which she
then was, prayed to be left alone. Elvira then went
out of the cabinet, and Agnes de Castro withdrew at
the same time.

It was in her own chamber, that Agnes examining more freely this adventure, found it as cruel as death. She loved Constantia sincerely, and had not till then anything more than an esteem, mixed with admiration, for the Prince of Portugal; which indeed, none could refuse to so many fine qualities. And looking on herself as the most unfortunate of her sex, as being the cause of all the sufferings of the Princess, to whom she was obliged for the greatest bounties, she spent the whole night in tears and complaints, sufficient to have revenged Constantia for all the griefs she made her suffer.

The Prince, on his side, was in no great tranquillity; the generosity of his Princess increased his remorse, without diminishing his love: he feared, and with reason, that those who were the occasion of Constantia's seeing those verses, should discover his passion to the King, from whom he hoped for no indulgence: and he would most willingly have given his life, to have been free from this extremity.

In the meantime the afflicted Princess languished in a most deplorable sadness: she found nothing in those who were the cause of her misfortunes, but things fitter to move her tenderness than her anger. It was in vain that jealousy strove to combat the inclination she had to love her fair rival; nor was there any occasion of making the Prince less dear to her: and she felt neither hatred, nor so much as indifference for innocent Agnes.

While these three disconsolate persons abandoned themselves to their melancholy, Elvira, not to leave her vengeance imperfect, studied in what manner she might bring it to the height of its effects. Her brother, on whom she depended, showed her a great deal of friendship, and judging rightly that the love of Don Pedro to Agnes de Castro would not be approved by the King, she acquainted Don Alvaro her brother with it, who was not ignorant of the passion the Prince had once protested to have for his

sister. He found himself very much interested in
this news, from a second passion he had for Agnes ;
which the business of his fortune had hitherto hindered him from discovering. And he expected a
great many favours from the King, that might render
the effort of his heart the more considerable.

He hid not from his sister this one thing, which he
found difficult to conceal ; so that she was now possessed with a double grief, to find Agnes sovereign of
all the hearts to which she had a pretension.

Don Alvaro was one of those ambitious men, that
are fierce without moderation, and proud without
generosity ; of a melancholy, cloudy humour, of a
cruel inclination, and to effect his ends, found nothing
difficult or unlawful. Naturally he loved not the
Prince, who, on all accounts, ought to have held the
first rank in the heart of the King, which should
have set bounds to the favour of Don Alvaro ; who
when he knew the Prince was his rival, his jealousy
increased his hate of him : and he conjured Elvira
to employ all her care, to oppose an engagement that
could not but be destructive to them both ; she
promised him, and he not very well satisfied, relied
on her promise.

Don Alvaro, who had too lively a representation
within himself, of the beauties and grace of the
Prince of Portugal, thought of nothing, but how to
combat his merits, he himself not being handsome, or
well made. His fashion was as disagreeable as his
humour, and Don Pedro had all the advantages that
one man may possibly have over another. In fine, all
that Don Alvaro wanted, adorned the Prince : but as
he was the husband of Constantia, and depended upon
an absolute father, and that Don Alvaro was free,
and master of a good fortune, he thought himself
more assured of Agnes, and fixed his hopes on that
thought.

He knew very well, that the passion of Don Pedro
could not but inspire a violent anger in the soul of

the King. Industrious in doing ill, his first business was to carry this unwelcome news to him. After he had given time to his grief, and had composed himself to his desire, he then besought the King to interest himself in his amorous affair, and to be the protector of his person.

Though Don Alvaro had no other merit to recommend him to the King, than a continual and blind obedience to all his commands; yet he had favoured him with several testimonies of his vast bounty; and considering the height to which the King's liberality had raised him, there were few ladies that would have refused his alliance. The King assured him of the continuation of his friendship and favour, and promised him, if he had any authority, he would give him the charming Agnes.

Don Alvaro, perfectly skilful in managing his master, answered the King's last bounty with a profound submission. He had yet never told Agnes what he felt for her; but he thought now he might make a public declaration of it, and sought all means to do it.

The gallantry which Coimbra seemed to have forgotten, began now to be awakened. The King to please Don Alvaro, under pretence of diverting Constantia, ordered some public sports, and commanded that everything should be magnificent.

Since the adventure of the verses, Don Pedro endeavoured to lay a constraint on himself, and to appear less troubled; but in his heart he suffered always alike: and it was not but with great uneasiness he prepared himself for the tournament. And since he could not appear with the colours of Agnes, he took those of his wife, without device, or any great magnificence.

Don Alvaro adorned himself with the liveries of Agnes de Castro; and this fair maid, who had yet found no consolation from what the Princess had told her, had this new cause of being displeased.

Don Pedro appeared in the list with an admirable grace; and Don Alvaro, who looked on this day as his own, appeared there all shining with gold, mixed with stones of blue, which were the colours of Agnes; and there were embroidered all over his equipage, flaming hearts of gold on blue velvet, and nets for the snares of love, with abundance of double *A's;* his device was a love coming out of a cloud, with these verses written underneath:

> Love from a cloud breaks like the god of day,
> And to the world his glories does display;
> To gaze on charming eyes, and make them know,
> What to soft hearts, and to his power they owe.

The pride of Don Alvaro was soon humbled at the feet of the Prince of Portugal, who threw him against the ground with twenty others, and carried alone the glory of the day. There was in the evening a noble assembly at Constantia's, where Agnes would not have been, unless expressly commanded by the Princess. She appeared there all negligent and careless in her dress, but yet she appeared all beautiful and charming. She saw, with disdain, her name, and her colours, worn by Don Alvaro, at a public triumph; and if her heart was capable of any tender motions, it was not for such a man as he for whom her delicacy destined them. She looked on him with a contempt, which did not hinder him from pressing so near, that there was a necessity for her to hear what he had to declare to her.

She treated him not uncivilly, but her coldness would have rebated the courage of any but Alvaro. 'Madam,' said he (when he could be heard of none but herself), 'I have hitherto concealed the passion you have inspired me with, fearing it should displease you; but it has committed a violence on my respect; and I could no longer conceal it from you.' 'I never reflected on your actions,' answered Agnes with all the indifference of which she was capable, 'and if you

think you offend me, you are in the wrong to make
me perceive it.' 'This coldness is but an ill omen for
me,' replied Don Alvaro, 'and if you have not found
me out to be your lover to-day, I fear you will never
approve my passion.'

'Oh! what a time have you chosen to make it
appear to me?' pursued Agnes. 'Is it so great an
honour for me, that you must take such care to show
it to the world? And do you think that I am so
desirous of glory, that I must aspire to it by your
actions? If I must, you have very ill maintained it
in the tournament; and if it be that vanity that you
depend upon, you will make no great progress on
a soul that is not fond of shame. If you were
possessed of all the advantages, which the Prince has
this day carried away, you yet ought to consider
what you are going about; and it is not a maid like
me, who is touched with enterprises, without respect
or permission.'

The favourite of the King was too proud to hear
Agnes, without indignation: but as he was willing to
conceal it, and not offend her, he made not his resentment appear; and considering the observation she
made on the triumphs of Don Pedro (which increased
his jealousies), 'If I have not overcome at the tournament,' replied he, 'I am not the less in love for being
vanquished, nor less capable of success on occasion.'

They were interrupted here, but from that day,
Don Alvaro, who had opened the first difficulties,
kept no more his wonted distance, but perpetually
persecuted Agnes; yet, though he were protected by
the King, that inspired in her never the more consideration for him. Don Pedro was always ignorant
by what means the verses he had lost in the garden,
fell into the hands of Constantia. As the Princess
appeared to him indulgent, he was only concerned
for Agnes; and the love of Don Alvaro, which was
then so well known, increased the pain: and had he
been possessed of the authority, he would not have

suffered her to have been exposed to the persecutions
of so unworthy a rival. He was also afraid of the
King's being advertised of his passion, but he thought
not at all of Elvira, nor apprehended any malice from
her resentment.

While she burned with a desire of destroying
Agnes, against whom she vented all her venom, she
was never weary of making new reports to her brother,
assuring him, that though they could not prove that
Agnes made any returns to the tenderness of the
Prince, yet that was the cause of Constantia's grief:
and, that if this Princess should die of it, Don Pedro
might marry Agnes. In fine, she so incensed the
jealous Don Alvaro's jealousy, that he could not
hinder himself from running immediately to the King,
with the discovery of all he knew, and all he guessed,
and who, he had the pleasure to find, was infinitely
enraged at the news. 'My dear Alvaro,' said the
King, 'you shall instantly marry this dangerous
beauty : and let possession assure your repose and
mine. If I have protected you on other occasions,
judge what a service of so great an importance for
me, would make me undertake ; and without any
reserve, the forces of this State are in your power, and
almost anything that I can give shall be assured you,
so you render yourself master of the destiny of
Agnes.'

Don Alvaro pleased, and vain with his master's
bounty, made use of all the authority he gave him.
He passionately loved Agnes, and would not, on the
sudden, make use of violence ; but resolved with
himself to employ all possible means to win her
fairly ; yet if that failed, to have recourse to force, if
she continued always insensible.

While Agnes de Castro (importuned by his assiduities, despairing at the grief of Constantia, and perhaps
made tender by those she had caused in the Prince of
Portugal) took a resolution worthy of her virtue ; yet,
amiable as Don Pedro was, she found nothing in him,

but his being husband to Constantia, that was dear to
her.   And, far from encouraging the power she had
got over his heart, she thought of nothing but removing from Coimbra.   The passion of Don Alvaro,
which she had no inclination to favour, served her as
a pretext; and pressed with the fear of causing, in
the end, a cruel divorce between the Prince and his
Princess, she went to find Constantia, with a trouble,
which all her care was not able to hide from her.

The Princess easily found it out; and their common misfortunes having not changed their friendship,
'What ails you, Agnes?' said the Princess to her, in
a soft tone, and with her ordinary sweetness.   'And
what new misfortune causes that sadness in thy
looks?'   'Madam,' replied Agnes, shedding a rivulet
of tears, 'the obligations and ties I have to you, put
me upon a cruel trial.   I had bounded the felicity of
my life in hope of passing it near your Highness, yet
I must carry to some other part of the world this
unlucky face of mine, which renders me nothing but
ill offices.   And it is to obtain that liberty, that I am
come to throw myself at your feet; looking upon you
as my sovereign.'

Constantia was so surprised and touched with the
proposition of Agnes, that she lost her speech for
some moments.   Tears, which were sincere, expressed her first sentiments: and after having shed
abundance, to give a new mark of her tenderness to
the fair afflicted Agnes, she with a sad and melancholy
look, fixed her eyes upon her, and holding out her
hand to her, in a most obliging manner, sighing, cried,
'You will then, my dear Agnes, leave me; and expose
me to the griefs of seeing you no more?'   'Alas,
madam,' interrupted this lovely maid, 'hide from the
unhappy Agnes a bounty which does but increase her
misfortunes.   It is not I, madam, that would leave
you; it is my duty, and my reason that orders my
fate.   And those days which I shall pass far from
you, promise me nothing to oblige me to this design,

if I did not see myself absolutely forced to it. I am
not ignorant of what passes at Coimbra ; and I shall
be an accomplice of the injustice there committed, if
I should stay there any longer.' 'Ah, I know your
virtue,' cried Constantia, 'and you may remain here
in all safety, while I am your protectress ; and let
what will happen, I will accuse you of nothing.'
'There's no answering for what's to come,' replied
Agnes, sadly, 'and I shall be sufficiently guilty, if my
presence cause sentiments, which cannot be innocent.
Besides, madam, the importunities of Don Alvaro are
insupportable to me ; and though I find nothing but
aversion to him, since the King protects his insolence, and he's in a condition of undertaking anything, my flight is absolutely necessary. But, madam,
though he has nothing but what seems odious to me ;
I call Heaven to witness, that if I could cure the
Prince by marrying Don Alvaro, I would not consider
of it a moment ; and finding in my punishment the
consolation of sacrificing myself to my Princess,
I would support it without murmuring. But if I were
the wife of Don Alvaro, Don Pedro would always
look upon me with the same eyes. So that I find
nothing more reasonable for me, than to hide myself
in some corner of the world ; where, though I shall
most certainly live without pleasure, yet I shall preserve the repose of my dearest mistress.' 'All the
reason you find in this design,' answered the Princess,
'cannot oblige me to approve of your absence. Will
it restore me the heart of Don Pedro ? And will he
not fly away with you ? His grief is mine, and my
life is tied to his ; do not make him despair then, if
you love me. I know you, I tell you so once more ;
and let your power be ever so great over the heart of
the Prince, I will not suffer you to abandon us.'

Though Agnes thought she had perfectly known
Constantia, yet she did not expect to find so entire
a virtue in her, which made her think herself more
happy, and the Prince more criminal. 'Oh, wisdom !

Oh, bounty without example!' cried she. 'Why is it, that the cruel destinies do not give you all you deserve? You are the disposer of my actions,' continued she, in kissing the hand of Constantia, 'I'll do nothing but what you'll have me. But consider, and weigh well the reasons that ought to counsel you in the measures you oblige me to take.'

Don Pedro, who had not seen the Princess all that day, came in then, and finding them both extremely troubled, with a fierce impatience, demanded the cause: 'Sir,' answered Constantia, 'Agnes too wise, and too scrupulous, fears the effects of her beauty, and will live no longer at Coimbra; and it was on this subject (which cannot be agreeable to me) that she asked my advice.' The Prince grew pale at this discourse, and snatching the words from her mouth (with more concern than possessed either of them) cried with a voice very feeble, 'Agnes cannot fail, if she follow your counsel, madam: and I leave you full liberty to give it her.' He then immediately went out, and the Princess, whose heart he perfectly possessed, not being able to hide her displeasure, said, 'My dear Agnes, if my satisfaction did not only depend on your conversation, I should desire it of you, for Don Pedro's sake; it is the only advantage that his unfortunate love can hope. And would not the world have reason to call me barbarous, if I contribute to deprive him of that?' 'But the sight of me will prove a poison to him,' replied Agnes. 'And what should I do, my Princess, if after the reserve he has hitherto kept, his mouth should add anything to the torments I have already felt, by speaking to me of his flame?' 'You would hear him sure, without causing him to despair,' replied Constantia, 'and I should put this obligation to the account of the rest you have done.' 'Would you then have me expect those events which I fear, madam?' replied Agnes. 'Well—I will obey, but just Heaven,' pursued she, 'if they prove fatal, do not punish an innocent heart for it.' Thus this conversation ended. Agnes withdrew into her chamber, but it was not to be more at ease.

What Don Pedro had learned of the design of Agnes, caused a cruel agitation in his soul; he wished he had never loved her, and desired a thousand times to die. But it was not for him to make vows against a thing which fate had designed him; and whatever resolutions he made, to bear the absence of Agnes, his tenderness had not force enough to consent to it.

After having, for a long time, combated with himself, he determined to do what was impossible for him to let Agnes do. His courage reproached him with the idleness, in which he passed the most youthful and vigorous part of his days: and making it appear to the King, that his allies, and even the Prince Don John Emanuel, his father-in-law, had concerns in the world which demanded his presence on the frontiers, he easily obtained liberty to make this journey, to which the Princess would put no obstacle.

Agnes saw him part without any concern, but it was not upon the account of any aversion she had to him. Don Alvaro began then to make his importunity an open persecution; he forgot nothing that might touch the insensible Agnes, and made use, a long time, only of the arms of love. But seeing that this submission and respect was to no purpose, he formed strange designs.

As the King had a deference for all his counsels, it was not difficult to inspire him with what he had a mind to. He complained of the ungrateful Agnes, and forgot nothing that might make him perceive that she was not cruel to him on his account, but from the too much sensibility she had for the Prince. The King, who was extremely angry at this, reiterated all the promises he had made him.

The King had not yet spoken to Agnes in favour of Don Alvaro; and not doubting but his approbation would surmount all obstacles, he took an occasion to entertain her with it. And removing some distance

from those who might hear him, 'I thought Don
Alvaro had merit enough,' said he to her, 'to have
obtained a little share in your esteem ; and I could
not imagine there would have been any necessity of
my soliciting it for him : I know you are very charming,
but he has nothing that renders him unworthy of you;
and when you shall reflect on the choice my friendship
has made of him from among all the great men of my
Court, you will do him at the same time justice. His
fortune is none of the meanest, since he has me for
his protector. He is nobly born, a man of honour
and courage ; he adores you, and it seems to me that
all these reasons are sufficient to vanquish your pride.'

The heart of Agnes was so little disposed to give
itself to Don Alvaro, that all the King of Portugal
had said had no effect on her in his favour. 'If Don
Alvaro, sir,' answered she, 'were without merit, he
possesses advantages enough in the bounty your
Majesty is pleased to honour him with, to make him
master of all things. It is not that I find any defect
in him that I answer not his desires. But, sir, by
what obstinate power would you that I should love,
if Heaven has not given me a soul that is tender?
And why should you pretend that I should submit to
him, when nothing is dearer to me than my liberty?'
'You are not so free, nor so insensible, as you say,'
answered the King, blushing with anger ; 'and if your
heart were exempt from all sorts of affection, he might
expect a more reasonable return than what he finds.
But imprudent maid, conducted by an ill fate,' added
he in fury, 'what pretensions have you to Don Pedro?
Hitherto I have hid the chagrin, which his weakness
and yours give me ; but it was not the less violent for
being hid. And since you oblige me to speak out,
I must tell you, that if my son were not already
married to Constantia, he should never be your husband ; renounce then those vain ideas, which will cure
him, and justify you.'

The courageous Agnes was scarce mistress of the

first transports, at a discourse so full of contempt; but calling her virtue to the aid of her anger, she recovered herself by the assistance of reason. And considering the outrage she received, not as coming from a great King, but a man blinded and possessed by Don Alvaro, she thought him not worthy of her resentment; her fair eyes animated themselves with so shining a vivacity, they answered for the purity of her sentiments; and fixing them steadfastly on the King, 'If the Prince Don Pedro have weaknesses,' replied she, with an air disdainful, 'he never communicated them to me; and I am certain, I never contributed wilfully to them. But to let you see how little I regard your defiance, and to put my glory in safety, I will live far from you, and all that belongs to you. Yes, sir, I will quit Coimbra with pleasure; and for this man, who is so dear to you,' answered she with a noble pride and fierceness, of which the King felt all the force, 'for this favourite, so worthy to possess the most tender affections of a great prince, I assure you, that into whatever part of the world fortune conducts me, I will not carry away the least remembrance of him.' At these words she made a profound reverence, and made such haste from his presence, that he could not oppose her going if he would.

The King was now more strongly convinced than ever, that she favoured the passion of Don Pedro, and immediately went to Constantia, to inspire her with the same thought; but she was not capable of receiving such impressions, and following her own natural inclinations, she generously defended the virtue of his actions. The King, angry to see her so well intentioned to her rival, whom he would have had her hate, reproached her with the sweetness of her temper, and went thence to mix his anger with Don Alvaro's rage, who was totally confounded when he saw the negotiation of his master had taken no effect. 'The haughty maid braves me then, sir,' said he to the

King, 'and despises the honour which your bounty offered her! Why cannot I resist so fatal a passion? But I must love her, in spite of myself; and if this flame consume me, I can find no way to extinguish it.' 'What can I further do for you?' replied the King. 'Alas, sir,' answered Don Alvaro, 'I must do by force, what I cannot otherwise hope from the proud and cruel Agnes.' 'Well, then,' added the King, 'since it is not fit for me to authorise publicly a violence in the midst of my kingdom, choose those of my subjects whom you think most capable of serving you, and take away by force the beauty that charms you; and if she do not yield to your love, put that power you are master of into execution, to oblige her to marry you.'

Don Alvaro, ravished with this proposition, which at the same time flattered both his love and his anger, cast himself at the feet of the King, and renewed his acknowledgments by fresh protestations, and thought of nothing but employing his unjust authority against Agnes.

Don Pedro had been about three months absent, when Alvaro undertook what the King counselled him to; though the moderation was known to him, yet he feared his presence, and would not attend the return of a rival, with whom he would avoid all disputes.

One night when the said Agnes, full of her ordinary inquietudes, in vain expected the god of sleep, she heard a noise, and after saw some men unknown enter her chamber, whose measures being well consulted, they carried her out of the palace, and putting her in a close coach, forced her out of Coimbra, without being hindered by any obstacle. She knew not of whom to complain, nor whom to suspect. Don Alvaro seemed too puissant to seek his satisfaction this way; and she accused not the Prince of this attempt, of whom she had so favourable an opinion; whatever she could think or say, she could not hinder her ill fortune. They hurried her on with diligence, and before it was day, were a considerable way off from the town.

As soon as day began to break, she surveyed those that encompassed her, without so much as knowing one of them ; and seeing that her cries and prayers were all in vain with these deaf ravishers, she satisfied herself with imploring the protection of Heaven, and abandoned herself to its conduct.

While she sat thus overwhelmed with grief, uncertain of her destiny, she saw a body of horse advance towards the troop which conducted her. The ravishers did not shun them, thinking it to be Don Alvaro : but when he approached more near, they found it was the Prince of Portugal who was at the head of them, and who, without foreseeing the occasion that would offer itself of serving Agnes, was returning to Coimbra full of her idea, after having performed what he ought in this expedition.

Agnes, who did not expect him, changed now her opinion, and thought that it was the Prince that had caused her to be stolen away. 'Oh, sir!' said she to him, having still the same thought, 'is it you that have torn me from the Princess? And could so cruel a blow come from a hand that is so dear to her? What will you do with an unfortunate creature who desires nothing but death? And why will you obscure the glory of your life, by an artifice unworthy of you?' This language astonished the Prince no less than the sight of Agnes had done ; he found by what she had said, that she was taken away by force ; and immediately passing to the height of rage, he made her understand by one only look, that he was not the base author of her trouble. 'I tear you from Constantia, whose only pleasure you are!' replied he. 'What opinion have you of Don Pedro? No, madam, though you see me here, I am altogether innocent of the violence that has been done you ; and there is nothing I will refuse to hinder it.' He then turned himself to behold the ravishers, but his presence had already scattered them ; he ordered some of his men to pursue them, and to seize some of them, that he might know what authority it was that set them at work.

During this, Agnes was no less confused than before ; she admired the conduct of her destiny, that brought the Prince at a time when he was so necessary to her. Her inclinations to do him justice soon repaired the offence her suspicions had caused ; she was glad to have escaped a misfortune, which appeared certain to her : but this was not a sincere joy, when she considered that her lover was her deliverer, and a lover worthy of all her acknowledgments, but who owed his heart to the most amiable Princess in the world.

While the Prince's men were pursuing the ravishers of Agnes, he was left almost alone with her ; and though he had always resolved to shun being so, yet his constancy was not proof against so fair an occasion : 'Madam,' said he to her, 'is it possible that men born amongst those that obey us, should be capable of offending you ? I never thought myself destined to revenge such an offence ; but since Heaven has permitted you to receive it, I will either perish or make them repent it.' 'Sir,' replied Agnes, more concerned at this discourse than at the enterprise of Don Alvaro, 'those who are wanting in their respect to the Princess and you, are not obliged to have any for me. I do not in the least doubt but Don Alvaro was the undertaker of this enterprise ; and I judged what I ought to fear from him, by what his importunities have already made me suffer. He is sure of the King's protection, and he will make him an accomplice in his crime : but, sir, Heaven conducted you hither happily for me, and I am indebted to you for the liberty I have of serving the Princess yet longer.' 'You will do for Constantia,' replied the Prince, 'what 'tis impossible not to do for you ; your good-

ness attaches you to her, and my destiny engages me
to you for ever.'

The modest Agnes, who feared this discourse as
much as the misfortune she had newly shunned,
answered nothing but by downcast eyes; and the
Prince, who knew the trouble she was in, left her to go
to speak to his men, who brought back one of those
that belonged to Don Alvaro, by whose confession he
found the truth. He pardoned him, thinking not fit
to punish him, who obeyed a man whom the weakness
of his father had rendered powerful.

Afterwards they conducted Agnes back to Coimbra,
where her adventure began to make a great noise.
The Princess was ready to die with despair, and at
first thought it was only a continuation of the design
this fair maid had of retiring; but some women that
served her having told the Princess, that she was
carried away by violence, Constantia made her
complaint to the King, who regarded her not at all.

'Madam,' said he to her, 'let this fatal plague
remove itself, who takes from you the heart of your
husband; and without afflicting yourself for her
absence, bless Heaven and me for it.'

The generous Princess took Agnes's part with a
great deal of courage, and was then disputing her
defence with the King, when Don Pedro arrived at
Coimbra.

The first object that met the Prince's eyes was
Don Alvaro, who was passing through one of the
courts of the palace, amidst a crowd of courtiers,
whom his favour with the King drew after him. This
sight made Don Pedro rage; but that of the Princess
and Agnes caused in Alvaro another sort of emotion.
He easily divined, that it was Don Pedro, who had
taken her from his men, and, if his fury had acted
what it would, it might have produced very sad
effects.

'Don Alvaro,' said the Prince to him, 'is it thus
you make use of the authority which the King my

father hath given you? Have you received employ-
ments and power from him, for no other end but to
do these base actions, and to commit rapes on ladies?
Are you ignorant how the Princess interests herself
in all that concerns this maid? And do you not
know the tender and affectionate esteem she has for
her?' 'No,' replied Don Alvaro, with an insolence
that had like to have put the Prince past all patience,
'I am not ignorant of it, nor of the interest your
heart takes in her.' 'Base and treacherous as thou
art,' replied the Prince, 'neither the favour which
thou hast so much abused, nor the insolence which
makes thee speak this, should hinder me from punish-
ing thee, wert thou worthy of my sword; but there
are other ways to humble thy pride, and 'tis not fit for
such an arm as mine to seek so base an employment
to punish such a slave as thou art.'

Don Pedro went away at these words, and left
Alvaro in a rage, which is not to be expressed;
despairing to see himself defeated in an enterprise
he thought so sure; and at the contempt the Prince
showed him, he promised himself to sacrifice all to his
revenge.

Though the King loved his son, he was so prepossessed against his passion, that he could not pardon
him what he had done, and condemned him as much
for this last act of justice, in delivering Agnes, as if it
had been the greatest of crimes.

Elvira, whom the sweetness of hope flattered some
moments, saw the return of Agnes with a sensible
displeasure, which suffered her to think of nothing
but irritating her brother.

In fine, the Prince saw the King, but instead of
being received by him with a joy due to the success
of his journey, he appeared all sullen and out of
humour. After having paid him his first respects,
and given him an exact account of what he had done,
he spoke to him about the violence committed against
the person of Agnes de Castro, and complained to

him of it in the name of the Princess, and of his own.
'You ought to be silent in this affair,' replied the
King; 'and the motive which makes you speak is so
shameful for you, that I sigh and blush at it. What
is it to you, if this maid, whose presence is troublesome to me, be removed hence, since 'tis I that desire
it?' 'But, sir,' interrupted the Prince, 'what necessity
is there of employing force, artifice, and the night, when
the least of your orders had been sufficient? Agnes
would willingly have obeyed you; and if she continue
at Coimbra, it is perhaps against her will : but be it
as it will, sir, Constantia is offended, and if it were
not for fear of displeasing you (the only thing that
retains me), the ravisher should not have gone unpunished.' 'How happy are you,' replied the King,
smiling with disdain, 'in making use of the name of
Constantia to uphold the interest of your heart! You
think I am ignorant of it, and that this unhappy
Princess looks on the injury you do her with indifference. Never speak to me more of Agnes' (with
a tone very severe). 'Content yourself, that I pardon
what's passed, and think maturely of the considerations I have for Don Alvaro, when you would design
anything against him.' 'Yes, sir,' replied the Prince
with fierceness, 'I will speak to you no more of
Agnes; but Constantia and I will never suffer, that
she should be any more exposed to the insolence of
your favourite.' The King had like to have broke
out into a rage at this discourse; but he had yet
a rest of prudence left that hindered him. 'Retire,'
said he to Don Pedro, 'and go make reflections on
what my power can do, and what you owe me.'

During this conversation, Agnes was receiving from
the Princess, and from all the ladies of the Court,
great expressions of joy and friendship. Constantia
saw again her husband, with a great deal of satisfaction; and far from being sorry at what he had
lately done for Agnes, she privately returned him
thanks for it, and still was the same towards him, not-

withstanding all the jealousy which was endeavoured
to be inspired in her.

Don Alvaro, who found in his sister a maliciousness
worthy of his trust, did not conceal his fury from her.
After she had made vain attempts to moderate it,
in blotting Agnes out of his heart, seeing that his
disease was incurable, she made him understand, that
so long as Constantia should not be jealous, there
were no hopes: that if Agnes should once be suspected by her, she would not fail of abandoning her,
and that then it would be easy to get satisfaction, the
Prince being now so proud of Constantia's indulgence.
In giving this advice to her brother, she promised to
serve him effectually; and having no need of anybody
but herself to perform ill things, she recommended
Don Alvaro to manage well the King.

Four years were passed in that melancholy station,
and the Princess, besides her first dead child, and
Ferdinando, who was still living, had brought two
daughters into the world.

Some days after Don Pedro's return, Elvira, who
was most dexterous in the art of well governing any
wicked design, did gain one of the servants who
belonged to Constantia's chamber. She first spoke
her fair, then overwhelmed her with presents and
gifts; and finding in her as ill a disposition as in herself, she readily resolved to employ her.

After she was sure of her, she composed a letter,
which was after writ over again in an unknown hand,
which she deposited in that maid's hands, that she
might deliver to Constantia with the first opportunity,
telling her, that Agnes had dropped it. This was the
substance of it:—

I employ not my own hand to write to you, for reasons that
I shall acquaint you with. How happy am I to have overcome
all your scruples! And what happiness shall I find in the
progress of our intrigue! The whole course of my life shall
continually represent to you the sincerity of my affections;
pray think on the secret conversation that I require of you.
I dare not speak to you in public, therefore let me conjure you

here, by all that I have suffered, to come to-night to the place
appointed, and speak to me no more of Constantia ; for she
must be content with my esteem, since my heart can be only
yours.

The unfaithful Portuguese served Elvira exactly to
her desires ; and the very next day seeing Agnes go
out from the Princess, she carried Constantia the
letter ; which she took, and found there what she was
far from imagining.   Tenderness never produced an
effect more full of grief, than what it made her suffer.
'Alas ! they are both culpable,' said she, sighing, 'and
in spite of the defence my heart would make for them,
my reason condemns them.   Unhappy Princess, the
sad subject of the capriciousness of fortune !   Why
dost not thou die, since thou hast not a heart of
honour to revenge itself ?   O Don Pedro ! why did
you give me your hand, without your heart ?   And
thou, fair, and ungrateful ! wert thou born to be the
misfortune of my life, and perhaps the only cause of
my death ? '   After having given some moments to
the violence of her grief, she called the maid, who
brought her the letter, commanding her to speak of it
to nobody, and to suffer no one to enter into her
chamber.

She considered then of that Prince with more
liberty, whose soul she was not able to touch with the
least tenderness ; and of the cruel fair one that had
betrayed her.   Yet, even while her soul was upon the
rack, she was willing to excuse them, and ready to do
all she could for Don Pedro ; at least, she made a firm
resolution, not to complain of him.

Elvira was not long without being informed of what
had passed, nor of the melancholy of the Princess,
from whom she hoped all she desired.

Agnes, far from foreseeing this tempest, returned
to Constantia ; and hearing of her indisposition,
passed the rest of the day at her chamber-door, that
she might from time to time learn news of her health ;
for she was not suffered to come in, at which Agnes

was both surprised and troubled. The Prince had the same destiny, and was astonished at an order which ought to have excepted him.

The next day Constantia appeared, but so altered, that it was not difficult to imagine what she had suffered. Agnes was the most impatient to approach her, and the Princess could not forbear weeping. They were both silent for some time, and Constantia attributed this silence of Agnes to some remorse which she felt : and this unhappy maid being able to hold no longer, 'Is it possible, madam,' said she, 'that two days should have taken from me all the goodness you had for me? What have I done? And for what do you punish me?' The Princess regarded her with a languishing look, and returned her no answer but sighs. Agnes, offended with this reserve, went out with very great dissatisfaction and anger; which contributed to her being thought criminal. The Prince came in immediately after, and found Constantia more disordered than usual, and conjured her in a most obliging manner to take care of her health. 'The greatest good for me,' said she, 'is not the continuation of my life ; I should have more care of it if I loved you less : but——' She could not proceed ; and the Prince, excessively afflicted at her trouble, sighed sadly, without making her any answer, which redoubled her grief. Spite then began to mix itself; and all things persuading the Princess that they made a sacrifice of her, she would enter into no explanation with her husband, but suffered him to go away without saying anything to him.

Nothing is more capable of troubling our reason, and consuming our health, than secret notions of jealousy in solitude.

Constantia, who used to open her heart freely to Agnes, now believing she had deceived her, abandoned herself so absolutely to grief, that she was ready to sink under it ; she immediately fell sick with the violence of it, and all the Court was concerned at

this misfortune. Don Pedro was truly afflicted at it,
but Agnes more than all the world beside. Constantia's
coldness towards her, made her continually sigh ; and
her distemper created merely by fancy, caused her to
reflect on everything that offered itself to her memory :
so that at last she began even to fear herself, and to
reproach herself for what the Princess suffered.

But the distemper began to be such that they feared
Constantia's death, and she herself began to feel the
approaches of it. This thought did not at all disquiet
her : she looked on death as the only relief from all
her torments ; and regarded the despair of all that
approached her without the least concern.

The King, who loved her tenderly, and who knew
her virtue, was infinitely moved at the extremity she
was in. And Don Alvaro, who lost not the least
occasion of making him understand that it was
jealousy which was the cause of Constantia's distemper, did but too much incense him against
criminals, worthy of compassion. The King was
not of a temper to conceal his anger long : 'You
give fine examples,' said he to the Prince, 'and such
as will render your memory illustrious ! The death
of Constantia (of which you only are to be accused)
is the unhappy fruit of your guilty passion. Fear
Heaven after this : and behold yourself as a monster
that does not deserve to see the light. If the interest
you have in my blood did not plead for you, what ought
you not to fear from my just resentment ? But what
must not imprudent Agnes, to whom nothing ties
me, expect from my hands ? If Constantia dies, she,
who has the boldness, in my Court, to cherish a foolish
flame by vain hopes, and make us lose the most
amiable Princess, whom thou art not worthy to
possess, shall feel the effects of her indiscretion.'

Don Pedro knew very well, that Constantia was
not ignorant of his sentiments for Agnes ; but he
knew also with what moderation she received it. He
was very sensible of the King's reproaches ; but as

his fault was not voluntary, and that a commanding power, a fatal star, had forced him to love in spite of himself, he appeared afflicted and confused : 'You condemn me, sir,' answered he, 'without having well examined me ; and if my contentions were known to you, perhaps you would not find me so criminal. I would take the Princess for my judge, who you say I sacrifice, if she were in a condition to be consulted. If I am guilty of any weakness, her justice never reproached me for it ; and my tongue never informed Agnes of it. But suppose I have committed any fault, why would you punish an innocent lady, who perhaps condemns me for it as much as you ?' 'Ah, villain !' interrupted the King, 'she has but too much favoured you. You would not have loved thus long, had she not made you some returns.' 'Sir,' replied the Prince, pierced with grief for the outrage that was committed against Agnes, 'you offend a virtue, than which nothing can be purer ; and those expressions which break from your choler, are not worthy of you. Agnes never granted me any favours ; I never asked any of her ; and I protest to Heaven, I never thought of anything contrary to the duty I owe Constantia.'

As they thus argued, one of the Princess's women came all in tears to acquaint Don Pedro, that the Princess was in the last extremities of life : 'Go see thy fatal work,' said the King, 'and expect from a too-long patient father the usage thou deservest.'

The Prince ran to Constantia, whom he found dying, and Agnes in a swoon, in the arms of some of the ladies. What caused this double calamity, was, that Agnes, who could suffer no longer the indifference of the Princess, had conjured her to tell her what was her crime, and either to take her life from her, or re-store her to her friendship.

Constantia, who found she must die, could no longer keep her secret affliction from Agnes ; and after some words, which were a preparation to the sad explana-tion, she showed her that fatal billet, which Elvira

had caused to be written : 'Ah, madam!' cried out
the fair Agnes, after having read it, 'ah, madam!
how many cruel inquietudes had you spared me, had
you opened your heart to me with your wonted
bounty! 'Tis easy to see that this letter is counter-
feit, and that I have enemies without compassion.
Could you believe the Prince so imprudent, to make
use of any other hand but his own, on an occasion like
this? And do you believe me so simple to keep
about me this testimony of my shame, with so little
precaution? You are neither betrayed by your husband nor me ; I attest Heaven, and those efforts I
have made to leave Coimbra. Alas, my dear Princess !
how little have you known her, whom you have so
much honoured! Do not believe that when I have
justified myself, I will have any more communication
with the world. No, no ; there will be no retreat far
enough from hence for me. I will take care to hide
this unlucky face, where it shall be sure to do no more
harm.'

The Princess touched at this discourse, and the
tears of Agnes, pressed her hand, which she held in
hers ; and fixing looks upon her capable of moving
pity in the most insensible souls, ' If I have committed
any offence, my dear Agnes,' answered she, ' death,
which I expect in a moment, shall revenge it. I ought
also to protest to you, that I have not ceased loving
you, and that I believe everything you have said,
giving you back my most tender affections.'

It was at this time that the grief, which equally
oppressed them, put the Princess into such an extremity, that they sent for the Prince. He came, and
found himself almost without life or motion at this
sight. And what secret motive soever might call him
to the aid of Agnes, it was to Constantia he ran.
The Princess, who finding her last moments drawing
on, by a cold sweat that covered her all over ; and
finding she had no more business with life, and causing
those persons she most suspected to retire, ' Sir,' said

she to Don Pedro, 'if I abandon life without regret,
it is not without trouble that I part with you. But,
Prince, we must vanquish when we come to die; and
I will forget myself wholly, to think of nothing but
of you. I have no reproaches to make against you,
knowing that 'tis inclination that disposes hearts, and
not reason. Agnes is beautiful enough to inspire the
most ardent passion, and virtuous enough to deserve
the first fortunes in the world. I ask her, once more,
pardon for the injustice I have done her, and recommend her to you, as a person most dear to me.
Promise me, my dear Prince, before I expire, to give
her my place in your throne: it cannot be better
filled: you cannot choose a Princess more perfect for
your people, nor a better mother for our little children.
And you, my dear and faithful Agnes,' pursued she,
'listen not to a virtue too scrupulous, that may make
any opposition to the Prince of Portugal. Refuse
him not a heart of which he is worthy; and give him
that friendship which you had for me, with that which
is due to his merit. Take care of my little Fernando,
and the two young Princesses: let them find me in
you, and speak to them sometimes of me. Adieu, live
both of you happy, and receive my last embraces.'

The afflicted Agnes, who had recovered a little her
forces, lost them again a second time; her weakness
was followed with convulsions so vehement, that they
were afraid of her life; but Don Pedro never removed
from Constantia: 'What, madam,' said he, 'you will
leave me then; and you think 'tis for my good? Alas,
Constantia! if my heart has committed an outrage
against you, your virtue has sufficiently revenged you
on me in spite of you. Can you think me so barbarous?' As he was going on, he saw death shut the
eyes of the most generous Princess for ever; and he
was within a very little of following her.

But what loads of grief did this bring upon Agnes,
when she found in that interval, wherein life and
death were struggling in her soul, that Constantia

was newly expired! She would then have taken away
her own life, and have let her despair fully appear.

At the noise of the death of the Princess, the town
and the palace were all in tears. Elvira, who saw
then Don Pedro free to engage himself, repented of
having contributed to the death of Constantia; and
thinking herself the cause of it, promised in her griefs
never to pardon herself.

She had need of being guarded several days together; during which time she failed not incessantly
to weep. And the Prince gave all those days to
deepest mourning. But when the first emotions were
past, those of his love made him feel that he was still
the same.

He was a long time without seeing Agnes; but
this absence of his served only to make her appear
the more charming when he did see her.

Don Alvaro, who was afraid of the liberty of the
Prince, made new efforts to move Agnes de Castro,
who was now become insensible to everything but
grief. Elvira, who was willing to make the best of
the design she had begun, consulted all her woman's
arts, and the delicacy of her wit, to revive the flames
with which the Prince once burnt for her. But his
constancy was bounded, and it was Agnes alone that
was to reign over his heart. She had taken a firm
resolution, since the death of Constantia, to pass the
rest of her days in a solitary retreat. In spite of
the precaution she took to hide this design, the
Prince was informed of it, and did all he was able to
dispose his constancy and fortitude to it. He thought
himself stronger than he really was; but after he had
well consulted his heart, he found but too well how
necessary the presence of Agnes was to him. 'Madam,'
said he to her one day, with a heart big, and his eyes
in tears, 'which action of my life has made you determine my death? Though I never told you how much
I loved you, yet I am persuaded you are not ignorant
of it. I was constrained to be silent during some

years for your sake, for Constantia's, and my own;
but 'tis not possible for me to put this force upon my
heart for ever: I must once at least tell you how it
languishes. Receive then the assurances of a passion,
full of respect and ardour, with an offer of my fortune, which I wish not better, but for your advantage.'

Agnes answered not immediately to these words,
but with abundance of tears; which having wiped
away, and beholding Don Pedro with an air which
made him easily comprehend she did not agree with
his desires, 'If I were capable of the weakness with
which you'd inspire me, you'd be obliged to punish
me for it. What!' said she, 'Constantia is scarce
buried, and you would have me offend her! No, my
Prince,' added she with more softness, 'no, no, she
whom you have heaped so many favours on, will not
call down the anger of Heaven, and the contempt of
men upon her, by an action so perfidious. Be not
obstinate then in a design in which I will never show
you favour. You owe to Constantia, after her death,
a fidelity that may justify you: and I, to repair the
ills I have made her suffer, ought to shun all converse
with you.' 'Go, madam,' replied the Prince, growing
pale, 'go, and expect the news of my death; in that
part of the world, whither your cruelty shall lead you,
the news shall follow close after; you shall quickly
hear of it: and I will go seek it in those wars which
reign among my neighbours.'

These words made the fair Agnes de Castro perceive that her innocency was not so great as she
imagined, and that her heart interested itself in the
preservation of Don Pedro: 'You ought, sir, to preserve your life,' replied Agnes, 'for the sake of the
little Prince and Princesses, which Constantia has left
you. Would you abandon their youth,' continued
she, with a tender tone, 'to the cruelty of Don Alvaro?
Live! sir, live! and let the unhappy Agnes be the
only sacrifice.' 'Alas, cruel maid!' interrupted Don
Pedro, 'why do you command me to live, if I cannot

live with you? Is it an effect of your hatred?' 'No,
sir,' replied Agnes, 'I do not hate you; and I wish to
God that I could be able to defend myself against the
weakness with which I find myself possessed. Oblige
me to say no more, sir: you see my blushes, interpret
them as you please: but consider yet, that the less
aversion I find I have to you, the more culpable I am;
and that I ought no more to see, or speak to you. In
fine, sir, if you oppose my retreat, I declare to you,
that Don Alvaro, as odious as he is to me, shall serve
for a defence against you; and that I will sooner consent to marry a man I abhor, than to favour a passion
that cost Constantia her life.' 'Well then, Agnes,' replied the Prince, with looks all languishing and dying,
'follow the motions which barbarous virtue inspires
you with; take these measures you judge necessary
against an unfortunate lover, and enjoy the glory of
having cruelly refused me.'

At these words he went away; and troubled as
Agnes was, she would not stay him. Her courage
combated with her grief, and she thought now, more
than ever, of departing.

It was difficult for her to go out of Coimbra; and not
to defer what appeared to her so necessary, she went
immediately to the apartment of the King, notwithstanding the interest of Don Alvaro. The King received her with a countenance severe, not being able
to consent to what she demanded: 'You shall not go
hence,' said he, 'and if you are wise, you shall enjoy
here with Don Alvaro both my friendship and my
favour.' 'I have taken another resolution,' answered
Agnes, 'and the world has no part in it.' 'You will
accept Don Pedro,' replied the King, 'his fortune is
sufficient to satisfy an ambitious maid: but you will
not succeed Constantia, who loved you so tenderly;
and Spain has Princesses enough to fill up part of the
throne which I shall leave him.' 'Sir,' replied Agnes,
piqued at this discourse, 'if I had a disposition to love,
and a design to marry, perhaps the Prince might be

the only person on whom I would fix it. And you know, if my ancestors did not possess crowns, yet they were worthy to wear them. But let it be how it will, I am resolved to depart, and to remain no longer a slave in a place to which I came free.'

This bold answer, which showed the character of Agnes, angered and astonished the King. 'You shall go when we think fit,' replied he, 'and without being a slave at Coimbra, you shall attend our order.'

Agnes saw she must stay, and was so grieved at it, that she kept her chamber several days, without daring to inform herself of the Prince; and this retirement spared her the affliction of being visited by Don Alvaro.

During this, Don Pedro fell sick, and was in so great danger, that there was a general apprehension of his death. Agnes did not in the least doubt, but it was an effect of his discontent: she thought at first she had strength and resolution enough to see him die, rather than to favour him; but had she reflected a little, she had soon been convinced to the contrary. She found not in her heart that cruel constancy she thought there so well established. She felt pains and inquietude, shed tears, made wishes; and, in fine, discovered that she loved.

It was impossible to see the heir of the crown, a Prince that deserved so well, even at the point of death, without a general affliction. The people who loved him, passed whole days at the palace gate to hear news of him. The Court was all overwhelmed with grief.

Don Alvaro knew very well how to conceal a malicious joy, under an appearance of sadness. Elvira, full of tenderness, and perhaps of remorse, suffered also on her side. The King, although he condemned the love of his son, yet still had a tenderness for him, and could not resolve to lose him. Agnes de Castro, who knew the cause of his distemper, expected the end of it with strange anxieties.

In fine, after a month had passed away in fears, they
began to have a little hopes of his recovery. The
Prince and Don Alvaro were the only persons that
were not glad of it : but Agnes rejoiced enough for
all the rest.

Don Pedro, seeing that he must live whether he
would or no, thought of nothing but passing his days
in melancholy and discontent. As soon as he was in
a condition to walk, he sought out the most solitary
places, and gained so much upon his own weakness,
to go everywhere, where Agnes was not ; but her idea
followed him always, and his memory, faithful to
represent her to him with all her charms, rendered
her always dangerous.

One day, when they had carried him into the
garden, he sought out a labyrinth which was at the
farthest part of it, to hide his melancholy, during
some hours ; there he found the sad Agnes, whom
grief, little different from his, had brought thither;
the sight of her whom he expected not, made him
tremble. She saw by his pale and meagre face the
remains of his distemper ; his eyes full of languishment troubled her, and though her desire was so great
to have fled from him, an unknown power stopped
her, and it was impossible for her to go.

After some moments of silence, which many sighs
interrupted, Don Pedro raised himself from the place
where his weakness had forced him to sit ; he made
Agnes see, as he approached her, the sad marks of
his sufferings : and not content with the pity he saw
in her eyes, 'You have resolved my death then, cruel
Agnes,' said he, 'my desire was the same with yours ;
but Heaven has thought fit to reserve me for other
misfortunes, and I see you again, as unhappy, but
more in love than ever.'

There was no need of these words to move Agnes
to compassion, the languishment of the Prince spoke
enough : and the heart of this fair maid was but too
much disposed to yield itself. She thought then that

Constantia ought to be satisfied; love, which combated for Don Pedro, triumphed over friendship, and
found that happy moment, for which the Prince of
Portugal had so long sighed.

'Do not reproach me, for that which has cost me
more than you, sir,' replied she, 'and do not accuse
a heart, which is neither ungrateful nor barbarous:
and I must tell you, that I love you. But now I have
made you that confession, what is it farther that you
require of me?' Don Pedro, who expected not a
change so favourable, felt a double satisfaction; and
falling at the feet of Agnes, he expressed more by the
silence his passion created, than he could have done
by the most eloquent words.

After having known all his good fortune, he then
consulted with the amiable Agnes, what was to be
feared from the King; they concluded that the cruel
billet, which so troubled the last days of Constantia,
could come from none but Elvira and Don Alvaro.
The Prince, who knew that his father had searched
already an alliance for him, and was resolved on his
favourite's marrying Agnes, conjured her so tenderly
to prevent these persecutions, by consenting to a
secret marriage, that, after having a long time considered, she at last consented. 'I will do what you
will have me,' said she, 'though I presage nothing but
fatal events from it; all my blood turns to ice, when
I think of this marriage, and the image of Constantia
seems to hinder me from doing it.'

The amorous Prince surmounted all her scruples,
and separated himself from Agnes, with a satisfaction
which soon redoubled his forces; he saw her after-
ward with the pleasure of a mystery. And the day
of their union being arrived, Don Gill, Bishop of
Guarda, performed the ceremony of the marriage, in
the presence of several witnesses, faithful to Don
Pedro, who saw him possessor of all the charms of
the fair Agnes.

She lived not the more peaceable for belonging to

the Prince of Portugal; her enemies, who continually
persecuted her, left her not without troubles: and the
King, whom her refusal enraged, laid his absolute
commands on her to marry Don Alvaro, with threats
to force her to it, if she continued rebellious.

The Prince took loudly her part; and this, joined
to the refusal he made of marrying the Princess of
Aragon, caused suspicions of the truth in the King
his father.   He was seconded by those that were too
much interested, not to unriddle this secret.   Don
Alvaro and his sister acted with so much care, gave
so many gifts, and made so many promises, that they
discovered the secret engagements of Don Pedro and
Agnes.

The King wanted but little of breaking out into all
the rage and fury so great a disappointment could
inspire him with, against the Princess.   Don Alvaro,
whose love was changed into the most violent hatred,
appeased the first transports of the King, by making
him comprehend, that if they could break the marriage
of them, that would not be a sufficient revenge; and
so poisoned the soul of the King, to consent to the
death of Agnes.

The barbarous Don Alvaro offered his arm for this
terrible execution, and his rage was security for the
sacrifice.

The King, who thought the glory of his family dis-
graced by this alliance, and his own in particular in the
procedure of his son, gave full power to this murderer,
to make the innocent Agnes a victim to his rage.

It was not easy to execute this horrid design.
Though the Prince saw Agnes but in secret, yet all
his cares were still awake for her, and he was married
to her above a year, before Don Alvaro could find out
an opportunity so long sought for.

The Prince diverted himself but little, and very
rarely went far from Coimbra; but on a day, an
unfortunate day, and marked out by Heaven for an
unheard-of and horrid assassination, he made a party

to hunt at a fine house, which the King of Portugal had near the city.

Agnes loved everything that gave the Prince satisfaction; but a secret trouble made her apprehend some misfortune in this unhappy journey. 'Sir,' said she to him, alarmed, without knowing the reason why, 'I tremble, seeing you to-day as it were designed the last of my life. Preserve yourself, my dear Prince; and though the exercise you take be not very dangerous, beware of the least hazards, and bring me back all that I trust with you.' Don Pedro, who had never found her so handsome and so charming before, embraced her several times, and went out of the palace with his followers, with a design not to return till the next day.

He was no sooner gone, but the cruel Don Alvaro prepared himself for the execution he had resolved on; he thought it of that importance, that it required more hands than his own, and so chose for his companions Don Lopez Pacheo, and Pedro Cuello, two monsters like himself, whose cruelty he was assured of by the presents he had made them.

They waited the coming of the night, and the lovely Agnes was in her first sleep, which was the last of her life, when these assassins approached her bed. Nothing made resistance to Don Alvaro, who could do everything, and whom the blackest furies introduced to Agnes; she wakened, and opening her curtains, saw, by the candle burning in her chamber, the poniard with which Don Alvaro was armed; he having his face not covered, she easily knew him, and forgetting herself, to think of nothing but the Prince: 'Just Heaven,' said she, lifting up her fine eyes, 'if you will revenge Constantia, satisfy yourself with my blood only, and spare that of Don Pedro.' The barbarous man that heard her, gave her not time to say more; and finding he could never (by all he could do by love) touch the heart of the fair Agnes, he pierced it with his poniard: his accomplices gave her

several wounds, though there was no necessity of so
many to put an end to an innocent life.

What a sad spectacle was this for those who approached her bed the next day! And what dismal
news was this to the unfortunate Prince of Portugal!
He returned to Coimbra at the first report of this
adventure, and saw what had certainly cost him his
life, if men could die of grief. After having a
thousand times embraced the bloody body of Agnes,
and said all that a just despair could inspire him
with, he ran like a madman into the palace, demanding the murderers of his wife, of things that could not
hear him. In fine, he saw the King, and without observing any respect, he gave a loose to his resentment: after having railed a long time, overwhelmed
with grief, he fell into a swoon, which continued all
that day. They carried him into his apartment: and
the King, believing that his misfortune would prove
his cure, repented not of what he had permitted.

Don Alvaro, and the two other assassins, quitted
Coimbra. This absence of theirs made them appear
guilty of the crime; for which the afflicted Prince
vowed a speedy vengeance to the ghost of his lovely
Agnes, resolving to pursue them to the uttermost
part of the universe. He got a considerable number
of men together, sufficient to have made resistance,
even to the King of Portugal himself, if he should yet
take the part of the murderers: with these he ravaged
the whole country, as far as the Duero Waters, and
carried on a war, even till the death of the King, continually mixing tears with blood, which he gave to
the revenge of his dearest Agnes.

Such was the deplorable end of the unfortunate
love of Don Pedro of Portugal, and of the fair Agnes
de Castro, whose remembrance he faithfully preserved
in his heart, even upon the throne, to which he
mounted, by the right of his birth, after the death of
the King.

THE LOVER'S WATCH

OR THE ART OF MAKING LOVE

THE ARGUMENT

IT is in the most happy and august Court of the best and greatest monarch of the world, that Damon, a young nobleman, whom we will render under that name, languishes for a maid of quality, who will give us leave to call her Iris.

Their births are equally illustrious; they are both rich, and both young; their beauty such as I do not too nicely particularise, lest I should discover (which I am not permitted to do) who these charming lovers are. Let it suffice, that Iris is the most fair and accomplished person that ever adorned a Court; and that Damon is only worthy of the glory of her favour; for he has all that can render him lovely in the fair eyes of the amiable Iris. Nor is he master of those superficial beauties alone, that please at first sight; he can charm the soul with a thousand arts of wit and gallantry. And, in a word, I may say, without flattering either, that there is no one beauty, no one grace, no perfection of mind and body, that wants to complete a victory on both sides.

The agreement of age, fortunes, quality and humours in these two fair lovers, made the impatient Damon hope, that nothing would oppose his passion; and if he saw himself every hour languishing for the adorable maid, he did not however despair. And if Iris sighed, it was not for fear of being one day more happy.

In the midst of the tranquillity of these two lovers, Iris was obliged to go into the country for some months, whither it was impossible for Damon to wait on her, he being obliged to attend the King his master; and being the most amorous of his sex, suffered with extreme impatience the absence of his mistress. Nevertheless, he failed not to send to her every day, and gave up all his melancholy hours to thinking, sighing, and writing to her the softest letters that love could inspire. So that Iris even blessed that absence that gave her so tender and convincing proofs of his passion; and found this dear way of conversing, even recompensed all her sighs for his absence.

After a little intercourse of this kind, Damon bethought himself to ask Iris a discretion which he had won of her before she left the town; and in a billet-doux to that purpose, pressed her very earnestly for it. Iris being infinitely pleased with his importunity, suffered him to ask it often; and he never failed of doing so.

But as I do not here design to relate the adventures of these two amiable persons, nor give you all the billet-douxs that passed between them; you shall here find nothing but the watch this charming maid sent her impatient lover.

IRIS TO DAMON

IT must be confessed, Damon, that you are the most importuning man in the world. Your billets have a hundred times demanded a discretion, which you won of me; and tell me, will you not wait my return to be paid? You are either a very faithless creditor, or believe me very unjust, that you dun with such impatience. But to let you see that I am a maid of honour, and value my word, I will acquit myself of this obligation I have to you, and send you a watch of my fashion ; perhaps you never saw any so good. It is not one of those that have always something to be mended in it : but one that is without fault, very just and good, and will remain so as long as you continue to love me : but, Damon, know, that the very minute you cease to do so, the string will break, and it will go no more. 'Tis only useful in my absence, and when I return 'twill change its motion : and though I have set it but for the springtime, it will serve you the whole year round : and it will be necessary only that you alter the business of the hours (which my cupid, in the middle of my watch, points you out) according to the length of the days and nights. Nor is the dart of that little god directed to those hours, so much to inform you how they pass, as how you ought to pass them ; how you ought to employ those of your absence from Iris. 'Tis there you shall find the whole business of a lover, from his mistress ; for I have designed it a rule to all your actions. The consideration of the workman ought to make you set a value upon the work : and though it be not an accomplished and perfect piece ; yet, Damon, you ought to be grateful and esteem it, since I have made it for you alone. But however I may boast of the design, I know, as well as I believe you love me, that you will not suffer me to have the glory of it wholly, but will say in your heart :

> That Love, the great instructor of the mind,
>   That forms anew, and fashions every soul,
> Refines the gross defects of human kind ;
>   Humbles the proud and vain, inspires the dull ;
> Gives cowards noble heat in fight,
> And teaches feeble women how to write :
> That doth the universe command,
> Does from my Iris' heart direct her hand.

I give you the liberty to say this to your heart, if you please : and that you may know with what justice you do so, I will confess in my turn.

THE CONFESSION

That Love's my conduct where I go,
And Love instructs me all I do.
Prudence no longer is my guide,
Nor take I counsel of my pride.
In vain does honour now invade,
In vain does reason take my part,
If against Love it do persuade,
If it rebel against my heart.
If the soft evening do invite,
And I incline to take the air,
The birds, the spring, the flow'rs no more delight :
'Tis Love makes all the pleasure there :
Love, which about me still I bear ;
I'm charm'd with what I thither bring,
And add a softness to the spring.
If for devotion I design,
Love meets me, even at the shrine ;
In all my worship claims a part,
And robs even Heaven of my heart :
All day does counsel and control,
And all the night employs my soul.
No wonder then if all you think be true,
That Love's concerned in all I do for you.

And, Damon, you know that Love is no ill master ; and I must say, with a blush, that he has found me no unapt scholar ; and he instructs too agreeably not to succeed in all he undertakes.

Who can resist his soft commands?
When he resolves, what God withstands?

But I ought to explain to you my watch : the naked cupid which you will find in the middle of it, with his wings clipped, to show you he is fixed and constant, and will not fly away, points you out with his arrow the four-and-twenty hours that compose the day and the night : over every hour you will

find written what you ought to do, during its course;
and every half-hour is marked with a sigh, since the
quality of a lover is, to sigh day and night : sighs are
the children of lovers, that are born every hour.
And that my watch may always be just, Love himself
ought to conduct it; and your heart should keep
time with the movement :

> My present's delicate and new,
>   If by your heart the motion's set ;
> According as that's false or true,
> You'll find my Watch will answer it.

Every hour is tedious to a lover, separated from
his mistress : and to show you how good I am, I will
have my watch instruct you, to pass some of them
without inquietude ; that the force of your imagination may sometimes charm the trouble you have for
my absence :

> Perhaps I am mistaken here,
>   My heart may too much credit give :
> But, Damon, you can charm my fear,
> And soon my error undeceive.

But I will not disturb my repose at this time with
a jealousy, which I hope is altogether frivolous and
vain ; but begin to instruct you in the mysteries of
my watch. Cast then your eyes upon the eighth hour
in the morning, which is the hour I would have you
begin to wake : you will find there written :

EIGHT O'CLOCK

AGREEABLE REVERIE

Do not rise yet ; you may find thoughts agreeable
enough, when you awake, to entertain you longer in
bed. And 'tis in that hour you ought to recollect all
the dreams you had in the night. If you had
dreamed anything to my advantage, confirm yourself

in that thought; but if to my disadvantage, renounce it, and disown the injurious dream. It is in this hour also that I give you leave to reflect on all that I have ever said and done, that has been most obliging to you, and that gives you the most tender sentiments.

THE REFLECTIONS

Remember, Damon, while your mind
   Reflects on things that charm and please,
You give me proofs that you are kind,
   And set my doubting soul at ease:
For when your heart receives with joy
   The thoughts of favours which I give,
My smiles in vain I not employ,
   And on the square we love and live.

Think then on all I ever did,
   That e'er was charming, e'er was dear;
Let nothing from that soul be hid,
   Whose griefs and joys I feel and share.
All that your love and faith have sought,
All that your vows and sighs have bought,
Now render present to your thought.

And for what's to come, I give you leave, Damon, to flatter yourself and to expect, I shall still pursue those methods, whose remembrance charms so well. But, if it be possible, conceive these kind thoughts between sleeping and waking, that all my too forward complaisance, my goodness, and my tenderness, which I confess to have for you, may pass for half dreams: for it is most certain

That though the favours of the fair
Are ever to the lover dear;
Yet, lest he should reproach that easy flame,
That buys its satisfaction with its shame;
She ought but rarely to confess
How much she finds of tenderness;
Nicely to guard the yielding part,
And hide the hard-kept secret in her heart.

For, let me tell you, Damon, though the passion of a woman of honour be ever so innocent, and the lover ever so discreet and honest; her heart feels I know not what of reproach within, at the reflection of any favours she has allowed him. For my part, I never call to mind the least soft or kind word I have spoken to Damon, without finding at the same instant my face covered over with blushes, and my heart with sensible pain. I sigh at the remembrance of every touch I have stolen from his hand, and have upbraided my soul, which confesses so much guilty love, as that secret desire of touching him made appear. I am angry at the discovery, though I am pleased at the same time with the satisfaction I take in doing so ; and ever disordered at the remembrance of such arguments of too much love. And these unquiet sentiments alone are sufficient to persuade me, that our sex cannot be reserved too much. And I have often, on these occasions, said to myself:

THE RESERVE

Though Damon every virtue have,
  With all that pleases in his form,
That can adorn the just and brave,
  That can the coldest bosom warm ;
Though wit and honour there abound,
  Yet the pursuer's ne'er pursued,
And when my weakness he has found,
  His love will sink to gratitude :
While on the asking part he lives,
'Tis she th' obliger is who gives.

And he that at one throw the stake has won
Gives over play, since all the stock is gone.
And what dull gamester ventures certain store
With losers who can set no more ?

NINE O'CLOCK

DESIGN TO PLEASE NOBODY

I should continue to accuse you of that vice I have often done, that of laziness, if you remained past this hour in bed : it is time for you to rise ; my watch tells you it is nine o'clock. Remember that I am absent, therefore do not take too much pains in dressing yourself, and setting your person off.

THE QUESTION

Tell me ! What can he design,
Who in his mistress' absence will be fine ?
   Why does he cock, and comb, and dress ?
Why is his cravat string in print ?
   What does th' embroidered coat confess ?
   Why to the glass this long address,
If there be nothing in 't ?
If no new conquest is design'd,
If no new beauty fill his mind ?
Let fools and fops, whose talents lie
   In being neat, in being spruce,
Be dressed in vain, and tawdery ;
   With men of sense, 'tis out of use :
The only folly that distinction sets
Between the noisy fluttering fools and wits.
Remember, *Iris* is away ;
   And sighing to your valet cry,
Spare your perfumes and care to-day,
I have no business to be gay,
   Since Iris is not by.
I'll be all negligent in dress,
   And scarce set off for complaisance :
Put me on nothing that may please,
   But only such as may give no offence.

Say to yourself, as you are dressing, ' Would it please Heaven, that I might see Iris to-day ! But oh ! it is impossible : therefore all that I shall see will

be but indifferent objects, since it is Iris only that
I wish to see.'   And sighing, whisper to yourself:

THE SIGH

Ah ! charming object of my wishing thought !
   Ah ! soft idea of a distant bliss !
That only art in dreams and fancy brought,
   That give short intervals of happiness.
But when I waking find thou absent art,
   And with thee, all that I adore,
What pains, what anguish fills my heart !
   What sadness seizes me all o'er !
All entertainments I neglect,
   Since Iris is no longer there :
Beauty scarce claims my bare respect,
   Since in the throng I find not her.
Ah then ! how vain it were to dress, and show ;
Since all I wish to please, is absent now !

It is with these thoughts, Damon, that your mind
ought to be employed, during your time of dressing.
And you are too knowing in love, to be ignorant

That when a lover ceases to be blest
   With the object he desires,
Ah ! how indifferent are the rest !
   How soon their conversation tires !
Though they a thousand arts to please invent,
Their charms are dull, their wit impertinent.

TEN O'CLOCK

READING OF LETTERS

My cupid points you now the hour in which you
ought to retire into your cabinet, having already passed
an hour in dressing : and for a lover, who is sure not
to appear before his mistress, even that hour is too
much to be so employed. But I will think, you
thought of nothing less than dressing while you were

about it. Lose then no more minutes, but open your escritoire, and read over some of those billets you have received from me. Oh! what pleasures a lover feels about his heart, in reading those from a mistress he entirely loves!

THE JOY

Who, but a lover, can express
The joys, the pants, the tenderness,
That the soft amorous soul invades,
While the dear billet-doux he reads?
Raptures divine the heart o'erflow,
Which he that loves not cannot know.

A thousand tremblings, thousand fears,
The short-breathed sighs, the joyful tears!
The transport, where the love's confessed;
The change, where coldness is expressed;
The diff'ring flames the lover burns,
As those are shy, or kind, by turns.

However you find them, Damon, construe them all to my advantage: possibly, some of them have an air of coldness, something different from that softness they are usually too amply filled with; but where you find they have, believe there, that the sense of honour, and my sex's modesty, guided my hand a little against the inclinations of my heart; and that it was as a kind of an atonement, I believed I ought to make, for something I feared I had said too kind, and too obliging before. But wherever you find that stop, that check in my career of love, you will be sure to find something that follows it to favour you, and deny that unwilling imposition upon my heart; which, lest you should mistake, love shows himself in smiles again, and flatters more agreeably, disdaining the tyranny of honour and rigid custom, that imposition upon our sex; and will, in spite of me, let you see he reigns absolutely in my soul.

The reading my billet-doux may detain you an hour: I have had so much goodness to write you

enough to entertain you so long at least, and sometimes reproach myself for it ; but, contrary to all my
scruples, I find myself disposed to give you those
frequent marks of my tenderness. If yours be so
great as you express it, you ought to kiss my letters
a thousand times ; you ought to read them with attention, and weigh every word, and value every line. A
lover may receive a thousand endearing words from
a mistress, more easily than a billet. One says a great
many kind things of course to a lover, which one is
not willing to write, or to give testified under one's
hand, signed and sealed. But when once a lover has
brought his mistress to that degree of love, he ought
to assure himself, she loves not at the common rate.

LOVE'S WITNESS

Slight unpremeditated words are borne
    By every common wind into the air ;
Carelessly uttered, die as soon as born,
    And in one instant give both hope and fear :
Breathing all contraries with the same wind,
According to the caprice of the mind.

But billet-doux are constant witnesses,
    Substantial records to eternity ;
Just evidence, who the truth confess,
    On which the lover safely may rely ;
They're serious thoughts, digested and resolved ;
And last when words are into clouds devolved.

I will not doubt, but you give credit to all that
is kind in my letters ; and I will believe, you find
a satisfaction in the entertainment they give you, and
that the hour of reading them is not disagreeable to
you. I could wish, your pleasure might be extreme,
even to the degree of suffering the thought of my
absence not to diminish any part of it. And I could
wish too, at the end of your reading, you would sigh
with pleasure, and say to yourself :

THE TRANSPORT

O Iris !   While you thus can charm,
While at this distance you can wound and warm ;
My absent torments I will bless and bear,
That give me such dear proofs how kind you are.
Present, the valued store was only seen,
Now I am rifling the bright mass within.

Every dear, past, and happy day,
When languishing at Iris' feet I lay ;
When all my prayers and all my tears could move
No more than her permission, I should love :
Vain with my glorious destiny,
I thought, beyond, scarce any Heaven could be.

But, charming maid, now I am taught,
That absence has a thousand joys to give,
On which the lovers present never thought,
That recompense the hours we grieve.
Rather by absence let me be undone,
Than forfeit all the pleasures that has won.

With this little rapture, I wish you would finish the reading my letters, shut your escritoire, and quit your cabinet ; for my love leads to eleven o'clock.

ELEVEN O'CLOCK

THE HOUR TO WRITE IN

If my watch did not inform you it is now time to write, I believe, Damon, your heart would, and tell you also that I should take it kindly, if you would employ a whole hour that way ; and that you should never lose an occasion of writing to me, since you are assured of the welcome I give your letters. Perhaps you will say, an hour is too much, and that it is not the mode to write long letters.   I grant you, Damon, when we write those indifferent ones of gallantry in course, or necessary compliment; the handsome comprising of which in the fewest words, renders them the most agreeable: but in love we have a thousand foolish things to say, that of themselves bear no great sound, but have a mighty sense in love; for there is a peculiar eloquence natural alone to a lover, and to be understood by no other creature. To those, words have a thousand graces and sweetnesses; which, to the unconcerned, appear meanness, and easy sense, at the best. But, Damon, you and I are none of those ill judges of the beauties of love; we can penetrate beyond the vulgar, and perceive the fine soul in every line, through all the humble dress of phrase; when possibly they who think they discern it best in florid language, do not see it at all. Love was not born or bred in courts, but cottages; and, nursed in groves and shades, smiles on the plains, and wantons in the streams; all unadored and harmless. Therefore, Damon, do not consult your wit in this affair, but love alone; speak all that he and nature taught you, and let the fine things you learn in schools alone. Make use of those flowers you have gathered there, when you conversed with statesmen and the gown. Let Iris possess your heart in all its simple innocence, that is the best eloquence to her that loves: and that is my instruction to a lover that would succeed in his amours; for I have a heart very difficult to please, and this is the nearest way to it.

ADVICE TO LOVERS

Lovers, if you would gain the heart
   Of Damon, learn to win the prize;
He'll show you all its tend'rest part,
   And where its greatest danger lies;
The magazine of its disdain,
Where honour, feebly guarded, does remain.

If present, do but little say;
   Enough the silent lover speaks:
But wait, and sigh, and gaze all day;
   Such rhetoric more than language takes.
For words the dullest way do move;
And uttered more to show your wit than love.

Let your eyes tell her of your heart ;
  Its story is, for words, too delicate.
Souls thus exchange, and thus impart,
  And all their secrets can relate.
A tear, a broken sigh, she'll understand ;
Or the soft trembling pressings of the hand.

Or if your pain must be in words exprest,
  Let them fall gently, unassured, and slow ;
And where they fail, your looks may tell the rest :
  Thus Damon spoke, and I was conquered so.
The witty talker has mistook his art ;
The modest lover only charms the heart.

Thus, while all day you gazing sit,
  And fear to speak, and fear your fate,
You more advantages by silence get,
  Than the gay forward youth with all his prate.
Let him be silent here ; but when away,
Whatever love can dictate, let him say.

There let the bashful soul unveil,
  And give a loose to love and truth ;
Let him improve the amorous tale,
  With all the force of words, and fire of youth ;
There all, and anything let him express ;
Too long he cannot write, too much confess.

O Damon ! How well have you made me understand this soft pleasure ! You know my tenderness
too well, not to be sensible how I am charmed with
your agreeable long letters.

THE INVENTION

Ah ! he who first found out the way
Souls to each other to convey,
Without dull speaking, sure must be,
Something above humanity.
Let the fond world in vain dispute,
And the first sacred mystery impute
Of letters to the learned brood,
And of the glory cheat a god :
'Twas Love alone that first the art essayed,
And Psyche was the first fair yielding maid,
That was by the dear billet-doux betrayed.

It is an art too ingenious to have been found out
by man, and too necessary to lovers, not to have
been invented by the god of love himself. But,
Damon, I do not pretend to exact from you those
letters of gallantry, which, I have told you, are filled
with nothing but fine thoughts, and writ with all the
arts of wit and subtilty : I would have yours still all
tender unaffected love, words unchosen, thoughts un-
studied, and love unfeigned. I had rather find more
softness than wit in your passion ; more of nature
than of art ; more of the lover than the poet.

Nor would I have you write any of those little
short letters, that are read over in a minute ; in love,
long letters bring a long pleasure : do not trouble
yourself to make them fine, or write a great deal of
wit and sense in a few lines ; that is the notion of a
witty billet, in any affair but that of love. And have
a care rather to avoid these graces to a mistress ; and
assure yourself, dear Damon, that what pleases the
soul pleases the eye, and the largeness or bulk of
your letter shall never offend me ; and that I only am
displeased when I find them small. A letter is ever the
best and most powerful agent to a mistress, it almost
always persuades, it is always renewing little impressions, that possibly otherwise absence would
deface. Make use then, Damon, of your time while
it is given you, and thank me that I permit you to
write to me. Perhaps I shall not always continue in
the humour of suffering you to do so ; and it may so
happen, by some turn of chance and fortune, that you
may be deprived, at the same time, both of my
presence, and of the means of sending to me. I will
believe that such an accident would be a great misfortune to you, for I have often heard you say, that
'To make the most happy lover suffer martyrdom,
one need only forbid him seeing, speaking and writing
to the object he loves.' Take all the advantages then
you can, you cannot give me too often marks too
powerful of your passion . write therefore during this

hour, every day. I give you leave to believe, that
while you do so, you are serving me the most obligingly and agreeably you can, while absent; and that
you are giving me a remedy against all grief, uneasiness, melancholy, and despair; nay, if you exceed
your hour, you need not be ashamed. The time you
employ in this kind devoir, is the time that I shall be
grateful for, and no doubt will recompense it. You
ought not however to neglect heaven for me; I will
give you time for your devotion, for my watch tells
you it is time to go to the temple.

TWELVE O'CLOCK

INDISPENSABLE DUTY

There are certain duties which one ought never to
neglect: that of adoring the gods is of this nature;
and which we ought to pay, from the bottom of our
hearts: and that, Damon, is the only time I will dispense with your not thinking on me. But I would
not have you go to one of those temples, where the
celebrated beauties, and those that make a profession
of gallantry, go; and who come thither only to see,
and be seen; and whither they repair, more to show
their beauty and dress, than to honour the gods. If
you will take my advice, and oblige my wish, you
shall go to those that are least frequented, and you
shall appear there like a man that has a perfect
veneration for all things sacred.

THE INSTRUCTION

Damon, if your heart and flame,
You wish, should always be the same,
Do not give it leave to rove,
   Nor expose it to new harms:
Ere you think on't, you may love,
   If you gaze on beauty's charms:
If with me you would not part,
Turn your eyes into your heart.

If you find a new desire
In your easy soul take fire,
From the tempting ruin fly ;
 Think it faithless, think it base:
Fancy soon will fade and die,
 If you wisely cease to gaze.
Lovers should have honour too,
Or they pay but half Love's due.

Do not to the temple go,
With design to gaze or show :
Whate'er thoughts you have abroad,
 Though you can deceive elsewhere,
There's no feigning with your God ;
 Souls should be all perfect there.
The heart that's to the altar brought,
Only heaven should fill its thought.

Do not your sober thoughts perplex,
By gazing on the ogling sex :
Or if beauty call your eyes,
 Do not on the object dwell ;
Guard your heart from the surprise,
 By thinking Iris doth excel.
Above all earthly things I'd be,
Damon, most beloved by thee ;
And only heaven must rival me.

ONE O'CLOCK

FORCED ENTERTAINMENT

I perceive it will be very difficult to you to quit the temple, without being surrounded with compliments from people of ceremony, friends, and newsmongers, and several of those sorts of persons, who afflict and busy themselves, and rejoice at a hundred things they have no interest in ; coquettes and politicians, who make it the business of their whole lives, to gather all the news of the town ; adding or diminishing according to the stock of their wit and invention, and spreading it all abroad to the believing fools and gossips ; and perplexing everybody with a hundred

ridiculous novels, which they pass off for wit and
entertainment. Or else some of those recounters of
adventures, that are always telling of intrigues, and
that make a secret to a hundred people of a thousand
foolish things they have heard: like a certain pert
and impertinent lady of the town, whose youth and
beauty being past, set up for wit, to uphold a feeble
empire over hearts; and whose character is this:

THE COQUETTE

Milanda, who had never been
Esteem'd a beauty at fifteen,
Always amorous was, and kind:
   To every swain she lent an ear;
Free as air, but false as wind;
   Yet none complained she was severe.
She eased more than she made complain
Was always singing, pert, and vain.

Where'er the throng was, she was seen,
And swept the youths along the green
With equal grace she flattered all;
   And fondly proud of all address,
Her smiles invite, her eyes do call,
   And her vain heart her looks confess.
She rallies this, to that she bowed,
Was talking ever, laughing loud.

On every side she makes advance,
And everywhere a confidence;
She tells for secrets all she knows,
   And all to know she does pretend:
Beauty in maids she treats as foes:
   But every handsome youth as friend.

Scandal still passes off for truth;
And noise and nonsense, wit and youth.
Coquette all o'er, and every part,
Yet wanting beauty, even of art;
Herds with the ugly, and the old;
   And plays the critic on the rest:
Of men, the bashful, and the bold,
   Either, and all, by turns, likes best:
Even now, though youth be languished, she
Sets up for love and gallantry.

This sort of creature, Damon, is very dangerous; not that I fear you will squander away a heart upon her, but your hours; for, in spite of you, she'll detain you with a thousand impertinences, and eternal tattle. She passes for a judging wit; and there is nothing so troublesome as such a pretender. She, perhaps, may get some knowledge of our correspondence; and then, no doubt, will improve it to my disadvantage. Possibly she may rail at me; that is her fashion by the way of friendly speaking; and an awkward commendation, the most effectual way of defaming and traducing. Perhaps she tells you, in a cold tone, that you are a happy man to be beloved by me: that Iris indeed is handsome, and she wonders she has no more lovers; but the men are not of her mind; if they were, you should have more rivals. She commends my face, but that I have blue eyes, and it is a pity my complexion is no better: my shape but too much inclining to fat. Cries—she would charm infinitely with her wit, but that she knows too well she is mistress of it. And concludes, ——but altogether she is well enough. Thus she runs on without giving you leave to edge in a word in my defence; and ever and anon crying up her own conduct and management: tells you how she is oppressed with lovers, and fatigued with addresses; and recommending herself, at every turn, with a perceivable cunning. And all the while is jilting you of your good opinion; which she would buy at the price of anybody's repose, or her own fame, though but for the vanity of adding to the number of her lovers. When she sees a new spark, the first thing she does, she inquires into his estate; if she finds it such as may (if the coxcomb be well managed) supply her vanity, she makes advances to him, and applies herself to all those little arts, she usually makes use of to gain her fools; and according to his humour dresses and affects her own. But, Damon, since I point to no particular person in this character, I will

not name who you should avoid ; but all of this sort
I conjure you, wheresoever you find them.   But if
unlucky chance throw you in their way, hear all they
say, without credit or regard, as far as decency will
suffer you ; hear them without approving their foppery ; and hear them without giving them cause to
censure you.   But it is so much lost time to listen to
all the novels this sort of people will perplex you
with ; whose business is to be idle, and who even
tire themselves with their own impertinences.   And
be assured after all there is nothing they can tell
you that is worth your knowing.   And Damon, a
perfect lover never asks any news but of the maid
he loves.

THE INQUIRY

Damon, if your love be true
    To the heart that you possess,
Tell me what you have to do
    Where you have no tenderness?
Her affairs who cares to learn,
For whom he has not some concern?

If a lover fain would know
If the object loved be true,
Let her but industrious be
To watch his curiosity ;
Though ne'er so cold his questions seem,
They come from warmer thoughts within.

When I hear a swain inquire
    What gay Melinda does to live,
I conclude there is some fire
    In a heart inquisitive ;
Or 'tis, at least, the bill that's set
To show, the heart is to be let.

TWO O'CLOCK

DINNER-TIME

Leave all those fond entertainments or you will disoblige me, and make dinner wait for you; for my cupid tells you it is that hour. Love does not pretend to make you lose that; nor is it my province to order you your diet. Here I give you a perfect liberty to do what you please; and possibly, it is the only hour in the whole four-and-twenty that I will absolutely resign you, or dispense with your even so much as thinking on me. It is true, in seating yourself at table, I would not have you placed over against a very beautiful object; for in such a one there are a thousand little graces in speaking, looking, and laughing, that fail not to charm, if one gives way to the eyes, to gaze and wander that way; in which, perhaps, in spite of you, you will find a pleasure. And while you do so, though without design or concern, you give the fair charmer a sort of vanity in believing you have placed yourself there, only for the advantage of looking on her; and she assumes a hundred little graces and affectations which are not natural to her, to complete a conquest, which she believes so well begun already. She softens her eyes, and sweetens her mouth; and in fine, puts on another air than when she had no design, and when you did not, by your continual looking on her, rouse her vanity, and increase her easy opinion of her own charms. Perhaps she knows I have some interest in your heart, and prides herself, at least, with believing she has attracted the eyes of my lover, if not his heart; and thinks it easy to vanquish the whole, if she pleases; and triumphs over me in her secret imaginations. Remember, Damon, that while you act thus in the company and conversation of other beauties, every look or word you give in favour of them, is an indignity to my reputation; and which you cannot suffer if you love me truly, and with honour: and assure yourself, so much vanity as you inspire in her, so much fame you rob me of; for whatever praises you give another beauty, so much you take away from mine. Therefore, if you dine in company, do as others do: be generally civil, not applying yourself by words or looks to any particular person: be as gay as you please; talk and laugh with all, for this is not the hour for chagrin.

THE PERMISSION

My Damon, though I stint your love,
   I will not stint your appetite;
That I would have you still improve,
   By every new and fresh delight.
Feast till Apollo hides his head,
Or drink the amorous god to Thetis' bed.

Be like yourself: all witty, gay!
   And o'er the bottle bless the board;
The listening round will, all the day,
   Be charmed, and pleased with every word.
Though Venus' son inspire your wit,
'Tis the Silenian god best utters it.

Here talk of everything but me,
   Since ev'rything you say with grace:
If not disposed your humour be,
   And you'd this hour in silence pass;
Since something must the subject prove
Of Damon's thoughts, let it be me and Love.

But, Damon, this enfranchised hour,
   No bounds, or laws, will I impose;
But leave it wholly in your power,
   What humour to refuse or choose:
I rules prescribe but to your flame;
For I, your mistress, not physician, am

THREE O'CLOCK

VISITS TO FRIENDS

Damon, my watch is juster than you imagine; it would not have you live retired and solitary, but permits you to go and make visits. I am not one of those that believe love and friendship cannot find a place in one and the same heart. And that man would be very unhappy, who, as soon as he had a mistress, should be obliged to renounce the society of his friends. I must confess I would not that you should have so much concern for them, as you have for me; for I have heard a sort of a proverb that says ' He cannot be very fervent in love, who is not a little cold in friendship.' You are not ignorant, that when Love establishes himself in a heart, he reigns a tyrant there, and will not suffer even friendship, if it pretend to share his empire there.

CUPID

Love is a god, whose charming sway
Both heaven, and earth, and seas obey;
A power that will not mingled be
With any dull equality.
Since first from heaven, which gave him birth,
He ruled the empire of the earth;
Jealous of sov'reign power he rules,
And will be absolute in souls.

I should be very angry if you had any of those friendships which one ought to desire in a mistress only; for many times it happens that you have sentiments a little too tender for those amiable persons; and many times love and friendship are so confounded together, that one cannot easily discern one from the other. I have seen a man flatter himself with an opinion, that he had but an esteem for a woman, when by some turn of fortune in her life,

as marrying, or receiving the addresses of men, he
has found by spite and jealousies within, that that
was love, which he before took for complaisance or
friendship.   Therefore have a care, for such amities
are dangerous : not but that a lover may have fair
and generous female friends, whom he ought to
visit; and perhaps I should esteem you less, if I
did not believe you were valued by such, if I were
perfectly assured they were friends and not lovers.
But have a care you hide not a mistress under this
veil, or that you gain not a lover by this pretence :
for you may begin with friendship, and end with
love ; and I should be equally afflicted should you give
it or receive it.   And though you charge our sex with
all the vanity, yet I often find nature to have given
you as large a portion of that common crime, which
you would shuffle off, as ashamed to own ; and are
as fond and vain of the imagination of a conquest,
as any coquette of us all : though at the same time
you despise the victim, you think it adds a trophy
to your fame.   And I have seen a man dress and
trick, and adjust his looks and mien to make a visit
to a woman he loved not, nor ever could love, as for
those he made to his mistress ; and only for the
vanity of making a conquest upon a heart, even
unworthy of the little pains he has taken about it.
And what is this but buying vanity at the expense
of ease ; and with fatigue to purchase the name
of a conceited fop, besides that of a dishonest man ?
For he who takes pains to make himself beloved,
only to please his curious humour, though he should
say nothing that tends to it, more than by his looks,
his sighs, and now and then breaking into praises
and commendations of the object ; by the care he
takes, to appear well dressed before her, and in good
order, he lies in his looks, he deceives with his mien
and fashion, and cheats with every motion, and every
grace he puts on.   He cozens when he sings or
dances ; he dissembles when he sighs : and every-

thing he does that wilfully gains upon her, is malice prepense, baseness, and art below a man of sense or virtue: and yet these arts, these cozenages, are the common practices of the town. What is this but that damnable vice, of which they so reproach our sex; that of jilting for hearts? And it is in vain that my lover, after such foul play, shall think to appease me, with saying 'He did it to try how easy he could conquer, and of how great force his charms were; and why should I be angry if all the town loved him, since he loved none but Iris?' Oh foolish pleasure! How little sense goes to the making of such a happiness! And how little love must he have for one particular person, who would wish to inspire it into all the world, and yet himself pretend to be insensible! But this, Damon, is rather what is but too much practised by your sex, than any guilt I charge on you: though vanity be an ingredient that nature very seldom omits in the composition of either sex; and you may be allowed a tincture of it at least. And, perhaps, I am not wholly exempt from this leaven in my nature, but accuse myself sometimes of finding a secret joy of being adored, though I even hate my worshipper. But if any such pleasure touch my heart, I find it at the same time blushing in my cheeks with a guilty shame, which soon checks the petty triumphs; and I have a virtue at soberer thoughts, that I find surmounts my weakness and indiscretion; and I hope Damon finds the same: for, should he have any of those attachments, I should have no pity for him.

THE EXAMPLE

Damon, if you'd have me true,
   Be you my precedent and guide:
Example sooner we pursue,
   Than the dull dictates of our pride.
Precepts of virtue are too weak an aim:
'Tis demonstration that can best reclaim.

Show me the path you'd have me go ;
    With such a guide I cannot stray :
What you approve, whate'er you do,
    It is but just I bend the way.
If true, my honour favours your design ;
If false, revenge is the result of mine.

A lover true, a maid sincere,
    Are to be prized as things divine :
'Tis justice makes the blessing dear,
    Justice of love without design.
And she that reigns not in a heart alone,
Is never safe, or easy, on her throne.

FOUR O'CLOCK

GENERAL CONVERSATION

In this visiting-hour, many people will happen to meet at one and the same time together, in a place : and as you make not visits to friends, to be silent, you ought to enter into conversation with them; but those conversations ought to be general, and of general things : for there is no necessity of making your friend the confidant of your amours. It would infinitely displease me, to hear you have revealed to them all that I have reposed in you; though secrets ever so trivial, yet since uttered between lovers, they deserve to be prized at a higher rate. For what can show a heart more indifferent and indiscreet, than to declare in any fashion, or with mirth, or joy, the tender things a mistress says to her lover ; and which possibly, related at second hand, bear not the same sense, because they have not the same sound and air they had originally, when they came from the soft heart of her, who sighed them first to her lavish lover ? Perhaps they are told again with mirth, or joy, unbecoming their character and business; and then they lose their graces : (for love is the most solemn thing in nature, and the most unsuiting with gaiety). Perhaps the soft expressions suit not so

well the harsher voice of the masculine lover, whose
accents were not formed for so much tenderness; at
least, not of that sort: for words that have the same
meaning, are altered from their sense by the least
tone or accent of the voice; and those proper and
fitted to my soul, are not possibly so to yours,
though both have the same efficacy upon us; yours
upon my heart, as mine upon yours: and both will
be misunderstood by the unjudging world. Besides
this, there is a holiness in love that is true, that ought
not to be profaned. And as the poet truly says, at
the latter end of an ode, of which I will recite the
whole:

THE INVITATION

Amynta, fear not to confess
The charming secret of thy tenderness:
    That which a lover can't conceal,
    That which, to me, thou shouldst reveal;
And is but what thy lovely eyes express.
    Come, whisper to my panting heart,
That heaves and meets thy voice half-way;
    That guesses what thou wouldst impart,
And languishes for what thou hast to say.
Confirm my trembling doubt, and make me know,
Whence all these blessings, and these sighings flow.

Why dost thou scruple to unfold
A mystery that does my life concern?
    If thou ne'er speakest, it will be told;
For lovers all things can discern.
From every look, from every bashful grace,
That still succeed each other in thy face,
I shall the dear transporting secret learn:
    But 'tis a pleasure not to be exprest,
    To hear it by the voice confest,
    When soft sighs breathe it on my panting breast.

All calm and silent is the grove,
Whose shading boughs resist the day;
    Here thou may'st blush, and talk of love,
While only winds, unheeding, stay,
That will not bear the sound away:
    While I with solemn awful joy,
    All my attentive faculties employ;

Listening to every valued word ;
And in my soul the secret treasure hoard :
   There like some mystery divine,
   The wondrous knowledge I'll enshrine.
Love can his joys no longer call his own,
That the dear secret's kept unknown.

There is nothing more true than those two last lines :
and that love ceases to be a pleasure, when it ceases
to be a secret, and one you ought to keep sacred.
For the world, which never makes a right judgment
of things, will misinterpret love, as they do religion ;
everyone judging it, according to the notion he hath
of it, or the talent of his sense. Love (as a great
Duke said) is like apparitions ; everyone talks of
them, but few have seen them. Everybody thinks
himself capable of understanding love, and that he is
a master in the art of it ; when there is nothing so
nice, or difficult, to be rightly comprehended ; and
indeed cannot be, but to a soul very delicate. Nor
will he make himself known to the vulgar : there
must be an uncommon fineness in the mind that contains him ; the rest he only visits in as many dis-
guises as there are dispositions and natures, where he
makes but a short stay, and is gone. He can fit
himself to all hearts, being the greatest flatterer in
the world : and he possesses everyone with a confidence, that they are in the number of his elect ; and
they think they know him perfectly, when nothing
but the spirits refined possess him in his excellency.
From this difference of love, in different souls, proceed those odd fantastic maxims, which so many
hold of so different kinds. And this makes the most
innocent pleasures pass oftentimes for crimes, with
the unjudging crowd, who call themselves lovers.
And you will have your passion censured by as many
as you shall discover it to, and as many several ways.
I advise you therefore, Damon, to make no confidants
of your amours ; and believe, that silence has, with
me, the most powerful charm.

'Tis also in these conversations, that those indiscreetly civil persons often are, who think to oblige a good man, by letting him know he is beloved by someone or other; and making him understand how many good qualities he is master of, to render him agreeable to the fair sex, if he would but advance where love and good fortune call; and that a too constant lover loses a great part of his time, which might be managed to more advantage, since youth hath so short a race to run. This, and a thousand the like indecent complaisances, give him a vanity that suits not with that discretion, which has hitherto acquired him so good a reputation. I would not have you, Damon, act on these occasions, as many of the easy sparks have done before you, who receive such weakness and flattery for truth; and passing it off with a smile, suffer them to advance in folly, till they have gained a credit with them, and they believe all they hear, telling them they do so, by consenting gestures, silence, or open approbation. For my part, I should not condemn a lover that should answer a sort of civil brokers for love, somewhat briskly; and by giving them to understand they are already engaged, or directing them to fools, that will possibly hearken to them, and credit such stuff, shame them out of a folly so infamous and disingenuous. In such a case only I am willing you should own your passion; not that you need tell the object which has charmed you. And you may say, you are already a lover, without saying you are beloved. For so long as you appear to have a heart unengaged, you are exposed to all the little arts and addresses of this sort of obliging procurers of love, and give way to the hope they have of making you their proselyte. For your own reputation then, and my ease and honour, shun such conversations; for they are neither creditable to you, nor pleasing to me. And believe me, Damon, a true lover has no curiosity, but what concerns his mistress.

FIVE O'CLOCK

DANGEROUS VISITS

I foresee, or fear, that these busy impertinent friends will oblige you to visit some ladies of their acquaintance, or yours; my watch does not forbid you. Yet I must tell you, I apprehend danger in such visits; and I fear, you will have need of all your care and precaution, in these encounters, that you may give me no cause to suspect you. Perhaps you will argue, that civility obliges you to it. If I were assured there would no other design be carried on, I should believe it were to advance an enormous prudence too far, to forbid you. Only keep yourself upon your guard; for the business of most part of the fair sex, is, to seek only the conquest of hearts. All their civilities are but so many interests; and they do nothing without design. And in such conversations there is always a *Je ne sais quoi*, that is feared, especially when beauty is accompanied with youth and gaiety; and which they assume upon all occasions that may serve their turn. And I confess it is not an easy matter to be just in these hours and conversations: the most certain way of being so, is to imagine I read all your thoughts, observe all your looks, and hear all your words.

THE CAUTION

My Damon, if your heart be kind,
　　Do not too long with beauty stay;
For there are certain moments when the mind
　　Is hurried by the force of charms away.
In fate a minute critical there lies,
That waits on Love, and takes you by surprise.

A lover pleased with constancy,
Lives still as if the maid he loved were by :
 As if his actions were in view,
 As if his steps she did pursue ;
 Or that his very soul she knew.
Take heed ; for though I am not present there,
My Love, my genius waits you everywhere.

I am very much pleased with the remedy, you say,
you make use of to defend yourself from the attacks
that beauty gives your heart ; which in one of your
billets, you said was this, or to this purpose :

THE CHARM FOR CONSTANCY

Iris, to keep my soul entire and true,
It thinks, each moment of the day, on you.
 And when a charming face I see,
  That does all other eyes incline,
 It has no influence on me :
  I think it ev'n deformed to thine.
My eyes, my soul, and sense, regardless move
To all, but the dear object of my love.

But, Damon, I know all lovers are naturally flatterers, though they do not think so themselves ;
because everyone makes a sense of beauty according
to his own fancy. But perhaps you will say in your
own defence, that it is not flattery to say an un-
beautiful woman is beautiful, if he that says so believes she is so. I should be content to acquit you
of the first, provided you allow me the last : and if I
appear charming in Damon's eyes, I am not fond of
the approbation of any other. It is enough the world
thinks me not altogether disagreeable, to justify his
choice ; but let your good opinion give what increase
it pleases to my beauty, though your approbation
give me a pleasure, it shall not a vanity ; and I am
contented that Damon should think me a beauty,
without my believing I am one. It is not to draw
new assurances, and new vows from you, that I speak

this; though tales of love are the only ones we desire
to hear often told, and which never tire the hearers if
addressed to themselves. But it is not to this end I
now seem to doubt what you say to my advantage:
no, my heart knows no disguise, nor can dissemble
one thought of it to Damon; it is all sincere, and
honest as his wish. Therefore it tells you, it does not
credit everything you say; though I believe you say
abundance of truths in a great part of my character.
But when you advance to that, which my own sense,
my judgment, or my glass cannot persuade me to
believe, you must give me leave either to believe you
think me vain enough to credit you, or pleased that
your sentiments and mine are differing in this point.
But I doubt I may rather reply in some verses, a
friend of yours and mine sent to a person she thought
had but indifferent sentiments for her; yet, who nevertheless flattered her, because he imagined she had a
very great esteem for him. She is a woman that, you
know, naturally hates flattery: on the other side she
was extremely dissatisfied, and uneasy at his opinion
of his being more in her favour than she desired he
should believe. So that one night having left her full
of pride and anger, she next morning sent him these
verses, instead of a billet-doux.

THE DEFIANCE

> By Heaven 'tis false, I am not vain;
>   And rather would the subject be
> Of your indifference, or disdain,
>   Than wit or raillery.
>
> Take back the trifling praise you give,
>   And pass it on some easier fool,
> Who may the injuring wit believe,
>   That turns her into ridicule.
>
> Tell her, she's witty, fair and gay,
>   With all the charms that can subdue:
> Perhaps she'll credit what you say;
>   But curse me if I do.

If your diversion you design,
  On my good-nature you have prest:
Or if you do intend it mine,
  You have mistook the jest.

Philander, fly that guilty art:
  Your charming facile wit will find,
It cannot play on any heart,
  That is sincere and kind.

For wit with softness to reside,
  Good-nature is with pity stored;
But flattery's the result of pride,
  And fawns to be adored.

Nay, even when you smile and bow,
  'Tis to be rendered more complete:
Your wit, with ev'ry grace you show,
  Is but a popular cheat.

Laugh on, and call me coxcomb—do;
  And, your opinion to improve,
Think, all you think of me is true;
  And to confirm it, swear I love.

Then, while you wreck my soul with pain,
  And of a cruel conquest boast,
'Tis you, Philander, that are vain,
  And witty at my cost.

Possibly, the angry Amynta, when she writ these
verses, was more offended, that he believed himself
beloved, than that he flattered; though she would
seem to make that a great part of the quarrel, and
cause of her resentment. For we are often in a
humour to seem more modest in that point, than
naturally we are; being too apt to have a favourable
opinion of ourselves: and it is rather the effects of
a fear that we are flattered, than our own ill opinion
of the beauty flattered; and that the praiser thinks
not so well of it, as we do ourselves, or at least we
wish he should. Not but there are grains of allow-
ance for the temper of him that speaks. One man's
humour is to talk much; and he may be permitted
to enlarge upon the praise he gives the person he

pretends to, without being accused of much guilt. Another hates to be wordy; from such a one, I have known one soft expression, one tender thing, go as far as whole days' everlasting protestations urged with vows, and mighty eloquence. And both the one and the other, indeed, must be allowed in good manners, to stretch the compliment beyond the bounds of nice truth: and we must not wonder to hear a man call a woman a beauty, when she is not ugly; or another a great wit, if she have but common-sense above the vulgar; well bred, when well dressed; and good-natured, when civil. And as I should be very ridiculous, if I took all you said for absolute truth; so I should be very unjust, not to allow you very sincere in almost all you said besides; and those things, the most material to love, honour, and friendship. And for the rest, Damon, be it true or false, this believe, you speak with such a grace, that I cannot choose but credit you; and find an infinite pleasure in that faith, because I love you. And if I cannot find the cheat, I am contented you should deceive me on, because you do it so agreeably.

SIX O'CLOCK

WALK WITHOUT DESIGN

You yet have time to walk; and my watch foresaw you could not refuse your friends. You must to the Park, or to the Mall; for the season is fair and inviting, and all the young beauties love those places too well, not to be there. It is there that a thousand intrigues are carried on, and as many more designed. It is there that everyone is set out for conquest; and who aim at nothing less than hearts. Guard yours well, my Damon; and be not always admiring what you see. Do not, in passing by, sigh them silent

praises. Suffer not so much as a guilty wish to
approach your thoughts, nor a heedful glance to steal
from your fine eyes : those are regards you ought
only to have for her you love. But oh ! above all,
have a care of what you say. You are not reproach-
able, if you should remain silent all the time of your
walk ; nor would those that know you believe it the
effects of dulness, but melancholy. And if any of
your friends ask you why you are so, I will give
you leave to sigh, and say :

THE MALCONTENT

Ah ! wonder not if I appear
Regardless of the pleasures here ;
Or that my thoughts are thus confined
To the just limits of my mind.
My eyes take no delight to rove
O'er all the smiling charmers of the grove,
Since she is absent whom they love.

Ask me not, Why the flow'ry spring,
Or the gay little birds that sing,
Or the young streams no more delight,
Or shades and arbours can't invite ?
Why the soft murmurs of the wind,
Within the thick-grown groves confined,
No more my soul transport, or cheer ;
Since all that's charming—Iris, is not here ;
Nothing seems glorious, nothing fair.

Then suffer me to wander thus,
With downcast eyes, and arms across :
Let beauty unregarded go ;
The trees and flowers unheeded strow ;
Let purling streams neglected glide ;
With all the spring's adorning pride.
'Tis Iris only soul can give
To the dull shades, and plains, and make them thrive ;
Nature and my last joys retrieve.

I do not, for all this, wholly confine your eyes :
you may look indifferently on all, but with a particular regard on none. You may praise all the

beauties in general, but no single one too much. I
will not exact from you neither an entire silence.
There are a thousand civilities you ought to pay to
all your friends and acquaintance; and while I
caution you of actions, that may get you the reputation of a lover of some of the fair that haunt those
places, I would not have you, by an unnecessary and
uncomplaisant sullenness, gain that of a person too
negligent or morose. I would have you remiss in
no one punctilio of good manners. I would have
you very just, and pay all you owe; but in these
affairs be not over generous, and give away too much.
In fine, you may look, speak, and walk; but, Damon,
do it all without design : and while you do so, remember that Iris sent you this advice.

THE WARNING

Take heed, my Damon, in the grove,
Where beauties with design do walk ;
Take heed, my Damon, how you look and talk,
 For there are ambuscades of love.
The very winds that softly blow,
 Will help betray your easy heart ;
And all the flowers that blushing grow,
The shades about, and rivulets below,
 Will take the victor's part.

Remember, Damon, all thy safety lies
In the just conduct of your eyes.
The heart, by nature good and brave,
Is to those treacherous guards a slave.
 If they let in the fair destructive foe,
Scarce honour can defend her noble seat :
 Ev'n she will be corrupted too,
 Or driven to a retreat.
The soul is but the cully to the sight,
And must be pleased in what that takes delight.

Therefore examine yourself well; and conduct your
eyes, during this walk, like a lover that seeks nothing:
and do not stay too long in these places.

SEVEN O'CLOCK

VOLUNTARY RETREAT

It is time to be weary, it is night: take leave of your friends and retire home. It is in this retreat that you ought to recollect in your thoughts all the actions of the day, and all those things that you ought to give me an account of, in your letter. You cannot hide the least secret from me, without treason against sacred love. For all the world agrees that confidence is one of the greatest proofs of the passion of love; and that lover who refuses his confidence to the person he loves, is to be suspected to love but very indifferently, and to think very poorly of the sense and generosity of his mistress. But that you may acquit yourself like a man, and a lover of honour, and leave me no doubt upon my soul; think of all you have done this day, that I may have all the story of it in your next letter to me: but deal faithfully, and neither add nor diminish in your relation; the truth and sincerity of your confession will atone even for little faults that you shall commit against me, in some of those things you shall tell me. For if you have failed in any point or circumstance of love, I had much rather hear it from you than another: for it is a sort of repentance to accuse yourself; and would be a crime unpardonable, if you suffer me to hear it from any other: and be assured, while you confess it, I shall be indulgent enough to forgive you. The noblest quality of man is sincerity; and, Damon, one ought to have as much of it in love, as in any other business of one's life, notwithstanding the most part of men make no account of it there; but will believe there ought to be double-dealing,

and an art practised in love as well as in war.   But,
oh! beware of that notion.

SINCERITY

Sincerity ! thou greatest good !
   Thou virtue which so many boast !
And art so nicely understood !
   And often in the searching lost !
For when we do approach thee near,
   The fine idea framed of thee,
Appears not now so charming fair
   As the most useful flattery.
Thou hast no glitt'ring to invite ;
Nor takest the lover at first sight.

The modest virtue shuns the crowd,
   And lives, like Vestals, in a cell ;
In cities 'twill not be allowed,
   Nor takes delight in Courts to dwell ;
'Tis nonsense with the man of wit ;
   And ev'n a scandal to the great :
For all the young, and fair, unfit ;
   And scorned by wiser fops of state.
A virtue yet was never known
To the false trader, or the falser gown.

And, Damon, though thy noble blood
   Be most illustrious, and refined ;
Though ev'ry grace and ev'ry good
   Adorn thy person and thy mind :
Yet, if this virtue shine not there,
   This God-like virtue, which alone,
Wert thou less witty, brave, or fair,
   Would for all these, less prized, atone ;
My tender folly I'd control,
And scorn the conquest of thy soul.

EIGHT O'CLOCK

IMPATIENT DEMANDS

After you have sufficiently collected yourself of all the past actions of the day, call your page into your cabinet, or him whom you trusted with your last letter to me; where you ought to inquire of him a thousand things, and all of me. Ask impatiently, and be angry if he answers not your curiosity soon enough. Think that he has a dreaming in his voice, in these moments more than at other times; and reproach him with dulness: for 'tis most certain that when one loves tenderly, we would know in a minute, what cannot be related in an hour. Ask him, How I did? How I received his letter? And if he examined the air of my face, when I took it? If I blushed or looked pale? If my hand trembled, or I spoke to him with short interrupting sighs? If I asked him any questions about you, while I was opening the seal? Or if I could not well speak, and was silent? If I read it attentively, and with joy? And all this, before you open the answer I have sent you by him: which, because you are impatient to read, you, with the more haste and earnestness, demand all you expect from him; and that you may the better know what humour I was in, when I writ that to you. For, oh! a lover has a thousand little fears, and dreads, he knows not why. In fine, make him recount to you all that passed, while he was with me; and then you ought to read that which I have sent, that you may inform yourself of all that passes in my heart: for you may assure yourself, all that I say to you that way proceeds from thence.

THE ASSURANCE

How shall a lover come to know,
Whether he's beloved or no?
What dear things must she impart,
To assure him of her heart?
Is it when her blushes rise;
And she languish in her eyes;
Tremble when he does approach;
Look pale, and faint at ev'ry touch?

Is it, when a thousand ways
She does his wit and beauty praise;
Or she venture to explain,
In less moving words, a pain;
Though so indiscreet she grows,
To confirm it with her vows?

These some short-lived passion moves,
While the object's by she loves;
While the gay and sudden fire
Kindles by some fond desire:
And a coldness will ensue,
When the lover's out of view.
Then she reflects with scandal o'er
The easy scene that passed before:
Then, with blushes, would recall
The unconsidering criminal;
In which a thousand faults she'll find,
And chide the errors of her mind.
Such fickle weight is found in words,
As no substantial faith affords:
Deceived and baffled all may be,
Who trust that frail security.

But a well-digested flame,
That will always be the same;
And that does from merit grow,
Established by our reason too;
By a better way will prove,
'Tis th' unerring fire of love.
Lasting records it will give:
And, that all she says may live;
Sacred and authentic stand,
Her heart confirms it by her hand.
If this, a maid, well-born, allow;
Damon, believe her just and true.

NINE O'CLOCK

MELANCHOLY REFLECTIONS

You will not have much trouble to explain what my watch designs here. There can be no thought more afflicting, than that of the absence of a mistress: and which the sighings of the heart will soon make you find. Ten thousand fears oppress him; he is jealous of everybody, and envies those eyes and ears that are charmed by being near the object adored. He grows impatient, and makes a thousand resolutions, and as soon abandons them all. He gives himself wholly up to the torment of uncertainty; and by degrees, from one cruel thought to another, winds himself up to insupportable chagrin. Take this hour then, to think on your misfortunes, which cannot be small to a soul that is wholly sensible of love. And everyone knows, that a lover, deprived of the object of his heart, is deprived of all the world, and inconsolable: for though one wishes without ceasing for the dear charmer one loves, and though you speak of her every minute; though you are writing to her every day, and though you are infinitely pleased with the dear and tender answer; yet, to speak sincerely, it must be confessed, that the felicity of a true lover is to be always near his mistress. And you may tell me, O Damon! what you please; and say that absence inspires the flame, which perpetual presence would satiate. I love too well to be of that mind, and when I am, I shall believe my passion is declining. I know not whether it advances your love; but surely it must ruin your repose: and it is possible to be, at once, an absent lover, and happy too. For my part, I can meet with nothing that can please in the absence of Damon; but on the contrary I see all things with disgust. I will flatter myself, that it is so with you; and that

the least evils appear great misfortunes; and that all
those who speak to you of anything but of what you
love, increase your pain, by a new remembrance of
her absence.   I will believe that these are your sentiments, when you are assured not to see me in some
weeks; and if your heart do not betray your words,
all those days will be tedious to you.   I would not,
however, have your melancholy too extreme; and to
lessen it, you may persuade yourself, that I partake it
with you: for, I remember, in your last you told me,
you would wish we should be both grieved at the
same time, and both at the same time pleased; and
I believe I love too well not to obey you.

LOVE SECURED

Love, of all joys, the sweetest is,
   The most substantial happiness ;
The softest blessing life can crave,
The noblest passion souls can have.
Yet, if no interruption were,
   No difficulties came between,
'Twould not be rendered half so dear :
   The sky is gayest when small clouds are seen.
The sweetest flower, the blushing rose,
Amidst the thorns securest grows.
If love were one continued joy,
How soon the happiness would cloy !
The wiser god did this foresee ;
   And to preserve the bliss entire,
Mixed it with doubt and jealousy,
   Those necessary fuels to the fire ;
Sustained the fleeting pleasures with new fears ;
With little quarrels, sighs and tears ;
   With absence, that tormenting smart,
That makes a minute seem a day,
   A day a year to the impatient heart,
That languishes in the delay,
But cannot sigh the tender pain away ;
That still returns, and with a greater force,
Through every vein it takes its grateful course.
   But whatsoe'er the lover does sustain,
Though he still sigh, complain, and fear ;
   It cannot be a mortal pain,
When two do the affliction bear.

TEN O'CLOCK

REFLECTIONS

After the afflicting thoughts of my absence, make some reflections on your happiness. Think it a blessing to be permitted to love me ; think it so, because I permit it to you alone, and never could be drawn to allow it any other. The first thing you ought to consider, is, that at length I have suffered myself to be overcome, to quit that nicety that is natural to me, and receive your addresses ; nay, thought them agreeable : and that I have at last confessed, the present of your heart is very dear to me. It is true, I did not accept of it the first time it was offered me, nor before you had told me a thousand times, that you could not escape expiring, if I did not give you leave to sigh for me, and gaze upon me ; and that there was an absolute necessity for me, either to give you leave to love, or die. And all those rigours my severity has made you suffer, ought now to be recounted to your memory, as subjects of pleasure ; and you ought to esteem and judge of the price of my affections, by the difficulties you found in being able to touch my heart. Not but you have charms that can conquer at first sight ; and you ought not to have valued me less, if I had been more easily gained. But it is enough to please you, to think and know I am gained ; no matter when and how. When, after a thousand cares and inquietudes, that which we wish for succeeds to our desires, the remembrance of those pains and pleasures we encountered in arriving at it, gives us a new joy.

Remember also, Damon, that I have preferred you before all those that have been thought worthy of my esteem ; and that I have shut my eyes to all their pleading merits, and could survey none but yours.

Consider then, that you had not only the happiness to please me, but that you only found out the way of doing it, and I had the goodness at last to tell you so, contrary to all the delicacy and niceness of my soul, contrary to my prudence, and all those scruples, you know, are natural to my humour.

My tenderness proceeded further, and I gave you innocent marks of my new-born passion, on all occasions that presented themselves. For, after that from my eyes and tongue you knew the sentiments of my heart, I confirmed that truth to you by my letters. Confess, Damon, that if you make these reflections, you will not pass this hour very disagreeably.

BEGINNING LOVE

As free as wanton winds I lived,
   That unconcerned do play :
No broken faith, no fate I grieved ;
   No fortune gave me joy.
A dull content crowned all my hours,
   My heart no sighs opprest ;
I called in vain on no deaf powers,
   To ease a tortured breast.

The sighing swains regardless pined,
   And strove in vain to please :
With pain I civilly was kind,
   But could afford no ease.
Though wit and beauty did abound,
   The charm was wanting still,
That could inspire the tender wound,
   Or bend my careless will.

Till in my heart a kindling flame
   Your softer sighs had blown ;
Which I, with striving, love and shame,
   Too sensibly did own.
Whate'er the god before could plead ;
   Whate'er the youth's desert ;
The feeble siege in vain was laid
   Against my stubborn heart.

At first my sighs and blushes spoke,
   Just when your sighs would rise ;
And when you gazed, I wished to look,
   But durst not meet your eyes.
I trembled when my hand you pressed,
   Nor could my guilt control ;
But love prevailed, and I confessed
   The secrets of my soul.

And when upon the giving part,
   My present to avow,
By all the ways confirmed my heart,
   That honour would allow ;
Too mean was all that I could say,
   Too poorly understood :
I gave my soul the noblest way,
   My letters made it good.

You may believe I did not easily, nor suddenly,
bring my heart to this condescension ; but I loved,
and all things in Damon were capable of making me
resolve so to do. I could not think it a crime, where
every grace, and every virtue justified my choice.
And when once one is assured of this, we find not
much difficulty in owning that passion which will so
well commend one's judgment ; and there is no
obstacle that love does not surmount. I confessed
my weakness a thousand ways, before I told it you ;
and I remember all those things with pleasure, but
yet I remember them also with shame.

ELEVEN O'CLOCK

SUPPER

I will believe, Damon, that you have been so well
entertained during this hour, and have found so much
sweetness in these thoughts, that if one did not tell
you that supper waits, you would lose yourself in
reflections so pleasing, many more minutes. But you
must go where you are expected ; perhaps, among

the fair, the young, the gay; but do not abandon
your heart to too much joy, though you have so
much reason to be contented : but the greatest
pleasures are always imperfect, if the object beloved
do not partake of it. For this reason be cheerful
and merry with reserve : do not talk too much, I
know you do not love it; and if you do it, it will be
the effect of too much complaisance, or with some
design of pleasing too well; for you know your own
charming power, and how agreeable your wit and
conversation are to all the world. Remember, I am
covetous of every word you speak, that is not
addressed to me, and envy the happy listener, if I
am not by. And I may reply to you as Amynta did
to Philander, when he charged her of loving a talker :
and because, perhaps, you have not heard it, I will,
to divert you, send it to you; and at the same time
assure you, Damon, that your more noble quality, of
speaking little, has reduced me to a perfect abhorrence
of those wordy sparks, that value themselves upon
their ready and much talking upon every trivial
subject, and who have so good an opinion of their
talent that way, they will let nobody edge in a word,
or a reply; but will make all the conversation themselves, that they may pass for very entertaining
persons, and pure company. But the verses :

THE REFORMATION

Philander, since you'll have it so,
  I grant I was impertinent ;
And, till this moment, did not know,
  Through all my life what 'twas I meant.
Your kind opinion was the flattering glass,
In which my mind found how deformed it was.

In your clear sense, which knows no art,
  I saw the errors of my soul ;
And all the foibles of my heart
  With one reflection you control.
Kind as a god, and gently you chastise :
By what you hate, you teach me to be wise.

Impertinence, my sex's shame,
  That has so long my life pursued,
You with such modesty reclaim,
  As all the women has subdued.
To so divine a power what must I owe,
That renders me so like the perfect You?

That conversable thing I hate,
  Already, with a just disdain,
That prides himself upon his prate,
  And is, of words, that nonsense, vain :
When in your few appears such excellence,
As have reproached, and charmed me into sense.

For ever may I listening sit,
  Though but each hour a word be born ;
I would attend thy coming wit,
  And bless what can so well inform.
Let the dull world henceforth to words be damned ;
I'm into nobler sense than talking shamed.

I believe you are so good a lover, as to be of my
opinion ; and that you will neither force yourself
against nature, nor find much occasion to lavish out
those excellent things that must proceed from you,
whenever you speak. If all women were like me, I
should have more reason to fear your silence than
your talk : for you have a thousand ways to charm
without speaking, and those which to me show a
great deal more concern. But, Damon, you know
the greatest part of my sex judge the fine gentleman
by the volubility of his tongue, by his dexterity in
repartee, and cry 'Oh ! he never wants fine things to
say : he's eternally talking the most surprising
things.' But, Damon, you are well assured, I hope,
that Iris is none of these coquettes : at least, if she
had any spark of it once in her nature, she is by the
excellency of your contrary temper taught to know,
and scorn the folly. And take heed your conduct
never gives me cause to suspect you have deceived
me in your temper.

TWELVE O'CLOCK

COMPLAISANCE

Nevertheless, Damon, civility requires a little complaisance after supper; and I am assured, you can never want that, though I confess, you are not accused of too general a complaisance, and do not often make use of it to those persons you have an indifference for: though one is not the less esteemable for having more of this than one ought; and though an excess of it be a fault, it is a very excusable one. Have therefore some for those with whom you are: you may laugh with them, drink with them, dance or sing with them; yet think of me. You may discourse of a thousand indifferent things with them, and at the same time still think of me. If the subject be any beautiful lady, whom they praise, either for her person, wit, or virtue, you may apply it to me: and if you dare not say it aloud, at least, let your heart answer in this language:

> Yes, the fair object, whom you praise,
> Can give us love a thousand ways;
> Her wit and beauty charming are;
> But still my Iris is more fair.

Nobody ever spoke before me of a faithful lover, but still I sighed, and thought of Damon: and ever when they tell me tales of love, any soft pleasing intercourses of an amour; oh! with what pleasures do I listen! and with pleasure answer them, either with my eyes, or tongue:

> That lover may his Sylvia warm,
> But cannot, like my Damon, charm.

If I have not all these excellent qualities you meet with in those beautiful people, I am however very glad that love prepossesses your heart to my advantage : and I need not tell you, Damon, that a true lover ought to persuade himself, that all other objects ought to give place to her, for whom his heart sighs. But see, my Cupid tells you it is one o'clock, and that you ought not to be longer from your apartment ; where, while you are undressing, I will give you leave to say to yourself :

THE REGRET

Alas ! and must the sun decline,
   Before it have informed my eyes
Of all that's glorious, all that's fine,
   Of all I sigh for, all I prize ?
How joyful were those happy days,
When Iris spread her charming rays,
Did my unwearied heart inspire
With never-ceasing awful fire,
And ev'ry minute gave me new desire !
But now, alas ! all dead and pale,
   Like flow'rs that wither in the shade :
Where no kind sunbeams can prevail,
   To raise its cold and fading head,
   I sink into my useless bed.
I grasp the senseless pillow as I lie ;
A thousand times, in vain, I sighing cry,
Ah ! would to heaven my Iris were as nigh.

ONE O'CLOCK

IMPOSSIBILITY TO SLEEP

You have been up long enough ; and Cupid, who takes care of your health, tells you, it is time for you to go to bed. Perhaps you may not sleep as soon as you are laid, and possibly you may pass an hour in bed, before you shut your eyes. In this impossibility of sleeping, I think it very proper for you to imagine what I am doing where I am. Let your fancy take a little journey then, invisible, to observe my actions

and my conduct. You will find me sitting alone in
my cabinet (for I am one that do not love to go to
bed early) and will find me very uneasy and pensive,
pleased with none of those things that so well entertain others. I shun all conversation, as far as civility
will allow, and find no satisfaction like being alone,
where my soul may, without interruption, converse
with Damon. I sigh, and sometimes you will see
my cheeks wet with tears, that insensibly glide down
at a thousand thoughts that present themselves soft
and afflicting. I partake of all your inquietude.
On other things I think with indifference, if ever my
thoughts do stray from the more agreeable object.
I find, however, a little sweetness in this thought,
that, during my absence, your heart thinks of me,
when mine sighs for you. Perhaps I am mistaken,
and that at the same time that you are the entertainment of all my thoughts, I am no more in yours ;
and perhaps you are thinking of those things that
immortalise the young and brave, either by those
glories the Muses flatter you with, or that of Bellona,
and the god of war ; and serving now a monarch,
whose glorious acts in arms has outgone all the
feigned and real heroes of any age, who has, himself,
outdone whatever history can produce of great and
brave, and set so illustrious an example to the under-
world, that it is not impossible, as much a lover as
you are, but you are thinking now how to render
yourself worthy the glory of such a god-like master,
by projecting a thousand things of gallantry and
danger. And though I confess, such thoughts are
proper for your youth, your quality, and the place
you have the honour to hold under our sovereign,
yet let me tell you, Damon, you will not be without
inquietude, if you think of either being a delicate
poet, or a brave warrior ; for love will still interrupt
your glory, however you may think to divert him
either by writing or fighting. And you ought to
remember these verses :

LOVE AND GLORY

Beneath the kind protecting laurel's shade,
For sighing lovers, and for warriors made,
The soft Adonis, and rough Mars were laid.

Both were designed to take their rest ;
But Love the gentle boy opprest,
And false alarms shook the stern hero's breast.

This thinks to soften all his toils of war,
In the dear arms of the obliging fair ;
And that, by hunting, to divert his care.

All day, o'er hills and plains, wild beasts he chased,
Swift as the flying winds, his eager haste ;
In vain, the god of Love pursues as fast.

But oh ! no sports, no toils, divertive prove,
The evening still returns him to the grove,
To sigh and languish for the Queen of Love :

Where elegies and sonnets he does frame,
And to the listening echoes sighs her name,
And on the trees carves records of his flame.

The warrior in the dusty camp all day
With rattling drums and trumpets, does essay
To fright the tender flatt'ring god away.

But still, alas, in vain : whate'er delight,
What cares he takes the wanton boy to fright,
Love still revenges it at night.

'Tis then he haunts the royal tent,
The sleeping hours in sighs are spent,
And all his resolutions does prevent.

In all his pains, Love mixed his smart ;
In every wound he feels a dart ;
And the soft god is trembling in his heart.

Then he retires to shady groves,
And there, in vain, he seeks repose,
And strives to fly from what he cannot lose.

While thus he lay, Bellona came,
And with a gen'rous fierce disdain,
Upbraids him with his feeble flame.

Arise, the world's great terror, and their care ;
Behold the glitt'ring host from far,
That waits the conduct of the god of war.

Beneath these glorious laurels, which were made
To crown the noble victor's head,
Why thus supinely art thou laid ?

Why on that face, where awful terror grew,
Thy sun-parched cheeks why do I view
The shining tracks of falling tears bedew ?

What god has wrought these universal harms ?
What fatal nymph, what fatal charms,
Has made the hero deaf to war's alarms ?

Now let the conqu'ring ensigns up be furled :
Learn to be gay, be soft, and curled ;
And idle, lose the empire of the world.

In fond effeminate delights go on ;
Lose all the glories you have won :
Bravely resolve to love, and be undone.

'Tis thus the martial virgin pleads ;
Thus she the am'rous god persuades
To fly from Venus, and the flow'ry meads.

You see here that poets and warriors are oftentimes in affliction, even under the shades of their
protecting laurels ; and let the nymphs and virgins
sing what they please to their memory, under the
myrtles, and on flowery beds, they are much better
days than in the campaign. Nor do the crowns of
glory surpass those of love : the first is but an
empty name, which is now kept and lost with hazard ;
but love more nobly employs a brave soul, and all
his pleasures are solid and lasting ; and when one has
a worthy object of one's flame, glory accompanies
love too. But go to sleep, the hour is come ; though
it is now that your soul ought to be entertained in
dreams.

TWO O'CLOCK

CONVERSATION IN DREAMS

I doubt not but you will think it very bold and arbitrary, that my watch should pretend to rule even your sleeping hours, and that my cupid should govern your very dreams ; which are but thoughts disordered, in which reason has no part ; chimeras of the imagination, and no more. But though my watch does not pretend to counsel unreasonable, yet you must allow it here, if not to pass the bounds, at least to advance to the utmost limits of it. I am assured, that after having thought so much of me in the day, you will think of me also in the night. And the first dream my watch permits you to make, is to think you are in conversation with me.

Imagine, Damon, that you are talking to me of your passion, with all the transport of a lover, and that I hear you with satisfaction ; that all my looks and blushes, while you are speaking, give you new hopes and assurances ; that you are not indifferent to me ; and that I give you a thousand testimonies of my tenderness, all innocent and obliging.

While you are saying all that love can dictate, all that wit and good manners can invent, and all that I wish to hear from Damon, believe in this dream, all flattering and dear, that after having showed me the ardour of your flame, I confess to you the bottom of my heart, and all the loving secrets there ; that I give you sigh for sigh, tenderness for tenderness, heart for heart, and pleasure for pleasure. And I would have your sense of this dream so perfect, and your joy so entire, that if it happen you should awake with the satisfaction of this dream, you should find your heart still panting with the soft pleasure of the dear deceiving transport, and you should be ready to cry out :

> Ah ! how sweet it is to dream,
> When charming Iris is the theme !

For such, I wish, my Damon, your sleeping and your waking thoughts should render me to your heart.

THREE O'CLOCK

CAPRICIOUS SUFFERING IN DREAMS

It is but just to mix a little chagrin with these pleasures, a little bitter with your sweet ; you may be cloyed with too long an imagination of my favours : and I will have your fancy in dreams represent me to it, as the most capricious maid in the world. I know, here you will accuse my watch, and blame me with unnecessary cruelty, as you will call it : but lovers have their little ends, their little advantages, to pursue by methods wholly unaccountable to all, but that heart which contrives them. And as good a lover as I believe you, you will not enter into my design at first sight ; and though, on reasonable thoughts, you will be satisfied with this conduct of mine, at its first approach you will be ready to cry out :

THE REQUEST

> Oh Iris ! let my sleeping hours be fraught
> With joys, which you deny my waking thought.
> Is't not enough you absent are ?
>   Is't not enough I sigh all day,
> And languish out my life in care,
>   To ev'ry passion made a prey ?
> I burn with love, and soft desire ;
>   I rave with jealousy and fear :
> All day, for ease, my soul I tire ;
> In vain I search it ev'rywhere :
> It dwells not with the witty or the fair.

It is not in the camp or court,
In business, music, or in sport ;
The plays, the Park, the Mall afford
No more than the dull basset-board.
The beauties in the drawing-room,
With all their sweetness, all their bloom,
No more my faithful eyes invite,
    Nor rob my Iris of a sigh or glance,
Unless soft thoughts of her incite
    A smile, or trivial complaisance.
Then since my days so anxious prove,
    Ah, cruel tyrant ! give
A little loose to joys in love,
    And let your Damon live.

Let him in dreams be happy made,
    And let his sleep some bliss provide :
The nicest maid may yield in night's dark shade,
    What she so long by daylight had denied.
There let me think you present are,
And court my pillow for my fair.
There let me find you kind, and that you give
All that a man of honour dares receive.
And may my eyes eternal watches keep,
Rather than want that pleasure when I sleep.

Some such complaint as this I know you will
make ; but, Damon, if the little quarrels of lovers
render the reconciling moments so infinitely charming, you must needs allow, that these little chagrins
in capricious dreams must awaken you to more joy to
find them but dreams, than if you had met with no
disorder there. It is for this reason that I would have
you suffer a little pain for a coming pleasure ; nor,
indeed, is it possible for you to escape the dreams my
cupid points you out. You shall dream that I have
a thousand foibles, something of the lightness of my
sex ; that my soul is employed in a thousand vanities ;
that (proud and fond of lovers) I make advances for
the glory of a slave, without any other interest or design
than that of being adored. I will give you leave to
think my heart fickle, and that, far from resigning it
to anyone, I lend it only for a day, or an hour, and

take it back at pleasure; that I am a very coquette, even to impertinence.

All this I give you leave to think, and to offend me: but it is in sleep only that I permit it; for I would never pardon you the least offence of this nature, if in any other kind than in a dream. Nor is it enough affliction to you, to imagine me thus idly vain; but you are to pass on to a hundred more capricious humours: as that I exact of you a hundred unjust things; that I pretend you should break off with all your friends, and for the future have none at all; that I will myself do those things, which I violently condemn in you; and that I will have for others, as well as you, that tender friendship that resembles love, or rather love which people call friendship; and that I will not, after all, have you dare complain of me.

In fine, be as ingenious as you please to torment yourself; and believe, that I am become unjust, ungrateful, and insensible. But were I so indeed, O Damon! consider your awaking heart, and tell me, would your love stand the proof of all these faults in me? But know, that I would have you believe I have none of these weaknesses, though I am not wholly without faults, but those will be excusable to a lover; and this notion I have of a perfect one:

> Whate'er fantastic humours rule the fair,
> She's still the lover's dotage, and his care.

FOUR O'CLOCK

JEALOUSY IN DREAMS

Do not think, Damon, to wake yet; for I design you shall yet suffer a little more: jealousy must now possess you, that tyrant over the heart, that compels your very reason, and seduces all your good-nature. And in this dream you must believe that in sleeping,

which you could not do me the injustice to do when
awake.   And here you must explain all my actions
to the utmost disadvantage : nay, I will wish, that
the force of this jealousy may be so extreme, that it
may make you languish in grief, and be overcome
with anger.

You shall now imagine, that one of your rivals is
with me, interrupting all you say, or hindering all you
would say ; that I have no attention to what you
say aloud to me, but that I incline mine ear to
hearken to all that he whispers to me.   You shall
repine, that he pursues me everywhere, and is eternally at your heels if you approach me ; that I caress
him with sweetness in my eyes, and that vanity in my
heart, that possesses the humours of almost all the
fair; that is, to believe it greatly for my glory to have
abundance of rivals for my lovers.   I know you love me
too well not to be extremely uneasy in the company
of a rival, and to have one perpetually near me ; for
let him be beloved or not by the mistress, it must be
confessed, a rival is a very troublesome person.   But,
to afflict you to the utmost, I will have you imagine
that my eyes approve of all his thoughts ; that they
flatter him with hopes ; and that I have taken away
my heart from you, to make a present of it to this
more lucky man.   You shall suffer, while possessed
with this dream, all that a cruel jealousy can make a
tender soul suffer.

THE TORMENT

O jealousy ! thou passion most ingrate !
Tormenting as despair, envious as hate !
Spiteful as witchcraft, which th' Invoker harms ;
Worse than the wretch that suffers by its charms.
Thou subtile poison in the fancy bred,
Diffused through every vein, the heart and head,
And over all, like wild contagion spread,
Thou, whose sole property is to destroy,
Thou opposite to good, antipathy to joy ;
Whose attributes are cruel rage and fire,
Reason debauched, false sense, and mad desire.

In fine, it is a passion that ruffles all the senses, and disorders the whole frame of nature. It makes one hear and see what was never spoken, and what never was in view. It is the bane of health and beauty, an unmannerly intruder; and an evil of life worse than death. She is a very cruel tyrant in the heart; she possesses and pierces it with infinite unquiets; and we may lay it down as a certain maxim—

> She that would rack a lover's heart
> To the extent of cruelty,
> Must his tranquillity pervert
> To the most torturing jealousy.

I speak too sensibly of this passion, not to have loved well enough to have been touched with it. And you shall be this unhappy lover, Damon, during this dream, in which nothing shall present itself to your tumultuous thoughts, that shall not bring its pain. You shall here pass and repass a hundred designs, that shall confound one another. In fine, Damon, anger, hatred, and revenge, shall surround your heart.

> There they shall all together reign
> With mighty force, with mighty pain;
> In spite of reason, in contempt of love:
> Sometimes by turns, sometimes united move.

FIVE O'CLOCK

QUARRELS IN DREAMS

I perceive you are not able to suffer all this injustice, nor can I permit it any longer: and though you commit no crime yourself, yet you believe in this dream, that I complain of the injuries you do my fame; and that I am extremely angry with a jealousy so prejudicial to my honour. Upon this belief you accuse me of weakness; you resolve to see me no more, and are making a thousand feeble vows against love. You esteem me as a false one, and resolve to cease loving the vain coquette, and will say to me, as a certain friend of yours said to his false mistress:

THE INCONSTANT

Though, Sylvia, you are very fair,
  Yet disagreeable to me ;
And since you so inconstant are,
  Your beauty's damned with levity.
Your wit, your most offensive arms,
For want of judgment, wants its charms.

To every lover that is new,
  All new and charming you surprise ;
But when your fickle mind they view,
  They shun the danger of your eyes.
Should you a miracle of beauty show,
Yet you're inconstant, and will still be so.

It is thus you will think of me : and in fine, Damon, during this dream, we are in perpetual state of war.

Thus both resolve to break their chain,
And think to do't without much pain,
But oh ! alas ! we strive in vain.

For lovers, of themselves, can nothing do ;
There must be the consent of two :
You give it me, and I must give it you.

And if we shall never be free, till we acquit one another, this tie between you and I, Damon, is likely to last as long as we live ; therefore in vain you endeavour, but can never attain your end ; and in conclusion you will say, in thinking of me :

Oh ! how at ease my heart would live,
Could I renounce this fugitive ;
This dear, but false, attracting maid
That has her vows and faith betrayed !
Reason would have it so, but love
Dares not the dang'rous trial prove.

Do not be angry then, for this afflicting hour **is** drawing to an end, and you ought not to despair of coming into my absolute favour again :

> Then do not let your murm'ring heart,
> Against my int'rest, take your part.
> The feud was raised by dreams, all false and vain,
> And the next sleep shall reconcile again.

SIX O'CLOCK

ACCOMMODATION IN DREAMS

Though the angry lovers force themselves, all they can, to chase away the troublesome tenderness of the heart, in the height of their quarrels, love sees all their sufferings, pities and redresses them. And when we begin to cool, and a soft repentance follows the chagrin of the love-quarrel, it is then that love takes the advantage of both hearts, and renews the charming friendship more forcibly than ever, puts a stop to all our feuds, and renders the peace-making minutes the most dear and tender part of our life. How pleasing it is to see your rage dissolve! How sweet, how soft is every word that pleads for pardon at my feet! It is there that you tell me, your very sufferings are overpaid, when I but assure you from my eyes, that I will forget your crime. And your imagination shall here present me the most sensible of your past pain, that you can wish; and that all my anger being banished, I give you a thousand marks of my faith and gratitude; and lastly, to crown all, that we again make new vows to one another of inviolable peace :

> After these debates of love,
> Lovers thousand pleasures prove,
> Which they ever think to taste,
> Though oftentimes they do not last.

Enjoy then all the pleasures that a heart that is very amorous, and very tender, can enjoy. Think no more on those inquietudes that you have suffered; bless Love for his favours, and thank me for my graces: and resolve to endure anything, rather than enter upon any new quarrels. And however dear the reconciling moments are, there proceeds a great deal of evil from these little frequent quarrels; and I think the best counsel we can follow, is to avoid them as near as we can. And if we cannot, but that, in spite of love and good understanding, they should break out, we ought to make as speedy peace as possible; for it is not good to grate the heart too long, lest it grow hardened insensibly, and lose its native temper. A few quarrels there must be in love: love cannot support itself without them: and, besides the joy of an accommodation, love becomes by it more strongly united, and more charming. Therefore let the lover receive this as a certain receipt against declining love:

LOVE RECONCILED

He that would have the passion be
    Entire between the am'rous pair,
Let not the little feuds of jealousy
    Be carried on to a despair:
That palls the pleasure he would raise;
The fire that he would blow, allays.

When understandings false arise,
    When misinterpreted your thought,
If false conjectures of your smiles and eyes
    Be up to baneful quarrels wrought;
Let love the kind occasion take,
And straight accommodations make.

The sullen lover, long unkind,
    Ill-natured, hard to reconcile,
Loses the heart he had inclined;
    Love cannot undergo long toil;
He's soft and sweet, not born to bear
The rough fatigues of painful war.

SEVEN O'CLOCK

DIVERS DREAMS

Behold, Damon, the last hour of your sleep, and of my watch. She leaves you at liberty now, and you may choose your dreams : trust them to your imagination, give a loose to fancy, and let it rove at will, provided, Damon, it be always guided by a respectful love. For thus far I pretend to give bounds to your imagination, and will not have it pass beyond them. Take heed, in sleeping, you give no ear to a flattering cupid, that will favour your slumbering minutes with lies too pleasing and vain : you are discreet enough when you are awake ; will you not be so in dreams?

Damon, awake ; my watch's course is done : after this, you cannot be ignorant of what you ought to do during my absence. I did not believe it necessary to caution you about balls and comedies ; you know, a lover deprived of his mistress, goes seldom there. But if you cannot handsomely avoid these diversions, I am not so unjust a mistress, to be angry with you for it, go, if civility, or other duties oblige you. I will only forbid you, in consideration of me, not to be too much satisfied with those pleasures ; but see them so, as the world may have reason to say, you do not seek them, you do not make a business or pleasure of them ; and that it is complaisance, and not inclination, that carries you thither. Seem rather negligent than concerned at anything there ; and let every part of you say, Iris is not here.

I say nothing to you neither of your duty elsewhere ; I am satisfied you know it too well ; and have too great a veneration for your glorious master, to neglect any part of that for even love itself. And I very well know how much you love to be eternally near his illustrious person ; and that you scarce prefer your mistress before him, in point of love : in all things else, I give him leave to take place of Iris in the noble heart of Damon.

I am satisfied you pass your time well now at Windsor, for you adore that place; and it is not, indeed, without great reason; for it is most certainly now rendered the most glorious palace in the Christian world. And had our late gracious sovereign, of blessed memory, had no other miracles and wonders of his life and reign to have immortalised his fame (of which there shall remain a thousand to posterity) this noble structure alone, this building (almost divine) would have eternised the great name of glorious Charles II. till the world moulder again to its old confusion, its first chaos. And the painting of the famous Varrio, and noble carvings of the inimitable Gibbon, shall never die, but remain to tell succeeding ages, that all arts and learning were not confined to ancient Rome and Greece, but that England, too, could boast its mightiest share. Nor is the inside of this magnificent structure, immortalised with so many eternal images of the illustrious Charles and Catharine, more to be admired than the wondrous prospects without. The stupendous height, on which the famous pile is built, renders the fields, and flowery meadows below, the woods, the thickets, and the winding streams, the most delightful object that ever nature produced. Beyond all these, and far below, in an inviting vale, the venerable college, an old, but noble building, raises itself, in the midst of all the beauties of nature, high-grown trees, fruitful plains, purling rivulets, and spacious gardens, adorned with all variety of sweets that can delight the senses.

At farther distance yet, on an ascent almost as high as that to the royal structure, you may behold the famous and noble Clifdon rise, a palace erected by the illustrious Duke of Buckingham, who will leave this wondrous piece of architecture, to inform the future world of the greatness and delicacy of his mind; it being for its situation, its prospects, and its

marvellous contrivances, one of the finest villas of
the world; at least, were it finished as begun; and
would sufficiently declare the magnificent soul of the
hero that caused it to be built, and contrived all its
fineness. And this makes up not the least part of the
beautiful prospect from the Palace Royal, while on
the other side lies spread a fruitful and delightful park
and forest well stored with deer, and all that makes
the prospect charming; fine walks, groves, distant
valleys, downs, and hills, and all that nature could invent, to furnish out a quiet soft retreat for the most
fair and most charming of queens, and the most
heroic, good, and just of kings. And these groves
alone are fit and worthy to divert such earthly gods.

Nor can heaven, nature, or human art contrive an
addition to this earthly paradise, unless those great
inventors of the age, Sir Samuel Moreland, or Sir
Robert Gordon, could by the power of engines, convey the water so into the park and Castle, as to furnish
it with delightful fountains, both useful and beautiful.
These are only wanting, to render the place all perfection, and without exception.

This, Damon, is a long digression from the business
of my heart; but, you know I am so in love with that
charming Court, that when you gave me an occasion,
by your being there now, only to name the place,
I could not forbear transgressing a little, in favour of
its wondrous beauty; and the rather, because I would,
in recounting it, give you to understand how many
fine objects there are, besides the ladies that adorn it,
to employ your vacant moments in; and I hope you
will, without my instructions, pass a great part of your
idle time in surveying these prospects, and give that
admiration you should pay to living beauty, to those
more venerable monuments of everlasting fame.

Neither need I, Damon, assign you your waiting
times: your honour, duty, love, and obedience, will
instruct you when to be near the person of the King;
and, I believe, you will omit no part of that devoir.

You ought to establish your fortune and your glory: for I am not of the mind of those critical lovers, who believe it a very hard matter to reconcile love and interest, to adore a mistress, and serve a master at the same time. And I have heard those, who on this subject, say, 'Let a man be never so careful in these double duties, it is ten to one but he loses his fortune or his mistress.' These are errors that I condemn: and I know that love and ambition are not incompatible, but that a brave man may preserve all his duties to his sovereign, and his passion and his respect for his mistress. And this is my notion of it:

LOVE AND AMBITION

The nobler lover, who would prove
  Uncommon in address,
Let him Ambition join with Love;
  With Glory, Tenderness:
But let the virtues so be mixt,
  That when to Love he goes,
Ambition may not come betwixt,
  Nor Love his power oppose.
The vacant hours from softer sport,
Let him give up to interest and the court.

'Tis Honour shall his business be,
  And Love his noblest play:
Those two should never disagree,
  For both make either gay.
Love without Honour were too mean
  For any gallant heart;
And Honour singly, but a dream,
  Where Love must have no part.
A flame like this you cannot fear,
Where Glory claims an equal share.

Such a passion, Damon, can never make you quit any part of your duty to your Prince. And the monarch you serve is so gallant a master, that the inclination you have to his person obliges you to serve him, as much as your duty; for Damon's loyal

soul loves the man, and adores the monarch: for he is
certainly all that compels both, by a charming force
and goodness, from all mankind.

THE KING

Darling of Mars! Bellona's care!
The second deity of war!
Delight of heaven, and joy of earth!
Born for great and wondrous things,
Destined at his auspicious birth
T' outdo the numerous race of long-past kings.

Best representative of heaven,
To whom its chiefest attributes are given)
Great, pious, steadfast, just, and brave!
To vengeance slow, but swift to save!
Dispensing mercy all abroad!
Soft and forgiving as a god!

Thou saving angel who preserv'st the land
From the just rage of the avenging hand;
Stopt the dire plague, that o'er the earth was hurled,
And sheathing thy almighty sword,
Calmed the wild fears of a distracted world,
(As heaven first made it) with a sacred word!

But I will stop the low flight of my humble Muse,
who when she is upon the wing, on this glorious
subject, knows no bounds. And all the world has
agreed to say so much of the virtues and wonders of
this great monarch, that they have left me nothing
new to say; though indeed he every day gives us new
themes of his growing greatness, and we see nothing
that equals him in our age. Oh! how happy are we
to obey his laws; for he is the greatest of kings, and
the best of men.

You will be very unjust, Damon, if you do not
confess I have acquitted myself like a maid of honour,
of all the obligations I owe you, upon the account of
the discretion I lost to you. If it be not valuable
enough, I am generous enough to make it good: and

since I am so willing to be just, you ought to esteem me, and to make it your chiefest care to preserve me yours; for I believe I shall deserve it, and wish you should believe so too. Remember me, write to me, and observe punctually all the motions of my watch: the more you regard it, the better you will like it; and whatever you think of it at first sight, it is no ill present. The invention is soft and gallant; and Germany, so celebrated for rare watches, can produce nothing to equal this.

Damon, my watch is just and new;
And all a lover ought to do,
My cupid faithfully will show.
And ev'ry hour he renders there,
Except *l'heure du Bergère.*

THE CASE
FOR THE WATCH

DAMON TO IRIS

EXPECT not, O charming Iris! that I should choose
words to thank you in; (words, that least part of love,
and least the business of the lover) but will say all,
and everything that a tender heart can dictate, to
make an acknowledgment for so dear and precious
a present as this of your charming watch: while
all I can say will but too dully express my sense of
gratitude, my joy, and the pleasure I receive in the
mighty favour. I confess the present too rich, too
gay, and too magnificent for my expectation: and
though my love and faith deserve it, yet my humbler
hope never durst carry me to a wish of so great
a bliss, so great an acknowledgment from the maid
I adore. The materials are glorious, the work delicate, and the movement just, and even gives rules to
my heart, who shall observe very exactly all that the
cupid remarks to me; even to the minutes, which
I will point with sighs, though I am obliged to them
there but every half hour.

You tell me, fair Iris, that I ought to preserve it
tenderly, and yet you have sent it me without a case.
But that I may obey you justly, and keep it dear to
me, as long as I live, I will give it a case of my
fashion: it shall be delicate, and suitable to the fine

present, of such materials too. But because I would have it perfect, I will consult your admirable wit and invention in an affair of so curious a consequence.

THE FIGURE OF THE CASE

I design to give it the figure of the heart. Does not your watch, Iris, rule the heart? It was your heart that contrived it, and it was your heart you consulted in all the management of it; and it was your heart that brought it to so fine a conclusion. The heart never acts without reason, and all the heart projects, it performs with pleasure.

Your watch, my lovely maid, has explained to me a world of rich secrets of love: and where should thoughts so sacred be stored, but in the heart, where all the secrets of the soul are treasured up, and of which only Love alone can take a view? It is thence he take his sighs and tears, and all his little flatteries and arts to please; all his fine thoughts, and all his mighty raptures; nothing is so proper as the heart to preserve it, nothing so worthy as the heart to contain it; and it concerns my interest too much, not to be infinitely careful of so dear a treasure. And believe me, charming Iris, I will never part with it.

THE VOTARY

Fair goddess of my just desire,
Inspirer of my softest fire !
Since you, from out the num'rous throng
That to your altars do belong,
To me the sacred myst'ry have revealed,
From all my rival-worshippers concealed ;
And taught my soul with heav'nly fire,
Refined it from its grosser sense,
And wrought it to a higher excellence ;
It can no more return to earth,
Like things that thence receive their birth :
But still aspiring, upward move,
And teach the world new flights of love ;
New arts of secrecy shall learn,
And render youth discreet in love's concern.

In his soft heart, to hide the charming things
  A mistress whispers to his ear ;
  And ev'ry tender sigh she brings,
  Mix with his soul, and hide it there.
To bear himself so well in company,
  That if his mistress present be,
  It may be thought by all the fair,
  Each in his heart does claim a share,
  And all are more beloved than she.
But when with the dear maid apart,
  Then at her feet the lover lies ;
Opens his soul, shows all his heart,
  While joy is dancing in his eyes.
Then all that honour may, or take, or give,
  They both distribute, both receive.
A looker-on would spoil a lover's joy ;
For love's a game where only two can play.
  And 'tis the hardest of love's mysteries,
To feign love where it is not, hide it where it is.

After having told you, my lovely Iris, that I design to put your watch into a heart, I ought to show you the ornaments of the case. I do intend to have them crowned ciphers: I do not mean those crowns of vanity, which are put indifferently on all sorts of ciphers; no, I must have such as may distinguish mine from the rest, and may be true emblems of what I would represent. My four ciphers therefore shall be crowned with these four wreaths of olive, laurel, myrtle, and roses: and the letters that begin the names of Iris and Damon shall compose the ciphers; though I must intermix some other letters that bear another sense, and have another signification.

THE FIRST CIPHER

The first cipher is composed of an I and a D, which are joined by an L and an E ; which signifies Love Extreme. And it is but just, O adorable Iris! that love should be mixed with our ciphers, and that love alone should be the union of them.

Love ought alone the mystic knot to tie ;
Love, that great master of all arts :
And this dear cipher is to let you see,
Love unites names as well as hearts.

Without this charming union, our souls could not communicate those invisible sweetnesses, which complete the felicity of lovers, and which the most tender and passionate expressions are too feeble to make us comprehend. But, my adorable Iris, I am contented with the vast pleasure I feel in loving well, without the care of expressing it well ; if you will imagine my pleasure, without expressing it. For I confess, it would be no joy to me to adore you, if you did not perfectly believe I did adore you. Nay, though you loved me, if you had no faith in me, I should languish and love in as much pain, as if you scorned ; and at the same time believe I died for you. For surely, Iris, it is a greater pleasure to please than to be pleased ; and the glorious power of giving, is infinitely a greater satisfaction, than that of receiving : there is so great and god-like a quality in it. I would have your belief therefore equal to my passion, extreme ; as indeed all love should be, or it cannot bear that divine name : it can pass but for an indifferent affection. And these ciphers ought to make the world find all the noble force of delicate passion : for, O my Iris ! what would love signify, if we did not love fervently? Sisters and brothers love ; friends and relations have affections : but where the souls are joined, which are filled with eternal soft wishes, oh ! there is some excess of pleasure, which cannot be expressed !

Your looks, your dear obliging words, and your charming letters, have sufficiently persuaded me of your tenderness ; and you might surely see the excess of my passion by my cares, my sighs, and entire resignation to your will. I never think of Iris, but my heart feels double flames, and pants and heaves with double sighs ; and whose force makes its ardours known, by a thousand transports. And they are very much to blame, to give the name of love to feeble easy passions. Such transitory tranquil inclinations are at best but well-wishers to love ; and a heart that has such heats as those, ought not to put itself into the rank of those nobler victims that are offered at the shrine of Love. But our souls, Iris, burn with a more glorious flame, that lights and conducts us beyond a possibility of losing one another. It is this that flatters all my hopes ; it is this alone makes me believe myself worthy of Iris : and let her judge of its violence, by the greatness of its splendour.

Does not a passion of this nature, so true, so ardent, deserve to be crowned ? And will you wonder to see, over this cipher, a wreath of myrtles, those boughs so sacred to the Queen of Love, and so worshipped by lovers ? It is with these soft wreaths, that those are crowned, who understand how to love well and faithfully.

> The smiles, the graces, and the sports,
> That in the secret groves maintain their courts,
>   Are with these myrtles crowned :
> Thither the nymphs their garlands bring ;
> Their beauties, and their praises sing,
>   While echoes do the songs resound.
>
> Love, though a god, with myrtle wreaths
>   Does his soft temples bind ;
> More valued are those consecrated leaves,
>   Than the bright wealth in Eastern rocks confined :
> And crowns of glory less ambition move,
> Than those more sacred diadems of love.

THE SECOND CIPHER

Is crowned with olives ; and I add to the two letters of our names an R and L, for Reciprocal Love. Every time that I have given you, O lovely Iris, testimonies of my passion, I have been so blest, as to receive some from your bounty; and you have been pleased to flatter me with a belief, that I was not indifferent to you. I dare therefore say, that being honoured with the glory of your tenderness and care, I ought, as a trophy of my illustrious conquest, to adorn the watch with a cipher that is so advantageous to me. Ought I not to esteem myself the most fortunate and happy of mankind, to have exchanged my heart with so charming and admirable a person as Iris? Ah! how sweet, how precious is the change; and how vast a glory arrives to me from it! Oh! you must not wonder if my soul abandons itself to a thousand ecstasies! In the merchandise of hearts, oh, how dear it is to receive as much as one gives; and barter heart for heart! Oh! I would not receive mine again, for all the crowns the universe contains! Nor ought you, my adorable, make any vows or wishes, ever to retrieve yours; or show the least repentance for the blessing you have given me. The exchange we made, was confirmed by a noble faith; and you ought to believe, you have bestowed it well, since you are paid for it a heart that is so conformable to yours, so true, so just, and so full of adoration. And nothing can be the just recompense of love, but love: and to enjoy the true felicity of it, our hearts ought to keep an equal motion; and, like the scales of justice, always hang even.

It is the property of reciprocal love, to make the heart feel the delicacy of love, and to give the lover all the ease and softness he can reasonably hope. Such a love renders all things advantageous and prosperous: such a love triumphs over all other pleasures. And I put a crown of olives over the cipher of reciprocal love, to make known, that two hearts, where love is justly equal, enjoy a peace that nothing can disturb.

Olives are never fading seen ;
But always flourishing, and green.
  The emblem 'tis of Love and Peace ;
  For Love that's true, will never cease :
  And Peace does pleasure still increase.
Joy to the world, the peace of kings imparts ;
And peace in love distributes it to hearts.

THE THIRD CIPHER

The C and L, which are joined to the letters of our names in this cipher crowned with laurel, explains a Constant Love. It will not, my fair Iris, suffice, that my love is extreme, my passion violent, and my wishes fervent, or that our loves are reciprocal ; but they ought also to be constant: for in love, the imagination is oftener carried to those things that may arrive, and which we wish for, than to things that time has robbed us of. And in those agreeable thoughts of joys to come, the heart takes more delight to wander, than in all those that are past ; though the remembrance of them be very dear, and very charming. We should be both unjust, if we were not persuaded we are possessed with a virtue, the use of which is so admirable as that of constancy. Our loves are not of that sort that can finish, or have an end ; but such a passion, so perfect, and so constant, that it will be a precedent for future ages, to love perfectly; and when they would express an extreme passion, they will say 'They loved, as Damon did the charming Iris.' And he that knows the glory of constant love, will despise those fading passions, those little amusements, that serve for a day. What pleasure or dependence can one have in a love of that sort? What concern? What raptures can such an amour produce in a soul? And what satisfaction can one promise one's self in playing with a false gamester ; who though you are aware of him, in spite of all your precaution, puts the false dice upon you, and wins all?

Those eyes that can no better conquest make,
  Let them ne'er look abroad :
Such, but the empty name of lovers take,
  And so profane the god.
Better they never should pretend,
Than, ere begun, to make an end.

Of that fond flame what shall we say,
That's born and languished in a day ?
Such short-lived blessings cannot bring
The pleasure of an envying.
Who is't will celebrate that flame,
That's damned to such a scanty fame ?
While constant love the nymphs and swains
Still sacred make, in lasting strains
And cheerful lays throughout the plains.
A constant love knows no decay ;
But still advancing ev'ry day,
Will last as long as life can stay,
With ev'ry look and smile improves,
With the same ardour always moves,
With such as Damon charming Iris loves !

Constant love finds itself impossible to be shaken; it resists the attacks of envy, and a thousand accidents that endeavour to change it. Nothing can disoblige it but a known falseness, or contempt: nothing can remove it ; though for a short moment it may lie sullen and resenting, it recovers, and returns with greater force and joy. I therefore, with very good reason, crown this cipher of constant love with a wreath of laurel ; since such love always triumphs over time and fortune, though it be not her property to besiege : for she cannot overcome, but in defending herself ; but the victories she gains are nevertheless glorious.

For far less conquest, we have known
The victor wear the laurel crown.
The triumph with more pride let him receive ;
While those of love, at least, more pleasures give.

THE FOURTH CIPHER

Perhaps, my lovely maid, you will not find out what I mean by the S and the L, in this last cipher, that is crowned with roses. I will therefore tell you, I mean Secret Love. There are very few people who know the nature of that pleasure, which so divine a love creates: and let me say what I will of it, they must feel it themselves, who would rightly understand it, and all its ravishing sweets. But this there is a great deal of reason to believe, that the secrecy in love doubles the pleasures of it. And I am so absolutely persuaded of this, that I believe all those favours that are not kept secret, are dull and pallid, very insipid and tasteless pleasures: and let the favours be ever so innocent that a lover receives from a mistress, she ought to value them, set a price upon them, and make the lover pay dear; while he receives them with difficulty, and sometimes with hazard. A lover that is not secret, but suffers every one to count his sighs, has at most but a feeble passion, such as produces sudden and transitory desires which die as soon as born. A true love has not this character; for whensoever it is made public, it ceases to be a pleasure, and is only the result of vanity. Not that I expect our loves should always remain a secret. No, I should never, at that rate, arrive to a blessing, which, above all the glories of the earth, I aspire to; but even then there are a thousand joys, a thousand pleasures that I shall be as careful to conceal from the foolish world, as if the whole preservation of that pleasure depended on my silence; as indeed it does in a great measure.

To this cipher I put a crown of roses, which are not flowers of a very lasting date. And it is to let you see, that it is impossible love can be long hid. We see every day, with what fine dissimulation and pains, people conceal a thousand hates and malices, disgusts, disobligations, and resentments, without

being able to conceal the least part of their love : but
reputation has an odour as well as roses ; and a lover
ought to esteem that as the dearest and tenderest
thing : not only that of his own, which is, indeed, the
least part ; but that of his mistress, more valuable to
him than life. He ought to endeavour to give people
no occasion to make false judgments of his actions,
or to give their censures ; which most certainly are
never in the favour of the fair person : for likely,
those false censurers are of the busy female sex, the
coquettes of that number ; whose little spites and
railleries, joined to that fancied wit they boast of, set
them at odds with all the beautiful and innocent.
And how very little of that kind serves to give the
world a faith, when a thousand virtues, told of the
same persons, by more credible witnesses and judges,
shall pass unregarded ! so willing and inclined is all
the world to credit the ill, and condemn the good !
And yet, oh ! what pity it is we are compelled to
live in pain, to oblige this foolish scandalous world !
And though we know each other's virtue and honour,
we are obliged to observe that caution (to humour the
talking town) which takes away so great a part of
the pleasure of life. It is therefore that among those
roses, you will find some thorns ; by which you may
imagine, that in love, precaution is necessary to its
secrecy. And we must restrain ourselves, upon a
thousand occasions, with so much care, that, O Iris !
it is impossible to be discreet, without pain ; but it is
a pain that creates a thousand pleasures.

> Where should a lover hide his joys,
> Free from malice, free from noise ;
>   Where no envy can intrude ;
>   Where no busy rival's spy,
> Made, by disappointment, rude,
>   May inform his jealousy ?
> The heart will the best refuge prove ;
> Which nature meant the cabinet of love.
> What would a lover not endure,
> His mistress' fame and honour to secure ?

Iris, the care we take to be discreet,
Is the dear toil that makes the pleasure sweet :
The thorn that does the wealth inclose,
That with less saucy freedom we may touch the rose.

THE CLASP OF THE WATCH

Ah, charming Iris! Ah, my lovely maid! it is now, in a more peculiar manner, that I require your aid in the finishing of my design, and completing the whole piece to the utmost perfection ; and without your aid it cannot be performed. It is about the clasp of the watch ; a material in all appearance, the most trivial of any part of it. But that it may be safe for ever, I design it the image, or figure of two hands ; that fair one of the adorable Iris, joined to mine; with this motto, "Inviolable Faith." For in this case, this heart ought to be shut up by this eternal clasp. Oh! there is nothing so necessary as this! Nothing can secure love, but faith.

That virtue ought to be a guard to all the heart thinks, and all the mouth utters : nor can love say he triumphs without it. And when that remains not in the heart, all the rest deserves no regard. Oh! I have not loved so ill to leave one doubt upon your soul. Why then, will you want that faith, O unkind charmer, that my passion and my services so justly merit?

When two hearts entirely love,
And in one sphere of honour move,
Each maintains the other's fire,
With a faith that is entire.
For, what heedless youth bestows,
On a faithless maid, his vows?
Faith without love, bears Virtue's price ;
But love without her mixture, is a vice.
Love, like religion, still should be,
    In the foundation firm and true ;
In points of faith should still agree,
    Though innovations vain and new,
Love's little quarrels, may arise ;
In foundations still they're just and wise.

Then, charming maid, be sure of this;
  Allow me faith, as well as love :
Since that alone affords no bliss,
  Unless your faith your love improve.
Either resolve to let me die
By fairer play, your cruelty ;
Than not your love with faith impart,
And with your vows to give your heart.
In mad despair I'd rather fall,
Than lose my glorious hopes of conquering all.

So certain it is, that love without faith, is of no value.

In fine, my adorable Iris, this case shall be, as near as I can, like those delicate ones of filigrain work, which do not hinder the sight from taking a view of all within : you may therefore see, through this heart, all your watch. Nor is my desire of preserving this inestimable piece more, than to make it the whole rule of my life and actions. And my chiefest design in these ciphers, is to comprehend in them the principal virtues that are most necessary to love. Do not we know that reciprocal love is justice? Constant love, fortitude?   Secret love, prudence? Though it is true that extreme love, that is, excess of love, in one sense, appears not to be temperance ; yet you must know, my Iris, that in matters of love, excess is a virtue, and that all other degrees of love are worthy scorn alone. It is this alone that can make good the glorious title : it is this alone that can bear the name of love ; and this alone that renders the lovers truly happy, in spite of all the storms of fate, and shocks of fortune. This is an antidote against all other griefs : this bears up the soul in all calamity ; and is the very heaven of life, the last refuge of all worldly pain and care, and may well bear the title of divine.

THE ART OF LOVING WELL

That Love may all perfection be,
Sweet, charming to the last degree,
The heart, where the bright flames do dwell,
In faith and softness should excel :
Excess of love should fill each vein,
And all its sacred rites maintain.

The tend'rest thoughts heav'n can inspire,
Should be the fuel to its fire :
And that, like incense, burn as pure ;
Or that in urns should still endure.
No fond desire should fill the soul,
But such as honour may control.

Jealousy I will allow :
Not the amorous winds that blow,
Should wanton in my Iris' hair,
Or ravish kisses from my fair.
Not the flowers that grow beneath,
Should borrow sweetness of her breath,

If her bird she do caress,
How I grudge its happiness,
When upon her snowy hand
The wanton does triumphing stand !
Or upon her breast she skips,
And lays her beak to Iris' lips !
Fainting at my ravished joy,
I could the innocent destroy.

If I can no bliss afford
To a little harmless bird,
Tell me, O thou dear-loved maid !
What reason could my rage persuade,
If a rival should invade ?

If thy charming eyes should dart
Looks that sally from the heart ;
If you sent a smile, or glance,
To another though by chance ;
Still thou giv'st what's not thy own,
They belong to me alone.

All submission I would pay:
Man was born the fair t' obey.
Your very look I'd understand,
And thence receive your least command:
Never your justice will dispute;
But like a lover execute.

I would no usurper be,
But in claiming sacred thee.
I would have all, and every part;
No thought would hide within thy heart.
Mine a cabinet was made,
Where Iris' secrets should be laid.

In the rest, without control,
She should triumph o'er the soul!
Prostrate at her feet I'd lie,
Despising power and liberty;
Glorying more by love to fall,
Than rule the universal ball.

Hear me, O you saucy youth!
And from my maxims learn this truth:
Would you great and powerful prove?
Be a humble slave to love.
'Tis nobler far a joy to give,
Than any blessing to receive.

THE LADY'S LOOKING-GLASS
TO DRESS HERSELF BY

OR THE ART OF CHARMING

How long, O charming Iris! shall I speak in vain of your adorable beauty? You have been just, and believe I love you with a passion perfectly tender and extreme, and yet you will not allow your charms to be infinite. You must either accuse my flames to be unreasonable, and that my eyes and heart are false judges of wit and beauty; or allow that you are the most perfect of your sex. But instead of that, you always accuse me of flattery, when I speak of your infinite merit; and when I refer you to your glass, you tell me, that flatters as well as Damon: though one would imagine, that should be a good witness for the truth of what I say, and undeceive you of the opinion of my injustice. Look—— and confirm yourself, that nothing can equal your perfections. All the world says it, and you must doubt it no longer. O, Iris! will you dispute against the whole world?

But since you have so long distrusted your own glass, I have here presented you with one, which I know is very true; and having been made for you only, can serve only you. All other glasses present all objects, but this reflects only Iris: whenever you consult it, it will convince you; and tell you how much right I have done you, when I told you, you were the fairest person that ever nature made. When other beauties look into it, it will speak to all the fair ones: but let them do what they will, it will say nothing to their advantage.

> Iris, to spare what you call flattery,
>   Consult your glass each hour of the day :
> 'Twill tell you where your charms and beauties lie,
>   And where your little wanton graces play :
> Where love does revel in your face and eyes ;
> What look invites your slaves, and what denies.
>
> Where all the loves adorn you with such care,
>   Where dress your smiles, where arm your lovely eyes ;
> Where deck the flowing tresses of your hair :
>   How cause your snowy breasts to fall and rise.
> How this severe glance makes a lover die ;
> How that, more soft, gives immortality.
>
> Where you shall see what 'tis enslaves the soul ;
>   Where ev'ry feature, ev'ry look combines :
> When the adorning air, o'er all the whole,
>   To so much wit, and so nice virtue joins.
> Where the *belle taille*, and motion still afford
> Graces to be eternally adored.

But I will be silent now, and let your glass speak.

THE LADY'S LOOKING-GLASS

Damon (O charming Iris!) has given me to you, that you may sometimes give yourself the trouble, and me the honour of consulting me in the great and weighty affairs of beauty. I am, my adorable mistress! a faithful glass; and you ought to believe all I say to you.

THE SHAPE OF IRIS

I must begin with your shape, and tell you without flattery, it is the finest in the world, and gives love and admiration to all that see you. Pray observe how free and easy it is, without constraint, stiffness, or affectation : those mistaken graces of the fantastic, and the formal, who give themselves pain to show their will to please, and whose dressing makes the greatest part of their fineness, when they are more obliged to the tailor than to nature; who add or diminish, as occasion serves, to form a grace, where heaven never gave it. And while they remain on this wreck of pride, they are eternally uneasy, without pleasing anybody. Iris, I have seen a woman of your acquaintance, who, having a greater opinion of her own person than anybody else, has screwed her body into so fine a form (as she calls it) that she dares no more stir a hand, lift up an arm, or turn her head aside, than if, for the sin of such a disorder, she were to be turned into a pillar of salt; the less stiff and fixed statue of the two. Nay, she dares not speak or smile, lest she should put her face out of that order she had set it in her glass, when she last looked on herself: and is all over such a Lady Nice (excepting in her conversation) that ever made a ridiculous figure. And there are many ladies more, but too much tainted with that nauseous formality, that old-fashioned vice. But Iris, the charming, the all-perfect Iris, has nothing in her whole form that is not free, natural and easy; and whose every motion cannot but please extremely; and which has not given Damon a thousand rivals.

Damon, the young, the am'rous, and the true,
Who sighs incessantly for you ;
Whose whole delight, now you are gone,
Is to retire to shades alone,
And to the echoes make his moan.
By purling streams the wishing youth is laid,
Still sighing Iris ! lovely charming maid !
See, in thy absence, how thy lover dies !
While to his sighs the echo still replies.

Then with a stream he holds discourse :
O thou that bend'st thy liquid force
To lovely Thames ! upon whose shore
The maid resides whom I adore !
My tears of love upon thy surface bear :
And if upon thy banks thou seest my fair :
In all thy softest murmurs sing,
From Damon I this present bring ;

My ev'ry curl contains a tear !
Then at her feet thy tribute pay :
But haste, O happy stream ! away ;
Lest charmed too much, thou shouldst for ever stay.
And thou, O gentle, murm'ring breeze !
That plays in air, and wantons with the trees ;
On thy young wings, where gilded sunbeams play,
To Iris my soft sighs convey,
Still as they rise, each minute of the day :
But whisper gently in her ear ;
Let not the ruder winds thy message hear,
Nor ruffle one dear curl of her bright hair.
Oh ! touch her cheeks with sacred reverence,
　　And stay not gazing on her lovely eyes !
But if thou bear'st her rosy breath from thence,
'Tis incense of that excellence,
　　That as thou mount'st, 'twill perfume all the skies.

IRIS'S COMPLEXION

Say what you will, I am confident, if you will
confess your heart, you are, every time you view
yourself in me, surprised at the beauty of your
complexion ; and will secretly own, you never saw
anything so fair. I am not the first glass, by a
thousand, that has assured you of this. If you will
not believe me, ask Damon ; he tells it you every day,
but that truth from him offends you : and because he
loves too much, you think his judgment too little ; and
since this is so perfect, that must be defective. But
it is most certain your complexion is infinitely fine,
your skin soft and smooth as polished wax, or ivory,
extremely white and clear ; though if anybody speaks
but of your beauty, an agreeable blush casts itself
all over your face, and gives you a thousand new
graces.

And then two flowers newly born,
　Shine in your heav'nly face ;
The rose that blushes in the morn,
　Usurps the lily's place :
Sometimes the lily does prevail,
And makes the gen'rous crimson pale.

IRIS'S HAIR

Oh, the beautiful hair of Iris! it seems as if nature had crowned you with a great quantity of lovely fair brown hair, to make us know that you were born to rule, and to repair the faults of fortune that has not given you a diadem. And do not bewail the want of that (so much your merit's due) since heaven has so gloriously recompensed you with what gains more admiring slaves.

> Heav'n for sovereignty has made your form :
> And you were more than for dull empire born ;
> O'er hearts your kingdom shall extend,
> Your vast dominion know no end.
> Thither the Loves and Graces shall resort ;
> To Iris make their homage, and their court.
> No envious star, no common fate,
> Did on my Iris' birthday wait ;
> But all was happy, all was delicate.
> Here fortune would inconstant be in vain :
> Iris, and love, eternally shall reign.

Love does not make less use of your hair for new conquests, than of all the rest of your beauties that adorn you. If he takes our hearts with your fine eyes, it ties them fast with your hair; and if it weaves a chain, it is not easily broken. It is not of those sorts of hair, whose harshness discovers ill-nature ; nor of those whose softness shows us the weakness of the mind ; not that either of these arguments are without exception. But it is such as bears the character of a perfect mind, and a delicate wit ; and for its colour, the most faithful, discreet, and beautiful in the world ; such as shows a complexion and constitution, neither so cold to be insensible, nor so hot to have too much fire : that is, neither too white, nor too black ; but such a mixture of the two colours, as makes it the most agreeable in the world.

'Tis that which leads those captivated hearts,
   That bleeding at your feet do lie ;
'Tis that the obstinate converts,
   That dare the power of love deny :
'Tis that which Damon so admires ;
Damon, who often tells you so.
If from your eyes Love takes his fires,
   'Tis with your hair he strings his bow :
Which touching but the feathered dart,
It never missed the destined heart.

IRIS'S EYES

I believe, my fair mistress, I shall dazzle you with
the lustre of your own eyes. They are the finest blue
in the world : they have all the sweetness that ever
charmed the heart, with a certain languishment that's
irresistible ; and never any looked on them, that did
not sigh after them. Believe me, Iris, they carry un-
avoidable darts and fires ; and whoever expose themselves to their dangers, pay for their imprudence.

Cold as my solid crystal is,
   Hard and impenetrable too ;
Yet I am sensible of bliss,
   When your charming eyes I view ·
Even by me their flames are felt ;
And at each glance I fear to melt.

Ah, how pleasant are my days !
   How my glorious fate I bless !
Mortals never knew my joys,
   Nor monarch guessed my happiness.
Every look that's soft and gay,
Iris gives me every day.

Spite of her virtue and her pride,
   Every morning I am blest
With what to Damon is denied ;
   To view her when she is undrest.
All her heaven of beauty's shown
To triumphing me—alone.

THE LADY'S LOOKING-GLASS 291

Scarce the prying beams of light,
  Or th' impatient god of day,
Are allowed so near a sight,
  Or dare profane her with a ray;
When she has appeared to me,
Like Venus rising from the sea.

But oh! I must those charms conceal,
  All too divine for vulgar eyes:
Should I my secret joys reveal,
  Of sacred trust I break the ties;
And Damon would with envy die,
Who hopes one day to be as blest as I.

Extravagant with my joys, I have strayed beyond my limits; for I was telling you of the wondrous fineness of your eyes, which no mortal can resist, nor any heart stand the force of their charms, and the most difficult conquest they gain, scarce cost them the expense of a look. They are modest and tender, chaste and languishing. There you may take a view of the whole soul, and see wit and good nature (those two inseparable virtues of the mind) in an extraordinary measure. In fine, you see all that fair eyes can produce, to make themselves adored. And when they are angry, they strike an unresistible awe upon the soul; and those severities Damon wishes may perpetually accompany them, during their absence from him; for it is with such eyes, he would have you receive all his rivals.

Keep, lovely maid, the softness in your eyes,
  To flatter Damon with another day:
When at your feet the ravished lover lies,
  Then put on all that's tender, all that's gay:
And for the griefs your absence makes him prove,
Give him the softest, dearest looks of love.

His trembling heart with sweetest smiles caress,
  And in your eyes soft wishes let him find;
That your regret of absence may confess,
  In which no sense of pleasure you could find
And to restore him, let your faithful eyes
Declare, that all his rivals you despise.

THE MOUTH OF IRIS

I perceive your modesty would impose silence on me : but, O fair Iris! do not think to present yourself before a glass, if you would not have it tell you all your beauties. Content yourself that I only speak of them, *en passant ;* for should I speak what I would, I should dwell all day upon each particular, and still say something new. Give me liberty then to speak of your fine mouth : you need only open it a little, and you will see the most delicate teeth that ever you beheld ; the whitest, and the best set. Your lips are the finest in the world; so round, so soft, so plump, so dimpled, and of the loveliest colour. And when you smile, oh! what imagination can conceive how sweet it is, that has not seen you smiling? I cannot describe what I so admire ; and it is in vain to those who have not seen Iris.

O Iris! boast that one peculiar charm,
  That has so many conquests made ;
So innocent, yet capable of harm ;
  So just itself, yet has so oft betrayed :
Where a thousand graces dwell,
And wanton round in ev'ry smile.

A thousand loves do listen when you speak,
  And catch each accent as it flies :
Rich flowing wit, whene'er you silence break,
  Flows from your tongue, and sparkles in your eyes.
Whether you talk, or silent are,
Your lips immortal beauties wear.

THE NECK OF IRIS

All your modesty, all your nice care, cannot hide the ravishing beauties of your neck ; we must see it, coy as you are; and see it the whitest, and finest shaped, that ever was formed. Oh! why will you cover it? You know all handsome things would be seen. And oh! how often have you made your

lovers envy your scarf, or anything that hides so fine
an object from their sight. Damon himself complains of your too nice severity. Pray do not hide it
so carefully. See how perfectly turned it is! with
small blue veins, wandering and ranging here and
there, like little rivulets, that wanton over the flowery
meads! See how the round white rising breasts
heave with every breath, as if they disdained to be
confined to a covering; and repel the malicious
cloud that would obscure their brightness!

> Fain I would have leave to tell
> The charms that on your bosom dwell;
> Describe it like some flow'ry field,
> That does ten thousand pleasures yield;
> A thousand gliding springs and groves;
> All receptacles for loves:
> But oh! what Iris hides, must be
> Ever sacred kept by me.

THE ARMS AND HANDS OF IRIS

I shall not be put to much trouble to show you
your hands and arms, because you may view them
without my help; and you are very unjust, if you
have not admired them a thousand times. The
beautiful colour and proportion of your arm is inimitable, and your hand is dazzling, fine, small,
and plump; long pointed fingers delicately turned;
dimpled on the snowy outside, but adorned within
with rose, all over the soft palm. O Iris! nothing
equals your fair hand; that hand, of which Love so
often makes such use to draw his bow, when he
would send the arrow home with more success; and
which irresistibly wounds those, who possibly have
not yet seen your eyes. And when you have been
veiled, that lovely hand has gained you a thousand
adorers. And I have heard Damon say, 'Without
the aid of more beauties, that alone had been sufficient to have made an absolute conquest over his

soul.' And he has often vowed 'It never touched him but it made his blood run with little irregular motions in his veins, his breath beat short and double, his blushes rise, and his very soul dance.'

Oh! how the hand the lover ought to prize
'Bove any one peculiar grace,
While he is dying for the eyes
And doting on the lovely face!
The unconsid'ring little knows,
How much he to this beauty owes.

That, when the lover absent is,
Informs him of his mistress' heart;
'Tis that which gives him all his bliss,
When dear love-secrets 'twill impart.
That plights the faith the maid bestows;
And that confirms the tim'rous vows.

'Tis that betrays the tenderness,
Which the too bashful tongue denies:
'Tis that which does the heart confess,
And spares the language of the eyes.
'Tis that which treasure gives so vast;
Ev'n Iris 'twill to Damon give at last.

THE GRACE AND AIR OF IRIS

It is I alone, O charming maid! that can show you that noble part of your beauty: that generous air that adorns all your lovely person, and renders every motion and action perfectly adorable. With what a grace you walk! How free, how easy, and how unaffected! See how you move! for only here you can see it. Damon has told you a thousand times, that never any mortal had so glorious an air: but he could not half describe it, nor would you credit even what he said; but with a careless smile pass it off for the flattery of a lover. But here behold, and be convinced, and know, no part of your beauty can charm more than this. O Iris! confess, Love has adorned you with all his art and care. Your beauties are the themes of all the Muses; who tell you in daily

songs, that the Graces themselves have not more than
Iris. And one may truly say, that you alone know
how to join the ornaments and dress with beauty;
and you are still adorned, as if that shape and air
had a peculiar art to make all things appear gay and
fine. Oh! how well dressed you are! How everything becomes you! Never singular, never gaudy;
but always suiting with your quality.

> Oh! how that negligence becomes your air!
> That careless flowing of your hair,
> That plays about with wanton grace,
> With evrey motion of your face :
> Disdaining all that dull formality,
> That dares not move the lip, or eye,
> But at some fancied grace's cost ;
> And think, with it, at least, a lover lost.
> But the unlucky minute to reclaim,
> And ease the coquette of her pain,
> The pocket-glass adjusts the face again :
> Resets the mouth, and languishes the eyes ;
> And thinks, the spark that ogles that way—dies.
>
> Of Iris learn, O ye mistaken fair!
> To dress your face, your smiles, your air :
> Let easy nature all the business do,
> She can the softer graces show ;
> Which art but turns to ridicule,
> And where there's none serves but to show the fool.
>
> In Iris you all graces find ;
> Charms without art, a motion unconfined ;
> Without constraint, she smiles, she looks, she talks ;
> And without affectation, moves and walks.
> Beauties so perfect ne'er were seen :
> O ye mistaken fair! Dress ye by Iris' mien.

THE DISCRETION OF IRIS

But, O Iris! the beauties of the body are imperfect,
if the beauties of the soul do not advance themselves
to an equal height. But, O Iris! what mortal is
there so damned to malice, that does not, with adoration, confess, that you, O charming maid, have an

equal portion of all the braveries and virtues of the mind? And, who is it, that confesses your beauty, that does not at the same time acknowledge and bow to your wisdom? The whole world admires both in you; and all with impatience ask 'Which of the two is most surprising, your beauty, or your discretion?' But we dispute in vain on that excellent subject; for after all, it is determined, that the two charms are equal. It is none of those idle discretions that consists in words alone, and ever takes the shadow of reason for the substance; and that makes use of all the little artifices of subtlety, and florid talking, to make the outside of the argument appear fine, and leave the inside wholly misunderstood; who runs away with words, and never thinks of sense. But you, O lovely maid! never make use of these affected arts; but without being too brisk or too severe, too silent or too talkative, you inspire in all your hearers a joy, and a respect. Your soul is an enemy to that usual vice of your sex, of using little arguments against the fair; or, by a word or jest, making yourself and hearers pleasant at the expense of the fame of others.

Your heart is an enemy to all passions, but that of love. And this is one of your noble maxims, 'That every one ought to love, in some part of his life; and that in a heart truly brave, love is without folly: that wisdom is a friend to love, and love to perfect wisdom.' Since these maxims are your own, do not, O charming Iris! resist that noble passion: and since Damon is the most tender of all your lovers, answer his passion with a noble ardour. Your prudence never fails in the choice of your friends; and in choosing so well your lover, you will stand an eternal precedent to all unreasonable fair ones.

O thou that dost excel in wit and truth!
Be still a precedent for love and youth.
Let the dull world say what it will,
A noble flame's unblameable.

Where a fine sentiment and soft passion rules,
They scorn the censure of the fools.

Yield, Iris, then ; oh, yield to love !
  Redeem your dying slave from pain ;
The world your conduct must approve :
Your prudence never acts in vain.

THE GOODNESS AND COMPLAISANCE OF IRIS

Who but your lovers, fair Iris ! doubts but you are
the most complaisant person in the world ; and that
with so much sweetness you oblige all, that you
command in yielding. And as you gain the heart
of both sexes, with the affability of your noble
temper ; so all are proud and vain of obliging you.
And, Iris, you may live assured, that your empire is
eternally established by your beauty and your goodness : your power is confirmed, and you grow in
strength every minute : your goodness gets you
friends, and your beauty lovers.

This goodness is not one of those, whose folly
renders it easy to every desirer ; but a pure effect of
the generosity of your soul ; such as prudence alone
manages, according to the merit of the person to
whom it is extended ; and those whom you esteem,
receive the sweet marks of it, and only your lovers
complain ; yet even then you charm. And though
sometimes you can be a little disturbed, yet through
your anger your goodness shines ; and you are but
too much afraid, that that may bear a false interpretation. For oftentimes scandal makes that pass for
an effect of love, which is purely that of complaisance.

Never had anybody more tenderness for their
friends, than Iris : their presence gives her joy, their
absence trouble ; and when she cannot see them, she
finds no pleasure like speaking of them obligingly.
Friendship reigns in your heart, and sincerity on your
tongue. Your friendship is so strong, so constant,
and so tender, that it charms, pleases, and satisfies all,

that are not your adorers. Damon therefore is excusable, if he be not contented with your noble friendship alone ; for he is the most tender of that number.

No ! give me all, th' impatient lover cries ;
   Without your soul I cannot live :
Dull friendship cannot mine suffice,
   That dies for all you have to give.
The smiles, the vows, the heart must all be mine ;
I cannot spare one thought, or wish of thine.

I sigh, I languish all the day ;
   Each minute ushers in my groans :
To ev'ry god in vain I pray ;
   In ev'ry grove repeat my moans.
Still Iris' charms are all my sorrows' themes !
They pain me waking, and they rack in dreams.

Return, fair Iris ! Oh, return !
   Lest sighing long your slave destroys.
I wish, I rave, I faint, I burn ;
   Restore me quickly all my joys :
Your mercy else will come too late ;
Distance in love more cruel is than hate.

THE WIT OF IRIS

You are deceived in me, fair Iris, if you take me for one of those ordinary glasses, that represent the beauty only of the body ; I remark to you also the beauties of the soul. And all about you declares yours the finest that ever was formed ; that you have a wit that surprises, and is always new. It is none of those that loses its lustre when one considers it ; the more we examine yours, the more adorable we find it. You say nothing that is not at once agreeable and solid ; it is always quick and ready, without impertinence, that little vanity of the fair : who, when they know they have wit, rarely manage it so, as not to abound in talking ; and think, that all they say must please, because luckily they sometimes chance to do so. But Iris never speaks, but it is of use ; and gives a pleasure to all that hear her. She has the

perfect air of penetrating, even the most secret
thoughts. How often have you known, without being
told, all that has passed in Damon's heart! For all
great wits are prophets too.

> Tell me; oh, tell me! charming prophetess;
> For you alone can tell my love's success.
>> The lines in my dejected face,
> I fear, will lead you to no kind result:
>> It is your own that you must trace;
> Those of your heart you must consult.
> 'Tis there my fortune I must learn,
> And all that Damon does concern.
>
> I tell you that I love a maid,
>> As bright as heav'n, of angel-hue;
> The softest nature ever made,
>> Whom I with sighs and vows pursue.
> Oh, tell me, charming prophetess!
> Shall I this lovely maid possess?
>
> A thousand rivals do obstruct my way;
>> A thousand fears they do create:
> They throng about her all the day,
>> Whilst I at awful distance wait.
> Say, will the lovely maid so fickle prove,
> To give my rivals hope, as well as love?
>
> She has a thousand charms of wit,
>> With all the beauty heav'n e'er gave:
> Oh! let her not make use of it,
>> To flatter me into the slave.
> Oh! tell me truth, to ease my pain;
> Say rather, I shall die by her disdain.

THE MODESTY OF IRIS

I perceive, fair Iris, you have a mind to tell me,
I have entertained you too long with a discourse on
yourself. I know your modesty makes this declaration an offence, and you suffer me, with pain, to
unveil those treasures you would hide. Your modesty,
that so commendable a virtue in the fair, and so
peculiar to you, is here a little too severe. Did I

flatter you, you should blush: did I seek, by praising you, to show an art of speaking finely, you might chide. But, O Iris, I say nothing but such plain truths, as all the world can witness are so: and so far I am from flattery, that I seek no ornament of words. Why do you take such care to conceal your virtues? They have too much lustre, not to be seen, in spite of all your modesty: your wit, your youth, and reason, oppose themselves against this dull obstructer of our happiness. Abate, O Iris, a little of this virtue, since you have so many others to defend yourself against the attacks of your adorers. You yourself have the least opinion of your own charms: and being the only person in the world, that is not in love with them, you hate to pass whole hours before your looking-glass; and to pass your time, like most of the idle fair, in dressing, and setting off those beauties, which need so little art. You, more wise, disdain to give those hours to the fatigue of dressing, which you know so well how to employ a thousand ways. The Muses have blessed you, above your sex; and you know how to gain a conquest with your pen, more absolutely than all the industrious fair, who trust to dress and equipage.

I have a thousand things to tell you more, but willingly resign my place to Damon, that faithful lover; he will speak more ardently than I: for let a glass use all its force, yet, when it speaks its best, it speaks but coldly.

If my glass, O charming Iris, have the good fortune (which I could never entirely boast) to be believed, it will serve at least to convince you I have not been so guilty of flattery, as I have a thousand times been charged. Since then my passion is equal to your beauty (without comparison, or end), believe, O lovely maid! how I sigh in your absence; and be persuaded to lessen my pain, and restore me to my joys; for there is no torment so great, as the absence of a lover from his mistress; of which this is the idea.

THE EFFECTS OF ABSENCE FROM WHAT WE LOVE

Thou one continued sigh ! all over pain !
Eternal wish ! but wish, alas, in vain !
Thou languishing, impatient hoper on ;
A busy toiler, and yet still undone !
A breaking glimpse of distant day,
Enticing on, and leading more astray !
Thou joy in prospect, future bliss extreme ;
Never to be possessed, but in a dream !
Thou fab'lous goddess, which the ravished boy
In happy slumbers proudly did enjoy ;
But waking, found an airy cloud he prest ;
His arms came empty to his panting breast.
Thou shade, that only haunt'st the soul by night ;
And when thou shouldst in form thou fly'st the sight :
Thou false idea of the thinking brain,
That labours for the charming form in vain :
Which if by chance it catch, thou'rt lost again.

THE LUCKY MISTAKE

A NEW NOVEL

THE river Loire has on its delightful banks abundance of handsome, beautiful, and rich towns and villages, to which the noble stream adds no small graces and advantages, blessing their fields with plenty, and their eyes with a thousand diversions. In one of these happily situated towns, called Orleans, where abundance of people of the best quality and condition reside, there was a rich nobleman, now retired from the busy Court, where in his youth he had been bred, wearied with the toils of ceremony and noise, to enjoy that perfect tranquillity of life, which is nowhere to be found but in retreat, a faithful friend, and a good library ; and, as the admirable Horace says, in a little house and a large garden. Count Bellyaurd, for so was this nobleman called, was of this opinion ; and the rather, because he had one only son, called Rinaldo, now grown to the age of fifteen, who having all the excellent qualities and graces of youth by nature, he would bring him up in all virtues and noble sciences, which he believed the gaiety and lustre of the Court might divert. He therefore in his retirement spared no cost to those that could instruct and accomplish him ; and he had the best tutors and masters that could be purchased at Court : Bellyaurd making far less account of riches than of fine parts. He found his son capable of all impressions, having a wit suitable to his delicate person, so that he was the sole joy of his life, and the darling of his eyes.

In the very next house, which joined close to that of Bellyaurd's, there lived another Count, who had in his youth been banished the Court of France for some misunderstandings in some high affairs wherein he was concerned. His name was De Pais, a man of great birth, but of no fortune; or at least one not suitable to the grandeur of his origin. And as it is most natural for great souls to be most proud (if I may call a handsome disdain by that vulgar name) when they are most depressed; so De Pais was more retired, more estranged from his neighbours, and kept a greater distance, than if he had enjoyed all he had lost at Court; and took more solemnity and state upon him, because he would not be subject to the reproaches of the world, by making himself familiar with it. So that he rarely visited; and, contrary to the custom of those in France, who are easy of access, and free of conversation, he kept his family retired so close, that it was rare to see any of them; and when they went abroad, which was but seldom, they wanted nothing as to outward appearance, that was fit for his quality, and what was much above his condition.

This old Count had two only daughters, of exceeding beauty, who gave the generous father ten thousand torments, as often as he beheld them, when he considered their extreme beauty, their fine wit, their innocence, modesty, and above all their birth; and that he had not a fortune to marry them according to their quality; and below it, he had rather see them laid in their silent graves, than consent to it: for he scorned the world should see him forced by his poverty to commit an action below his dignity.

There lived in a neighbouring town, a certain nobleman, friend to De Pais, called Count Vernole, a man of about forty years of age, of low stature, complexion very black and swarthy, lean, lame, ex-

tremely proud and haughty ; extracted of a descent
from the blood-royal; not extremely brave, but very
glorious : he had no very great estate, but was in
election of a greater, and of an addition of honour
from the King, his father having done most worthy
services against the Huguenots, and by the high favour
of Cardinal Mazarin, was represented to his Majesty,
as a man related to the Crown, of great name, but
small estate : so that there were now nothing but
great expectations and preparations in the family of
Count Vernole to go to the Court, to which he daily
hoped an invitation or command.

Vernole's fortune being hitherto something akin to
that of De Pais, there was a greater correspondence
between these two gentlemen, than they had with
any other persons ; they accounting themselves above
the rest of the world, believed none so proper and fit
for their conversation, as that of each other; so that
there was a very particular intimacy between them.
Whenever they went abroad, they clubbed their train,
to make one great show ; and were always together,
bemoaning each other's fortune, and that from so
high a descent, as one from monarchs by the mother's
side, and the other from dukes of the father's side,
they were reduced by fate to the degree of private
gentlemen.   They would often consult how to
manage affairs most to advantage, and often De Pais
would ask counsel of Vernole, how best he should
dispose of his daughters, which now were about their
ninth year the eldest, and eighth the youngest.
Vernole had often seen those two buds of beauty,
and already saw opening in Atlante's face and mind
(for that was the name of the eldest, and Charlot the
youngest) a glory of wit and beauty, which could not
but one day display itself, with dazzling lustre, to the
wondering world.

Vernole was a great virtuoso, of a humour nice,
delicate, critical, and opinionative : he had nothing
of the French mien in him, but all the gravity of the

don. His ill-favoured person, and his low estate, put him out of humour with the world; and because that should not upbraid or reproach his follies and defects, he was sure to be beforehand with that, and to be always satiric upon it; and loved to live and act contrary to the custom and usage of all mankind besides.

He was infinitely delighted to find a man of his own humour in De Pais, or at least a man that would be persuaded to like his so well, to live up to it; and it was no little joy and satisfaction to him to find, that he kept his daughters in that severity, which was wholly agreeable to him, and so contrary to the manner and fashion of the French quality; who allow all freedoms, which to Vernole's rigid nature, seemed as so many steps to vice, and in his opinion, the ruiner of all virtue and honour in womankind. De Pais was extremely glad his conduct was so well interpreted, which was no other in him than a proud frugality; who, because they could not appear in so much gallantry as their quality required, kept them retired, and unseen to all, but his particular friends, of whom Vernole was the chief.

Vernole never appeared before Atlante (which was seldom) but he assumed a gravity and respect fit to have entertained a maid of twenty, or rather a matron of much greater years and judgment. His discourses were always of matters of state or philosophy; and sometimes when De Pais would (laughing) say 'He might as well entertain Atlante with Greek and Hebrew,' he would reply gravely, 'You are mistaken, sir, I find the seeds of great and profound matter in the soul of this young maid, which ought to be nourished now while she is young, and they will grow up to very great perfection: I find Atlante capable of the noble virtues of the mind, and am infinitely mistaken in my observations, and art of physiognomy, if Atlante be not born for greater things than her fortune does now promise. She will be very con-

siderable in the world (believe me), and this will
arrive to her perfectly from the force of her charms.'
De Pais was extremely overjoyed to hear such good
prophesied of Atlante, and from that time set a sort
of an esteem upon her, which he did not on Charlot
his younger; whom, by the persuasions of Vernole,
he resolved to put in a monastery, that what he had
might descend to Atlante: not but he confessed
Charlot had beauty extremely attractive, and a wit
that promised much, when it should be cultivated by
years and experience; and would show itself with
great advantage and lustre in a monastery. All this
pleased De Pais very well, who was easily persuaded,
since he had not a fortune to marry her well in the
world.

As yet Vernole had never spoken to Atlante of love,
nor did his gravity think it prudence to discover his
heart to so young a maid; he waited her more sensible years, when he could hope to have some return.
And all he expected from this her tender age, was by
his daily converse with her, and the presents he made
her suitable to her years, to ingratiate himself insensibly into her friendship and esteem, since she was
not yet capable of love; but even in that he mistook
his aim, for every day he grew more and more disagreeable to Atlante, and would have been her
absolute aversion, had she known she had every day
entertained a lover; but as she grew in years and
sense, he seemed the more despicable in her eyes as
to his person; yet as she had respect to his parts and
qualities, she paid him all the complaisance she could,
and which was due to him, and so must be confessed.
Though he had a stiff formality in all he said and
did, yet he had wit and learning, and was a great
philosopher. As much of his learning as Atlante was
capable of attaining to, he made her mistress of, and
that was no small portion; for all his discourse was
fine and easily comprehended, his notions of philosophy fit for ladies; and he took greater pains with

Atlante, than any master would have done with a scholar. So that it was most certain, he added very great accomplishment to her natural wit: and the more, because she took a great delight in philosophy; which very often made her impatient of his coming, especially when she had many questions to ask him concerning it, and she would often receive him with a pleasure in her face, which he did not fail to interpret to his own advantage, being very apt to flatter himself. Her sister Charlot would often ask her, 'How she could give whole afternoons to so disagreeable a man. What is it,' said she, 'that charms you so? his tawny leather-face, his extraordinary high nose, his wide mouth and eyebrows, that hang lowering over his eyes, his lean carcase, and his lame and halting hips?' But Atlante would discreetly reply, 'If I must grant all you say of Count Vernole to be true, yet he has a wit and learning that will atone sufficiently for all those faults you mention. A fine soul is infinitely to be preferred to a fine body; this decays, but that is eternal; and age that ruins one, refines the other.' Though possibly Atlante thought as ill of the Count as her sister, yet in respect to him, she would not own it.

Atlante was now arrived to her thirteenth year, when her beauty, which every day increased, became the discourse of the whole town, which had already gained her as many lovers as had beheld her; for none saw her without languishing for her, or at least, but what were in very great admiration of her. Everybody talked of the young Atlante, and all the noblemen, who had sons (knowing the smallness of her fortune, and the lustre of her beauty), would send them, for fear of their being charmed with her beauty, either to some other part of the world, or exhorted them, by way of precaution, to keep out of her sight. Old Bellyaurd was one of those wise parents; and timely prevention, as he thought, of Rinaldo's falling in love with Atlante, perhaps was the occasion of his being so. He had before heard of Atlante, and of her beauty, yet it had made no impressions on his heart; but his father no sooner forbid him loving, than he felt a new desire tormenting him, of seeing this lovely and dangerous young person. He wonders at his unaccountable pain, which daily solicits him within, to go where he may behold this beauty; of whom he frames a thousand ideas, all such as were most agreeable to him; but then upbraids his fancy for not forming her half so delicate as she was; and longs yet more to see her, to know how near she approaches to the picture he has drawn of her in his mind: and though he knew she lived the next house to him, yet he knew also she was kept within like a vowed nun, or with the severity of a Spaniard. And though he had a chamber, which had a jutting window, that looked just upon the door of Monsieur De Pais, and that he would watch many hours at a time, in hope to see them go out, yet he could never get a glimpse of her; yet he heard she often frequented the Church of Our Lady. Thither then young Rinaldo resolved to go, and did so two or three mornings; in which time, to his unspeakable grief, he saw no beauty appear that charmed him; and yet he fancied that Atlante was there, and that he had seen her; that some one of those young ladies that he saw in the church was she, though he had nobody to inquire of, and that she was not so fair as the world reported; for which he would often sigh, as if he had lost some great expectation However, he ceased not to frequent this church, and one day saw a young beauty, who at first glimpse made his heart leap to his mouth, and fall a-trembling again into its wonted place; for it immediately told him, that that young maid was Atlante: she was with her sister Charlot, who was very handsome, but not comparable to Atlante. He fixed his eyes upon her as she kneeled at the altar; he never moved from that charming face as long as she remained there; he forgot all devotion, but what he paid to her; he adored her, he burnt and languished already for her, and found he must possess Atlante or die. Often as he gazed upon her, he saw her fair eyes lifted up towards his, where they often met; which she perceiving, would cast hers down into her bosom, or on her book, and blush as if she had done a fault. Charlot perceived all the motions of Rinaldo, how he folded his arms, how he sighed and gazed on her sister; she took notice of his clothes, his garniture, and every particular of his dress, as young girls do; and seeing him so very handsome, and so much better dressed than all the young cavaliers that were in the church, she was very much pleased with him; and could not forbear saying, in a low voice, to Atlante, 'Look, look, my sister, what a pretty monsieur yonder is! see how fine his face is, how delicate his hair, how gallant his dress! and do but look how he gazes on you!' This would make Atlante blush anew, who durst not raise her eyes for fear she should encounter his. While he had the pleasure to imagine they were talking of him, and he saw in the pretty face of Charlot, that what she said was not to his disadvantage, and by the blushes of Atlante, that she was not displeased with what was spoken to her; he perceived the young one importunate with her; and Atlante jogging her with her elbow, as much as to say, 'Hold your peace': all this he made a kind interpretation of, and was transported with joy at the good omens. He was willing to flatter his new flame, and to compliment his young desire with a little hope; but the divine ceremony ceasing, Atlante left the church, and it being very fair weather, she walked home. Rinaldo, who saw her going, felt all the agonies of a lover, who parts with all that can make him happy; and seeing only Atlante attended with her sister, and a footman following with their books, he was a thousand times about to speak to them; but he no sooner advanced a step or two towards them to that purpose (for he

followed them) but his heart failed, and a certain awe
and reverence, or rather the fears and tremblings of a
lover, prevented him.   But when he considered, that
possibly he might never have so favourable an opportunity again, he resolved anew, and called up so
much courage to his heart, as to speak to Atlante;
but before he did so, Charlot looking behind her, saw
Rinaldo very near to them, and cried out with a voice
of joy, 'O sister, sister! look where the handsome
monsieur is, just behind us! sure he is somebody of
quality, for see he has two footmen that follow him,
in just such liveries, and so rich as those of our
neighbour Monsieur Bellyaurd.' At this Atlante
could not forbear, but before she was aware of it,
turned her head, and looked on Rinaldo; which
encouraged him to advance, and putting off his hat,
which he clapped under his arm, with a low bow, said,
'Ladies, you are slenderly attended, and so many
accidents arrive to the fair in the rude streets, that I
humbly implore you will permit me, whose duty it is
as a neighbour, to wait on you to your door.' 'Sir,'
said Atlante, blushing, 'we fear no insolence, and
need no protector; or if we did, we should not be so
rude to take you out of your way, to serve us.'
'Madam,' said he, 'my way lies yours. I live at the
next door, and am son to Bellyaurd, your neighbour.
But, madam,' added he, 'if I were to go all my life
out of the way, to do you service, I should take it for
the greatest happiness that could arrive to me; but,
madam, sure a man can never be out of his way, who
has the honour of so charming company.' Atlante
made no reply to this, but blushed and bowed. But
Charlot said, 'Nay, sir, if you are our neighbour, we
will give you leave to conduct us home; but pray,
sir, how came you to know we are your neighbours?
for we never saw you before, to our knowledge.' 'My
pretty miss,' replied Rinaldo, 'I knew it from that
transcendent beauty that appeared in your faces, and
fine shapes; for I have heard, there was no beauty in

the world like that of Atlante's; and I no sooner
saw her, but my heart told me it was she. 'Heart!'
said Charlot, laughing, 'why, do hearts speak?'
'The most intelligible of anything,' Rinaldo replied,
'when it is tenderly touched, when it is charmed and
transported.' At these words he sighed, and Atlante,
to his extreme satisfaction, blushed. 'Touched,
charmed, and transported,' said Charlot, 'what's that?
And how do you do to have it be all these things?
For I would give anything in the world to have my
heart speak.' 'Oh!' said Rinaldo, 'your heart is too
young, it is not yet arrived to the years of speaking;
about thirteen or fourteen, it may possibly be saying
a thousand soft things to you; but it must be first inspired by some noble object, whose idea it must
retain.' 'What,' replied this pretty prattler, 'I'll
warrant I must be in love?' 'Yes,' said Rinaldo,
'most passionately, or you will have but little conversation with your heart.' 'Oh!' replied she, 'I am
afraid the pleasure of such a conversation will not
make me amends for the pain that love will give
me.' 'That,' said Rinaldo, 'is according as the object
is kind, and as you hope; if he love, and you hope,
you will have double pleasure: and in this, how
great an advantage have fair ladies above us men!
It is almost impossible for you to love in vain, you
have your choice of a thousand hearts, which you
have subdued, and may not only choose your slaves,
but be assured of them; without speaking, you are
beloved, it need not cost you a sigh or a tear. But
unhappy man is often destined to give his heart,
where it is not regarded, to sigh, to weep, and
languish, without any hope of pity.' 'You speak so
feelingly, sir,' said Charlot, 'that I am afraid this is
your case.' 'Yes, madam,' replied Rinaldo, sighing,
'I am that unhappy man.' 'Indeed it is pity,' said
she. Pray, how long have you been so?' 'Ever
since I heard of the charming Atlante,' replied he,
sighing again. 'I adored her character; but now I

have seen her, I die for her.' 'For me, sir!' said
Atlante, who had not yet spoken, 'this is the common
compliment of all the young men, who pretend to be
lovers; and if one should pity all those sighers, we
should have but very little left for ourselves.' 'I
believe,' said Rinaldo, 'there are none that tell you
so, who do not mean as they say: yet among all
those adorers, and those who say they will die for
you, you will find none will be so good as their words
but Rinaldo.' 'Perhaps,' said Atlante, 'of all those
who tell me of dying, there are none that tell me of
it with so little reason as Rinaldo, if that be your
name, sir.' 'Madam, it is,' said he, 'and who am
transported with an unspeakable joy, to hear those
last words from your fair mouth: and let me, O lovely
Atlante! assure you, that what I have said, are not
words of course, but proceed from a heart that has
vowed itself eternally yours, even before I had the
happiness to behold this divine person; but now
that my eyes have made good all my heart before
imagined, and did but hope, I swear, I will die a
thousand deaths, rather than violate what I have said
to you; that I adore you; that my soul and all my
faculties are charmed with your beauty and innocence,
and that my life and fortune, not inconsiderable, shall
be laid at your feet.' This he spoke with a fervency
of passion, that left her no doubt of what he had
said; yet she blushed for shame, and was a little
angry at herself, for suffering him to say so much to
her, the very first time she saw him, and accused herself for giving him any encouragement. And in this
confusion she replied, 'Sir, you have said too much
to be believed; and I cannot imagine so short an
acquaintance can make so considerable an impression; of which confession I accuse myself much
more than you, in that I did not only hearken to
what you said, without forbidding you to entertain
me at that rate, but for unheedily speaking something, that has encouraged this boldness: for so I

must call it, in a man so great a stranger to me.'
'Madam,' said he, 'if I have offended by the sudden-
ness of my presumptuous discovery, I beseech you to
consider my reasons for it, the few opportunities I am
like to have, and the impossibility of waiting on you,
both from the severity of your father and mine; who,
ere I saw you, warned me of my fate, as if he foresaw
I should fall in love, as soon as I should chance to
see you; and for that reason has kept me closer
to my studies, than hitherto I have been. And from
that time I began to feel a flame, which was kindled
by report alone, and the description my father gave
of your wondrous and dangerous beauty. Therefore,
madam, I have not suddenly told you of my passion.
I have been long your lover, and have long languished
without telling of my pain; and you ought to pardon
it now, since it is done with all the respect and
religious awe, that it is possible for a heart to deliver
and unload itself in. Therefore, madam, if you have
by chance uttered anything, that I have taken advantage or hope from, I assure you it is so small, that
you have no reason to repent it; but rather, if you
would have me live, send me not from you, without a
confirmation of that little hope. See, madam,' said
he, more earnestly and trembling, 'see we are almost
arrived at our homes, send me not to mine in a
despair that I cannot support with life; but tell me, I
shall be blessed with your sight, sometimes in your
balcony, which is very near to a jutting window in
our house, from whence I have sent many a longing
look towards yours, in hope to have seen my soul's
tormentor.' 'I shall be very unwilling,' said she, 'to
enter into an intrigue of love or friendship with a
man, whose parents will be averse to my happiness,
and possibly mine as refractory, though they cannot
but know such an alliance would be very considerable,
my fortune not being suitable to yours: I tell you
this, that you may withdraw in time from an engagement, in which I find there will be a great many

obstacles.' 'Oh! madam,' replied Rinaldo, sighing, 'if my person be not disagreeable to you, you will have no occasion to fear the rest; it is that I dread, and that which is all my fear.' He, sighing, beheld her with a languishing look, that told her, he expected her answer; when she replied, 'Sir, if that will be satisfaction enough for you at this time, I do assure you, I have no aversion for your person, in which I find more to be valued, than in any I have yet seen; and if what you say be real, and proceed from a heart truly affected, I find, in spite of me, you will oblige me to give you hope.'

They were come so near their own houses, that he had not time to return her any answer; but with a low bow he acknowledged her bounty, and expressed the joy her last words had given him, by a look that made her understand he was charmed and pleased: and she bowing to him with an air of satisfaction in her face, he was well assured, there was nothing to be seen so lovely as she then appeared, and left her to go into her own house. But till she was out of sight, he had not power to stir, and then sighing, retired to his own apartment, to think over all that had passed between them. He found nothing but what gave him a thousand joys, in all she had said; and he blessed this happy day, and wondered how his stars came so kind, to make him in one hour at once see Atlante, and have the happiness to know from her mouth, that he was not disagreeable to her. Yet with this satisfaction, he had a thousand thoughts mixed which were tormenting, and those were the fear of their parents; he foresaw from what his father had said to him already, that it would be difficult to draw him to a consent of his marriage with Atlante. These joys and fears were his companions all the night, in which he took but little rest. Nor was Atlante without her inquietudes. She found Rinaldo more in her thoughts than she wished, and a sudden change of humour, that made her know something was the

matter with her more than usual ; she calls to mind
Rinaldo's speaking of the conversation with his
heart, and found hers would be tattling to her, if she
would give way to it ; and yet the more she strove to
avoid it, the more it importuned her, and in spite of
all her resistance, would tell her, that Rinaldo had
a thousand charms. It tells her, that he loves and
adores her, and that she would be the most cruel of
her sex, should she not be sensible of his passion.
She finds a thousand graces in his person and conversation, and as many advantages in his fortune, which
was one of the most considerable in all those parts ;
for his estate exceeded that of the most noble men in
Orleans, and she imagines she should be the most fortunate of all womankind in such a match. With these
thoughts she employed all the hours of the night ;
so that she lay so long in bed the next day, that
Count Vernole, who had invited himself to dinner,
came before she had quitted her chamber, and she
was forced to say, she had not been well. He had
brought her a very fine book, newly come out, of
delicate philosophy, fit for the study of ladies. But
he appeared so disagreeable to that heart, wholly
taken up with a new and fine object, that she could
now hardly pay him that civility she was wont to do ;
while on the other side that little state and pride
Atlante assumed, made her appear the more charming
to him : so that if Atlante had no mind to begin
a new lesson of philosophy, while she fancied her
thoughts were much better employed, the Count
every moment expressing his tenderness and passion,
had as little an inclination to instruct her, as she had
to be instructed. Love had taught her a new lesson,
and he would fain teach her a new lesson of love, but
fears it will be a diminishing his gravity and grandeur,
to open the secrets of his heart to so young a maid.
He therefore thinks it more agreeable to his quality
and years, being about forty, to use her father's
authority in this affair, and that it was sufficient for

him to declare himself to Monsieur De Pais, who he knew would be proud of the honour he did him. Some time passed, before he could be persuaded even to declare himself to her father. He fancies the little coldness and pride he saw in Atlante's face, which was not usual, proceeded from some discovery of passion, which his eyes had made, or now and then a sigh, that unawares broke forth; and accuses himself of a levity below his quality, and the dignity of his wit and gravity; and therefore assumes a more rigid and formal behaviour than he was wont, which rendered him yet more disagreeable than before; and it was with greater pain than ever, she gave him that respect which was due to his quality.

Rinaldo, after a restless night, was up very early in the morning; and though he was not certain of seeing his adorable Atlante, he dressed himself with all that care, as if he had been to have waited on her, and got himself into the window, that overlooked Monsieur De Pais's balcony, where he had not remained long, before he saw the pretty Charlot come into it, not with any design of seeing Rinaldo, but to look and gaze about her a little. Rinaldo saw her, and made her a very low reverence, and found some disordered joy on the sight of even Charlot, since she was sister to Atlante. He called to her (for the window was so near her, he could easily he heard by her), and told her 'He was infinitely indebted to her bounty, for giving him an opportunity yesterday of falling on that discourse, which had made him the happiest man in the world.' He said, 'If she had not by her agreeable conversation encouraged him, and drawn him from one word to another, he should never have had the confidence to have told Atlante, how much he adored her.' 'I am very glad,' replied Charlot, 'that I was the occasion of the beginning of an amour which was displeasing to neither one nor the other; for I assure you for your comfort, my sister nothing but thinks on you: we lie together, and you have taught

her already to sigh so, that I could not sleep for her.'
At this his face was covered all over with a rising joy,
which his heart could not contain : and after some
discourse, in which this innocent girl discovered more
than Atlante wished she should, he besought her to
become his advocate; and she had no brother, to give
him leave to assume that honour, and call her sister.
Thus, by degrees, he flattered her into a consent of
carrying a letter from him to Atlante; which she,
who believed all as innocent as herself, and being not
forbid to do so, immediately consented to ; when he
took his pen and ink, that stood in the window, with
paper, and wrote Atlante this following letter :—

RINALDO TO ATLANTE

If my fate be so severe, as to deny me the happiness
of sighing out my pain and passion daily at your feet, if
there be any faith in the hope you were pleased to give me
(as it were a sin to doubt), O charming Atlante ! suffer me
not to languish, both without beholding you, and without
the blessing of now and then a billet, in answer to those
that shall daily assure you of my eternal faith and vow; it
is all I ask, till fortune, and our affairs, shall allow me the
unspeakable satisfaction of claiming you : yet if your charity
can sometimes afford me a sight of you, either from your
balcony in the evening, or at a church in the morning, it
would save me from that despair and torment, which must
possess a heart so unassured, as that of your eternal adorer,

RIN. BELLYAURD.

He having writ and sealed this, tossed it into the
balcony to Charlot, having first looked about to see if
none perceived them. She put it in her bosom, and
ran in to her sister, whom by chance she found alone;
Vernole having taken De Pais into the garden, to
discourse him concerning the sending Charlot to the
monastery, which work he desired to see performed,
before he declared his intentions to Atlante : for
among all his other good qualities, he was very

avaricious; and as fair as Atlante was, he thought
she would be much fairer with the addition of
Charlot's portion. This affair of his with Monsieur
De Pais, gave Charlot an opportunity of delivering
her letter to her sister; who no sooner drew it from
her bosom, but Atlante's face was covered over with
blushes. For she imagined from whence it came, and
had a secret joy in that imagination, though she
thought she must put on the severity and niceness
of a virgin, who would not be thought to have surrendered her heart with so small an assault, and the
first too. So she demanded from whence Charlot
had that letter; who replied with joy, 'From the
fine young gentleman, our neighbour.' At which
Atlante assumed all the gravity she could, to chide
her sister; who replied, 'Well, sister, had you this day
seen him, you would not have been angry to have
received a letter from him; he looked so handsome,
and was so richly dressed, ten times finer than he was
yesterday; and I promised him you should read it:
therefore, pray let me keep my word with him; and
not only so, but carry him an answer.' 'Well,' said
Atlante, 'to save your credit with Monsieur Rinaldo,
I will read it.' Which she did, and finished with
a sigh. While she was reading, Charlot ran into the
garden, to see if they were not likely to be surprised;
and finding the Count and her father set in an arbour,
in deep discourse, she brought pen, ink, and paper to
her sister, and told her, she might write without the
fear of being disturbed: and urged her so long to what
was enough her inclination, that she at last obtained
this answer :—

ATLANTE TO RINALDO

Charlot, your little importunate advocate, has at last subdued me to a consent of returning you this. She has put
me on an affair with which I am wholly unacquainted; and
you ought to take this very kindly from me, since it is the
very first time I ever wrote to one of your sex, though perhaps I might with less danger have done it to any other man.

I tremble while I write, since I dread a correspondence of this nature, which may insensibly draw us into an inconvenience, and engage me beyond the limits of that nicety I ought to preserve. For this way we venture to say a thousand little kind things, which in conversation we dare not do: for now none can see us blush. I am sensible I shall this way put myself too soon into your power; and though you have abundance of merit, I ought to be ashamed of confessing, I am but too sensible of it—— But hold—I shall discover for your repose (which I would preserve) too much of the heart of ATLANTE.

She gave this letter to Charlot; who immediately ran into the balcony with it, where she still found Rinaldo in a melancholy posture, leaning his head on his hand. She showed him the letter, but was afraid to toss it to him, for fear it might fall to the ground; so he ran and fetched a long cane, which he cleft at one end, and held it while she put the letter into the cleft, and stayed not to hear what he said to it. But never was man so transported with joy, as he was at the reading of this letter; it gives him new wounds; for to the generous, nothing obliges love so much as love: though it is now too much the nature of that inconstant sex, to cease to love as soon as they are sure of the conquest. But it was far different with our cavalier; he was the more inflamed, by imagining he had made some impressions on the heart of Atlante, and kindled some sparks there, that in time might increase to something more; so that he now resolves to die hers: and considering all the obstacles that may possibly hinder his happiness, he found none but his father's obstinacy, perhaps occasioned by the meanness of Atlante's fortune. To this he urged again, that he was his only son, and a son whom he loved equal to his own life; and that certainly, as soon as he should behold him dying for Atlante, which if he were forced to quit her he must be, he then believed the tenderness of so fond a parent would break forth into pity, and plead

within for his consent. These were the thoughts that
flattered this young lover all the day ; and whether
he were riding the great horse, or at his study of
philosophy, or mathematics, singing, dancing, or
whatsoever other exercise his tutors ordered, his
thoughts were continually on Atlante. And now
he profited no more, whatever he seemed to do ;
every day he failed not to write to her by the
hand of the kind Charlot; who, young as she was,
had conceived a great friendship for Rinaldo, and
failed not to fetch her letters, and bring him answers,
such as he wished to receive. But all this did not
satisfy our impatient lover ; absence killed, and he
was no longer able to support himself, without a sight
of this adorable maid. He therefore implores, she
will give him that satisfaction · and she at last grants
it, with a better will than he imagined. The next
day was the appointed time, when she would, under
pretence of going to church, give him an assignation.
And because all public places were dangerous, and
might make a great noise, and they had no private
place to trust to, Rinaldo, under pretence of going up
the river in his pleasure-boat, which he often did, sent
to have it made ready by the next day at ten of the
clock. This was accordingly done, and he gave
Atlante notice of his design of going an hour or two
on the river in his boat, which lay near to such
a place, not far from the church. She and Charlot
came thither : and because they durst not come out
without a footman or two, they taking one, sent him
with a 'How-do-ye' to some young ladies, and told
him, he should find them at church. So getting rid
of their spy, they hastened to the river-side, and
found a boat and Rinaldo, waiting to carry them on
board his little vessel, which was richly adorned, and
a very handsome collation ready for them, of cold
meats, salads and sweetmeats.

As soon as they were come into the pleasure-boat,
unseen of any, he kneeled at the feet of Atlante, and

there uttered so many passionate and tender things to her, with a voice so trembling and soft, with eyes so languishing, and a fervency and a fire so sincere, that her young heart, wholly incapable of artifice, could no longer resist such language, and such looks of love. She grows tender, and he perceives it in her fine eyes, who could not dissemble; he reads her heart in her looks, and found it yielding apace; and therefore assaults it anew, with fresh forces of sighs and tears. He implores she would assure him of her heart, which she could no other way do, than by yielding to marry him. He would carry her to the next village, there consummate that happiness, without which he was able to live no longer; for he had a thousand fears, that some other lover was, or would suddenly be provided for her; and therefore he would make sure of her while he had this opportunity: and to that end, he answered all the objections she could make to the contrary. But ever, when he named marriage, she trembled, with fear of doing something that she fancied she ought not to do without the consent of her father. She was sensible of the advantage, but had been so used to a strict obedience, that she could not without horror think of violating it; and therefore besought him, as he valued her repose, not to urge her to that. And told him further, that if he feared any rival, she would give him what other assurance and satisfaction he pleased, but that of marriage; which she could not consent to, till she knew such an alliance would not be fatal to him: for she feared, as passionately as he loved her, when he should find she had occasioned him the loss of his fortune, or his father's affection, he would grow to hate her. Though he answered to this all that a fond lover could urge, yet she was resolved, and he forced to content himself with obliging her by his prayers and protestations, his sighs and tears, to a contract, which they solemnly made each other, vowing on either side, they would never marry any other. This being solemnly concluded, he assumed a look more gay and contented than before: he presented her a very rich ring, which she durst not put on her finger, but hid it in her bosom.   And beholding each other now as man and wife, she suffered him all the decent freedoms he could wish to take; so that the hours of this voyage seemed the most soft and charming of his life: and doubtless they were so; every touch of Atlante transported him, every look pierced his soul, and he was all raptures of joy, when he considered this charming lovely maid was his own.

Charlot all this while was gazing above - deck, admiring the motion of the little vessel, and how easily the wind and tide bore her up the river.   She had never been in anything of this kind before, and was very well pleased and entertained, when Rinaldo called her down to tea; where they enjoyed themselves, as well as was possible: and Charlot was wondering to see such a content in their eyes.

But now they thought it was high time for them to return; they fancy the footman missing them at church, would go home and alarm their father, and the Knight of the Ill-favoured Countenance, as Charlot called Count Vernole, whose severity put their father on a greater restriction of them, than naturally he would do of himself.   At the name of this Count, Rinaldo changed colour, fearing he might be some rival; and asked Atlante, if this Vernole was akin to her?   She answered no; but was a very great friend to her father, and one who from their infancy had had a particular concern for their breeding, and was her master for philosophy.   'Ah!' replied Rinaldo, sighing, 'this man's concern must proceed from something more than friendship for her father'; and therefore conjured her to tell him, whether he was not a lover.   'A lover!' replied Atlante, 'I assure you, he is a perfect antidote against that passion.'   And though she suffered his ugly presence now, she should loathe and hate him, should he but name love to her.

She said 'she believed she need not fear any such persecution, since he was a man who was not at all amorous; that he had too much of the satire in his humour, to harbour any softness there: and nature had formed his body to his mind, wholly unfit for love. And that he might set his heart absolutely at rest, she assured him her father had never yet proposed any marriage to her, though many advantageous ones were offered him every day.

The sails being turned to carry them back from whence they came; after having discoursed of a thousand things, and all of love, and contrivance to carry on their mutual design, they with sighs parted; Rinaldo staying behind in the pleasure-boat, and they going ashore in the wherry that attended: after which he cast many an amorous and sad look, and perhaps was answered by those of Atlante.

It was past church-time two or three hours, when they arrived at home, wholly unprepared with an excuse, so absolutely was Atlante's soul possessed with softer business. The first person they met was the footman, who opened the door, and began to cry out how long he had waited in the church, and how in vain; without giving them time to reply. De Pais came towards them, and with a frowning look demanded where they had been. Atlante, who was not accustomed to excuses and untruth, was a while at a stand; when Charlot with a voice of joy cried out, 'O sir! we have been aboard of a fine little ship. At this Atlante blushed, fearing she would tell the truth. But she proceeded on, and said, that they had not been above a quarter of an hour at church, when the Lady ——, with some other ladies and cavaliers, were going out of the church, and that spying them, they would needs have them go with them. 'My sister, sir,' continued she, 'was very loth to go, for fear you should be angry; but my Lady —— was so importunate with her on one side, and I on the other, because I never saw a little ship in my life, that at last we prevailed with her; therefore, good sir, be not angry.' He promised them he was not. And when they came in, they found Count Vernole, who had been inspiring De Pais with severity, and counselled him to chide the young ladies, for being too long absent, under pretence of going to their devotion. Nor was it enough for him to set the father on, but himself with a gravity, where concern and malice were both apparent, reproached Atlante with levity; and told her he believed she had some other motive than the invitation of a lady, to go on ship-board; and that she had too many lovers, not to make them doubt that this was a designed thing; and that she had heard love from someone, for whom it was designed. To this she made but a short reply, that if it was so, she had no reason to conceal it, since she had sense enough to look after herself; and if anybody had made love to her, he might be assured, it was someone whose quality and merit deserved to be heard: and with a look of scorn, she passed on to another room, and left him silently raging within with jealousy: which, if before she tormented him, this declaration increased it to a pitch not to be concealed. And this day he said so much to the father, that he resolved forthwith to send Charlot to a nunnery: and accordingly the next day he bid her prepare to go. Charlot, who was not yet arrived to the years of distinction, did not much regret it; and having no trouble but leaving her sister, she prepared to go to a nunnery, not many streets from that where she dwelt. The Lady Abbess was her father's kinswoman, and had treated her very well, as often as she came to visit her: so that with satisfaction enough, she was condemned to a mon-astic life, and was now going for her probation-year. Atlante was troubled at her departure, because she had nobody to bring and to carry letters between Rinaldo and she: however, she took her leave of her, and promised to come and see her as often as she

should be permitted to go abroad; for she feared
now some constraint extraordinary would be put
upon her: and so it happened.

Atlante's chamber was that to which the balcony
belonged; and though she durst not appear there in
the daytime, she could in the night, and that way
give her lover as many hours of conversation as she
pleased, without being perceived. But how to give
Rinaldo notice of this, she could not tell; who not
knowing Charlot was gone to a monastery, waited
many days at his window to see her: at last, they
neither of them knowing who to trust with any
message, one day, when he was, as usual, upon his
watch, he saw Atlante step into the balcony, who
having a letter, in which she had put a piece of lead,
she tossed it into his window, whose casement was
open, and ran in again unperceived by any but himself. The paper contained only this :—

My chamber is that which looks into the balcony; from
whence, though I cannot converse with you in the day,
I can at night, when I am retired to go to bed: therefore
be at your window. Farewell.

There needed no more to make him a diligent
watcher: and accordingly she was no sooner retired
to her chamber, but she would come into the balcony,
where she failed not to see him attending at his
window. This happy contrivance was thus carried
on for many nights, where they entertained one
another with all the endearment that two hearts
could dictate, who were perfectly united and assured
of each other; and this pleasing conversation would
often last till day appeared, and forced them to part.

But old Bellyaurd perceiving his son frequent that
chamber more than usual, fancied something extraordinary must be the cause of it; and one night asking for his son, his valet told him, he was gone into
the Great Chamber, so this was called. Bellyaurd
asked the valet what he did there; he told him he

could not tell; for often he had lighted him thither, and that his master would take the candle from him at the chamber-door, and suffer him to go no farther. Though the old gentleman could not imagine what affairs he could have alone every night in that chamber, he had a curiosity to see: and one unlucky night, putting off his shoes, he came to the door of the chamber, which was open; he entered softly, and saw the candle set in the chimney, and his son at a great open bay-window. He stopped awhile to wait when he would turn, but finding him unmovable, he advanced something farther, and at last heard the soft dialogue of love between him and Atlante, whom he knew to be she, by his often calling her by her name in their discourse. He heard enough to confirm him how matters went; and unseen as he came, he returned, full of indignation, and thought how to prevent so great an evil, as this passion of his son might produce. At first he thought to round him severely in the ear about it, and upbraid him for doing the only thing he had thought fit to forbid him; but then he thought that would but terrify him for a while, and he would return again, where he had so great an inclination, if he were near her; he therefore resolves to send him to Paris, that by absence he might forget the young beauty that had charmed his youth. Therefore, without letting Rinaldo know the reason, and without taking notice that he knew anything of his amour, he came to him one day, and told him, all the masters he had for the improving him in noble sciences were very dull, or very remiss; and that he resolved he should go for a year or two to the Academy at Paris. To this the son made a thousand evasions; but the father was positive, and not to be persuaded by all his reasons: and finding he should absolutely displease him if he refused to go, and not daring to tell him the dear cause of his desire to remain at Orleans, he therefore, with a breaking heart, consents to go, nay, resolves it, though

it should be his death. But alas! he considers that
this parting will not only prove the greatest torment
upon earth to him, but that Atlante will share in his
misfortunes also. This thought gives him a double
torment, and yet he finds no way to evade it.

The night that finished this fatal day, he goes
again to his wonted station, the window; where he
had not sighed very long, but he saw Atlante enter
the balcony: he was not able a great while to speak
to her, or to utter one word. The night was light
enough to see him at the wonted place; and she
admires at his silence, and demands the reason in
such obliging terms as adds to his grief; and he, with
a deep sigh, replied, 'Urge me not, my fair Atlante,
to speak, lest by obeying you I give you more cause
of grief than my silence is capable of doing': and
then sighing again, he held his peace, and gave her
leave to ask the cause of these last words. But when
he made no reply but by sighing, she imagined it
much worse than indeed it was; and with a trembling
and fainting voice, she cried, 'Oh! Rinaldo, give me
leave to divine that cruel news you are so unwilling
to tell me: is it that,' added she, 'you are destined to
some more fortunate maid than Atlante?' At this
tears stopped her speech, and she could utter no
more. 'No, my dearest charmer,' replied Rinaldo,
elevating his voice, 'if that were all, you should see
with what fortitude I would die, rather than obey any
such commands. I am vowed yours to the last
moment of my life; and will be yours in spite of all
the opposition in the world: that cruelty I could
evade, but cannot this that threatens me.' 'Ah!'
cried Atlante, 'let Fate do her worst, so she still continue Rinaldo mine, and keep that faith he hath
sworn to me entire. What can she do beside, that
can afflict me?' 'She can separate me,' cried he,
'for some time from Atlante.' 'Oh!' replied she,
'all misfortunes fall so below that which I first
imagined, that methinks I do not resent this, as I

should otherwise have done; but I know, when I
have a little more considered it, I shall even die with
the grief of it, absence being so greater an enemy to
love, and making us soon forget the object beloved.
This, though I never experienced, I have heard, and
fear it may be my fate.' He then convinced her
fears with a thousand new vows, and a thousand imprecations of constancy. She then asked him if
their loves were discovered, that he was with such
haste to depart? He told her nothing of that was
the cause; and he could almost wish it were discovered, since he could resolutely then refuse to go
but it was only to cultivate his mind more effectually
than he could do here; it was the care of his father
to accomplish him the more; and therefore he could
not contradict it. 'But,' said he, ' I am not sent where
seas shall part us, nor vast distances of earth, but to
Paris,' from whence he might come in two days to see
her again; and that he would expect from that
balcony, that had given him so many happy moments,
many more when he should come to see her. He besought her to send him away with all the satisfaction
she could, which she could no otherwise do, than by
giving him new assurances that she would never give
away that right he had in her to any other lover.
She vows this with innumerable tears; and is almost
angry with him for questioning her faith. He tells
her he has but one night more to stay, and his grief
would be unspeakable, if he should not be able to
take a better leave of her, than at a window; and
that, if she would give him leave, he would by a rope
or two, tied together, so as it may serve for steps,
ascend her balcony; he not having time to provide a
ladder of ropes. She tells him she has so great a
confidence in his virtue and love, that she will refuse
him nothing, though it would be a very bold venture
for a maid, to trust herself with a passionate young
man, in silence of night: and though she did not
extort a vow from him to secure her, she expected

he would have a care of her honour. He swore to her, his love was too religious for so base an attempt. There needed not many vows to confirm her faith; and it was agreed on between them, that he should come the next night into her chamber.

It happened that night, as it often did, that Count Vernole lay with Monsieur De Pais, which was in a ground-room, just under that of Atlante's. As soon as she knew all were in bed, she gave the word to Rinaldo, who was attending with the impatience of a passionate lover below, under the window; and who no sooner heard the balcony open, but he ascended with some difficulty, and entered the chamber, where he found Atlante trembling with joy and fear. He throws himself at her feet, as unable to speak as she; who nothing but blushed and bent down her eyes, hardly daring to glance them towards the dear object of her desires, the lord of all her vows. She was ashamed to see a man in her chamber, where yet none had ever been alone, and by night too. He saw her fear, and felt her trembling; and after a thousand sighs of love had made way for speech, he besought her to fear nothing from him, for his flame was too sacred, and his passion too holy to offer anything but what honour with love might afford him. At last he brought her to some courage, and the roses of her fair cheeks assumed their wonted colour, not blushing too red, nor languishing too pale. But when the conversation began between them, it was the softest in the world: they said all that parting lovers could say; all that wit and tenderness could express. They exchanged their vows anew; and to confirm his, he tied a bracelet of diamonds about her arm, and she returned him one of her hair, which he had long begged, and she had on purpose made, which clasped together with diamonds; this she put about his arm, and he swore to carry it to his grave. The night was far spent in tender vows, soft sighs and tears on both sides, and it was high time to part: but, as if death had been to have arrived to them in that minute, they both lingered away the time, like lovers who had forgot themselves; and the day was near approaching when he bid farewell, which he repeated very often: for still he was interrupted by some commanding softness from Atlante, and then lost all his power of going; till she, more courageous and careful of his interest and her own fame, forced him from her: and it was happy she did, for he was no sooner got over the balcony, and she had flung him down his rope, and shut the door, but Vernole, whom love and contrivance kept waking, fancied several times he heard a noise in Atlante's chamber. And whether in passing over the balcony, Rinaldo made any noise or not, or whether it was still his jealous fancy, he came up in his night-gown, with a pistol in his hand. Atlante was not so much lost in grief, though she were all in tears, but she heard a man come up, and imagined it had been her father, she not knowing of Count Vernole's lying in the house that night; if she had, she possibly had taken more care to have been silent: but whoever it was, she could not get to bed soon enough, and therefore turned herself to her dressing-table, where a candle stood, and where lay a book open of the story of Ariadne and Theseus. The Count turning the latch, entered halting into her chamber in his night-gown clapped close about him, which betrayed an ill-favoured shape, his night-cap on, without a periwig, which discovered all his lean withered jaws, his pale face, and his eyes staring: and made altogether so dreadful a figure, that Atlante, who no more dreamt of him than of a devil, had possibly have rather seen the last. She gave a great shriek, which frightened Vernole; so both stood for a while staring on each other, till both were recollected. He told her the care of her honour had brought him thither; and then rolling his small eyes round the chamber, to see if he could discover anybody, he proceeded, and cried, 'Madam, if I had no other motive than your being up at this time of night, or rather of day, I could easily guess how you have been entertained.' 'What insolence is this,' said she, all in a rage, 'when to cover your boldness of approaching my chamber at this hour, you would question how I have been entertained! Either explain yourself, or quit my chamber; for I am not used to see such terrible objects here.' 'Possibly those you do see,' said the Count, 'are indeed more agreeable, but I am afraid have not that regard to your honour as I have': and at that word he stepped to the balcony, opened it, and looked out; but seeing nobody, he shut it to again. This enraged Atlante beyond all patience; and snatching the pistol out of his hand, she told him he deserved to have it aimed at his head, for having the impudence to question her honour, or her conduct; and commanded him to avoid her chamber as he loved his life, which she believed he was fonder of than of her honour. She speaking this in a tone wholly transported with rage, and at the same time holding the pistol towards him made him tremble with fear; and he now found, whether she were guilty or not, it was his turn to beg pardon. For you must know, however it came to pass that his jealousy made him come up in that fierce posture, at other times Vernole was the most tame and passive man in the world, and one who was afraid of his own shadow in the night. He had a natural aversion for danger, and thought it below a man of wit, or common-sense, to be guilty of that brutal thing, called courage or fighting. His philosophy told him, 'It was safe sleeping in a whole skin'; and possibly he apprehended as much danger from this virago, as ever he did from his own sex. He therefore fell on his knees, and besought her to hold her fair hand, and not to suffer that, which was the greatest mark of his respect, to be the cause of her hate or indignation. The pitiful faces he made, and the signs of mortal fear in him, had almost made her laugh, at least it allayed her anger;

and she bid him rise and play the fool hereafter somewhere else, and not in her presence. Yet for once
she would deign to give him this satisfaction, that she
was got into a book, which had many moving stories
very well written ; and that she found herself so well
entertained, she had forgotten how the night passed.
He most humbly thanked her for this satisfaction,
and retired, perhaps not so well satisfied as he pretended.

After this, he appeared more submissive and respectful towards Atlante ; and she carried herself
more reserved and haughty towards him ; which was
one reason, he would not yet discover his passion.

Thus the time ran on at Orleans, while Rinaldo
found himself daily languishing at Paris. He was
indeed in the best academy in the city, amongst
a number of brave and noble youths, where all things
that could accomplish them, were to be learned by
those that had any genius; but Rinaldo had other
thoughts, and other business : his time was wholly
passed in the most solitary parts of the garden, by
the melancholy fountains, and in the most gloomy
shades, where he could with most liberty breathe out
his passion and his griefs. He was past the tutorage
of a boy ; and his masters could not upbraid him, but
found he had some secret cause of grief, which made
him not mind those exercises, which were the delight
of the rest ; so that nothing being able to divert his
melancholy, which daily increased upon him, he
feared it would bring him into a fever, if he did not
give himself the satisfaction of seeing Atlante. He
had no sooner thought of this, but he was impatient
to put it in execution ; he resolved to go (having very
good horses) without acquainting any of his servants
with it. He got a very handsome and light ladder of
ropes made, which he carried under his coat, and
away he rode for Orleans, stayed at a little village, till
the darkness of the night might favour his design.
And then walking about Atlante's lodgings, till he

saw a light in her chamber, and then making that
noise on his sword, as was agreed between them, he
was heard by his adorable Atlante, and suffered to
mount her chamber, where he would stay till almost
break of day, and then return to the village, and take
horse, and away for Paris again. This, once in a
month, was his exercise, without which he could not
live; so that his whole year was passed in riding
between Orleans and Paris, between excess of grief,
and excess of joy by turns.

It was now that Atlante, arrived to her fifteenth
year, shone out with a lustre of beauty greater than
ever; and in this year, in the absence of Rinaldo, had
carried herself with that severity of life, without the
youthful desire of going abroad, or desiring any
diversion, but what she found in her own retired
thoughts, that Vernole, wholly unable longer to conceal his passion, resolved to make a publication of it,
first to the father, and then to the lovely daughter, of
whom he had some hope, because she had carried herself very well towards him for this year past; which
she would never have done, if she had imagined he
would ever have been her lover. She had seen no
signs of any such misfortune towards her in these
many years he had conversed with her, and she had
no cause to fear him. When one day her father taking
her into the garden, told her what honour and happiness was in store for her; and that now the glory of
his fallen family would rise again, since she had a
lover of an illustrious blood, allied to monarchs; and
one whose fortune was newly increased to a very
considerable degree, answerable to his birth. She
changed colour at this discourse, imagining but too
well who this illustrious lover was; when De Pais
proceeded and told her, 'indeed his person was not
the most agreeable that ever was seen: but he
married her to glory and fortune, not the man: 'And
a woman,' says he, 'ought to look no further.'

She needed not any more to inform her who this

intended husband was; and therefore, bursting forth
into tears, she throws herself at his feet, imploring
him not to use the authority of a father, to force her
to a thing so contrary to her inclination: assuring
him, she could not consent to any such thing; and
that she would rather die than yield. She urged
many arguments for this her disobedience; but none
would pass for current with the old gentleman, whose
pride had flattered him with hopes of so considerable
a son-in-law. He was very much surprised at Atlante's
refusing what he believed she would receive with joy;
and finding that no arguments on his side could draw
hers to an obedient consent, he grew to such a rage,
as very rarely possessed him: vowing, if she did not
conform her will to his, he would abandon her to all
the cruelty of contempt and poverty. So that at last
she was forced to return him this answer, 'That she
would strive all she could with her heart; but she
verily believed she should never bring it to consent
to a marriage with Monsieur the Count.' The father
continued threatening her, and gave her some days to
consider of it: so leaving her in tears, he returned to
his chamber, to consider what answer he should give
Count Vernole, who he knew would be impatient to
learn what success he had, and what himself was to
hope. De Pais, after some consideration, resolved
to tell him, she received the offer very well, but that
he must expect a little maiden-nicety in the case: and
accordingly did tell him so; and he was not at all
doubtful of his good fortune.

But Atlante, who resolved to die a thousand deaths
rather than break her solemn vows to Rinaldo, or to
marry the Count, cast about how she should avoid
it with the least hazard of her father's rage. She
found Rinaldo the better and the more advantageous
match of the two, could they but get his father's consent. He was beautiful and young; his title was
equal to that of Vernole, when his father should die;
and his estate exceeded his: yet she dares not make

a discovery, for fear she should injure her lover ; who at this time, though she knew it not, lay sick of a fever, while she was wondering that he came not as he used to do. However, she resolved to send him a letter, and acquaint him with the misfortune ; which she did in these terms :—

ATLANTE TO RINALDO

My father's authority would force me to violate my sacred vows to you, and give them to the Count Vernole, whom I mortally hate, yet could wish him the greatest monarch in the world, that I might show you I could even then despise him for your sake. My father is already too much enraged by my denial, to hear reason from me, if I should confess to him my vows to you: so that I see nothing but a prospect of death before me ; for assure yourself, my Rinaldo, I will die rather than consent to marry any other. Therefore come, my Rinaldo, and come quickly, to see my funeral, instead of those nuptials they vainly expect from your faithful

ATLANTE.

This letter Rinaldo received ; and there needed no more to make him fly to Orleans. This raised him soon from his bed of sickness, and getting immediately to horse, he arrived at his father's house; who did not so much admire to see him, because he heard he was sick of a fever, and gave him leave to return, if he pleased. He went directly to his father's house, because he knew somewhat of the business, he was resolved to make his passion known, as soon as he had seen Atlante, from whom he was to take all his measures. He therefore failed not, when all were in bed, to rise and go from his chamber into the street ; where finding a light in Atlante's chamber, for she every night expected him, he made the usual sign, and she went into the balcony ; and he having no conveniency of mounting up into it, they discoursed, and said all they had to say. From thence she tells him of the Count's passion, of her father's resolution, and that her own was rather to die his, than live for anybody else. And at last, as their refuge, they resolved to discover the whole matter: she to her father, and he to his, to see what accommodation they could make; if not, to die together. They parted at this resolve, for she would permit him no longer to stay in the street after such a sickness; so he went home to bed, but not to sleep.

The next day, at dinner, Monsieur Bellyaurd believing his son absolutely cured, by absence, of his passion; and speaking of all the news in the town, among the rest, told him he was come in good time to dance at the wedding of Count Vernole with Atlante, the match being agreed on. 'No, sir,' replied Rinaldo, 'I shall never dance at the marriage of Count Vernole with Atlante; and you will see in Monsieur De Pais's house a funeral sooner than a wedding.' And thereupon he told his father all his passion for that lovely maid; and assured him, if he would not see him laid in his grave, he must consent to this match. Bellyaurd rose in a fury, and told him he had rather see him in his grave, than in the arms of Atlante: 'Not,' continued he, 'so much for any dislike I have to the young lady, or the smallness of her fortune; but because I have so long warned you from such a passion, and have with such care endeavoured by your absence to prevent it.' He traversed the room very fast, still protesting against this alliance: and was deaf to all Rinaldo could say. On the other side the day being come, wherein Atlante was to give her final answer to her father concerning her marriage with Count Vernole; she assumed all the courage and resolution she could, to withstand the storm that threatened a denial. And her father came to her, and demanding her answer, she told him she could not be the wife of Vernole, since she was wife to Rinaldo, only son to Bellyaurd. If her father stormed before, he grew like a man distracted at her confession; and Vernole hearing them loud, ran to the chamber to learn the cause; where just as he entered he found De Pais's sword drawn, and ready to kill his daughter, who lay all in tears at his feet. He withheld his hand; and asking the cause of his rage, he was told all that Atlante had confessed; which put Vernole quite beside all his gravity, and made him discover the infirmity of anger, which he used to say ought to be dissembled by all wise men. So that De Pais forgot his own to appease his, but it was in vain, for he went out of the house, vowing revenge to Rinaldo. And to that end, being not very well assured of his own courage, as I said before, and being of the opinion, that no man ought to expose his life to him who has injured him; he hired Swiss and Spanish soldiers to attend him in the nature of footmen; and watched several nights about Bellyaurd's door, and that of De Pais's, believing he should some time or other see him under the window of Atlante, or perhaps mounting into it: for now he no longer doubted but this happy lover was he, whom he fancied he heard go from the balcony that night he came up with his pistol; and being more a Spaniard than a Frenchman in his nature, he resolved to take him any way unguarded or unarmed, if he came in his way.

Atlante, who heard his threatenings when he went from her in a rage, feared his cowardice might put him on some base action, to deprive Rinaldo of his life; and therefore thought it not safe to suffer him to come to her by night, as he had before done; but sent him word in a note, that he should forbear her window, for Vernole had sworn his death. This note came, unseen by his father, to his hands: but this could not hinder him from coming to her window, which he did as soon as it was dark: he came thither, only attended with his valet, and two footmen; for now he cared not who knew the secret. He had no sooner made the sign, but he found himself encompassed with Vernole's bravos; and himself standing

at a distance cried out 'That is he.' With that they
all drew on both sides, and Rinaldo received a wound
in his arm. Atlante heard this, and ran crying out
'That Rinaldo pressed by numbers, would be killed.'
De Pais, who was reading in his closet, took his
sword, and ran out ; and, contrary to all expectation,
seeing Rinaldo fighting with his back to the door,
pulled him into the house, and fought himself with
the bravos : who being very much wounded by Rinaldo, gave ground, and sheered off; and De Pais,
putting up old Bilbo into the scabbard, went into his
house, where he found Rinaldo almost fainting with
loss of blood, and Atlante, with her maids binding up
his wound ; to whom De Pais said, 'This charity,
Atlante, very well becomes you, and is what I can
allow you ; and I could wish you had no other motive
for this action.' Rinaldo by degrees recovered of his
fainting, and as well as his weakness would permit
him, he got up and made a low reverence to De Pais,
telling him he had now a double obligation to pay
him all the respect in the world ; first, for his being
the father of Atlante ; and secondly, for being the
preserver of his life : two ties that should eternally
oblige him to love and honour him, as his own
parent. De Pais replied, he had done nothing but
what common humanity compelled him to do. But
if he would make good that respect he professed
towards him, it must be in quitting all hopes of
Atlante, whom he had destined to another, or an
eternal enclosure in a monastery. He had another
daughter, whom if he would think worthy of his
regard, he should take his alliance as a very great
honour ; but his word and reputation, nay his vows
were passed, to give Atlante to Count Vernole.
Rinaldo, who before he spoke took measure from
Atlante's eyes, which told him her heart was his,
returned this answer to De Pais, 'That he was
infinitely glad to find by the generosity of his offer,
that he had no aversion against his being his son-in-

law; and that, next to Atlante, the greatest happiness he could wish would be his receiving Charlot from his hand; but that he could not think of quitting Atlante, how necessary soever it would be, for glory, and his—(the further) repose.' De Pais would not let him at this time argue the matter further, seeing he was ill, and had need of looking after; he therefore begged he would for his health's sake retire to his own house, whither he himself conducted him, and left him to the care of his men, who were escaped the fray; and returning to his own chamber, he found Atlante retired, and so he went to bed full of thoughts. This night had increased his esteem for Rinaldo, and lessened it for Count Vernole; but his word and honour being passed, he could not break it, neither with safety nor honour: for he knew the haughty resenting nature of the Count, and he feared some danger might arrive to the brave Rinaldo, which troubled him very much. At last he resolved, that neither might take anything ill at his hands, to lose Atlante, and send her to the monastery where her sister was, and compel her to be a nun. This he thought would prevent mischief on both sides; and accordingly, the next day (having in the morning sent word to the Lady Abbess what he would have done), he carries Atlante, under pretence of visiting her sister (which they often did), to the monastery, where she was no sooner come, but she was led into the enclosure. Her father had rather sacrifice her, than she should be the cause of the murder of two such noble men as Vernole and Rinaldo.

The noise of Atlante being enclosed, was soon spread all over the busy town, and Rinaldo was not the last to whom the news arrived. He was for a few days confined to his chamber; where, when alone, he raved like a man distracted. But his wounds had so incensed his father against Atlante, that he swore he would see his son die of them, rather than suffer him to marry Atlante; and was extremely overjoyed

to find she was condemned for ever, to the monastery.
So that the son thought it the wisest course, and
most for the advantage of his love, to say nothing
to contradict his father; but being almost assured
Atlante would never consent to be shut up in a
cloister, and abandon him, he flattered himself with
hope, that he should steal her from thence, and marry
her in spite of all opposition. This he was impatient
to put in practice. He believed, if he were not permitted to see Atlante, he had still a kind advocate in
Charlot, who was now arrived to her thirteenth year,
and infinitely advanced in wit and beauty. Rinaldo
therefore often goes to the monastery, surrounding it,
to see what possibility there was of accomplishing
his design; if he could get her consent, he finds it
not impossible, and goes to visit Charlot; who had
command not to see him, or speak to him. This was
a cruelty he looked not for, and which gave him an
unspeakable trouble, and without her aid it was
wholly impossible to give Atlante any account of his
design. In this perplexity he remained many days,
in which he languished almost to death; he was distracted with thought, and continually hovering about
the nunnery walls, in hope, at some time or other, to
see or hear from that lovely maid, who alone could
make his happiness. In these traverses he often met
Vernole, who had liberty to see her when he pleased.
If it happened that they chanced to meet in the daytime, though Vernole was attended with an equipage
of ruffians, and Rinaldo but only with a couple of
footmen, he could perceive Vernole shun him, grow
pale, and almost tremble with fear sometimes, and
get to the other side of the street; and if he did not,
Rinaldo having a mortal hate to him, would often
bear up so close to him, that he would jostle him
against the wall, which Vernole would patiently put
up, and pass on; so that he could never be provoked
to fight by daylight, how solitary soever the place
was where they met. But if they chanced to meet

at night, they were certain of a skirmish, in which he would have no part himself; so that Rinaldo was often like to be assassinated, but still came off with some slight wound. This continued so long, and made so great a noise in the town, that the two old gentlemen were mightily alarmed by it; and Count Bellyaurd came to De Pais, one day, to discourse with him of this affair; and Bellyaurd, for the preservation of his son, was almost consenting, since there was no remedy, that he should marry Atlante. De Pais confessed the honour he proffered him, and how troubled he was, that his word was already passed to his friend, the Count Vernole, whom he said she should marry, or remain for ever a nun; but if Rinaldo could displace his love from Atlante, and place it on Charlot, he should gladly consent to the match. Bellyaurd, who would now do anything for the repose of his son, though he believed this exchange would not pass, yet resolved to propose it, since by marrying him he took him out of the danger of Vernole's assassinates, who would never leave him till they had despatched him, should he marry Atlante.

While Rinaldo was contriving a thousand ways to come to speak to, or send billets to Atlante, none of which could succeed without the aid of Charlot, his father came and proposed this agreement between De Pais and himself, to his son. At first Rinaldo received it with a changed countenance, and a breaking heart; but swiftly turning from thought to thought, he conceived this the only way to come at Charlot, and so consequently at Atlante: he therefore, after some dissembled regret, consents, with a sad put-on look: and Charlot had notice given her to see and entertain Rinaldo. As yet they had not told her the reason; which her father would tell her, when he came to visit her, he said. Rinaldo overjoyed at this contrivance, and his own dissimulation, goes to the monastery, and visits Charlot; where he ought to have said something of this proposition:

but wholly bent upon other thoughts, he solicits her
to convey some letters, and presents to Atlante;
which she readily did, to the unspeakable joy of the
poor distressed. Sometimes he would talk to Charlot
of her own affairs; asking her, if she resolved to
become a nun. To which she would sigh, and say,
if she must, it would be extremely against her inclinations; and, if it pleased her father, she had rather
begin the world with any tolerable match.

Things passed thus for some days, in which our
lovers were happy, and Vernole assured he should
have Atlante. But at last De Pais came to visit
Charlot, who asked her, if she had seen Rinaldo.
She answered, she had. 'And how does he entertain you?' replied De Pais. 'Have you received
him as a husband? and has he behaved himself like
one?' At this a sudden joy seized the heart of
Charlot; and loth to confess what she had done for
him to her sister, she hung down her blushing face
to study for an answer. De Pais continued, and told
her the agreement between Bellyaurd and him, for
the saving of bloodshed.

She, who blessed the cause, whatever it was, having
always a great friendship and tenderness for Rinaldo,
gave her father a thousand thanks for his care; and
assured him, since she was commanded by him, she
would receive him as her husband.

And the next day, when Rinaldo came to visit
her, as he used to do, and bringing a letter with him,
wherein he proposed the sight of Atlante; he found
a coldness in Charlot, as soon as he told her his
design, and desired her to carry the letter. He asked
the reason of this change: she tells him she was
informed of the agreement between their two fathers,
and that she looked upon herself as his wife, and
would act no more as a confidante; that she had
ever a violent inclination of friendship for him, which
she would soon improve into something more soft.

He could not deny the agreement, nor his promise;

but it was in vain to tell her, he did it only to get a correspondence with Atlante. She is obstinate, and he as pressing, with all the tenderness of persuasion. He vows he can never be any but Atlante's, and she may see him die, but never break his vows. She urges her claim in vain, so that at last she was overcome, and promised she would carry the letter; which was to have her make her escape that night. He waits at the gate for her answer, and Charlot returns with one that pleased him very well; which was, that night her sister would make her escape, and that he must stand in such a place of the nunnery wall, and she would come out to him.

After this she upbraids him with his false promise to her, and of her goodness to serve him after such a disappointment. He receives her reproaches with a thousand sighs, and bemoans her misfortune in not being capable of more than friendship for her; and vows, that next Atlante, he esteems her of all womankind. She seems to be obliged by this, and assured him, she would hasten the flight of Atlante; and taking leave, he went home to order a coach, and some servants to assist him.

In the meantime Count Vernole came to visit Atlante; but she refused to be seen by him: and all he could do there that afternoon, was entertaining Charlot at the grate; to whom he spoke a great many fine things, both of her improved beauty and wit; and how happy Rinaldo would be in so fair a bride. She received this with all the civility that was due to his quality; and their discourse being at an end, he took his leave, it being towards the evening.

Rinaldo, wholly impatient, came betimes to the corner of the dead wall, where he was appointed to stand, having ordered his footmen and coach to come to him as soon as it was dark. While he was there walking up and down, Vernole came by the end of the wall to go home: and looking about, he saw, at the other end, Rinaldo walking, whose back was towards him, but he knew him well; and though he feared and dreaded his business there, he durst not encounter him, they being both attended but by one footman apiece. But Vernole's jealousy and indignation were so high, that he resolved to fetch his bravos to his aid, and come and assault him: for he knew he waited there for some message from Atlante.

In the meantime it grew dark, and Rinaldo's coach came with another footman; which were hardly arrived, when Vernole, with his assistants, came to the corner of the wall, and screening themselves a little behind it, near to the place where Rinaldo stood, who waited now close to a little door, out of which the gardeners used to throw the weeds and dirt, Vernole could perceive anon the door to open, and a woman come out of it, calling Rinaldo by his name, who stepped up to her, and caught her in his arms with signs of infinite joy. Vernole being now all rage, cried to his assassinates, 'Fall on, and kill the ravisher.' And immediately they all fell on. Rinaldo, who had only his two footmen on his side, was forced to let go the lady; who would have run into the garden again, but the door fell to and locked: so that while Rinaldo was fighting, and beaten back by the bravos, one of which he laid dead at his feet, Vernole came to the frightened lady, and taking her by the hand, cried, 'Come, my fair fugitive, you must go along with me.' She, wholly scared out of her senses, was willing to go anywhere out of the terror she heard so near her, and without reply, gave herself into his hand, who carried her directly to her father's house; where she was no sooner come, but he told her father all that had passed, and how she was running away with Rinaldo, but that his good fortune brought him just in the lucky minute. Her father turning to reproach her, found by the light of a candle that this was Charlot, and not Atlante, whom Vernole had brought home.

At which Vernole was extremely astonished. Her father demanded of her why she was running away with a man, who was designed her by consent? 'Yes,' said Charlot, 'you had his consent, sir, and that of his father; but I was far from getting it: I found he resolved to die rather than quit Atlante; and promising him my assistance in his amour, since he could never be mine, he got me to carry a letter to Atlante; which was, to desire her to fly away with him. Instead of carrying her this letter, I told her, he was designed for me, and had cancelled all his vows to her. She swooned at this news; and being recovered a little, I left her in the hands of the nuns, to persuade her to live; which she resolves not to do without Rinaldo. Though they pressed me, yet I resolved to pursue my design, which was to tell Rinaldo she would obey his kind summons. He waited for her; but I put myself into his hands in lieu of Atlante; and had not the Count received me, we had been married by this time, by some false light that could not have discovered me. But I am satisfied, if I had, he would never have lived with me longer than the cheat had been undiscovered; for I find them both resolved to die, rather than change. And for my part, sir, I was not so much in love with Rinaldo, as I was out of love with the nunnery; and took any opportunity to quit a life absolutely contrary to my humour.' She spoke this with a gaiety so brisk, and an air so agreeable, that Vernole found it touched his heart; and the rather because he found Atlante would never be his; or if she were, he should be still in danger from the resentment of Rinaldo: he therefore bowing to Charlot, and taking her by the hand, cried, 'Madam, since Fortune has disposed you thus luckily for me, in my possession, I humbly implore you would consent she should make me entirely happy, and give me the prize for which I fought, and have conquered with my sword.' 'My lord,' replied Charlot, with a modest air, 'I am superstitious enough to believe, since Fortune, so contrary to all our designs, has given me into your hands, that she from the beginning destined me to the honour, which, with my father's consent, I shall receive as becomes me.' De Pais transported with joy, to find all things would be so well brought about, it being all one to him, whether Charlot or Atlante gave him Count Vernole for his son-in-law, readily consented ; and immediately a priest was sent for, and they were that night married. And it being now not above seven o'clock, many of their friends were invited, the music sent for, and as good a supper as so short a time would provide, was made ready.

All this was performed in as short a time as Rinaldo was fighting; and having killed one, and wounded the rest, they all fled before his conquering sword, which was never drawn with so good a will. When he came where his coach stood, just against the back-garden door, he looked for his mistress : but the coachman told him, he was no sooner engaged, but a man came, and with a thousand reproaches on her levity, bore her off.

This made our young lover rave ; and he is satisfied she is in the hands of his rival, and that he had been fighting, and shedding his blood, only to secure her flight with him. He lost all patience, and it was with much ado his servants persuaded him to return ; telling him in their opinion, she was more likely to get out of the hands of his rival, and come to him, than when she was in the monastery.

He suffers himself to go into his coach and be carried home ; but he was no sooner alighted, than he heard music and noise at De Pais's house. He saw coaches surround his door, and pages and footmen, with flambeaux. The sight and noise of joy made him ready to sink at the door ; and sending his footmen to learn the cause of this triumph, the pages that waited told him, that Count Vernole was this night married to Monsieur De Pais's daughter. He needed no more to deprive him of all sense; and staggering against his coach, he was caught by his footmen and carried into his house, and to his chamber, where they put him to bed, all senseless as he was, and had much ado to recover him to life. He asked for his father, with a faint voice, for he desired to see him before he died. It was told him he was gone to Count Vernole's wedding, where there was a perfect peace agreed on between them, and all their animosities laid aside. At this news Rinaldo fainted again; and his servants called his father home, and told him in what condition they had brought home their master, recounting to him all that was past. He hastened to Rinaldo, whom he found just recovered of his swooning; who, putting his hand out to his father, all cold and trembling, cried, 'Well, sir, now you are satisfied, since you have seen Atlante married to Count Vernole. I hope now you will give your unfortunate son leave to die; as you wished he should, rather than give him to the arms of Atlante.' Here his speech failed, and he fell again into a fit of swooning. His father ready to die with fear of his son's death, kneeled down by his bedside; and after having recovered a little, he said, 'My dear son, I have been indeed at the wedding of Count Vernole, but it is not Atlante to whom he is married, but Charlot; who was the person you were bearing from the monastery, instead of Atlante, who is still reserved for you, and she is dying till she hear you are reserved for her. Therefore, as you regard her life, make much of your own, and make yourself fit to receive her; for her father and I have agreed to the marriage already.' And without giving him leave to think, he called to one of his gentlemen, and sent him to the monastery, with this news to Atlante. Rinaldo bowed himself as low as he could in his bed, and kissed the hand of his father, with tears of joy. But his weakness continued all the next day; and they were fain to bring Atlante to him, to confirm his happiness.

It must only be guessed by lovers, the perfect joy these two received in the sight of each other. Bellyaurd received her as his daughter ; and the next day made her so, with very great solemnity, at which were Vernole and Charlot.   Between Rinaldo and him was concluded a perfect peace, and all thought themselves happy in this double union

THE COURT OF
THE KING OF BANTAM

THIS money certainly is a most devilish thing! I'm
sure the want of it had like to have ruined my dear
Philibella, in her love to Valentine Goodland; who
was really a pretty deserving gentleman, heir to
about fifteen hundred pounds a year; which, however, did not so much recommend him, as the sweetness of his temper, the comeliness of his person,
and the excellence of his parts. In all which circumstances my obliging acquaintance equalled him,
unless in the advantage of their fortune. Old Sir
George Goodland knew of his son's passion for
Philibella; and though he was generous, and of a
humour sufficiently complying, yet he could by no
means think it convenient, that his only son should
marry with a young lady of so slender a fortune as
my friend, who had not above five hundred pound,
and that the gift of her uncle, Sir Philip Friendly:
though her virtue and beauty might have deserved,
and have adorned the throne of an Alexander or a
Cæsar.

Sir Philip himself, indeed, was but a younger
brother, though of a good family, and of a generous
education; which, with his person, bravery, and wit,
recommended him to his Lady Philadelphia, widow
of Sir Bartholomew Banquier, who left her possessed
of two thousand pounds per annum, besides twenty

thousand pounds in money and jewels; which obliged him to get himself dubbed, that she might not descend to an inferior quality. When he was in town, he lived—let me see! in the Strand; or, as near as I can remember, somewhere about Charing Cross; where, first of all Mr. Would-be King, a gentleman of a large estate in houses, land and money, of a haughty, extravagant and profuse humour, very fond of every new face, had the misfortune to fall passionately in love with Philibella, who then lived with her uncle.

This Mr. Would-be it seems had often been told, when he was yet a stripling, either by one of his nurses, or his own grandmother, or by some other gipsy, that he should infallibly be what his surname implied, a king, by Providence or chance, ere he died, or never. This glorious prophecy had so great an influence on all his thoughts and actions, that he distributed and dispersed his wealth sometimes so largely, that one would have thought he had undoubtedly been king of some part of the Indies; to see a present made to-day of a diamond ring, worth two or three hundred pounds, to Madam Flippant; to-morrow, a large chest of the finest china to my Lady Fleece-well; and next day, perhaps, a rich necklace of large Oriental pearl, with a locket to it of sapphires, emeralds, rubies, etc., to pretty Miss Ogle-me, for an amorous glance, for a smile, and (it may be, though but rarely) for the mighty blessing of one single kiss. But such were his largesses, not to reckon his treats, his balls, and serenades besides, though at the same time he had married a virtuous lady, and of good quality. But her relation to him (it may be feared) made her very disagreeable: for a man of his humour and estate can no more be satisfied with one woman, than with one dish of meat; and to say truth, it is something unmodish. However, he might have died a pure celibate, and altogether unexpert of women, had his good or bad hopes only terminated in Sir Philip's niece. But the brave and haughty Mr. Would-be

was not to be baulked by appearances of virtue,
which he thought all womankind only did affect;
besides, he promised himself the victory over any
lady whom he attempted, by the force of his damned
money, though her virtue were ever so real and strict.

With Philibella he found another pretty young
creature, very like her, who had been a quondam mistress to Sir Philip. He, with young Goodland, was
then diverting his mistress and niece at a game at
cards, when Would-be came to visit him; he found
them very merry, with a flask or two of claret before
them, and oranges roasting by a large fire, for it was
Christmas-time. The Lady Friendly understanding
that this extraordinary man was with Sir Philip in
the parlour, came in to them, to make the number of
both sexes equal, as well as in hopes to make up a
purse of guineas towards the purchase of some new
fine business that she had in her head, from his accustomed design of losing at play to her. Indeed, she
had part of her wish, for she got twenty guineas of
him; Philibella ten; and Lucy, Sir Philip's quondam,
five. Not but that Would-be intended better fortune
to the young ones, than he did to Sir Philip's lady;
but her ladyship was utterly unwilling to give him
over to their management, though at the last, when
they were all tired with the cards, after Would-be had
said as many obliging things as his present genius
would give him leave, to Philibella and Lucy, especially to the first, not forgetting his *baisemains*
to the Lady Friendly, he bid the Knight and Goodland adieu; but with a promise of repeating his visit
at six o'clock in the evening on twelfth-day, to renew
the famous and ancient solemnity of choosing king
and queen; to which Sir Philip before invited him,
with a design yet unknown to you, I hope.

As soon as he was gone, everyone made their
remarks on him, but with very little or no difference
in all their figures of him. In short, all mankind,
had they ever known him, would have universally

agreed in this his character, that he was an original; since nothing in humanity was ever so vain, so haughty, so profuse, so fond, and so ridiculously ambitious, as Mr. Would-be King. They laughed and talked about an hour longer, and then young Goodland was obliged to see Lucy home in his coach ; though he had rather have sat up all night in the same house with Philibella, I fancy, of whom he took but an unwilling leave; which was visible enough to everyone there, since they were all acquainted with his passion for my fair friend.

About twelve o'clock on the day prefixed, young Goodland came to dine with Sir Philip, whom he found just returned from Court, in a very good humour. On the sight of Valentine, the Knight ran to him, and embracing him, told him, that he had prevented his wishes, in coming thither before he sent for him, as he had just then designed. The other returned, that he therefore hoped he might be of some service to him, by so happy a prevention of his intended kindness. 'No doubt,' replied Sir Philip, 'the kindness, I hope, will be to us both ; I am assured it will, if you will act according to my measures.' 'I desire no better prescriptions for my happiness,' returned Valentine, 'than what you shall please to set down to me : but is it necessary or convenient that I should know them first?' 'It is,' answered Sir Philip, 'let us sit, and you shall understand them. I am very sensible,' continued he, 'of your sincere and honourable affection and pretension to my niece, who, perhaps, is as dear to me as my own child could be, had I one; nor am I ignorant how averse Sir George your father is to your marriage with her, insomuch that I am confident he would disinherit you immediately upon it, merely for want of a fortune somewhat proportionable to your estate : but I have now contrived the means to add two or three thousand pounds to the five hundred I have designed to give with her; I mean, if you marry her, Val, not other-

wise; for I will not labour so for any other man.'
'What inviolable obligations you put upon me!'
cried Goodland. 'No return, by way of compliments,
good Val,' said the Knight. "Had I not engaged to
my wife, before marriage, that I would not dispose of
any part of what she brought me, without her consent, I would certainly make Philibella's fortune
answerable to your estate. And besides, my wife is
not yet full eight-and-twenty, and we may therefore
expect children of our own, which hinders me from
proposing anything more for the advantage of my
niece. But now to my instructions; King will be
here this evening without fail, and, at some time
or other to-night, will show the haughtiness of his
temper to you, I doubt not, since you are in a manner
a stranger to him. Be sure therefore you seem to
quarrel with him before you part, but suffer as much
as you can first from his tongue; for I know he will
give you occasions enough to exercise your passive
valour. I must appear his friend, and you must retire
home, if you please, for this night, but let me see you
as early as your convenience will permit to-morrow:
my late friend Lucy must be my niece too. Observe
this, and leave the rest to me.' 'I shall most punctually,
and will in all things be directed by you,' said Valentine. 'I had forgot to tell you,' said Friendly, 'that
I have so ordered matters, that he must be king
to-night, and Lucy queen, by the lots in the cake.'
'By all means,' returned Goodland; 'it must be
Majesty.'

Exactly at six o'clock came Would-be in his coach-
and-six, and found Sir Philip, and his lady, Goodland,
Philibella, and Lucy ready to receive him; Lucy as
fine as a duchess, and almost as beautiful as she was
before her fall. All things were in ample order for his
entertainment. They played till supper was served
in, which was between eight and nine. The treat was
very seasonable and splendid. Just as the second
course was set on the table, they were all on a sudden

surprised, except Would-be, with a flourish of violins, and other instruments, which proceeded to entertain them with the best and newest airs in the last new plays, being then in the year 1683. The ladies were curious to know to whom they owed the cheerful part of their entertainment : on which he called out, 'Hey! Tom Farmer! Aleworth! Eccles! Hall! and the rest of you! Here's a health to these ladies, and all this honourable company.' They bowed ; he drank, and commanded another glass to be filled, into which he put something yet better than the wine, I mean, ten guineas. 'Here, Farmer,' said he then, 'this for you and your friends.' We humbly thank the honourable Mr. Would-be King. They all returned, and struck up with more sprightliness than before. For gold and wine, doubtless, are the best rosin for musicians.

After supper they took a hearty glass or two to the King, Queen, Duke, etc. And then the mighty cake, teeming with the fate of this extraordinary personage, was brought in, the musicians playing an overture at the entrance of the Alimental Oracle; which was then cut and consulted, and the royal bean and pea fell to those to whom Sir Philip had designed them. It was then the Knight began a merry bumper, with three huzzas, and 'Long live King Would-be!' to Good-land, who echoed and pledged him, putting the glass about to the harmonious attendants ; while the ladies drank their own quantities among themselves, to his aforesaid Majesty. Then of course you may believe Queen Lucy's health went merrily round, with the same ceremony. After which he saluted his royal consort, and condescended to do the same honour to the two other ladies.

Then they fell a-dancing, like lightning; I mean, they moved as swift, and made almost as little noise ; but his Majesty was soon weary of that; for he longed to be making love both to Philibella and Lucy, who (believe me) that night might well enough have passed for a queen.

They fell then to questions and commands; to cross purposes: 'I think a thought, what is it like?' etc. In all which, his Would-be Majesty took the opportunity of showing the excellence of his parts, as, How fit he was to govern! How dexterous at mining and countermining! and, how he could reconcile the most contrary and distant thoughts! The music, at last, good as it was, grew troublesome and too loud; which made him dismiss them. And then he began to this effect, addressing himself to Philibella: 'Madam, had fortune been just, and were it possible that the world should be governed and influenced by two suns, undoubtedly we had all been subjects to you, from this night's chance, as well as to that lady, who indeed alone can equal you in the empire of beauty, which yet you share with her Majesty here present, who only could dispute it with you, and is only superior to you in title.' 'My wife is infinitely obliged to your Majesty,' interrupted Sir Philip, 'who in my opinion, has greater charms, and more than both of them together.' 'You ought to think so, Sir Philip,' returned the new dubbed King, 'however you should not so liberally have expressed yourself, in opposition and derogation to Majesty. Let me tell you it is a saucy boldness that thus has loosed your tongue! What think you, young kinsman and counsellor?' said he to Goodland. 'With all respect due to your sacred title,' returned Valentine, rising and bowing, 'Sir Philip spoke as became a truly affectionate husband; and it had been presumption in him, unpardonable, to have seemed to prefer her Majesty, or that other sweet lady, in his thoughts, since your Majesty has been pleased to say so much and so particularly of their merits. It would appear as if he durst lift up his eyes, with thoughts too near the heaven you only would enjoy.' 'And only can deserve, you should have added,' said King, no longer Would-be. 'How! may it please your Majesty,' cried Friendly, 'both my nieces! though you deserve

ten thousand more, and better, would your Majesty
enjoy them both?' 'Are they then both your nieces?'
asked Chance's King. 'Yes, both, sir,' returned the
Knight, 'her Majesty's the eldest, and in that Fortune
has shown some justice.' 'So she has,' replied the
titular monarch. 'My lot is fair,' pursued he, 'though
I can be blessed but with one.

> Let Majesty with Majesty be joined,
> To get and leave a race of kings behind.

'Come, madam,' continued he, kissing Lucy, 'this, as
an earnest of our future endeavours.' 'I fear,' returned the pretty Queen, 'your Majesty will forget
the unhappy Statira, when you return to the embraces
of your dear and beautiful Roxana.' 'There is none
beautiful but you,' replied the titular King, 'unless
this lady, to whom I yet could pay my vows most
zealously, were it not that fortune has thus pre-
engaged me. But, madam,' continued he, 'to show
that still you hold our royal favour, and that, next to
our royal consort, we esteem you, we greet you thus'
(kissing Philibella), 'and as a signal of our continued
love, wear this rich diamond' (here he put a diamond
ring on her finger, worth three hundred pounds).
'Your Majesty,' pursued he to Lucy, 'may please to
wear this necklace, with this locket of emeralds.'
'Your Majesty is bounteous as a god!' said Valentine.
'Art thou in want, young spark?' asked the King of
Bantam; 'I'll give thee an estate shall make thee
merit the mistress of thy vows, be she who she will.'
'That is my other niece, sir,' cried Friendly. 'How!
how! presumptuous youth! How are thy eyes and
thoughts exalted? ha!' 'To bliss your Majesty must
never hope for,' replied Goodland. 'How now! thou
creature of the basest mould! Not hope for what
thou dost aspire to!' 'Mock-King; thou canst not,
darest not, shalt not hope it,' returned Valentine in
a heat. 'Hold, Val,' cried Sir Philip, 'you grow
warm, forget your duty to their Majesties, and abuse

your friends, by making us suspected. Good-night,
dear Philibella, and my Queen!' 'Madam, I am your
ladyship's servant,' said Goodland; 'farewell, Sir
Philip. Adieu thou pageant! thou Property-King!
I shall see thy brother on the stage ere long; but
first I'll visit thee: and in the meantime, by way of
return to thy proffered estate, I shall add a real terri-
tory to the rest of thy empty titles; for from thy
education, barbarous manner of conversation, and
complexion, I think I may justly proclaim thee, King
of Bantam—so, hail, King that Would-be! Hail,
thou King of Christmas! All hail, Would-be King
of Bantam,' and so he left them. They all seemed
amazed, and gazed on one another, without speaking
a syllable, till Sir Philip broke the charm, and sighed
out, 'Oh, the monstrous effects of passion!' Say
rather, 'Oh, the foolish effects of a mean education!'
interrupted his Majesty of Bantam. 'For passions
were given us for use, reason to govern and direct us
in the use, and education to cultivate and refine that
reason. But,' pursued he, 'for all his impudence to
me, which I shall take a time to correct, I am obliged
to him, that at last he has found me out a kingdom
to my title; and if I were monarch, of that place
believe me, ladies, I would make you all princesses
and duchesses; and thou, my old companion, Friendly,
shouldst rule the roast with me. But these ladies
should be with us there, where we could erect temples
and altars to them; build golden palaces of love, and
castles——' 'In the air,' interrupted her Majesty,
Lucy. I, smiling. ''Gad take me,' cried King
Would-be, 'thou dear partner of my greatness, and
shalt be, of all my pleasures! thy pretty satirical
observation has obliged me beyond imitation.' 'I
think your Majesty is got into a vein of rhyming
to-night,' said Philadelphia. 'Ay! pox of that young
insipid fop, we could else have been as great as an
Emperor of China, and as witty as Horace in his
wine; but let him go, like a pragmatical, captious,

giddy fool as he is! I shall take a time to see him.'
'Nay, sir,' said Philibella, 'he has promised your
Majesty a visit in our hearing. Come, sir, I beg
your Majesty to pledge me this glass to your long
and happy reign; laying aside all thoughts of ungoverned youth. Besides, this discourse must needs
be ungrateful to her Majesty, to whom, I fear, he will
be married within this month!' 'How!' cried King
and no King 'married to my Queen! I must not,
cannot suffer it!' 'Pray restrain yourself a little, sir,'
said Sir Philip, 'and when once these ladies have left
us, I will discourse your Majesty further about this
business.' 'Well, pray Sir Philip, said his lady, 'let
not your Worship be pleased to sit up too long for his
Majesty. About five o'clock I shall expect you; it is
your old hour.' 'And yours, madam, to wake to receive me coming to bed——' 'Your ladyship under-
stands me,' returned Friendly. 'You're merry, my
love, you're merry,' cried Philadelphia. 'Come, niece,
to bed! to bed!' 'Ay,' said the Knight, 'go, both of
you and sleep together, if you can, without the thoughts
of a lover, or a husband.' His Majesty was pleased
to wish them a good repose; and so, with a kiss, they
parted for that time.

'Now we're alone,' said Sir Philip, 'let me assure
you, sir, I resent this affront done to you by Mr.
Goodland, almost as highly as you can: and though
I can't wish that you should take such satisfaction, as
perhaps some other hotter sparks would; yet let me
say, his miscarriage ought not to go unpunished in
him.' 'Fear not,' replied the other, 'I shall give him
a sharp lesson.' 'No, sir,' returned Friendly, 'I would
not have you think of a bloody revenge; for it is that
which possibly he designs on you: I know him brave
as any man. However, were it convenient that the
sword should determine betwixt you, you should not
want mine. The affront is partly to me, since done in
my house; but I've already laid down safer measures
for us, though of more fatal consequence to him: that

is, I've formed them in my thoughts. Dismiss your coach and equipage, all but one servant, and I will discourse it to you at large. It is now past twelve; and if you please, I would invite you to take up as easy a lodging here, as my house will afford.' (Accordingly they were dismissed, and he proceeded.) 'As I hinted to you before, he is in love with my youngest niece Philibella; but her fortune not exceeding five hundred pounds, his father will assuredly disinherit him, if he marries her: though he has given his consent that he should marry her eldest sister, whose father dying ere he knew his wife was with child of the youngest, left Lucy three thousand pounds, being as much as he thought convenient to match her handsomely; and accordingly the nuptials of young Goodland and Lucy are to be celebrated next Easter.' 'They shall not, if I can hinder them,' interrupted his offended Majesty. 'Never endeavour the obstruction,' said the Knight, 'for I'll show you the way to a dearer vengeance. Women are women, your Majesty knows; she may be won to your embraces before that time, and then you antedate him your creature.' 'A cuckold, you mean,' cried King in Fancy; 'oh, exquisite revenge! but can you consent that I should attempt it?' 'What is it to me? We live not in Spain, where all the relations of the family are obliged to vindicate a whore. No, I would wound him in his most tender part.' 'But how shall we compass it?' asked the other. 'Why thus, throw away three thousand pounds on the youngest sister, as a portion, to make her as happy as she can be in her new lover Sir Frederick Flygold, an extravagant young fop, and wholly given over to gaming; so, ten to one, but you may retrieve your money of him, and have the two sisters at your devotion.' 'Oh, thou my better genius than that which was given to me by heaven at my birth! What thanks, what praises shall I return and sing to thee for this!' cried King Conundrum. 'No thanks, no praises, I beseech your Majesty, since in this I gratify myself.

You think I am your friend? and, you will agree to this?' said Friendly, by way of question. 'Most readily,' returned the fop King: 'would it were broad day, that I might send for the money to my banker's; for in all my life, in all my frolics, encounters, and extravagances, I never had one so grateful, and so pleasant as this will be, if you are in earnest, to gratify both my love and revenge!' 'That I am in earnest, you will not doubt, when you see with what application I shall pursue my design. In the meantime, my duty to your Majesty; to our good success in this affair.' While he drank, the other returned, 'With all my heart'; and pledged him. Then Friendly began afresh: 'Leave the whole management of this to me; only one thing more I think necessary, that you make a present of five hundred guineas to her Majesty, the bride that must be.' 'By all means,' returned the wealthy King of Bantam; 'I had so designed before.' 'Well, sir,' said Sir Philip, 'what think you of a set party or two at piquet, to pass away a few hours, till we can sleep?' 'A seasonable and welcome proposition,' returned the King; 'but I won't play above twenty guineas the game, and forty the lurch.' 'Agreed,' said Friendly; 'first call in your servant; mine is here already.' The slave came in, and they began, with unequal fortune at first; for the Knight had lost a hundred guineas to Majesty, which he paid in specie; and then proposed fifty guineas the game, and a hundred the lurch. To which the other consented; and without winning more than three games, and those not together, made shift to get three thousand two hundred guineas in debt to Sir Philip; for which Majesty was pleased to give him bond, whether Friendly would or no,

Sealed and delivered in the presence of,

The mark of (W.) Will. Watchful.
And, (S.) Sim. Slyboots.

A couple of delicate beagles, their mighty attendants

It was then about the hour that Sir Philip's (and, it may be, other ladies) began to yawn and stretch; when the spirits refreshed, trolled about, and tickled the blood with desires of action; which made Majesty and Worship think of a retreat to bed: where in less than half an hour, or before ever he could say his prayers, I'm sure the first fell fast asleep; but the last, perhaps, paid his accustomed devotion, ere he began his progress to the shadow of death. However, he waked earlier than his cully Majesty, and got up to receive young Goodland, who came according to his word, with the first opportunity. Sir Philip received him with more than usual joy, though not with greater kindness, and let him know every syllable and accident that had passed between them till they went to bed: which you may believe was not a little pleasantly surprising to Valentine, who began then to have some assurance of his happiness with Phili-bella. His friend told him, that he must now be reconciled to his Mock-Majesty, though with some difficulty; and so taking one hearty glass apiece, he left Valentine in the parlour to carry the ungrateful news of his visit to him that morning. King —— was in an odd sort of taking, when he heard that Valentine was below; and had been, as Sir Philip informed Majesty, at Majesty's palace, to inquire for him there. But when he told him, that he had already schooled him on his own behalf for the affront done in his house, and that he believed he could bring his Majesty off without any loss of present honour, his countenance visibly discovered his past fear, and present satisfaction; which was much increased too, when Friendly showing him his bond for the money he won of him at play, let him know, that if he paid three thousand guineas to Philibella, he would immediately deliver him up his bond, and not expect the two hundred guineas overplus. His Majesty of Bantam was then in so good a humour, that he could have made love to Sir Philip; nay, I believe he could have kissed Valentine, instead of seeming angry. Down they came, and saluted like gentlemen : but after the greeting was over, Goodland began to talk something of affront, satisfaction, honour, etc., when immediately Friendly interposed, and after a little seeming uneasiness and reluctancy, reconciled the hot and choleric youth to the cold phlegmatic King.

Peace was no sooner proclaimed, than the King of Bantam took his rival and late antagonist with him in his own coach, not excluding Sir Philip by any means, to Locket's, where they dined. Thence he would have them to Court with him, where the met the Lady Flippant, the Lady Harpy, the Lady Crocodile, Madam Tattlemore, Miss Medler, Mrs. Gingerly, a rich grocer's wife, and some others, besides knights and gentlemen of as good humours as the ladies; all whom he invited to a ball at his own house, the night following; his own lady being then in the country. Madam Tattlemore, I think, was the first he spoke to in Court, and whom first he surprised with the happy news of his advancement to the title of King of Bantam. How wondrous hasty was she to be gone, as soon as she heard it! It was not in her power, because not in her nature, to stay long enough to take a civil leave of the company; but away she flew, big with the empty title of a fantastic King, proclaiming it to every one of her acquaintance, as she passed through every room, till she came to the presence-chamber, where she only whispered it; but her whispers made above half the honourable company quit the presence of the King of Great Britain, to go make their court to his Majesty of Bantam : some cried 'God bless your Majesty!' Some 'Long live the King of Bantam!' Others, 'All hail to your Sacred Majesty!' In short, he was congratulated on all sides. Indeed I don't hear that his Majesty King Charles II. ever sent an ambassador to compliment him; though possibly, he saluted him by his title the first time he saw him afterwards : for, you know, he

is a wonderful good-natured and well-bred gentleman.

After he thought the Court of England was universally acquainted with his mighty honour, he was
pleased to think fit to retire to his own more private
palace, with Sir Philip and Goodland, whom he entertained that night very handsomely, till about seven
o'clock; when they went together to the play, which
was that night, *A King and no King*. His attendant-
friends could not forbear smiling, to think how aptly
the title of the play suited his circumstances. Nor
could he choose but take notice of it behind the
scenes, between jest and earnest; telling the players
how kind Fortune had been the night past, in dis-
posing the bean to him; and justifying what one of
her prophetesses had foretold some years since. ' I
shall now no more regard,' said he, ' that old doating
fellow Pythagoras's saying, *Abstineto a fabis*, that is,'
added he, by way of construction, "Abstain from
beans": for I find the excellence of them in cakes and
dishes; from the first, they inspire the soul with
mighty thoughts; and from the last our bodies
receive a strong and wholesome nourishment.' ' That
is,' said a wag among those sharp youths, I think it
was my friend the Count, ' these puff you up in mind,
sir, those in body.' They had some further discourse
among the nymphs of the stage, ere they went into
the pit; where Sir Philip spread the news of his
friend's accession to the title, though not yet to the
throne of Bantam; upon which he was there again
complimented on that occasion. Several of the
ladies and gentlemen who saluted him, he invited to
the next night's ball at his palace.

The play done, they took each of them a bottle at
the ' Rose,' and parted till seven the night following;
which came not sooner than desired: for he had
taken such care, that all things were in readiness
before eight, only he was not to expect the music
till the end of the play. About nine, Sir Philip, his

Lady, Goodland, Philibella, and Lucy came. Sir Philip returned him *Rabelais*, which he had borrowed of him, wherein the Knight had written, in an old odd sort of a character, this prophecy of his own making; with which he surprised the Majesty of Bantam, who vowed he had never taken notice of it before; but he said, he perceived it had been long written, by the character; and here it follows, as near as I can remember:—

> When M. D. C. come L. before,
> Three XXX's, two II's and one I. more;
> Then K I N G, though now but name to thee,
> Shall both thy name and title be.

They had hardly made an end of reading it, ere the whole company, and more than he had invited, came in, and were received with a great deal of formality and magnificence. Lucy was there attended as his Queen; and Philibella, as the Princess her sister. They danced then till they were weary; and afterwards retired to another large room, where they found the tables spread and furnished with all the most seasonable cold meat; which was succeeded by the choicest fruits, and the richest dessert of sweet-meats that luxury could think on, or at least that this town could afford. The wines were almost excellent in their kind; and their spirits flew about through every corner of the house. There was scarce a spark sober in the whole company, with drinking repeated glasses to the health of the King of Bantam, and his Royal Consort, with the Princess Philibella's, who sat together under a royal canopy of state, his Majesty between the two beautiful sisters: only Friendly and Goodland wisely managed that part of the engagement where they were concerned, and pre-served themselves from the heat of the debauch.

Between three and four most of them began to draw off, laden with fruit and sweetmeats, and rich favours composed of yellow, green, red and white,

the colours of his new Majesty of Bantam. Before
five they were left to themselves; when the Lady
Friendly was discomposed, for want of sleep, and her
usual cordial, which obliged Sir Philip to wait on her
home, with his two nieces. But his Majesty would
by no means part with Goodland; whom, before nine
that morning, he made as drunk as a lord, and by
consequence, one of his peers; for Majesty was then,
indeed, as great as an Emperor. He fancied himself
Alexander, and young Valentine his Hephestion;
and did so be-buss him, that the young gentleman
feared he was fallen into the hands of an Italian.
However, by the kind persuasions of his condescend-
ing and dissembling Majesty, he ventured to go into
bed with him; where King Would-be fell asleep hand-
over-head: and not long after, Goodland, his new-made
peer, followed him to the cool retreats of Morpheus.

About three the next afternoon they both waked,
as by consent, and called to dress. And after that
business was over, I think they swallowed each of
them a pint of old hock, with a little sugar, by the
way of healing. Their coaches were got ready in
the meantime; but the peer was forced to accept of
the honour of being carried in his Majesty's to Sir
Philip's, whom they found just risen from dinner,
with Philadelphia and his two nieces. They sat
down, and asked for something to relish a glass of
wine, and Sir Philip ordered a cold chine to be set
before them, of which they ate about an ounce
apiece; but they drank more by half, I daresay.

After their little repast, Friendly called the Would-
be-Monarch aside, and told him, that he would have
him go to the play that night, which was 'The
London-Cuckolds'; promising to meet him there in
less than half an hour after his departure: telling him
withal, that he would surprise him with a much
better entertainment than the stage afforded. Majesty
took the hint, imagining, and that rightly, that the
Knight had some intrigue in his head, for the promo-

tion of the Commonwealth of Cuckoldom. In order therefore to his advice, he took his leave about a quarter of an hour after.

When he was gone, Sir Philip thus bespoke his pretended niece : 'Madam, I hope your Majesty will not refuse me the honour of waiting on you to a place where you will meet with better entertainment than your Majesty can expect from the best comedy in Christendom. Val,' continued he, 'you must go with us, to secure me against the jealousy of my wife.' 'That, indeed,' returned his lady, 'is very material ; and you are mightily concerned not to give me occasion, I must own.' 'You see I am now,' replied he : 'But —— come ! on with hoods and scarf !' pursued he, to Lucy. Then addressing himself again to his lady : 'Madam,' said he, 'we'll wait on you.' In less time than I could have drunk a bottle to my share, the coach was got ready, and on they drove to the play-house. 'By the way,' said Friendly to Val, 'your Honour, noble peer, must be set down at Long's ; for only Lucy and I must be seen to his Majesty of Bantam. And now, I doubt not, you understand what you must trust to.'—'To be robbed of her Majesty's company, I warrant,' returned the other, 'for these long three hours.' 'Why,' cried Lucy, 'you don't mean, I hope, to leave me with his Majesty of Bantam ?' 'It is for thy good, child ! It is for thy good,' returned Friendly. To the 'Rose' they got then ; where Goodland alighted, and expected Sir Philip ; who led Lucy into the King's box, to his new Majesty ; where, after the first scene, he left them together. The overjoyed fantastic monarch would fain have said some fine obliging things to the Knight, as he was going out ; but Friendly's haste prevented them, who went directly to Valentine, took one glass, called a reckoning, mounted his chariot, and away home they came : where I believe he was welcome to his lady ; for I never heard anything to the contrary.

In the meantime, his Majesty had not the patience to stay out half the play, at which he was saluted by above twenty gentlemen and ladies by his new and mighty title: but out he led Miss Majesty ere the third act was half done; pretending, that it was so damned a bawdy play, that he knew her modesty had been already but too much offended at it; so into his coach he got her. When they were seated, she told him she would go to no place with him, but to the lodgings her mother had taken for her, when she first came to town, and which still she kept. 'Your mother, madam,' cried he, 'why, is Sir Philip's sister living then?' 'His brother's widow is, sir,' she replied. 'Is she there?' he asked. 'No, sir,' she returned; 'she is in the country.' 'Oh, then we will go thither to choose.' The coachman was then ordered to drive to Jermain Street; where, when he came in to the lodgings, he found them very rich and modishly furnished. He presently called one of his slaves, and whispered him to get three or four pretty dishes for supper; and then getting a pen, ink and paper wrote a note to C——d the goldsmith with Temple Bar, for five hundred guineas; which Watchful brought him, in less than an hour's time, when they were just in the height of supper; Lucy having invited her landlady, for the better colour of the matter. His Bantamite Majesty took the gold from his slave, and threw it by him in the window, that Lucy might take notice of it (which you may assure yourself she did, and after supper winked on the goodly matron of the house to retire, which she immediately obeyed). Then his Majesty began his court very earnestly and hotly, throwing the naked guineas into her lap; which she seemed to refuse with much disdain; but upon his repeated promises, confirmed by unheard-of oaths and imprecations, that he would give her sister three thousand guineas to her portion, she began by degrees to mollify, and let the gold lie quietly in her lap. And the next night, after he had drawn notes on two

or three of his bankers, for the payment of three
thousand guineas to Sir Philip, or order, and received
his own bond, made for what he had lost at play,
from Friendly, she made no great difficulty to admit
his Majesty to her bed. Where I think fit to leave
them for the present; for (perhaps) they had some
private business.

The next morning before the titular King was
(I won't say up, or stirring, but) out of bed, young
Goodland and Philibella were privately married; the
bills being all accepted and paid in two days' time.
As soon as ever the fantastic monarch could find in
his heart to divorce himself from the dear and charming embraces of his beautiful bedfellow, he came
flying to Sir Philip, with all the haste that imagination
big with pleasure could inspire him with, to discharge
itself to a supposed friend. The Knight told him,
that he was really much troubled to find that his
niece had yielded so soon and easily to him; however,
he wished him joy: to which the other returned, that
he could never want it, whilst he had the command of
so much beauty, and that without the ungrateful
obligations of matrimony, which certainly are the
most nauseous, hateful, pernicious and destructive of
love imaginable. 'Think you so, sir?' asked the
Knight; 'we shall hear what a friend of mine will
say on such an occasion, to-morrow about this time:
but I beseech your Majesty to conceal your sentiments of it to him, lest you make him as uneasy as
you seem to be in that circumstance.' 'Be assured
I will,' returned the other: 'but when shall I see the
sweet, the dear, the blooming, the charming Philibella?' 'She will be with us at dinner.' 'Where's
her Majesty?' asked Sir Philip. 'Had you inquired
before, she had been here; for, look, she comes!'
Friendly seems to regard her with a kind of displeasure, and whispered Majesty, that he should
express no particular symptoms of familiarity with
Lucy in his house, at any time, especially when

Goodland was there, as then he was above with his lady and Philibella, who came down presently after to dinner.

About four o'clock, as his Majesty had intrigued with her, Lucy took a hackney-coach, and went to her lodgings; whither, about an hour after, he followed her. Next morning, at nine, he came to Friendly's, who carried him up to see his new-married friend. But (O damnation to thoughts!) what torments did he feel, when he saw young Goodland and Philibella in bed together; the last of which returned him humble and hearty thanks for her portion and husband, as the first did for his wife. He shook his head at Sir Philip, and without speaking one word, left them, and hurried to Lucy, to lament the ill-treatment he had met with from Friendly. They cooed and billed as long as he was able; she (sweet hypocrite) seeming to bemoan his misfortunes; which he took so kindly, that when he left her, which was about three in the afternoon, he caused a scrivener to draw up an instrument, wherein he settled a hundred pounds a year on Lucy for her life, and gave her a hundred guineas more against her lying-in: (for she told him, and indeed it was true, that she was with child, and knew herself to be so from a very good reason), and indeed she was so by the Friendly Knight. When he returned to her, he threw the obliging instrument into her lap (it seems, he had a particular kindness for that place); then called for wine, and something to eat; for he had not drunk a pint to his share all the day (though he had plied it at the chocolate house). The landlady, who was invited to sup with them, bid them good-night, about eleven: when they went to bed, and partly slept till about six; when they were entertained by some gentlemen of their acquaintance, who played and sang very finely, by way of epithalamium, these words and more:—

Joy to great Bantam !
Live long, love and wanton !
And thy Royal Consort !
For both are of one sort, etc.

The rest I have forgot. He took some offence at
the words ; but more at the visit that Sir Philip, and
Goodland, made him, about an hour after, who found
him in bed with his Royal Consort ; and after having
wished them joy, and thrown their Majesties' own
shoes and stockings at their head, retired. This gave
Monarch in Fancy so great a caution, that he took
his Royal Consort into the country (but above forty
miles off the place where his own lady was), where,
in less than eight months, she was delivered of a
princely babe, who was christened by the heathenish
name of Hayoumorecake Bantam, while her Majesty
lay in like a pretty Queen.

THE ADVENTURE OF
THE BLACK LADY

ABOUT the beginning of last June (as near as I can remember) Bellamora came to town from Hampshire, and was obliged to lodge the first night at the same inn where the stage-coach set up. The next day she took coach for Covent Garden, where she thought to find Madam Brightly, a relation of hers, with whom she designed to continue for about half a year undiscovered, if possible, by her friends in the country: and ordered therefore her trunk, with her clothes, and most of her money and jewels, to be brought after her to Madam Brightly's by a strange porter, whom she spoke to in the street as she was taking coach; being utterly unacquainted with the neat practices of this fine city. When she came to Bridges Street, where indeed her cousin had lodged near three or four years since, she was strangely surprised that she could not learn anything of her; no, nor so much as meet with any one that had ever heard of her cousin's name. Till, at last, describing Madam Brightly to one of the housekeepers in that place, he told her, that there was such a kind of lady, whom he had sometimes seen there about a year and a half ago; but that he believed she was married and removed towards Soho. In this perplexity she quite forgot her trunk and money, etc., and wandered in her hackney-coach all over St. Anne's parish; inquiring for Madam Brightly,

still describing her person, but in vain ; for no soul
could give her any tale or tidings of such a lady.
After she had thus fruitlessly rambled, till she, the
coachman, and the very horses were even tired, by
good fortune for her, she happened on a private house,
where lived a good, discreet, ancient gentlewoman,
who was fallen to decay, and forced to let lodgings
for the best part of her livelihood. From whom she
understood, that there was such a kind of lady who
had lain there somewhat more than a twelvemonth,
being near three months after she was married ; but
that she was now gone abroad with the gentleman
her husband, either to the play, or to take the fresh
air ; and she believed would not return till night.
This discourse of the good gentlewoman's so elevated
Bellamora's drooping spirits, that after she had begged
the liberty of staying there till they came home, she
discharged the coachman in all haste, still forgetting
her trunk, and the more valuable furniture of it.

When they were alone, Bellamora desired she might
be permitted the freedom to send for a pint of sack ;
which, with some little difficulty, was at last allowed
her. They began then to chat for a matter of half an
hour of things indifferent : and at length the ancient
gentlewoman asked the fair innocent (I must not say
foolish) one, of what country, and what her name
was : to both which she answered directly and truly,
though it might have proved not discreetly. She
then inquired of Bellamora if her parents were living,
and the occasion of her coming to town. The fair
unthinking creature replied, that her father and
mother were both dead ; and that she had escaped
from her uncle, under the pretence of making a visit
to a young lady, her cousin, who was lately married,
and lived above twenty miles from her uncle's, in the
road to London, and that the cause of her quitting
the country, was to avoid the hated importunities of
a gentleman, whose pretended love to her she feared
had been her eternal ruin. At which she wept and

sighed most extravagantly. The discreet gentle-woman endeavoured to comfort her by all the softest and most powerful arguments in her capacity; promising her all the friendly assistance that she could expect from her, during Bellamora's stay in town: which she did with so much earnestness, and visible integrity, that the pretty innocent creature was going to make her a full and real discovery of her imaginary insupportable misfortunes; and (doubtless) had done it, had she not been prevented by the return of the lady, whom she hoped to have found her Cousin Brightly. The gentleman her husband just saw her within doors, and ordered the coach to drive to some of his bottle-companions; which gave the women the better opportunity of entertaining one another, which happened to be with some surprise on all sides. As the lady was going up into her apart-ment, the gentlewoman of the house told her there was a young lady in the parlour, who came out of the country that very day on purpose to visit her. The lady stepped immediately to see who it was, and Bella-mora approaching to receive her hoped-for cousin, stopped on the sudden just as she came to her; and sighed out aloud, 'Ah, madam! I am lost; it is not your ladyship I seek.' 'No, madam,' returned the other, 'I am apt to think you did not intend me this honour. But you are as welcome to me, as you could be to the dearest of your acquaintance: have you for-gotten me, Madam Bellamora?' continued she. That name startled the other: however, it was with a kind of joy. 'Alas! madam,' replied the young one, 'I now remember that I have been so happy to have seen you; but where and when, my memory cannot tell me.' 'It is indeed some years since,' returned the lady, 'but of that another time. Meanwhile, if you are unprovided of a lodging, I dare undertake, you shall be welcome to this gentlewoman.' The un-fortunate returned her thanks; and whilst a chamber was preparing for her, the lady entertained her in her own. About ten o'clock they parted, Bellamora being conducted to her lodging by the mistress of the house, who then left her to take what rest she could amidst her so many misfortunes; returning to the other lady, who desired her to search into the cause of Bellamora's retreat to town.

The next morning the good gentlewoman of the house coming up to her, found Bellamora almost drowned in tears, which by many kind and sweet words she at last stopped; and asking whence so great signs of sorrow should proceed, vowed a most profound secrecy if she would discover to her their occasion; which, after some little reluctancy, she did, in this manner.

'I was courted,' said she, 'above three years ago, when my mother was yet living, by one Mr. Fondlove, a gentleman of good estate, and true worth; and one who, I dare believe, did then really love me. He continued his passion for me, with all the earnest and honest solicitations imaginable, till some months before my mother's death; who, at that time, was most desirous to see me disposed of in marriage to another gentleman, of much better estate than Mr. Fondlove; but one whose person and humour did by no means hit with my inclinations. And this gave Fondlove the unhappy advantage over me. For, finding me one day all alone in my chamber, and lying on my bed, in as mournful and wretched a condition to my then foolish apprehension, as now I am, he urged his passion with such violence, and accursed success for me, with reiterated promises of marriage, whensoever I pleased to challenge them, which he bound with the most sacred oaths, and most dreadful execrations: that partly with my aversion to the other, and partly with my inclinations to pity him, I ruined myself.' Here she relapsed into a greater extravagance of grief than before; which was so extreme that it did not continue long. When therefore she was pretty well come to herself, the ancient gentlewoman asked her, why she imagined herself ruined. To which she answered, 'I am great with child by him, madam, and wonder you did not perceive it last night. Alas! I have not a month to go: I am ashamed, ruined, and damned, I fear, for ever lost.' 'Oh! fie, madam, think not so,' said the other, 'for the gentleman may yet prove true, and marry you.' 'Ay, madam,' replied Bellamora, 'I doubt not that he would marry me; for soon after my mother's death, when I came to be at my own disposal, which happened about two months after, he offered, nay most earnestly solicited me to it, which still he perseveres to do.' 'This is strange!' returned the other, 'and it appears to me to be your own fault, that you are yet miserable. Why did you not, or why will you not consent to your own happiness?' 'Alas!' cried Bellamora, 'it is the only thing I dread in this world: for, I am certain, he can never love me after. Besides, ever since I have abhorred the sight of him: and this is the only cause that obliges me to forsake my uncle, and all my friends and relations in the country, hoping in this populous and public place to be most private, especially, madam, in your house, and in your fidelity and discretion.' 'Of the last you may assure yourself, madam,' said the other: 'but what provision have you made for the reception of the young stranger that you carry about you?' 'Ah, madam!' cried Bellamora, 'you have brought to my mind another misfortune.' Then she acquainted her with the supposed loss of her money and jewels, telling her withal, that she had but three guineas and some silver left, and the rings she wore, in her present possession. The good gentlewoman of the house told her, she would send to inquire at the inn where she lay the first night she came to town; for haply, they might give some account of the porter to whom she had entrusted her trunk; and withal repeated her promise of all the help in her power, and for that time left her much more composed than she found her. The good gentlewoman went directly to the other lady, her lodger, to whom she recounted Bellamora's mournful confession; at which the lady appeared mightily concerned: and at last she told her landlady, that she would take care that Bellamora should lie in according to her quality: 'for,' added she, 'the child, it seems, is my own brother's.'

As soon as she had dined, she went to the Exchange, and bought child-bed linen; but desired that Bellamora might not have the least notice of it. And at her return despatched a letter to her brother Fondlove in Hampshire, with an account of every particular; which soon brought him up to town, without satisfying any of his or her friends with the reason of his sudden departure. Meanwhile, the good gentlewoman of the house had sent to the Star Inn on Fish Street Hill, to demand the trunk, which she rightly supposed to have been carried back thither: for by good luck, it was a fellow that plied thereabouts, who brought it to Bellamora's lodgings that very night, but unknown to her. Fondlove no sooner got to London, but he posts to his sister's lodgings, where he was advised not to be seen of Bellamora till they had worked farther upon her, which the landlady began in this manner. She told her that her things were miscarried, and she feared lost; that she had but a little money herself, and if the Overseers of the Poor (justly so called from their overlooking them) should have the least suspicion of a strange and unmarried person, who was entertained in her house big with child, and so near her time as Bellamora was, she should be troubled, if they could not give security to the parish of twenty or thirty pounds, that they should not suffer by her, which she could not; or otherwise she must be sent to the house of correction, and her child to a parish nurse. This discourse, one may imagine, was very dreadful to a person of her youth, beauty, education, family and estate: however, she resolutely protested, that she had rather undergo all this, than be exposed to the scorn of her friends and relations in the country. The other told her then, that she must write down to her uncle a farewell letter, as if she were just going aboard the packet-boat for Holland, that he might not send to inquire for her in town, when he should understand she was not at her new-married cousin's in the country; which accordingly she did, keeping herself close prisoner to her chamber; where she was daily visited by Fondlove's sister and the landlady, but by no soul else, the first dissembling the knowledge she had of her misfortunes. Thus she continued for above three weeks, not a servant being suffered to enter her chamber, so much as to make her bed, lest they should take notice of her great belly: but for all this caution, the secret had taken wind, by the means of an attendant of the other lady below, who had overheard her speaking of it to her husband. This soon got out of doors, and spread abroad, till it reached the long ears of the wolves of the parish, who next day designed to pay her a visit. But Fondlove, by good providence, prevented it; who, the night before, was ushered into Bellamora's chamber by his sister, his brother-in-law, and the landlady. At the sight of him she had like to have swooned away: but he taking her in his arms, began again, as he was wont to do, with tears in his eyes, to beg that she would marry him ere she was delivered; if not for his, nor her own, yet for the child's sake, which she hourly expected; that it might not be born out of wedlock, and so be made incapable of inheriting either of their estates; with a great many more pressing arguments on all sides. To which at last she consented; and an honest officious gentleman, whom they had before provided, was called up, who made an end of the dispute. So to bed they went together that night; next day to the Exchange, for several pretty businesses that ladies in her condition want. Whilst they were abroad, came the vermin of the parish (I mean the Overseers of the

Poor, who eat the bread from them), to search for
a young black-haired lady (for so was Bellamora)
who was either brought to bed, or just ready to lie
down. The landlady showed them all the rooms in
the house, but no such lady could be found. At last
she bethought herself, and led them into her parlour,
where she opened a little closet door, and showed
them a black cat that had just kittened: assuring
them, that she should never trouble the parish as
long as she had rats or mice in the house; and so
dismissed them like loggerheads as they came.

FINIS

PLYMOUTH: WILLIAM BRENDON AND SON, LTD.
PRINTERS